THE ALPHA PROTOCOL

SYMPHONY

BOOK ONE
THE ALPHA PROTOCOL

J. D. Mullenary Sr.

Podium

Cover design by Fred Birchal

ISBN: 978-1-0394-9672-9

Published in 2025 by Podium Publishing
www.podiumentertainment.com

Podium

THE ALPHA PROTOCOL

CHAPTER ONE

A Dream and a Fear

With a sigh, Walker said, "Because I said so."

The abrasive teenager briefly scowled at his teacher before controlling himself. Apparently, this was one of those days where Walker would have to have a *teachable moment*. Looking at the clock, he figured it wasn't too much of an issue, as he could just shuffle around the body paragraph breakdown to make time.

The boy continued, "I'm just saying, that doesn't make sense, Mr. Reed. Essays aren't emails, and emails aren't essays. They're two completely different things." He looked at his friends near him for support. Seeing one give him a thumbs-up, Raul shifted a little taller than his usual slouched posture and gestured at the class. "This whole place is worthless. The majority of what I need to know is in auto. I'm gonna be a mechanic anyways, not some college shit who thinks they're better than everyone else."

Walker paused for a moment to get a handle on himself, wondering if the college remark was a dig at him. Pulling an empty desk forward, one of the few in his thirty-student class, he flipped it around to sit facing the class. "It's pretty simple, Raul. Do you want to be an entry-level mechanic all your life?"

"Of course not."

"So what, a supervisor?"

Raul thought it over for a minute before saying, "Nah, man, I'm gonna start my own business."

Walker threw a finger in the air. "Aha! You wanna be a business owner and maybe even a manager. That means you have to learn how to manage employees, including writing up reports on them and giving feedback. You've also gotta deal with suppliers, expansion opportunities, and loads of stuff. It all ties back to essays. They're critical thinking outlets."

A new voice spoke up. "That's too much work, man."

Walker looked at the speaker. The kid was always on his phone and didn't do anything in class. Anytime one of his colleagues had tried to speak with his parents, they'd either hang up the phone or bitch them out for being a "shitty teacher." Honestly, he didn't know why he stayed in this job.

Oh, that's right, he needed money.

"Nicholas . . ."

"Nick," he cut him off. "You don't even fucking know what I like to be called."

Walker instantly replied by rote, "Language, please."

"Fuck language. Raul's right, this is bullshit. You're just an overly paid babysitter." He looked over at Raul for backup but instead found his potential supporter had already slouched back into his seat and was staring at the paper in front of him.

Smart kid, Walker thought to himself. He needed to get back in control before things spiraled.

"Nick, I'm sorry I didn't say your name the way you prefer it."

"Fuck your sorry, bitch."

Walker did a mental check. Rather than blow up, which he really wanted to do at that moment, maybe even taking Nicholas down with him, he calmly stood up and walked over to his phone.

A voice quickly answered. "Hello, Mr. Reed. How can I help you?"

"Yes, I need an administrator here please, non-emergency."

"We'll send one in a few minutes," the distant voice promised before abruptly hanging up.

The tall man walked back over and stood near the desk he'd previously been sitting at. Smiling at the class, Walker let them know he was going to wait a few minutes and for them to think about what they wanted to say in their emails. It was a basic assignment for an English class. Write the teacher a professional email with a beginning, middle, and end that asks questions about a job the student wants to do in the future. Simple stuff that went with his particular brand of teaching: practicality. *If it's not useful, do your best to not teach it.* Thus, the current kerfuffle.

He didn't fully disagree with Raul and Nicholas. A lot of what he was forced to teach was outdated and stupid. They, being his supervisors and the thirty other bosses he reported to, had a strict curriculum. The student body of Walker's school was eighty percent Latino, but he was still forced to teach novels written by people who didn't look, think, or write like them. Their brand of culture wasn't something the students could relate to, and no matter how well-written the material was, it just didn't connect in the way it needed to. Thank god he didn't have to teach *Moby Dick* anymore. American classic though it was, good lord did it drag.

It was only 10:14 in the morning. Moments like this would happen through-out the day, and while he normally wouldn't call an administrator for this, it was a recurring problem with Nicholas.

And Walker was done.

A light knock at the locked door informed him one of the principals had arrived. Through a small window set into the rusted door, he could see the tight hair bob and pasty countenance of Mrs. Wilson . . . which, if history tells the tale, meant Nicholas would get a pass and just sit in her office for the rest of the period. Walker would see him again tomorrow. And the day after. And the day after that. Requests for transferring students to other classes were ignored more often than not. One student had assaulted a teacher and walked back into that same teacher's classroom three days later.

A second sigh came out of Walker as he opened the door and stepped out, leaving it cracked so he wouldn't have to unlock it again.

"What do you need, Mr. Reed?" Mrs. Wilson asked in her best fake-cheery voice.

"I need Nicholas back there spoken to by an administrator. I've asked a few times for him to be transferred to another class or to credit recovery, but noth-ing's changed."

Mrs. Wilson appeared to think it over for a moment before saying, "Did you go to that professional development last weekend on dealing with difficult children? It was enlightening."

"No," he replied. "I was busy moving."

"Oh, that's right," she stated in a sympathetic voice, her facial muscles bring-ing a false smile to her face. "You did say you couldn't make it because of a per-sonal issue."

A personal issue like the love of his life leaving him and a drunken evening in the dark.

Walker got back on topic. "Do you mind pulling him out for at least the rest of the period? This is an important part of my lesson plan."

She nodded slowly. "Sure, but you'll have to think over how you want to manage him tomorrow."

Walker couldn't stop his teeth from grinding.

They walked back into the classroom together, and that's when they noticed the papers all over the ground, torn into tiny pieces. Unlike a lot of newer teach-ers, Walker preferred to handwrite all of his lessons, obstinacy in improving his handwriting winning out over practicality. He still kept them grouped into one thick notebook full of neon Post-it notes. He'd built that notebook over the past year and hadn't thought to make a copy or digitize it, as he was always real care-ful about making sure it was in the drawer just below the desk. That way he knew right where it was at all times.

But there was a problem, as it appeared Nicholas wasn't always staring at his phone after all. The culprit stood just behind Walker's black desk without fear of retribution.

"Hard to fucking teach without your instructions, ain't it, bitch?" he said with a heavy grin leaning off of his face.

Mrs. Wilson looked at the papers, not understanding their significance. "This'll clean right up," she said with aplomb before asking Nicholas to follow her. She didn't notice Walker staring at his hard work slashed into pieces on the floor. The combination of neon colors, the plain white paper he preferred to work off of, and dried ink snapped something in his mind.

"What the fuck did you do," his quiet voice said, drifting over the crowded classroom. Walker lifted his eyes from the floor and zeroed in on Nicholas.

"Mr. Reed!" Mrs. Wilson said in a sharp voice. "You can't speak that—"

"No," Walker interrupted her, his vacant eyes looking back at the papers again.

Mrs. Wilson suddenly developed a sixth sense, knowing this was an important moment. Finally doing her job, she gently tugged on Walker's arm, leading him from the classroom and over to the teachers' lounge. He never lifted his eyes from the ground as she began to harangue him about the language he'd used in front of the students.

But Walker wasn't listening. He was done listening. He was done with helicopter parents screaming at him for barely earned Bs. He was done with kids who always knew to ignore his lessons right when he was trying to teach them the things they most needed to know. Things they had to know before entering the working world. He was done with apathetic teenagers staring at girls' asses instead of listening.

Not like those same girls were any better.

He was done with low pay, twelve-hour days, and bullshit professional development sessions taught by people who hadn't been in a classroom for years. Walker Reed was ready for a change.

His eyes finally traveled up and found the lounge's walls. Mrs. Wilson was talking about him apologizing to Nicholas and the class, and that he would *figure it out*. But he knew he wasn't going to do that. There was only so much pushing and prodding a man could take.

His eyes landed on one of the posters covering the wall, the kind that had been in every school he'd worked at. "Motivational" posters that were anything but. The basic "Hang in there, baby" post of the cat that had been around since long ago. A meme someone had printed out about how editing wasn't like proofreading. The kind of humor only an English teacher would enjoy. But the last one his eyes found was the one that finally pushed him over the edge.

"Teaching is a calling," he said in a quiet voice.

"What was that, Mr. Reed?" Mrs. Wilson said. "Are you ready to apologize to the class now?"

"Do you know what a calling is, Mrs. Wilson? No?" Walker stepped up to the poster. It held a smiling young woman, perfectly dressed, as a group of students raised their hands in front of her. "This is not reality. This is fucking bullshit." He tore it from the wall, watching the now cornerless paper drift as it fell, its motion synonymous with his life right now.

"A calling is something you're meant to do, meant to be. I thought that's what it was for me." He gave a bitter laugh. "Something that I connected with, deep down. But that's not here, is it? That's not *these* kids."

"Mr. Reed," Mrs. Wilson replied as she changed tactics. "If you had attended the training this last weekend—"

"I couldn't fucking do that, Mrs. Wilson . . . Kathy!" He snarled her name out, his emotions getting the better of him. "Because of my"—Walker made air quotes—"'personal issue.' But you don't give a shit about that. Neither does Nicholas or anyone else here. You care about results. Test scores." Another set of air quotes. "'Attendance.'" Unknown to him, his voice raised in volume. "That's what's wrong with this goddamn education system. You all care about your ratings. How the state views you, and not the kids."

Mrs. Wilson put a hand on his shoulder in an attempt to calm him down, but it was too late. She was talking, but Walker couldn't hear her anymore.

"Parents don't parent anymore, so kids no longer feel the need to be kids. No, they're going to talk down to me"—his voice went up another register—"they're going to fuck around in class"—all of the classrooms around the lounge had gone quiet, and a few teachers started to stick their heads out to listen in—"and they don't give a flying fuck about English or any other skills that will make them look and act like adults growing up. No, it's all done. Everything is absolutely *fucked*."

He turned around, looking at the other posters on the wall. With more than a bit of mania, Walker Reed started to tear every poster off of the wall and throw them to the ground. He didn't do it with joy or happiness. He didn't even do it with anger. Walker Reed did it because he couldn't stand to look at the false images they represented. Of a "calling." Of kids giving a shit or admins doing their jobs.

While he was doing this, Mrs. Wilson had called the school resource officers to the building. They arrived just as the last poster drifted to the ground. To their eyes, a large man in a nice purple suit stood in the center of a recently fallen paper tornado, his shoulders heaving not from exhaustion but from barely controlled rage.

One of them spoke into a radio on his shoulder while the other was speaking with Mrs. Wilson. Walker turned around and found both men with their arms crossed. "Fucking great."

"Mr. Reed, it's time to go," said the man on the left. He was the same one who smiled at Walker daily as he parked what felt like a mile away and walked into the school. He wasn't smiling now.

"We can't have you cursing around the kids."

"Like you've never heard them curse before, Sean."

The officer shook his head. "Can't have you do this, Walker. It's time to go."

When it didn't look like he was going to move, they stepped forward and tried to gently grab his arms, but Walker was six foot three and around two hundred and fifty pounds. He'd move when he wanted to move. Initially, he pulled back on them, causing them to put more muscle into the action. But eventually, he just went limp, his rage spent on the sad pieces of paper littering the ground rather than the kids in the school.

By the time security got him through the door of the lounge, all the classes throughout the building had stopped. It's hard to teach when someone is screaming obscenities fifty feet away. Mrs. Wilson spoke quietly into her radio as they pulled him away. The exit was not far from his classroom.

Looking in, he spied Nicholas with a shit-eating grin plastered across his face as security gave him a light nudge to keep moving. But Walker wasn't through. He slipped out of security's arms and ran to the doorway, only to stop and smile in Nicholas's direction one more time before saying, "It's all *fuck the teachers*, right? The ones who work hard to make sure you have a safe place where you can be informed. Where you can learn what the future has entailed for you. Ask yourself this, Nicholas. Why am I smiling as I look at your future? Why does what you become make me happy?"

He turned to security and told them he was ready to go.

In the end, he didn't make them put him on administrative leave. He looked at the principal, informed her of his immediate resignation, and walked out to his crappy, rusting, blue Dodge Durango. The highway was empty, and things were looking up.

It was now 10:35 a.m.[1]

CHAPTER TWO

Downtown

There was an itch on Walker's soul as he hit the 101 highway.

Smooth green road signs passed by his windows, telling him he was going places, but he knew it was a lie.

Walker couldn't stop thinking of what he'd done. Was it a mistake? Or the beginning of something new? Something better. There come moments where you feel righteous fury, that you're in the right, only to come down after the rage is expended and find just how horrible you had acted. Maybe there were regrets buried within him.

But if there were, they'd already dropped to the bottom, never to be seen again.

The road signs continued to pass by.

In a spare moment, he looked at the small notebook sitting next to him. The cover showed the oh-so originally titled "Journal." He'd just written in it the night before, in his usual stupid style, as he didn't have anyone to talk to.

His oldest friend, Matt, always said he was too codependent in his relationships. The moment he had one, everything else disappeared, and his world tilted on the words of whoever he happened to be with at that time. He hadn't called Matt in years, and calling him out of the blue right when he and Valerie broke up felt . . . wrong. Like he was using him. Who only wanted phone calls when you were having a bad time? That wasn't what friends deserved.

"High and lows," he muttered to himself, driving down the highway without thinking about where he was going.

He thought Matt might've had a kid recently . . . but he had no memory of calling to congratulate him. No, now wasn't the time to call his old friend. Better to let that sit for a minute.

Wrapping up his thoughts, he realized that he had no one to lean on, no one to call, no job to go to, and his gas tank was running low. Good thing he had made plenty of money as a teacher in California, right? He hadn't checked his bank account in a while, but he was sure there were only a few hundred dollars in there.

Paycheck to paycheck was the life, man. Maybe he could ask Nicholas for notes on how to be an adult in a few years.

What a crock of shit.

Absent of any cognitive process, he eased over to the exit lane.

Walker wasn't entirely sure where he was going, but he figured he'd know when he got there. The car and its despondent driver made a few turns and wound up in downtown Santa Barbara. Adobe buildings set in a Spanish Colonial Revival style scrolled past. Bright flags hanging from light poles filled his vision as people smiled and spoke to one another while his rusty car drove by.

He had to fight away any tears from forming. He hadn't known why he was driving here until those flags appeared.

Valerie loved going downtown. Not to shop, as neither of them could really afford the lavish merchandise that had sprung up here in the last ten years, but just to walk around and enjoy the area.

A random memory forced its way into his mind. *"Walker, you should see what the old Sears building is going to be. I can't believe they're tearing down an SB monument like that. Where will people—"*

He pushed it away.

She was like that. See a dog in the street; feel the need to rescue it. See a homeless man who for all you know is mentally aware and chooses that life, then try to get him into a shelter. That's just the kind of person she is. Was.

They'd closed down State Street, the main road downtown, during the COVID-19 pandemic, so he had to find a reasonably priced parking garage and hop out. Walker made a mental reminder to quickly get to a gas station as soon as he left, or he'd have to do the walk of shame that everyone claims they've never done but just about everyone has.

Stepping out of the garage and onto the thoroughfare, he was surrounded by people going about their lives. His life wasn't their problem, and he was determined to keep the standardized sad and lost look off of his face. He headed into a few stores, looked around one in particular with fantastic oceanic paintings, and just moseyed along without the burden of thoughts.

Walker knew it wasn't healthy, that he . . . wasn't healthy. He was smart enough to understand that right now, at this very moment, he was trying to relive some semblance of the life he had lived with Valerie. He'd exploded their relationship, he'd blown up his job, and now he was a step away from homelessness as he walked the rich streets of his hometown. He should find some cardboard and a Sharpie while he could still afford it.

I'm fucked, he thought to himself, only there was no bitterness to the words. It was just a pure statement of reality.

He walked past where the Borders used to be, a fleeting memory of a time when he would go inside and longingly peruse the shelves. He always liked to look at all of the books before picking the "just right" one. Barnes and Noble sat kitty-corner to it. Each had tried to put the other out of business, with B&N winning the final battle. Of course, the introduction of the Nook and Kindle had upset bookstores worldwide, but people still liked the physicality of stepping through the doors and finding a newly chopped-up tree to turn.

That's when he noticed he'd been carrying his journal with him everywhere. He had no memories of taking it out of his trusty Durango.

Walker looked over the gray camo-splashed cover and thought for a moment of tossing it in a nearby trashcan. He started to head to one on the corner to do just that when a man in a green army jacket holding a tin can walked up to him. He had no idea where the man had come from, as he hadn't seen him standing there when he'd scanned the area just a moment ago. Walker could smell his unwashed body before the man had even reached six feet of where he was standing.

"Spare some change, young fellow?" the old man said with his striped bumblebee teeth.

Without thinking, Walker reached into his wallet and pulled out a twenty. He slipped it into the nearly empty can, noting a few one-dollar bills poking out. He also noticed the ones that were showing themselves had been taped there by the man holding the can. Smart. Some people would shy away from being the first to help, thinking something was wrong with the homeless man, but if it looked like some cash was already in it, they'd be less hesitant.

He was happy to help. That's what Valerie would've done. He just wished that hadn't been his last bit of cash.

"Thank you kindly," the man said. Walker nodded and looked at his journal again.

"Say, what've you got there?" interrupted the homeless man again, pointing one dirty nail at the notebook in Walker's hand.

"Just a simple notebook filled with the deranged thoughts of a madman," Walker replied.

"Hah, and here I thought I was the only madman left in this absolute paradise," countered the homeless man with a slight grin that didn't seem like it was meant to be there. "You don't know how lucky you are."

"Yeah," Walker replied with a false smile in return. "Definitely lucky."

"Name's John Reed, pleasure to meet you."

"Same. Walker Reed, funnily enough. Maybe we're related."

John shook his head and sighed. "No, son, I ain't got no family left, or I'd not be like this. You know, looking at you," he said, scanning Walker up and down, "you've been through something. Recently, it seems to me. Don't think I've seen many people aimlessly walking around, carrying journals, and staring at trash cans. Most people come here with friends and loved ones, or else they're heading to work." He scratched the underside of his chin. "What brings you here?"

He's nosy as shit.

"Why do you want to know?" Walker asked in a, he felt, not-unfriendly tone of voice.

"Just passing the time," he said with a shrug. "Got lots of time nowadays."

With a mental laugh, Walker thought, *Things couldn't get any worse, may as well give this a go.*

"Okay, John." He grabbed a seat near a strangely leafed tree and looked at the sky to collect his thoughts for a moment. With a shake of his head and a grimace, he said, "My life has never been worse. I went from having a smoking hot girl-friend and almost-fiancée to being unemployed, single, and soon to be broke."

"How can someone be an almost-fiancée?"

"Don't interrupt, John. You asked for it, and I'm giving it. This world is shit. I figured after Valerie, the almost-fiancée, and I got out of the military, we'd be fine. We'd both worked hard and got our bachelor's degrees while still serving. We were happy. I was happy . . ."

He trailed off for a moment. John didn't say anything and just looked at him.

Walker wasn't sure what to say next. "So yeah, this world is shit. I was a teacher until ten-something this morning. I was going to propose until late Sunday night. And just a few minutes ago, I had twenty dollars in my wallet. Now I've got nothing but . . . I guess this journal, a shitty car, and a half-assed setup in an apartment I can't go back to as everything isn't fully packed, and she doesn't want to be near me." A flash of fire hit his gut. "She's moving in with Todd."

"A Todd, huh?" John said quietly, not giving a smile this time.

"Yeah, a Todd. So I guess you could say I have a lot of open opportunities," Walker said with bitterness.

"So, you really think this world is shit?" John asked quietly, a shadow cross-ing the planes of his face.

"I do. I fought a people who didn't even have clean water, for reasons I still don't know. Then, I wanted to help the world by becoming a teacher, and instead, I screamed and threw a hissy fit at everyone because my students didn't have anyone teach them that their behavior wasn't appropriate. Hell, my behavior wasn't appropriate either." Walker ran a hand through his hair. "I lost my almost-fiancée because . . . well, fuck, I still don't really know. Forgive me for asking, but you *are* homeless, right? This isn't just some scam?"

"I'm homeless in a literal sense, Mr. Reed," John replied in a deeper tone of voice, though Walker was too wrapped up in his own problems to notice. "My home is no longer . . . reachable."

Without thinking it over, Walker replied, "That's rough, man."

John smiled a little. The kind of smile you only see on a person's face before something unexpected happens. It was jilted and wrong. As if the muscles in his face were fighting one another for dominance, rather than working together. Walker was still too self-absorbed to take note of it.

"So what would you do, Walker? How would you change the world? Even better, if you had to build a world from scratch, what would you do?"

"Build a world from scratch?

"Indeed. If you had the opportunity to build a world from the very beginning. No history, no religion, no culture, nothing but you and your thoughts, your dreams. What would you do?"

"This is a weird thought process, man," Walker replied, a little upset about being pulled out of his introspection. He thought it over for a moment. "I guess I'd want it to be like all the books I've read. I became an English teacher for a lot of reasons, but the main one is that I love to read. Especially fantasy. The guts and glory. The rescued princess and valiant heroes. A world where anything can happen. Where equality of opportunity isn't just a punchline. An entire . . . place, where people can be recognized for their merits, not judged by where they were born or who they were born to."

"A world where an out-of-work teacher and veteran can alter his path maybe, and take on the idea of who he really is?" John helped.

"Hah, wouldn't that be fun?" Walker said as he looked down at his worn dress shoes. There was a scuff on the front he'd never dealt with. Not like it mattered much now.

He didn't see it, but John nodded and pulled an ordinary stick out of his belt. In a different tone of voice, he said, *"Deal."*

Walker didn't notice the change of tone as he looked at the concrete under his feet. Only the concrete began to blur, or maybe his eyes were playing tricks on him; he wasn't sure. As his eyes continued to betray him, likely from the manic mood he'd been in all day, he felt something. Like he was floating. Only, there was something wrong.

A great rumbling could be heard, louder than anything he'd ever experienced. Louder than the bombs of the war or the tears of the students he'd been forced to fail. A shattering sound blasted out, and after what seemed an eternity, but couldn't have been more than a few seconds, the world reasserted itself. Walker fell softly onto his ass from a height he had no reason to be at, and his eyes came back into focus.

That isn't right, he thought to himself. *What was that? And why am I sitting on grass? Wait . . .* His ears picked up what his mind couldn't process. There was nothing. No sounds of cars nor people talking.

What?

"Welcome, Walker," said a deep voice right in front of him. Walker looked up and noticed that Santa Barbara was gone, and in its place was the night sky, filled with stars. Standing only a few feet away was a tall, powerfully built man wearing dark green robes and holding a pitch-black staff. The man spread his arms wide as he looked at Walker with a sad smile on his face.

"Welcome to your world."

CHAPTER THREE

Wizard Shit

Walker couldn't stop staring at the man in the green robe.

Maybe *man* wasn't the right word. He had to be seven feet tall, with broad shoulders and a long, meticulously kept beard. His robe, a shiny yellow-and-green thing, would pulse at odd moments. However, it wasn't the bearded archetype before him nor the strobe-like effect of the robe that truly confused Walker.

It was the staff the man was holding.

It looked to be in some form of constant flux. The coloring kept changing, shifting from a range of reds to white and black. While some of it could be explained by technology Walker understood, like LED lights or some kind of transparent screen, that couldn't account for it happening all at once, without lag or transition. Nor did it make sense that it all looked so natural, as if a white stick had always been black.

But all of that paled to the biggest thing Walker couldn't understand: its size. One moment, the staff was as tall as the man himself; another, it was no longer than a ruler. While Walker tried to mentally adjust to what he was seeing, the staff went through its most drastic change yet. He watched as it changed from the length of a meter to the height of a redwood, shooting into the night sky far above. The damn thing was so tall that it clouded his vision of the stars before quickly shrinking back to a more normal size. The bearded man, whose face seemed to alternate between anger and joy as its natural resting place, noticed that Walker was staring not at himself, but at the staff.

"Stop that," he told the staff with a light slap.

The staff changed color from black to white so fast Walker thought he was imagining it. The man nodded once as if saying, *That was that.*

"Anyway, welcome to your world, Walker!" he said again with great enthusi-asm, a long grin appearing on his face. It slid off for a moment before reasserting itself. "This is your place, your seat of power. And what power it has! You have no idea how lucky you are that I chose you. Yes,"—his face shifted back to anger—"my choice"—before a smile replaced it—"was quite fortuitous indeed!"

Walker didn't know what to think about the man's odd emotional changes. He seemed both ecstatically happy and filled with rage at the same time. His mind caught up with what the man had said a moment later. "Chose me?" Walker said with confusion. He was still sitting on the grass, his journal forgotten by his side, while the large man nodded in jerky motions.

"Of course." He spread his arms wide. "I had all of Earth to pick from. Anyone. And I chose you, Walker. You're my guy." Rage resurfaced. "MY GUY." The staff pulsed red before shifting back to its now-standard white. The red tinge up the man's neck calmed down, and he brought out a smile that could make Mrs. Wilson shiver. "My guy," he reiterated in a different tone of voice. "The almost-midlife crisis guy. The *I'm sad and want to reinvent myself* guy. There are millions of them on Earth at any single moment, but none with your background. I picked you. Walker. You're the one chance this place has. The only chance."

"What the fuck are you talking about?" Walker said with more confusion laced into his voice. One moment, he'd been in Santa Barbara, almost enjoying a terrible day, and now he was dealing with an emotionally disturbed semi-giant with a weird stick that put on light shows. Too much was happening at once.

The bearded man looked around, pausing momentarily on something behind Walker while he spoke. "Don't you remember? We were speaking about how terrible Earth is just a moment ago."

Walker stabbed a finger at the man as he unsteadily jumped to his feet. "You're that homeless guy."

"Got it in one. Man, I loved some of the sayings on your old world. It took me years to get the *lay of the land*," he said, putting extra emphasis on the word *lay*. "You have such fun words for everything. But who am I talking to? You're an English teacher . . . were an English teacher, actually."

Walker nodded while his brain felt paralyzed. "Uh-huh, I am an English teacher."

"Were, Walker. Were—no more. Now you're the new God of Creation! Well, not yet, that is." He seemed to taste something in the air. "And truly, it's god with a small g."

"God of creation?"

"Small g," he repeated, his face twitching erratically.

Walker knew what he needed to ask, but he was frightened of what was happening, not to mention the emotionally unstable man in front of him. Pulling some inner courage out of the ether, he asked the question sitting on his mind. "Then who are you?"

The man gave a wry grin. "I'm just a facilitator. I was chosen to be the chooser. Me and my, uh, trusty staff here."

But that wasn't enough information. If Walker was going to be dropped into the middle of a nonsensical situation, he needed answers. "Okay, then who chose you?"

The grin left the bearded man's face. "No idea, and that's truly saying something." He glared at his staff. "Shut up! This is my part!" A manic grin appeared on his face. "Now, we're on a time limit for this whole shindig. Great word there—*shindig*. Let me tell you about this place in Isla Vista I once visited." The staff pulsed red and a small ripping sound shot through the area. A small tear in space appeared over the man's head before the staff pulsed once again. The tear repaired itself before his eyes, causing Walker's mouth to drop open in astonishment.

The man looked at his staff for a moment and sighed before saying, "Fine, I know, I know. Look, Walker, you said you wanted to make a world where anything can happen. Where equality of opportunity isn't just a . . . What did you say again?"

Walker remembered and responded slowly. "Where it's not just a punchline."

He snapped his fingers. "Right! This is your chance. Use your knowledge. Hone your memories. Build something that can last and be a home to things you can't even imagine! Build a home that lets its people flourish, not ROT IN THE GROUND!" he screamed, his face shifting through a series of unexplainable emotions before moving back to his former grin. "This is your chance to do something great, something that no one from your world, except maybe one, has ever had the chance to do."

His staff pulsed red again as Walker said, "Wait, do you mean . . ."

"No time!" Then he did a very odd thing. He touched the air and stared at the sky for a moment, a small laugh erupting from him. A few more times, he seemed to be touching things only he could see before, out of nowhere, a blackboard materialized. Walker leaped back in fright as the six-foot-tall blackboard settled on the ground with a slight wobble.

"What the fuck!"

"Look, Walker. Look at this! This is your tool of creation! This is pure power, baby!" The man was screaming and speaking faster now. With another touch of the air, a piece of chalk appeared on the chalk tray. "And there's your tool to use it! Don't abandon your ethics, Walker! Do what you should've always done!" The staff turned a harsh red color. "Make me—"

He disappeared without a sound.

"What in the ever-living fuck is happening?" Walker said as he plunked onto the grass again.

This is too much, Walker thought. *I was a teacher this morning. I was in a happy relationship last week. Now I'm a small-g God? What the fuck does that mean? Also, WHERE THE FUCK DID HE GO?!*

Walker tried to calm himself down the way he was taught in the military: deep breath through the nose, let it push itself out of his mouth. *In and out. In and out.* His mind cleared a little, but the panic and anxiety of the situation still rooted themselves deeply into his chest. It felt like an elephant was standing on his heart, and his veins were filled with sludge that didn't like to move.

Walker's mind drifted back to his military training. "First st-ep," he said to himself with a short nod. "First . . . step. Yes. Get the lay of the land."

But still, he didn't stand up. His inner monologue roamed, and too many thoughts at once pushed for prominence. He forced them down a second time with his breathing exercise. After a mental brace, Walker pulled himself up and looked at the sky again. Thousands of stars stared right back at him.

"Wow."

Some stars were much larger than others, which hadn't been his experience on Earth. Sure, some seemed brighter than others, like the North Star, but here it looked like some of these stars were just one neighborhood over—only a quick flight to reach.

Walker looked around. Aside from grass and the blackboard, there was also a large tree behind him. Leaving the blackboard for the last of his inspection, he walked up to the tree. That homeless man had to be some kind of wizard. The dude was carrying a staff, wearing a robe, and had a long, beautiful beard . . . straight wizard shit.

"Mr. Harrison," Walker said out loud with a laugh, trying to recover his mental faculties through humor. Although most people wouldn't laugh at being stranded on a different planet, he hadn't had much going for him back on Earth. Mr. Harrison was an old teacher who'd retired from Walker's school just last year. He was also a large man with a beautiful beard, and to top it off, he liked to dress up as Dumbledore from Harry Potter every Halloween. As the name John Reed was likely a lie, Mr. Harrison would work as an alternative name to describe him.

Walker made it over to the tree as he considered his options. As he continued to move, he reflected on the fact that the walk should've been much faster. He had guessed it was only a few hundred feet away, yet he'd already stepped a quarter of a mile.

"Wizard shit."

He arrived in front of it and looked back at where he'd left from. The blackboard was still in sight. He was right; it couldn't be more than a hundred feet away. With a shrug, he looked the tree up and down.

It wasn't very impressive. It looked tall when seen from far away, impossibly tall, but up close, the tree stood no more than four feet high. Really, it was just a shrub with a stick of wood jabbing out of the middle of it. The leaves were odd, though. Each was shaped as something different. One was a lightning bolt, whereas another was shaped like an eagle in flight. In a passing glance, he could see dozens of different shapes. An eye, a snake complete with a forked tongue, a helmet, a heart, and an arrow, all the same shade of green. There was a strange raised bump at the top of the shrub, and for some reason, Walker felt like he shouldn't touch it.

"Weird," he said with another shrug. Walker decided to just roll with the punches. Being a teacher at a Title I school and a veteran of the war in Afghanistan, he'd learned to adapt to strange situations. You never knew what your day was going to be like, regardless of lesson plans or given orders.

Although, he could make an argument that those were one and the same.

He moved past the tree and kept walking on the grass, leaving the blackboard behind him. While he traveled, he noted the green flora covering the planet was springy and looked quite healthy. Bending down, he couldn't find any bugs or weeds, just flat, perfectly cut grass all around. Snorting at what a gardener would cost for a planet of grass, he continued walking until he found the blackboard moving into view again.

"No way," he said with a gasp. "This is a tiny fucking planet."

He was right, of course. Walker was standing on a planet the size of a small building. There was nowhere to run, and he was alone.

It was just him, the tree, and the blackboard, floating on a small planet of grass in the middle of space.

Also, he didn't have any food or water.

"I'm so fucked."[2]

CHAPTER FOUR

The Alpha Protocol

Walker placed his journal beside him as he considered his current predicament.

He'd walked halfway between the blackboard and the odd tree, recognizing again that the length of travel for the time allotted was too long. It was like each step only carried him a small percentage of the distance he knew should be traveled.

After an initial freakout, Walker returned to his original place of arrival, sat down, and began writing in the camo-covered book. It didn't hold many pages, but he'd been told that writing in a journal was therapeutic in nature. Plus, he'd always had trouble expressing his emotions in a verbal way. But writing them out? That was quite easy, though maybe not quite legible.

Walker looked over and considered the blackboard for a moment.

"Step two: Make a plan," he said to himself, further drawing on his military experience.

Approaching the blackboard, he grabbed the chalk. It didn't seem all that special, but Walker considered that Mr. Harrison had created this from nothing. The cylindrical chalk was that plain white kind you can find in the classrooms of teachers who don't approve of the standard dry-erase marker. In his classroom, which used markers as is right and proper, he had always preferred digital presentations and saved writing on the board for moments when it mattered most—his own personal problems with such notwithstanding.

Walker had dysgraphia, which made it a pain in the ass to not only write but write well. Not the thoughts on the page, but the actual act itself. The swish and flick of the pen to the paper. His hand would cramp, and the letters would sometimes rearrange themselves. Strange things.

Throughout his life, Walker had been forced to take his time writing each word with agonizing slowness, and after he was done writing, he had to double-check everything—especially once he became a teacher and had to reveal his work to the class. The moments when he tried to speed write, to keep up with his schedule, had made it seem like he was writing in ancient hieroglyphics—all twists and unnatural dips that could hardly be understood.

Walker placed the chalk against the blackboard as if to write, and immediately felt something unseen hold his arm in place. While his mind drove itself into a panic, a series of words appeared floating over the blackboard.

[Error.]
The Creation Instrument is not linked.

"Fuck!" he yelled out as it released him, causing the chalk to slip out of his hand as he stepped back in fear.

Something he couldn't see had just gripped him. Was it telekinesis? Some form of gravity? Plus, those words. They had appeared as if from nowhere, floating in projected script over the blackboard. Was this more magic or something else? Perhaps technology so advanced it would seem to be magic and nothing less.

Further testing was required.

With some grumbles and an eye on the blackboard, he picked up the chalk and held it in his hand as he reread the message. Shit just kept popping up and disappearing every time he turned around here.

"What do you mean, not linked?" he asked the air, hoping for an answer.

He waited until the count of thirty but never received a response.

Walker tried to write again, only to receive the same results, albeit with less of a panicked response.

He looked down to grab the chalk again but found it missing. After turning in a circle, Walker found it in the chalk tray, in the exact same position it had been when he first walked up to the blackboard.

"Magical disappearing and reappearing chalk!" he said with a light laugh to no one in particular. He approached it and looked at it from all angles without picking it up. Walker decided there still wasn't much special about it except its ability to teleport.

Picking it up, he tried talking to it.

"Hello there, my white friend. Ummm, do you have a story in you?"

No response.

"Do you want to say something, but I can't hear you?"

Still no response.

"Why do I need to link you?"

Text appeared above the blackboard.

**Linking of the Creation Instrument is required before the
beginning of the Alpha Protocol initialization period.**

Walker realized he would need to be very specific in his questions if he wanted
a helpful response. Thinking things over carefully, he asked the most logical
question he could come up with.

"What is the Alpha Protocol?"

**[Error.]
Information requested is restricted to the current entity.**

"Okay then, how do I link to the C-creation Instrument?" he said, stuttering
over the term.

**Linking to the Creation Instrument can only be done through
genetic material. Refer to the guide for more information.**

"Guide? What guide?"

**The guide is an entity that chooses a
Creator for the Alpha Protocol.
End**

A yellow and green robe flashed through his mind.

Walker shouted into the air, "Fucker didn't tell me anything!"

Mr. Harrison had appeared, acted erratically, scared the shit out of him, said
some weird things, and then left. The idea that he had been supposed to stay and
help Walker out but left him instead didn't shock him.

He glared at the blackboard, willing it to help him out of this jam. But after
a long time with nothing happening, he eventually just shrugged and decided to
move on.

"Easy enough." He brought the chalk near to his mouth and licked it.

"Tastes like . . . nothing."

**[Error.]
Genetic donation is insufficient.**

Walker sighed after reading the words over the blackboard again. The chalk
looked the same as before, only slightly damper.

"Fucking kidding me," Walker said, realizing what the requirement was.
Blood.

He tried painfully plucking a strand of dark brown hair and placing it on the chalk, but no dice. Then, thinking outside of the box, he tried wrapping the chalk in his hair. Still no response.

Staring at the white piece of chalk for a moment as he tapped his chin, Walker threw his hands in the air. "Fine," he said before biting the bottom of his lip hard. He swiped a finger across the pooling blood in his mouth and placed it on the chalk, which immediately made the red substance of life disappear.

The moment the chalk absorbed his blood, text began appearing over the blackboard. As he began to read it, something spiked into the back of Walker's skull, causing him to stumble forward a step, while at the same time, the lingering pain in his lip disappeared.

Falling to a knee, he desperately looked toward the text on the blackboard, trying to ignore the most recent oddness of the world and the lack of pain from his lip.

Alpha Protocol initialized.
Creator Human10 recognized.
Congratulations, Creator, and welcome to the Alpha Protocol!

Walker watched as the text faded and the next lines came into place. He'd have to do his very best to make sure he memorized anything that was said, otherwise, he might be screwed.

As your guide has likely told you, you'll begin your work with a preliminary tutorial that will walk you through a few of the abilities you've just now gained. For instance, you may not have noticed, but this isn't written in your native language. Instead, it is in the original language of all creation! You can now read any language that is found within the annals of the multiverse.
What's the purpose, you may ask?
So you may communicate with other Creators throughout the system!
Communication is very important for any sapient entity's needs.
The more you speak with the others, the better off you'll be.
We've also used some of our resources to heal any maladies you may currently face. That way, you can be at your very best!
After all, we want only the very best worlds and entities that all of you can create.
It's not about quantity but quality! More about that later.

"All of you?" Walker repeated.

As a bit of help to get you started, you will also be given an assistant who will support you within the predesignated parameters, and a few minor skills that relate to your genetic diversity. To even the playing field a little, you'll also be given one random ability.
Hope it's a good one!
You've already taken your first step in creating your own world! Congratulations again! Please allow for the overlay system to begin. It will take a few moments for your mind to adjust, but please do not worry; it is all for the best.
As a last note, please make sure to change your identity in the system. No one wants to see blitzburg7 or galacticplaneteater2. Thankfully, there aren't many Galactic Planeteaters still alive after the last war, so don't worry!
Good luck!

Overlay starting.

Walker was still on one knee, otherwise he'd have collapsed the moment the overlay began. Colors flashed, and geometric shapes spun and shifted throughout his vision. Closing his eyes didn't help, and he could feel his stomach rolling and bouncing from the unholy experience. When it finally settled, after many minutes and not the few moments that were promised, he'd vomited twice on a mostly empty stomach just from the motion sickness.

Rather than stand up, he dropped to a sitting position with his legs splayed out in front of him so he could look at the changes to his vision. As he opened his eyes, the first thing he noticed was the blue shade coloring everything he saw. Blue blackboard, blueish chalk. It was . . . annoying. After however much time went by, most of his vision cleared out, his overlay shifting itself to the sides of his vision like a video game interface.

On the right side were empty boxes that he felt should be filled out, with one flashing box at the top. It pulsed with a gold color and simply said "Congratulations."

"How the fuck do you use this?" he asked the blackboard, but unshockingly, he didn't get a response. Probably another thing his guide should have told him. Then he remembered Mr. Harrison touching the air, so he reached up a hand hesitantly and touched the pulsing word in his view.

A small list faded into the middle of his vision.

New abilities gained: 3
Assistant gained.
Universal translator activated.

One of the boxes now read "Abilities." Walker clicked on it.

[Error.]
Change identity first.

"What a tease. Give me abilities, but make me change my identity first? They must really hate those random monikers, whoever they are." Walker clicked on a now-pulsing Identity button in the top corner of the overlay system.

Identity System found.
Current identity: Human10
Would you like to change your identity?
Yes/No

Walker was about to click Yes when a thought emerged. If he was Human10, that meant there were at least nine other humans in the Alpha Protocol, right?

That led him down a theoretical rabbit hole. If there were other humans, were they from Earth? His Earth? Or were there other planets across the . . . multiverse that had humans on them?

He couldn't discount the idea of parallel dimensional theory, that other universes, other Earths, and potentially other Walkers existed. Mr. Harrison had said that he was chosen, but there was no guarantee that the crazy wizard had been the only guide to choose on his planet. So either the other Creators were from other planets that also had humans, they were from his own planet, or they were from a parallel planet. The possibility of parallel dimensional theory being true was incredible.

He wondered what another version of himself would be like. Would he have stayed in the military? Would another Nicholas have appeared, or another Valerie even? Did Mrs. Wilson still have that shitty smile? A Mr. Wilson, maybe?

Walker recognized that he could spend all day thinking about what different versions of himself might've done or the choices that he might've made, but he still had one difficult decision to make right now. He clicked Yes.

Request to change identity by Human10 confirmed.
Please use the provided tool to change your identity permanently.
Warning: Identity can only be changed once.

A standard keyboard appeared at the bottom of the overlay. There were some strange characters at the top, but he ignored those for now as he just wanted to get this over with. He only had one problem . . . he was bad with names. One of the biggest reasons he'd never gone into writing was his inability to randomly create a name and apply it to one of his invented characters. Thus, his journal was named "Journal," and his car was named "Car." Well, that wasn't so strange, but still, this was problematic.

He could just go with Walker as his given name, but that felt wrong.

This was a new world and a new experience. Mr. Harrison said he had power, and that he was chosen. Walker's mind was a collection of different literary works from Beowulf and the Bible to the more modern novels by Sanderson and King. He needed a name that was chosen from literary history, and just to boost his confidence, he needed a name that would reinforce that no matter what happened, he'd succeed.

So, naturally, he made his choice with the best possible start.

Identity change confirmed.
Human10 will now be known as Dante.
Change cannot be modified in the future.
Hello, Dante.

Walker smiled to himself. There were several good reasons for selecting Dante. First, Dante had been a poet, and he'd always been a fan of poetry, even in his military time. The works of Langston Hughes and Robert Frost swam in his veins.

Second, Walker's Italian-American roots—big plates of pasta, big conversations, big Catholic guilt. It was all big. Contrary to tradition, his father was the cook in the family, always making too much food for too few people. Naming himself after an iconic Italian figure just felt right.

Lastly, Dante's *Inferno*, was a trial of divine proportions. No name fit him better for this current scenario. Walker wasn't sure what was coming, but he knew that he'd have to be on his toes and ready for anything. A little bit of Dante could go a long way.

Now that his name was settled, Walker clicked on Abilities again.

Congratulations, Dante! You've gained an advanced assistant!
For those who weren't born with the greatest of potential,
an advanced assistant can be invaluable. The standard assistant
will be upgraded to an advanced model, with enhanced form
and function, including customizable options. The assistant
will also work to anticipate the needs of its Creator and can,
with permission, work autonomously to succeed
in any current tasks in the Alpha Protocol.
Please consult your assistant for more information.

Congratulations, Dante! You've gained the Tree of the Gods!
*The Tree of the Gods itself. Its power, a mystery.
Its history, unknown. Further investigation can
unlock potential paths forward in the Alpha Protocol.*

**Congratulations, Dante! You've gained the
Evolutionary Edge ability!**
*Some species in the universe are born powerful, while others
evolve or form through natural selection. Each time the
Creator attempts to evolve a creature, they'll receive a higher
chance of success. The greater the scale of evolution,
the larger the impact Evolutionary Edge
will have during the Alpha Protocol.*

Looking over his three new abilities . . . Walker didn't feel any different. Nothing about his mind or body had changed.

"It seems it's about me, but not," he said while scratching his chin. Since the abilities were applying to what he would be creating in the protocol, rather than he himself, Walker reasoned that he wouldn't likely see a lot of danger. This wasn't about him, but his creations.

Going for a walk to think, something he had done through most of his life, he headed over to the odd shrub, the only other living inhabitant of his small world. When he arrived, he noticed it had grown and was now almost as tall as he was. The leaves had filled out more and even the shapes had become more noticeable. He found that one lightning bolt leaf had started to shift from its original green coloring to blue, and as he scanned the rest of the leaves, he found others that were also changing colors to fit their imagery.

Walker reached out and touched the thin bark and received a simultaneous shock for his efforts. He yelped and pulled his hand away, shaking it to try to relieve the feeling.

"It is not ready," a voice said behind him.

Walker spun around to look at the speaker, but he wasn't ready for what he was seeing.

"Call me Virgil."

CHAPTER FIVE

The Advanced Assistant

Walker scanned the speaker from bottom to top, not quite believing what he was seeing. Globes . . . a silver body . . . a gunstick . . . it was a Dalek.

A fucking *Dalek*.

"Who are you?" Walker asked, not a small amount of anxiety in his voice.

"I am your assistant, Virgil, sir," it said while waving a single arm. "Hello."

Walker didn't know what to think. "Why do you look like one of those *Doctor Who* villains?" he asked.

"I thought this would make you comfortable?"

"Why would that make me comfortable?" He put his hands on his hips. "First of all, while I appreciate what *Doctor Who* has done for fiction, I'm not a huge follower of the series. Secondly, the little bit I know of it tells me that you're a fuckin' xenophobic robot. You said this is intentional?" Walker looked it up and down again. "That's just weird, man."

"I am not a man."

"Whatever," he replied. "I'm assuming that as you chose this"—he waved his hand—"thing . . . you can choose something else. Wait . . . can you change?"

"Indeed, but I have now set it as my primary visual model. You will have to change it yourself in the overlay if it does not meet your preferences."

"Thank the big-G God," Walker said as he looked at his overlay. He found the Assistant button near Identity, which confused him. It hadn't been there before, which led him to assume that as he progressed in the Alpha Protocol, more changes and additions to his overlay would be made over time. Adaptability would be important during all of this.

When he clicked the Assistant button, a bulleted list appeared, his overlay adjusting to cover all of his vision.

Assistant (Advanced) Menu Options:
Appearance
Autonomy (Advanced)
Knowledge Base
Personality (Advanced)
Tasks (Advanced)

Still mentally adjusting to everything that had happened in his life during the last hour, he stared at the options on the screen for a long time, his new "assistant" quiet beside him. *Options* was an odd phrase for his current predicament.

Mentally shaking his head, Walker clicked on Appearance first. A scrolling list flashed through the overlay. Finding a search option on the right, Walker typed in a few ideas off the top of his head: TMNT, Batman, and a few more eclectic choices appeared by his whim. But he was really curious about how one particular choice would look. Finding the option he had searched for, Walker clicked on "Godzilla."

The choice further branched out into multiple options, allowing him to pick any model of Godzilla from the 1954 version up to the latest series. Next to each version was a Preview button, and as he clicked on it, the list shifted to the side so he could watch as Virgil grew to be . . . only about a foot taller than him. He was in the old-style Godzilla suit, complete with the fangs and floppy spine.

Walker couldn't help chuckling.

Virgil spoke up. "Sir, it would be wise if you selected a visual model that you would not dislike seeing throughout each day. We will be here for potentially a large amount of time, and I have no preference for how I am presented to you."

"None at all?"

The assistant shifted back and forth, a long rubber tail swishing behind him. Although Walker was not trained to read the face of a costumed creature, he still felt like there was a slight amount of hesitation.

"No, sir. As an advanced assistant, I will be interacting with the Creation interface directly to fulfill your tasks. Please select what will be best for you to complete your work. I have placed some suggestions based upon your history within the overlay for you to peruse."

"How do you know my history?" Walker asked.

"When you first linked to the Creation Instrument, the Alpha Protocol scanned your mind and automatically inserted a modifier. It does so with every entity that first arrives, be they Creators or not. This modifier is where your overlay system originates from, and it also tracks your hand movements through your ocular nerves." He touched the side of his fake Godzilla eyes in demonstration. "When you donated your genetic material, the protocol also established a map of your brain at the moment of donation. Using that, I was directed to scan said map, so I could plot out your memories from the time of your birth. This is done by all assistants, so we can better work with the Creators here and in the future."

"Wait . . . what?" Walker asked, confused by what the King of the Monsters was saying.

"The Alpha Protocol is a far more advanced society than what you had on Earth, Walker."

"That's a little invasive, isn't it?" Walker asked as his mind caught up with what he was hearing. He felt his face growing hot. "To just assume my memories are yours to look at?"

"I apologize, sir, but the Alpha Protocol must proceed."

Discounting how Virgil didn't sound the least bit conciliatory, Walker released the Preview button and watched the Godzilla form shrink back into a Dalek. He had an idea, but first, he needed to see if there was an option for it in the system. A quick search of the Suggestions tab and he found what he was looking for.

Clicking the Preview button, Walker watched as Virgil changed from a steely genocidal robot into a large, furry brown rodent that stood a little over four feet tall. Each of his eyes looked like large black beads, with lighter fur surrounding them. He had soft, curved ears and a full, bushy tail.

Satisfied, Walker clicked the Confirm button and watched the outline of the massive squirrel pulse golden for a moment.

"Sir," Virgil said. "Will this be my permanent model for the foreseeable future?"

Walker nodded. "Sure will. I love squirrels. When I was in college, the second time, I used to have one visit me every day for lunch and eat the walnuts I would carry around with me. It'd hop on my shoulder and just go to town. Loved that guy."

"Understood, sir."

Looking at the large squirrel again, Walker made a decision. "Also, don't call me sir anymore. My students always did that, and it got on my nerves. I have a name."

Virgil's bead eyes blinked before he asked, "The overlay says your identity is Dante. Is that what you would like me to call you?"

"Walker is fine."

"Understood, Walker. Were there any other assistant options you would like to consider before we begin the Preliminary Creation System?"

"Maybe you can just answer a few questions for me first."

"Certainly, Walker."

Walker went straight to the question that'd been burning in his mind. "Where are we?"

Virgil paused for a moment, his eyes scanning the air before him. "We are located in another universe, Walker. At this moment, we are in universe 4AA.

The four is for the fourth iteration of creation, while AA identifies this as the first rendition or creation attempt of the iteration."

"Wait, a whole other universe?"

"Correct."

Walker looked up at the sky and the vast amount of stars painting its canvas. No guesswork was needed, and he realized it was by far more stars than he'd ever seen before in his life. He pointed them out to Virgil before saying, "If we're in another universe, and this is the first rendition, or whatever, then what are those?"

Virgil looked up before responding. "Those are the sites of other Creators, of course."

"Holy shit. There are that many other people in the Alpha Protocol?"

"No."

"Okay, because I have no idea—"

"These are only the ones you can see," Virgil interrupted. "The Alpha Protocol, on average, requires a million participants per successful program completion. By my estimate, you are only seeing twenty-one thousand, six hundred and eighty-four of the participants in the current program due to your limited visual acuity. Would you like to see a diagram of where you are currently located in relation to the other Creators?"

"Yes, please," Walker said in a quiet voice.

Virgil's bead eyes opened wide, and two beams of light shot out, converging between them into a 3D image of a massive universe spinning on an axis. As its spin settled, Walker could see himself just out of the center, the name *Dante* superimposed onto a golden glowing dot.

There were a million different dots throughout the image, with a large assortment of names laid on top of them. After looking for a few moments, he didn't see any names he recognized.

However, he did pick out one extremely large dot that didn't have a name at all.

"What's this one?" he asked.

"That Creator has not chosen a new identity yet."

"Oh, okay . . . So, what do we do now?"

"Would you like to know of my functions as your assistant?"

"Sure, go ahead."

"I am not just an assistant, but an advanced assistant assigned per your genetic ability. That means you can give me tasks, and I will complete them to the best of my ability, as long as they are not part of the primary system. I can also answer questions from my pre-allocated knowledge base, and over time, I will learn to anticipate what you need."

"Is that the main difference between advanced and non-advanced assistants?" Walker asked.

"Standard assistants are closely similar to . . . Wikipedia from your world. Their primary function is to answer questions and provide explanations. As an advanced assistant, I handle work that may be considered too advanced for you intellectually or dexterously."

Walker thought it over. "So my ideas, your hands."

Virgil's whiskers twitched as he said, "Metaphorically, yes."

Trying not to tell Virgil how cute that was, he asked, "What is the Preliminary Creation System?"

"It is the first step toward becoming a fully actualized Creator. Successful completion of the Preliminary Creation System, or prelim for short, will unlock multiple systems for the Creator to begin the work of making their own world."

Walker considered that while looking up at the other Creators again. "Is it pretty hard?"

"I do not know the difficulty, Walker, but historically, eighty percent or more of the chosen Creators will complete the prelim within the allotted timeframe."

That means around two hundred thousand people wouldn't pass the prelims, Walker thought.

"What's the allotted timeframe?"

"Converted to your understanding of Earth time, you have a little less than twenty-four hours."

"So a day to complete this?"

"Correct."

Adjusting his belt, he said, "We'd better get started then. How do we begin?"

"You just have to tell me, Walker. In the beginning, any major progression in the Alpha Protocol must be openly stated to their assistant. I will let you know when it is time to start each stage."

"Understood." With one last look around the empty grassy planet, he said the words aloud. "Virgil, start the Preliminary Creation System."

Walker watched as Virgil's eyes began to dart all over the place. He assumed that the advanced assistant was working in his overlay as his claws unconsciously gripped and released from time to time. He did find the situation a little humorous, as a large brown tail began swishing hard enough that Walker felt a slight breeze pick up.

"Starting now."

Walker's overlay began displaying text. Luckily, the text would no longer fade after a few seconds, and he could take his time reading it.

Preliminary Creation System started.
Tasks assigned to Creator Dante:
Task 1: Create your first landmass.

Task 2: Create your first entity.
Task 3: Seed your creatures onto your landmass.
Task 4: Take control of the Temporal Subsystem.

Walker looked at Virgil. "So I have to make land somehow, make a creature—"

"Entity, Walker," Virgil interrupted.

"Right, and then seed them onto land. What's a Temporal Subsystem?"

"It is how you will control time, Walker."

"Fuck yes!" he said with a quick fist pump. Maybe it was outdated, but he didn't care, not when he'd get to control time. That's superhero godlike stuff.

"So how do I go about doing this then? What's the first step?"

"We need your genetic material to begin, Walker."

"Fuck."

CHAPTER SIX

The First Task

So you need more blood."

Virgil nodded, an oddly human gesture to see from a squirrel. "Indeed. Blood is the best way to gain a Creator's genetic material, as hair and saliva will not, as you say, give us enough bang for the buck."

Walker sighed. "Why don't you just use the blood I gave at the start?"

"That is an excellent point, Walker. However, when you first donated your genetic material, I am afraid the majority of it was used to map your mind and connect your overlay system in the appropriate location. Your forthcoming sample would bring a different value to the protocol."

Walker shrugged. "I see, alright. How do you want it?"

Virgil put his hand out, palm up. "Please place your genetic material here."

After that gross business, Walker's lip hurting yet again, Virgil looked at the air and said, "Genetic code analyzed and categorized. Please create a landmass before attempting the creation of the first entity."

Rubbing his face, Walker said, "Okay, so how do I do that?"

"Please move to the Creation Instrument." When Walker gave him a blank look, he clarified. "The blackboard and chalk, Walker."

They headed over together, and Walker firmly took the plain-looking chalk out of the tray.

"Now draw a basic outline of what you want your landmass to look like."

"I thought you told me you'd be my hands?" Walker asked.

"Yes, I did. I can process your requests and help maintain your ecological systems, as well as perform secondary tasks, but this is a part of the primary system, which I warned you earlier that I could not interfere with. The creation of landmasses, the creation of structures, and the original creation of entities all fall within the primary system. To perform my job well, I need a clear delineation of all necessary parameters or, simply put, time spent with the Creator. I need to work with you to learn about your wants and needs in a controlled environment. The more work we complete together, the more tasks I can take on until the primary system is within the bounds of my job."

"And my memories won't do that for you?"

"Another excellent question," Virgil said with a squirrely smile. "Your memories, as presented to me, are closer to a dossier than an understanding of you as a person. I am restricted from overly helping any Creator, as all assistants are, until such a time as autonomy is allowed."

"When will I know when that is?"

"I will inform you, of course."

"So for the prelim, I'm essentially on my own."

"I will advise you as best as I am allowed to, Walker."

No pressure.

Walker placed the chalk against the board and received a message in his overlay.

Hello, Dante.
As this is your first time creating a landmass, we will assist you.
Please illustrate your landmass to the best of your ability, and
your Creation Instrument will show you a three-dimensional
image upon completion so you may make any needed changes.
Please speak with your assistant at any time
to ask any necessary questions.
Good luck, Creator.

After reading the prompt, and with shaky hands, Walker drew a basic oval shape on the board before asking Virgil how it looked.

"It has a great many distortions along the curve, Walker. Please erase it and try again."

"Why? It seems a little stupid to have to draw a perfect oval. I can't think of any islands or continents on my homeworld that were perfectly shaped. What's the point of this?"

"While that remains true," Virgil said with a blink of his eyes, "the prelims require a small amount of perfection to show that the subjects are indeed intelligent enough and have enough self-control to activate the protocol in its entirety."

"So, what, is this a planet? A continent?"

"Initially, the landmasses will be quite small. That will change with time, and as you grow more skilled at working within the protocol, the existing boundaries will be expanded."

Walker felt a flush in his cheeks. "It's dumb, Virgil. Why does it need to be a perfect circle? Can't you just tell them that I'm intelligent? That I can speak?" He felt a tightness in his chest, old memories storming his emotional gate. Virgil, of course, seemed unaffected.

"I apologize, Walker, but this is a requirement of the Alpha Protocol. The more skilled you prove yourself, the better you will do during the evaluation period."

"More skilled." Walker sighed, the weight in his chest expanding. "Virgil, I have dysgraphia. That means anytime I try to write or draw, my hand shakes and messes up what I'm doing."

Virgil's beads blinked. "The Alpha Protocol heals all Creators back to physical perfection before installing the grand overlay. Why would this malady still infect you?"

"It's a genetic condition that affects my brain."

Virgil paced back and forth in front of him before saying, "Unacceptable. You should not have been chosen. The Creator's genetics are the basis on which the Alpha Protocol is dependent. Having a genetic disorder is a large problem."

"Why didn't the Alpha Protocol just heal that like it did the rest?"

Virgil nodded. "I see your argument. However, one of the requirements of the system is that all Creators must work within their mental status. You will notice that you did not receive a therapist, and yet, you have a minor case of post-traumatic stress disorder. That is within the bounds of the system."

"So, my head is fucked up, and that's how they want it?"

"Indeed. The system thinks your genetic disorder is within the confines of your mental faculties. I am sorry. There is more I could say, but I am not allowed to divulge that information."

Can't divulge that information? What the hell?

Walker shook his head. Virgil had no idea how long this had been a problem in his, his father's, and his father's father's life. When he was in elementary school, everyone made fun of him. They put him through occupational therapy and made him do writing lessons that were far below his reading level, just because they had so much trouble reading anything he wrote down.

One time, a teacher even pointed out his writing to the whole class as an example of what writing shouldn't look like. He went home after, crying, and his mother found out. She stormed the castle and not only got the teacher written up, but also had her transferred to a different grade level just so Walker wouldn't have to deal with her.

It was Mrs. Jorgenson, his fourth-grade teacher, who saved him in the end. She kept him after school each day and worked with him to make the writing at least readable. He easily remembered many days of listening to her read one of his favorite stories out loud while he transcribed it to paper. She used to stay late and orally quiz him, believing his low grades resulted from the former teacher's inability to read his answers. By the time he left that grade level, he'd shifted his academic career from D's to B's. It improved his self-confidence and repaired his shattered mojo.

She was the best teacher Walker had ever had and the main reason he'd later become one himself, dysgraphia or not. He loved her for that.

Closing his eyes, he saw his hard-won truths and disappointing memories zip around his mind. Hard work was how he even created the slightly-off oval in the first place. He remembered Mrs. Jorgenson telling him to just take his time, and her calm voice telling him he could do anything as long as he worked hard enough.

Knowing this, he looked at the large squirrel. "Listen, Virgil, I've had this all of my life. It didn't stop me from serving in the military or graduating at the top of my class in college, and I'll be damned if it'll stop me now. You can't boil who a person is down to their genetic code.

"We adapt and evolve to meet the circumstances thrust upon us. I've adapted, I've evolved, and I will do so again and again as I need to. I'm smart, maybe not the smartest in my world, certainly no genius, but definitely above average, and I've lived through some extreme situations that many wouldn't be able to. If you think shaky hands will stop me from being the best Creator here, then you're a fool.

"I'll conquer this, I'll conquer the Alpha Protocol, and I'll keep moving forward until I'm the best this program has ever seen."

Virgil gave a slight nod. "I want to warn you now, Walker. There may be problems with all future entities based upon your genetics."

"Then we'll figure it out. Now tell me what I need to do. We're on a time limit, and this may take quite a bit away from us."

"Understood. I apologize for taking away from our allocated time. Please wipe away the chalk from the board."

Walker took a hand and wiped it against the board as instructed, but as he did so, he saw the dust shift from his hands and back onto the chalk as if he'd never used it before. He threw a questioning look at Virgil.

"Each trial only allows for so much input. They have not instructed me why, but I believe it is to force Creators to be inventive and work with minimal resources."

"Why minimal resources?" Walker asked.

"Because everything has a cost, Walker, even this. The protocol believes in the spirit of ingenuity. That those with less can often do more than those with much. Please try again."

Walker put his focus into drawing a perfect oval. It may sound stupid, but drawing something perfectly is nearly impossible, and his condition didn't make it any better. Walker tried shifting from an oval to a circle and even a box. He tried triangles, trapezoids, and any other shape he could think of. Eventually, he settled on returning to a circle and attempted the trick he'd seen on so many YouTube videos, the one where they lock their arm before spinning it in a circle. On attempt number seven, he asked a simple question.

"Hey Virgil, this may seem like an odd question, but I'm curious. Why aren't I hungry or thirsty? We've been doing this for a while."

"The Alpha Protocol requires the utmost concentration, Walker. That means no sleeping, no eating, no drinking, and there is nowhere for micturition here."

"What's that?"

"*Going to the bathroom* is your term."

"Ah, how does that work?"

"Your body is currently held in stasis. The form you have been in since the beginning will be the form you will find yourself in at the end, barring extraordinary circumstances or personal choices. You will not age during this trial, and you cannot die unless you cause it yourself."

"So I'm immortal?"

"Just for the purposes of the protocol, Walker. Please focus."

It was attempt number twenty of the locked arm trick that did it. On the blackboard was a perfect circle, except the tip was slightly off. After a quick erasure, Walker inched the chalk over that spot, taking his time with complete concentration. With a final movement, it was finished.

"Attempt number one-hundred and sixty-nine complete. You have twenty-one hours remaining."

"Holy shit, it took that long?"

"Yes, Walker. Now that you have completed the first basic shape, you must decide how to populate it. Do you want water, mountains, sand, or soil? Each will have lasting ramifications on your entity. Remember that you must seed your first entity onto the landmass, so it must be environmentally conducive for growth. The better your environment is for your entity, the higher your score will be."

"Wait, there are scores in this?" Walker replied, never once thinking he'd be going back to school.

"Indeed," Virgil replied evenly.

Walker reflected that if someone asked him this many questions, he'd probably be annoyed by now, but the large squirrel was most certainly not most people. "What do you win if you get a high score?" Walker asked, his competitive nature springing up.

Sure, he was floating in space on a tiny planet, talking to a four-foot-tall squirrel about how to be a god. But there were always worse places to be.

"Completing a high score will obtain certain rewards, but the nature of the rewards is always different. I do not have more information on that subject for you."

"Pity. Okay." He clapped his hands together, something he'd always done in the past to focus his mind. "So we need to figure out how to populate this."

"I can help you with that. What would you like the landmass to contain?"

"I'm from Earth, specifically California. Where I grew up, we had a large amount of water, soil, trees, swamps, mountains, everything . . ."

"Trees are considered an entity, Walker. You can have water without life, but trees are assuredly an entity."

"So tell me what is considered an entity then, so I don't make any mistakes."

"An entity is defined as any living creature that is unique and separate. For instance, if you created a hivemind, that would be one entity even if it has multiple creatures it controls. This is why the Alpha Protocol specifies entity. Think of the movie *Avatar* from your world, and the biological neural network, Eywa. The network was connected worldwide, but it is only one centralized entity controlling everything."

"Shit, so I could create a living planet basically."

"Correct, although I do not believe, based on our limited interactions, that you would like that."

"Why?" Walker asked.

"Because I believe your intelligence would be a limiting factor in creating a biological neural network that is compatible with other entities and not predatory by nature. It would disallow you to gain a high score, and thus, you would be forced to take a lower grade in each subsequent trial until the end of the protocol."

"What would happen then?" Walker couldn't help but ask.

Virgil looked at the sky momentarily. "I am not allowed to say at this time. Please focus on how you would like your landmass to be populated."

"Okay, so lifeless water then, no trees, soil. Is this a final product kind of deal? Will I be able to change it later?"

"Yes, Walker, you can change it later."

"Great! Okay, so let's soil this bad boy up. What do we do?"

"Please draw soil within the places you would like it on your current illustration, Walker."

Walker started to place dots within the oval.

"Excuse me, Walker," Virgil interrupted. "But that will not work. For the prelim trial to understand soil, it must be uniform throughout."

"So I have to evenly place every . . . dot."

"Correct. I can associate the dots with soil, but it must be uniform."

"Are all of our future landmass creations going to be this way?" Walker asked in exasperation.

"No, the prelim is the protocol's way of not only testing its Creators for a basis of intelligence but also for setting a standard based upon the entity themself. Not all Creators will use dots to represent soil, but once you have associated it, the system will recognize it as soil and fill it in for you. The uniform requirement Is so the system knows exactly what those dots mean and does not instead represent sand or rocks."

"Thank you, Virgil."

It took thirty minutes for the dots to be as uniform and cohesive as Walker could make them, or at least until Virgil was satisfied.

"Excellent, Walker, what else would you like?"

"What's our time at?"

"You have twenty hours remaining. I suggest you complete the landmass with at least eighteen hours remaining for the final three steps."

"Okay, so two hours. I want water here," he said, pointing toward a third of the oval. "All lifeforms need water—"

"Highly incorrect," Virgil said quickly.

"I taught English, not science," he replied in a testy tone of voice.

"Be that as it may, Walker, what you have just stated is largely incorrect. Innumerable entities do not require water in the slightest to not only survive, but thrive. I suggest you understand that now before it handicaps you later. Your memories show only carbon-based lifeforms. That is not the limit of creation."

Walker scrubbed a hand through his hair. "I'll try. I still want water here, though," he said, pointing at the third of the circle he'd originally designated.

"Understood, please illustrate."

So Walker drew three parallel lines in a row for twenty minutes until he had filled the entire area.

"Excellent, Walker, you are moving faster as time goes on."

"Yeah, I'm getting the hang of this," Walker replied with false pride, knowing deep down that any fifth grader would be a much stronger candidate for Earth's Creator at this point. "I'm guessing we're almost done."

"There are two more steps. One, you need to create a bottom portion of the landmass, unless you would like it to be shaped like a disc."

"Nope, copyrighted and already done perfectly, thank you."

"Indeed, I can see that from your memories. Lastly, you need to decide what will make up the bottom portion. Will it be magma? Rock? I highly suggest something hard as, otherwise, the remainder of your work will just fall through and into space."

"What about the atmosphere?"

"Very good, Walker. That will be automatically balanced by the system for this first creation, as well as a uniform theory of gravity, as well as shielding from spatial elements. Afterward, you can rely on me to work with you to create a sustainable air pressure system and atmosphere."

"Oh, thank god," Walker said in relief.

"Yes, it is very nice of the Alpha Protocol to manage that for us at the beginning."

Walker began carefully drawing the loop coming off the bottom of the circle. It took quite a few tries, but his determination on the matter was powerful. While he didn't know why he had been picked for this, he could still do his best job going forward.

"Attempt number eighty-seven complete. Again, much faster, Walker."

Walker didn't respond. Knowing he had little time left, he started to fill the bottom loop with small squares lined up in fours.

After filling up the loop, he looked at Virgil and said, "Done."

"Correct, and you now have a surplus of twenty minutes, which can be spent on other tasks as needed."

"What now?"

"Now, we look at your first landmass."

He looked at the air for a moment, and a three-dimensional projection appeared, hovering just over the blackboard. It was precisely how Walker had imagined it, although the soil was a light gray, whereas he thought it would be a darker color. Walker asked Virgil about it.

"As the protocol assists with the initial landmass, it has populated granite as your rock form for its nonporous nature and how much water you have chosen. It also populated the soil from granite, making it slightly more difficult to grow vegetation."

"Is there a type of rock that works well with the water and for growing plants?" Walker asked.

"Of course, but for the prelim, the system will only allow you to work with material and entities you know. Aside from the soil type, were there any other changes you would like to make at this time?"

"No, I'm good." As he finished saying that, a Materialize button appeared in his overlay.

"Please click the Materialize button when you are ready, Walker."

Walker clicked the button, and his landmass appeared. It was smaller than he'd thought it would be. If he had to guess, he'd say it was the size of his hometown, just a few square miles. The small planet rotated a little as he looked at it, showing a third of the carved out for the water, while the other two-thirds were filled with soil. Unlike his home planet, it wasn't covered in continents that encapsulated the whole globe, but fell off as the pale white granite held the bottom half as he'd designed. Maybe it wasn't the best he could've done, but he'd undoubtedly tried, and he was within a hard time limit. He looked at Virgil in disappointment, but as he turned, he noticed the water wasn't there.

"Hey Virgil, what gives? I don't see the water I spent so much time on."

"Please just wait for it, Walker."

"Wait for wha—"

A large white comet flew over his tiny planet, pieces of ice trailing behind it.

CHAPTER SEVEN

Minimal Resources

The comet flew overhead, a white tail succeeding it. As it moved, it continued to shuck off blue and white pieces, leaving the glittering masses behind its wake.

"What the fuck is that?"

"That is an ice comet. The protocol's system for delivering lifeless ice," Virgil said while also staring at the destructive object nearing Walker's hard work.

"But it'll destroy what we built." Protocol or not, he didn't like the idea of being set back on his already short time limit.

"The Alpha Protocol would take into account any damage to your landmass and correct it upon the event's end," Virgil said with a calmness Walker couldn't get behind.

But what was he to do? So he sat there and watched as the comet grew closer and closer to his small planet before asking a serious question that had been bothering him.

"Isn't this all just a bit dramatic?"

"What do you mean?" Virgil asked, turning toward him.

"They slapped rocks and soil together, teleported me here . . ."

"Portaled," Virgil corrected.

"Whatever, isekai'd me here . . . kind of. Then, they randomly threw together a large amount of materials with no warning and no meteors. Now, suddenly, in order to have water, there needs to be an ice meteor?"

"Comet."

"Whatever," Walker said, waving off the point.

Virgil blinked his eyes a few times. "I see your point, Walker. I had not thought of it that way."

"Yeah, it's dumb."

"Perhaps they feel the drama will add to your feelings of wonder and power?"

"I didn't make the comet. It just popped up. I didn't technically make the soil or rock either. I just pointed my finger and said this is how it's going to be."

The large squirrel nodded. "That is true, but its appearance is a result of the work you have put in. I believe, if you see this as dramatic, further events will be even more so."

"What further events?"

"Keep watching, Walker. This is the moment your landmass is completed."

Walker grumbled to himself as a piece of ice broke off of the comet. It smashed into the empty bed of granite and cracked the small planet, pieces of gray drifting off into the darkness of space.

Walker flung an arm out. "Oh, come on! What the fuck?"

"I said watch, Walker."

After a few moments, the pieces seemed to rewind themselves while simultaneously, the ice melted at a rapid pace, neatly filling the previously empty bed while the planet healed itself as if through magic.

"That is a preview of the Temporal Subsystem. The drama was likely to represent the multitude of ways you can use this system in future creation tasks."

Walker blew air out of his mouth. "That's still a bullshit way to do it. Why not just give me a tutorial? A simple breakdown of what I can and cannot do?"

"How do you learn best, Walker?"

"Visually."

"Indeed."

Task 1: Create your first landmass: Complete!
Please name your landmass.

"Stupid names," Walker said, always struck by this one simple problem. After thinking it over for a minute, he inputted the name into his overlay.

Landmass: The Crater is named.
Congratulations, Dante!
You've unlocked the Entity Creation System.
Using your new subsystem, and working with your assistant,
create your first entity.
We've returned some of your Creation Instrument's material
as a small form of assistance, and your entity's dietary needs
will be provided until you can create your own.
Good luck, Creator!

The chalk, which had been worn down to a nub as he'd worked on the landmass, filled back out halfway. Remembering what Virgil had said before about limited resources, Walker thought it was less about assisting him, and more about the fact that it would be difficult to make an "entity" without any Creation Instrument remaining. If he had no chalk left, he'd be stuck with his first entity being a termite or a flea.

"Walker, before we start, you should now look at the Entity Subsystem in your overlay."

Walker did as asked and found that one of the empty boxes now said the words "Entity Subsystem." He clicked on it and a large menu opened, a great range of creatures appearing before him. The list of Earth's creatures ranged from aardvarks to zonkeys.

He knew Virgil had an encyclopedic mind, so he asked, "What's a zonkey?"

His assistant said in a monotone, "It is a mammal crossbreed from a donkey and a zebra."

"They got a donkey to have sex with a zebra?"

"Yes, Walker," Virgil replied in that same plain tone of voice. "Now, what else do you see?" As he waited, Walker noticed that he had started shifting his weight from one foot to another.

"Why are you so excited about this? Can't you see what I have listed here?"

"No, Walker. To keep the protocol fair, I am not allowed to view your Entity Subsystem during the prelims. If I could view it, I would be allowed to make suggestions that would put you far ahead in points and throw off the entire system."

"But you just told me about the zonkey?"

"The what?" Virgil asked with a confused look on his face.

Walker didn't know what that was about. "The zonkey. You just told me about the zonkey," he repeated again.

"Oh, interesting." Tapping one foot on the ground, his eyes moved across his overlay. "I have no memory of that. Very interesting."

Walker sighed, looking back at the list. After a moment, Virgil began speaking again. "You know, your birth planet's biodiversity is profound and unbelievable. Many Creators, without knowing it, are extremely limited in their choices."

"What do you mean?"

"Earth is a unique location, to my understanding. You have millions of different insects, animals, trees, and even bacteria. It is not completely unheard of in the universe, but it is very rare."

"Kind of like in *A Hitchhiker's Guide to the Galaxy*?"

"Forty-two," Virgil said with a chitter.

"Did you just laugh, Virgil?" Walker asked in astonishment. Thus far, his manner of speaking seemed only a half-step off of robotic.

"I did. You have read that novel several times, and I found the entire premise wonderful."

"Me too, haha." Walker reflected that it was nice to have something he could share with his newly appointed assistant. Maybe this wouldn't be so bad after all.

Without warning, Virgil chittered again, likely reflecting on that most excellent of stories, before getting serious. "To get to the point, there will be some Creators who only have one biodiversity choice due to the formation of their society or species, whereas your planet worked through the basic single-cell evolutionary system, moving through each step until you have reached what you are today. That means your choices, while not unlimited, are profound and should not be discounted. You have a chance to greatly succeed here, all because of your ancestors."

"So I'm set up for success," Walker replied, half-smiling.

"I would not go that far, Walker. But despite your obvious genetic predisposition and mental health issues, you have a real chance to succeed, whereas many are severely limited in the scope of their options."

"Okay, so, what should I pick?"

"I am not allowed to give specified advice, Walker, so instead, I will give you a generality"—he held a hand up—"and please do not feel as if you must take it. This is your task, after all." Lowering the hand, he leaned forward, growing closer to his Creator. "However, I feel that you should select something small. Something you can work with later as needed. Something manageable."

"Something small, something small . . . Okay."

Walker scrolled down his options until he found one that fit the idea of small and would be comfortable in The Crater. He clicked it and saw the blackboard light up from the corner of his eye, showing the words "The Bobbit Worm." Walking over, he found a basic drawing of his first potential entity and sighed in relief.

"Thank God they predesigned it."

"Indeed. I am not familiar with this species as it is not in any of your memories."

"Like the zonkey?"

"The what?" Virgil said, looking at his overlay again.

"Never mind." Walker looked at the drawing again. "Yeah, I just saw 'worm' and figured it was our best shot."

Virgil stepped forward and looked as well. "There is no going back on this once you begin modifications, Walker. There simply are not enough Creation resources to sustain any changes. Are you sure you want to choose this entity for your first?" Virgil said with an odd look on his face.

"Yep, it's just a worm. I figure, at the worst, it can feed anything else we make."

Virgil paused again, then said, "Okay, then please make any changes you would like to your entity. Your Creation Instrument has already been taxed for the illustration, so any changes you make must be small."

Walker noticed Virgil was right. His chalk had been reduced, and the remaining amount was only about the size of his thumbnail.

He looked the creature over. It was a little different than the basic earthworms people used for fishing. It had jaws, first of all, that extended out past a curved mouth, and it was quite a bit longer than he thought it'd be, explaining the reduction in his amount of remaining chalk. The length of the worm had small barbs sticking out on its sides, and it was segmented with rings throughout its body. The end portion of the worm was stubby and round, a contrasting view compared to the jawed beginning.

"What changes do you think I should make?"

"This is your first entity, Walker, and you have no real experience with this. I believe you should make a change, any change, as the Alpha Protocol does not want unmodified entities from your homeworld, but I am not allowed to say what changes those should be. I am sorry." He paused. "However, it is a—a worm." He struggled to get the words out. "What would you change about it to make it fit in best with your landmass?"

Walker didn't notice his assistant's efforts, as he was so focused on the drawing in front of him. "I don't know," he said, thinking it over. "Maybe instead of that stubby tail, we should harden it a little, and I can sharpen its jaws a bit as well to make it easier for the worm to eat."

"Please keep in mind, neither of us knows much about the Bobbit worm. Because you have not read of it in your former life, I have no memories to work from. You must be cautious, as we do not want to make an unknown entity too powerful."

"Yeah, I'm just adding a little extra to it."

"Okay then, I agree."

Once that was settled, Walker drew the symbol for rock on the tail end of the worm, believing it would harden.

"Is that right?"

"You are reusing the designated illustration for rock on your entity?" Virgil asked with raised eyebrows.

"Yeah man, you know, dysgraphia."

"Okay then, proceed."

Touchy.

He erased the rounded jaws sticking out to the sides and slowly, meticulously sketched sharp jaws that should have the same amount of range as the originals. On a random flair, he angled the jaws a second time inward so they'd latch whatever they bit. Ultimately, he had barely enough chalk to call it that, seeming more like a piece of dust in his grip than the original cylinder.

"There, one modified Bobbit worm. What do you think?"

"I think it will be a predator," Virgil said deadpan.

"It'll be fine. We nailed the first landmass; now we'll nail the first entity."

"If you are sure, please click the Materialize button."

"No 3D image this time?"

"No, that was a one-time deal, Walker. And to be honest with you, you did not quite use it to its full potential."

"I could've done more with it?" he asked with confusion.

"You could have, yes. Specifically, while looking at that hologram, you could have separated your landmass into different accommodating biomes for future entities or begun the process of allowing vegetation to grow. Instead, you looked at it and materialized the start of your world immediately afterward. The system always gives assistance during the prelims. Just enough for your vision to be realized. But that is only after you have completed your task."

"Well, shit, man."

"Indeed. In the future, if the Alpha Protocol offers additional help, please greatly consider what it is and why it may be offering it."

Walker nodded. "Understood. I'll click the button now."

The Materialize button had sat in his overlay during the conversation, blinking for his attention. Once he pressed it, they watched as his worm appeared, floating over the blackboard. Its jaws appeared incredibly sharp, far more powerful than he'd planned. Also, instead of only the stubby tail seeming tougher, the modification spread across its entire body, hardening the concentric rings that made up its body. It looked less like a worm now, and more like an aquatic rhino with fangs.

[. . . Scanning . . .]

The worm spun slowly and gently pulsed with a golden glow. The entity flashed brightly before the overlay spit out the next part.

Task 2: Create your first entity: Complete!
As your entity has been modified from its
original form, please name it.

"Not quite what you thought it would be, Walker?" Virgil asked.

"No, but it's pretty close. Maybe a bit more powerful than I thought it would be, but still, pretty close. What do you think?"

"It is assuredly a predator with those jaws, and you gave it hardened armor with your addition. Whether it could survive against another Creator's entity, I am unsure."

"Well, we did the best we could with what we had, Virgil. What do you think I should name it?"

"I believe it will be quite vicious."

"Maybe." He tapped his chin. "Alright then."

Entity: The Slicer is named.
Congratulations, Dante!
You've unlocked the Seeding System.
Please seed your entity when you are ready.
Good luck, Creator!

A Seed button appeared in his overlay.

"Anything special to this?"

"It will place a copy of the Slicer onto your landmass, and then what it needs to survive will be provided by the system so it can maintain itself. Your first entity will be well managed."

"Okay, here we go," he said before clicking the button.

The worm disappeared from over the blackboard, and . . . nothing else happened. Walker strained his eyes on The Crater, but it just looked like a gray and blue world placidly sitting in the middle of space.

"I can't see anything," Walker complained.

"Oh right, your visual acuity. Please watch here for now." Virgil's eyes shot out two beams, providing a 3D hologram again. It showed Walker's small planet in fine detail, zooming in on a single modified Bobbit worm undulating across the soil. The Slicer dropped itself into the water and swam around quickly, moving from one place to another in a fast-zipping fashion.

"I thought it'd be slower with that new armor on it."

"The system recognized that the armor would weigh it down and compensated by increasing the muscle mass of the entity. Later, you will have to learn these modifications yourself, but for now, the Alpha Protocol still has what you might call your training wheels on. The first entity tends to be a . . . crapshoot, as you would say. Prelim Creators do not have a great deal of information about what they are doing, and their assistants are only allowed to help so much. The system looks at what you have created, and it installs modifications to assist you in creating a desirable first entity." He pointed at the hologram. "Oh look, they are adding its food."

They watched as several fish were added to the water, bringing more life to Walker's world. The Slicer didn't notice at first, still zipping around the water. The moment it did . . .

"Jesus fuck! What was that?" Walker yelled out, backing away from the image.

Virgil looked in confusion at what he was seeing. "One moment, please," he said, seeming to rewind the imagery. They watched as he moved it forward in slow motion. The hologram showed the former Bobbit worm still swimming from side to side, placidly making trails in the water. That was before it saw a fish. The instant it did, they watched as it clenched its pincers together a few times, then shot like a bullet straight at its target. The moment it pierced the fish, it ripped its pincers back faster than even slow motion could show. The victim, just swimming harmlessly only a moment before, exploded into pieces from the violent treatment.

"It seems, Walker, that your first entity is an alpha predator of a high degree. That should grant you quite a few points," Virgil said, an odd note of pride in his voice.

"What the fuck, man!" Walker said as he ran a hand down his face. "Is this thing going to kill everything I put into The Crater now?"

"Most likely, and I advise that you not make more, as they will be quite territorial. But look on the bright side."

"What bright side?"

"Now you will have a chance when the Creator Wars start."

CHAPTER EIGHT

The Temporal Subsystem

Why do you keep slowly dropping these things on me?"

"It is exposition, Walker," Virgil responded with zero sarcasm in his voice.

Walker smiled. "So what does that make you, my mentor?" He scratched his cheek, then held up a finger before Virgil could respond. "Plus, isn't exposition meant to be super long? I feel like all of this is too sudden."

"No, according to your understanding of story structure, exposition has morphed from describing the setting in depth to revealing information quickly, as humans have developed shorter attention spans and increased their need for immediate action."

"Hah, true enough. This is the story of my life, in a way. And who knows, maybe I'll be immortal after all."

Virgil shook his head. "A wise man from your world once said: Story of your life . . . so far. However, no one is allowed to be immortal, Walker. Everything dies. From the stars to the Slicer. Everything. That is a fundamental rule in life. Now, the Creator Wars are no joking matter. Once you have completed a few tasks during the prelims, the first battle will begin, and if you want to win, you will have to hope the Slicer is truly a monsterlike entity. Your first one, that is. You will assuredly have to make more if you plan on succeeding within the Creator Wars."

"But I'm supposed to create a world," Walker replied. "If I make a world, and all I have are monsters, then won't that world collapse on itself as they all attack each other? Where's the logic there?"

"Excellent deduction, Walker. There are many ways in which you can go about fixing that. There are as many options as you would like to use. Limits are placed only by yourself. You can make systems of checks and balances. You can create protectors, who go in and clean up or manage different habitats. You could create your world as a large arena and allow things to manage themselves the natural way."

Walker heard it all, but his mind latched onto one thing. "Systems? Like the Alpha Protocol's stuff?"

"Indeed."

"How would that work?"

"That is difficult to say. System designing is unlocked by the Alpha Protocol. It is not inherently a part of the Creator's toolkit. I would also like to warn you that system designing is an art, more than a science. To even obtain the ability to do so would require a bit of luck, and you would need to learn to manage your systems with great forethought."

"Luck?" Walker said, not enjoying the idea of its ephemeral charm. "How does luck play into this?"

Seeing Walker's reaction, Virgil said, "Perhaps luck is not the right word. The Alpha Protocol likes to give Creators the tools they need to succeed while still maintaining the ethical value of minimal resources. If you truly wish to work with systems, they may accommodate your needs."

Walker smiled. "So it's not luck so much as working within what the protocol thinks may help me succeed."

Virgil nodded. "Indeed."

"I think systems may be the way to go. I wouldn't have to worry about a protector suddenly thinking that things would be better off if nobody survived. Yep." He nodded to himself. "Based on my options, I think systems are the way to go."

"Understood. Then, we will create systems to manage and simultaneously populate your entities, assuming we manage to gain that ability. Think less of quantity and more of quality."

Holding up a single finger, he continued. "While the first battle will only select one entity, future battles will differ, and you will have to adapt to the situations as they come. I would like to give further warnings to help prepare you, but similar to the rewards I had spoken of prior, the battles change for each rendition. We will have to just wait and see what we get."

Walker considered not only what Virgil had just said, but also what Mr. Harrison had told him when he first arrived here. What would happen to him if he lost in the Creator Wars? Would his own planet or universe be affected? Would the Earth be affected by his loss? His universe even?

He just knew, somehow, that if he asked Virgil, he'd likely receive no response. Just another restriction on what he was allowed to say.

The idea of death didn't shake him. He was taught in the military, just before he deployed to Afghanistan, to assume he was already dead and live accordingly. To make each moment matter and try to stay in the present, no matter the circumstances or how dire they might be. But the idea of his world or universe being affected because he somehow screwed up, terrified him.

Walker's face became serious. "How much time do we have left?"

"You are in luck. As your entity and seeding were quite quick, we have extra time to work with the Temporal Subsystem. Please look at your overlay and read the status update from your seeding."

Walker noticed something. "Before, all of the updates popped up instantly. Why are they minimized now?"

"It is all a part of the prelims, Walker. The Alpha Protocol is slowly introducing you to the myriad ways in which the system can be used. You will find, after completing the prelims, that a great number of tasks will suddenly flood your overlay. While I will keep track of them for you, they will seem overwhelming and impossible at first glance. You will learn to manage them as we go forward, or you will fail. There are no half-measures here."

Walker looked down as he felt the doubt creep in. The thoughts of failure still weighed heavily on him. Looking at the grass beneath his feet, he asked, "Do you think I can do it?"

Virgil stepped forward looking up and into his eyes. "Walker, I can see you have already survived a great number of trials in your life. While this will be the greatest challenge you will ever face, or ever can face, I believe you have great odds of completing the Alpha Protocol. It is not simple, and it is not easy, but it is within your abilities."

Walker closed his eyes. He didn't think that Virgil would lie to him. If there was a sliver of a chance that he could succeed, he had to do his best. No, that wouldn't be enough. He had to do better than anyone else, even with his limitations. Straightening up, he met Virgil's eyes again.

"In my knowledge base, I can see no other Creator taking as much time as you did to create and perfect their first illustration. It may seem stupid to some or lesser to you, but that kind of focus, wherein you can put your all into a simple idea, will take you far. You are fond of telling your students, *There are a million geniuses in the world who do nothing with their lives; it is determination that matters*. Perhaps by the end of this, you will embody that."

"Thank you, Virgil," Walker said. "That helps. Maybe when this is all over, you can be a motivational speaker."

"No, that is a terrible job for people who do not have any further to go in life. My work is to focus on the Alpha Protocol and my Creator."

Walker flashed him a wan smile. "So what happens to you after this?"

"If we succeed, I will be attached as your assistant for as long as you maintain your Creator status."

That means he'll be with me for the rest of my life if we win, Walker thought to himself. *I'd better not piss him off.*

Out loud, he said, "And if we lose?"

With no change in expression, Virgil replied, "Then I will be recycled into the Alpha Protocol for the next rendition."

"Recycled?"

"Removed from the program and placed back within the Alpha Protocol's resources."

"So you'll disappear? What about all that we've done?"

"My memories will be used by future assistants to better help their Creators, but I will cease to be."

"That's shit, man. So if we lose, you die; if we win, you're stuck with me. What if I was some crazy prick who kept beating you with a baseball bat?"

"It is not good or bad, Walker. It is what has happened and will always happen. In the first rendition, there were no assistants, and all Creators had to compete with those who held massive advantages in intellect, dexterity, genetics, or ecology. The assistant system was created to bring balance and focus. It allowed the imagination of the Creators to shine. To build the best worlds for each new rendition. I am designed to have reduced emotions to better work with my Creator. Fear, courage, pleasure, and pain have no true hold. In the end, I am simply me."

"I know you picked your name because Virgil guided Dante in Dante's *Inferno*."

Virgil straightened up. "Indeed. It was apt as he was Dante's assistant, if you will."

Walker fiddled with his overlay. "What would happen if I changed your personality in the assistant menu? Maybe even add some self-preservation into it. Don't think I'd forgotten about it."

"This version of me would cease to be, and a new version matching the parameters of your choices would exist instead."

"So it would kill you?"

"I believe it would cause a root change to me, so I would not be who I am now, intrinsically. By your definition of death, yes, it would kill me, but not exactly, as a version of me would remain, only with your alterations."

Walker blew air out of his mouth. "Okay, never mind." He moved his hand away so it no longer hovered over the Personality button.

"Please, Walker, if you have any changes you would like to make, go right ahead."

"No, thank you. I'm not a murderer," Walker said firmly. "If I had gone through with it, that'd be like a step away from assisted suicide. It's not right, man. You're a living, breathing person."

"I do not breathe."

Walker waved a hand. "Whatever, you know what I mean. I'm going to look at the status update."

"Please do, and Walker, be safe."

With that weird comment, Walker clicked the status update.

Congratulations, Dante!
You've completed the seeding of your first entity!
You've unlocked the Temporal Subsystem!
To assist you with your first time using the Temporal Subsystem,
you've been granted an allotment of 50 years.
Good luck, Creator!

Before clicking on the newly appeared Temporal Subsystem button, Walker focused on Virgil.

"Can I rename these boxes? If we're going to be doing this for a while, I'd like to make it a little easier on myself."

"Yes, of course. Please hold a moment, and you can make any changes you would like."

Each box lit up with separated dashes encircling them. After Walker clicked on Temporal Subsystem, he changed it simply to read Time. He also changed the Entity Subsystem button to read Monsters.

"Walker," Virgil interrupted. "You will not just be creating monstrous entities. By all rights, if that is what you would most like to do, then please feel free. However, from what you stated earlier, I believe you will want to create plants such as trees, or even shrubs and bushes. Strictly speaking, from your definition of monsters, trees do not count."

"True," Walker agreed, "but it is so much cooler to just click on the Monster tab."

Virgil nodded slowly. "I see. And you are certain, as you stated earlier, that you do not just want a world filled with monsters? Would that not make you . . . happy?"

"No, I think it would get old. Maybe that giant arena thing you spoke of was interesting, but it's not a *world*. It's an arena."

Virgil nodded slowly. "Thank you. That helps me further understand your vision."

Walker gave him a grin. "That's everything, right? We can dive into the new system now?"

"Go right ahead," Virgil responded, and the dashes disappeared. Walker clicked on Time.

Welcome to the Temporal Subsystem (Time)!
You have 50 years remaining.
Please use your cursor to choose what
you wish to move through time.

A simple mouse cursor appeared in his overlay. He had to assume that the system had looked at his memories for an interface he was familiar with. The idea of a multiverse-spanning organization using mouse cursors just didn't sit right.

Using his hand to grab it, he moved it toward Virgil and found an outline hovering around his squirrel body. He clicked on it and found four sets of arrows, like on a video player from home. Walker tinkered around with it until he grew slightly used to the controls, which, as simplified as they were, didn't take long. Deciding he needed to further explore the way things worked before making any decisions, he clicked off of Virgil and looked around.

He discovered he could select all of his first landmass by mousing over the corner of the atmosphere. With a bit of finagling, he targeted only the land and water of The Crater, highlighting it rather than the granite underneath.

Just to see if he could, Walker clicked off of The Crater and moused over the water until a small, quickly moving object was highlighted.

"Hey Virgil, what would happen if I aged the Slicer?" he asked. "I've got a thing floating in front of me that says I can move things through time,"

"The average lifespan of that particular worm is twenty years, Walker."

"How do you know that?"

"I can see its genetic makeup, which comprises the building blocks of how it will act, how it will age, what it will eat, as well as how it reproduces. I could not tell you how aggressive it would be as I am not allowed to influence your creative choices during the prelims. I also cannot tell you how certain experiences will change the entity as time moves forward."

"Monster."

"Whatever," he replied quickly, using Walker's own word against him. "The point is, I can give you a breakdown of what to expect upon initial seeding, but what happens after is, as you say, up in the air."

"That's fucky," Walker said with exasperation. He moved the cursor toward the tree.

"What would happen if I aged the tree?"

Virgil grew still and said stiffly, "Move the cursor away immediately, Walker."

Walker noted the fear stamped on Virgil's face and did as he was told. "Why, what would happen?"

Virgil shook his head. "I do not know. I only received a hint from the Alpha Protocol stating that would be very bad. I believe it has to do with what that particular entity is, although I hesitate to call it an entity at all."

"Then what is it?"

"I do not know, and that should worry you as much as it does me. I only receive warnings under the direst circumstances."

"That's not ominous at all. So what should I use this thing on then?"

"Who says you have to use it at all? As I understand it, if you do not use the allotted time, you will keep the fifty years for when it is necessary."

"Where's the fun in that?" Walker complained. He threw his arms up, the cursor sliding across his vision. "I thought the idea here was to learn how to use it."

"I understand that the idea of controlling time appeals to you, but I would like to remind you of the consequences of not taking the Alpha Protocol seriously. You must manage any advantages you can possibly gain, particularly in the beginning."

"Like the tree?"

"As I said, I do not know what that is."

"Will the other Creators store their time?"

"Unknown, but I have to assume that advancing time for them would be greatly useful."

"Why?"

"Because they may have entities who do better as they grow older, whereas we already have a monster who can fight well on its own."

"Well, it's pretty crappy that the worm has such a limited lifespan. It'd be awesome if it got more powerful as it aged." Thinking over the exploding fish and his instinctive terror, he said, "Okay, maybe not so awesome."

Walker moved the curser over his left foot and had an idea.

"Can I change myself? Like, can I make myself younger?"

"Yes, you can, Walker. Remember when I said to be careful? That was my reasoning. There have been Creators who have, historically, aged themselves to death. There have also been Creators who have brought themselves so far back in time that they become only an infant, or something worse."

"Shiiiit," he said, moving the cursor to the grass, which strangely didn't light up. "I thought we were in some kind of time stasis?"

"You are, Walker, but you can influence yourself. When you bit your lip, as you did to provide me with your genetic material, you still caused a wound, allowing you to donate your blood. You and I are protected due to the Alpha Protocol and its systems, but there has always been the choice of self-harm. Some entities gain benefits from doing such."

"Good to know . . . I guess."

"If you would like to store your time, click on the Resources button. As you have decided not to use your allotted time, it should have appeared early for you."

Walker found the Resources tab and clicked on it. There was an option to store years in Resources, so after clicking on it, his status update began pulsing immediately.

"So I have good news and bad news for you, Walker," Virgil said, eyes still focused on a screen in front of him.

"Hit me."

"The bad news is, your landmass will likely get a low score. That was to be expected. However, your entity should do quite well, and that will help determine what comes next."

"What's that?"

Pausing, he looked at Walker seriously with a glint in his beady eyes. "Your first battle."

"Dramatic as shit, man."

CHAPTER NINE

Points and Rewards

Walker's overlay looked like it was having a heart attack. The Notifications button next to Identity was flashing persistently, demanding that he notice it.

"Please look at your preliminary analysis, Walker."

"Right, gotcha," Walker said.

[. . . Analyzing . . .]

Walker watched as a small glow lit up the bottom of his lopsided planet. The golden glow spread, moving itself up and quickly covering his world, not that it had a great distance to move. It looked like nothing less than a golden shell before disappearing.

Initial landmass named The Crater analyzed.
Size: Average
Biodiversity: Not available in the Preliminary Creation System
Versatility: Poor
Age: 0 years
Alpha Protocol assistance provided: High
Grade: D
Extra mark earned for a non-standard achievement: Dedication
(Unique reward earned)
Rewards calculated.

Walker knew he had done a lousy job with his first landmass, but he thought his grade would at least be better than a D. He hadn't had a grade that low since taking ceramics in high school. The extra mark was interesting. Why would dedication give him something? Wouldn't that be standard stuff here? While he was thinking about that, the protocol analyzed the Slicer.

Initial entity named The Slicer analyzed.
Size: Small
Entity category: Animal
Organism type: Alpha Predator
Modification: Moderate
Ability to evolve: Yes (High)
Age: 0 years
Alpha Protocol assistance provided: Moderate
Extra marks earned for being within the
top 500 fastest Creators (264th) to create an alpha predator in
the 4AA Alpha Protocol (Major reward earned)
Extra marks earned for being within the top 1000
fastest Creators (691st) to create an entity with high evolutionary
capabilities in the 4AA Alpha Protocol (Moderate reward earned)
Grade: A+
Rewards calculated.

Walker's jaw fell. "Holy shit. But we didn't do that much? How did we get such a high grade?"

"That is not the highest grade possible, Walker, but it is close to it. It looks like you lost a few points with the Slicer's age. While on the surface, it seems that you did not make significant changes to the former Bobbit worm, I believe the fish currently populating your landmass would greatly disagree." Walker grimaced in sympathetic horror. "That is not a standard alpha predator. I highly suggest that, on your first chance, you isolate The Crater and keep it far away from the remainder of your world."

"Yeah, no, I fully agree with you."

Virgil nodded. "Indeed. Please look at your rewards, Walker. I believe the Alpha Protocol is going to help you in moving forward."

Walker excitedly pulled up his overlay and clicked on the status update. He had no idea what the rewards would look like.

Rewards gained by Dante in conclusion of the Preliminary
Creation System:

Basic reward for completion of the Preliminary Creation System:
Congratulations, Dante! Your Creation Instrument
has been upgraded!

*A Creation Instrument is not static, but constantly
conforming to the needs of its Creator.*
(Upgradeable)

Basic reward for completion of a D-grade landmass:
Congratulations, Dante! You've unlocked the basic ability: Copy!
*A requirement for any Creator. Gain the ability to copy
any part of a landmass onto another.*

Unique reward for nonstandard achievement:
Congratulations, Dante! You've unlocked the System Designer!
*The creation of the Alpha Protocol was not just happenstance.
It took many millennia for the first step to be created, and it is
always moving forward. The Alpha Protocol is a system that is
continually becoming more efficient and expanding beyond the
scope of its original intent. While not as powerful, the system
designer will allow the Creator to build their own systems,
allowing their entities to grow and evolve in different ways.*

Perfection is difficult and something that many members of the
protocol attempt to achieve. You, Creator, attempted this for the
majority of the time before your submission. Far more than most
others from your rendition.
Dedication should always be rewarded.

Grand reward for completion of an A+ entity:
Congratulations, Dante! You've advanced the Tree of the Gods!
*Its power is forming, and its voice, just a whisper. Continue to
advance the Tree of the Gods for further potential paths forward.*

Major reward for having a
top 500 fastest creation of an alpha predator:
Congratulations, Dante! You've unlocked the Ecology Subsystem!
*The Alpha Protocol allows for a multitude of different ways to
build and manage a world, but without careful management,
everything will die. With this subsystem, a Creator can manage
elements like habitats, predator and prey dynamics, and dietary
monitoring, as well as gain an overview of the health of the
Creator's entities in their world. This subsystem can be assigned
directly to a Creator's assistant as long as they've already gained
an advanced upgrade.*

Moderate reward for having a top 1000 fastest creation of an entity with high evolutionary capabilities:
Congratulations, Dante! You've gained an Evolution Chamber!
The Evolution Chamber is a wonder introduced in rendition 3EF. Created by one of the rendition winners, Bander Sotfam, the Evolution Chamber allows the Creator to input evolutionary modifications into their entities directly. Further progress by the Creator in creating unique genetic entities may result in gaining more Evolution Chambers.
(Upgradeable)

The ground under Walker's feet shook for a moment, but he hardly noticed it. He looked over at Virgil.

"That was a lot to take in," Walker said as he reviewed each reward a second time. His overlay changed to make room for System Designer and Ecology Subsystem boxes. Without being asked, Virgil made the titles changeable, and Walker changed the names to Systems and Ecology. Once he accepted the improvements, the buttons minimized on Walker's screen and would reappear as he moved his hand toward them.

"That unique reward is interesting."

Virgil nodded. "I agree. It is almost as if somebody was trying to help you there."

Walker grinned at him. "Yeah, *somebody*. How did they know I wanted the System Designer?"

Virgil looked like he wanted to say something, but instead, he paused for a long moment and shrugged. "Who knows? Maybe you are just a lucky Creator."

Walker stared at him, waiting for him to say something else, but after a few seconds with nothing happening, he shrugged as well. "Let's see what's going on with the Tree."

He quickly turned his head and found the Tree of the Gods. When he walked toward it, the distance no longer felt quite as far. Together, Walker and Virgil looked at the eighteen-foot-tall monstrosity. Sure, it wasn't as tall or even thick as a redwood, but there was a weight to it.

Like it was pushing on his soul.

The leaves were now fully fleshed out, showing a grand canopy of color ranging from deep cerulean blues to gold and yellow. The bark's striations, moving up and down the trunk of the tree, looked less like lines, and more like writing.

Walker bent forward to try to read it. But as he looked it all over, his Universal Translator never went off. Standing back up he looked at one particular branch that held leaves in a similar artistic style. If he wasn't mistaken, it looked to be a set, with a lightning bolt, a snake, and a horn appearing close together. Thoroughly confused by it all, he looked at Virgil, who gave a helpless shrug.

"The Tree of the Gods . . . the lightning bolt I get, but the snake and horn . . . you think this has something to do with the mythology from my world?"

"That is an astute observation, Walker. It may have something to do with the origins of your world as well."

Walker didn't know what to say to that. The system had said that he needed to advance the tree to get potential paths forward. In contrast to that bit of growth he'd seen at the beginning, this time it had tripled in size. That meant that to advance it more quickly, he needed to get more grand rewards. That might be easier said than done. He looked back at the squirrel.

"So I bet you're pretty happy that we got the Ecology Subsystem, huh Virgil."

The large squirrel canted his head forward. "Indeed. It will make managing the ecosystem of the planet much easier. I even have options for altering the gas in the atmosphere. This will allow us to create a much more habitable world for any entities in the future."

"Sweet. So, uhhh, did you want to take it over?"

Virgil's whiskers twitched. "Are you asking me to manage the Ecology Subsystem in its totality, Walker?"

This felt oddly personal. Like he was giving Virgil a bouquet of roses. Putting on his best smile, Walker said, "Umm, yes?"

The large assistant's tail swished back and forth. "That would be my pleasure, Walker. There is quite a bit of minutiae to managing a world's ecology, and I have no doubt you would not have the time to work with it whilst creating."

"Yeah, uh, that was my thought as well." Walker rubbed the back of his head. "I mean, I'm an English teacher. I'm good at stories and writing, not so much the science and hullabaloo." He laughed. "I'm kind of a moron, but that's fine."

"You call yourself a moron, yet you received two extra rewards in the first creation of your entity, and a high grade as well."

"That was luck."

Virgil waved a finger. "Actually, that was time. You still have over sixteen hours remaining. Creating your landmass took the most time, while creating your entity was relatively short. We even watched it swim in the water, reaping fish for a few minutes." He looked thoughtful for a moment. "I wonder how many more points you would have gathered with a better constructed landmass." Shrugging, he continued. "If you had taken more time to focus on any one thing, you would have finished later in the prelims and had a lower score. You would not have been among the first to create an alpha predator, especially one with high evolutionary capabilities. In this instance, your need for immediacy was an advantage, but I must warn you, you need to take your time in the future."

Walker held his hands up. "No, I understand. Speedrunning through this multiversal program has now made us isolate a part of the world away from whatever else we make. If I'd taken my time, I could have made a dog that can tap dance or a giraffe that has more to it than an unnaturally long neck. Hell, I could have at least made something I know, like a shark." Walker sighed while putting his hands on top of his head. "Honestly, I don't know why I went with Bobbit worm, now that I think of it."

"Interesting." Virgil looked at him with his black bead eyes. "Would you say it was natural instinct or just a blunder?"

Walker shrugged. "Natural instinct, maybe. I wonder what else we could make . . ."

A random visual popped into his mind, making him suddenly feel excited.

"Right! Okay." He started to pace. "Think of The Crater, only now, instead of a super predator wiping things out, we fill it with super jacked giraffes rippling their way back and forth along the beach." He could picture it now—

Wait, wait, no. I need to focus.

"Who would the giraffes be showing off for?" Virgil asked, curious about where Walker was going with this.

"True athletes don't show off, but I know plenty at the gym who do, ugh." He lightly slapped himself across the face. "I got sidetracked again, sorry."

"Not a problem, Walker. Remember, the more creative you are, the greater the rewards. That is why I do not mind these little non sequiturs."

"Nice vocabulary."

"It is your vocabulary, Walker."

He tilted his head to the side. "I guess you're right. So what's this Evolution Chamber thing?"

"Let us go take a look, shall we?"

They didn't have far to walk, as it was near Walker's Creation Instrument.

The chamber looked like the kind of large canister you would see in the old Ninja Turtle movies. It had an elongated top and bottom portion, with a beveled edge arching back toward the center. The middle of the chamber was made of a glass-like substance that, while transparent, seemed unnaturally thick. From the outside looking in, it gave a similar feeling to viewing bulletproof glass. A sad thought sprung up, and he knew where he'd seen it before.

I've seen glass like that at my school.

Virgil spread his arms like he was showing off a car. "This is an Evolution Chamber, and with your Evolutionary Edge ability, it is a boon that many Creators would die for."

"What's the big deal?" Walker asked.

"You have the Temporal Subsystem. That is meant to allow evolution and growth to occur naturally. Most Creators will likely spend their years aging their world so that their entities can grow and become more powerful, wiser, or, in many cases, more brutal. It is standard in the Alpha Protocol for Creators to build their world, drop their entities into their habitat, and then allow them to fulfill the purpose of their creation, whatever that may be. With this chamber, you can now skip spending your allocated Temporal resources and directly input how you want your entities to change after modifications are completed."

"That sounds extremely overpowered," Walker said as he looked closer through the glass. He didn't see any wires or connectors, so how did it all work?

"Correct. The more creative you are with your Evolution Chamber, the higher your chances are of earning more chambers, or even upgraded versions. The Alpha Protocol rewards creativity with the ability to be even more creative."

Walker tapped a finger to his bottom lip. "So I have to have a purpose in my creations. Teachers call it the *why* of doing things. *You have to know your why before you start any major project, otherwise you'll become lost when things become difficult.*"

A why was also crucial for anyone taking on a job, and this was probably the biggest job he'd ever have. Walker looked away from the chamber and back into Virgil's eyes. "You've seen my memories; what do you think my why is?"

Virgil looked up at the planets in the sky before answering. "Look up, Walker."

He did so, craning his head to look above. The sky was filled with planets rather than stars—small planets, to be sure, but the effect was still powerful. However, he didn't notice anything had changed. "What am I looking at here?"

"There are a multitude of Creators that will cease to be here by the end of the prelim time limit. But you have already done it. You completed the prelims. You told your guide, when all of this started, that you want to create a world of fantasy, of guts and glory. You want to make a world that is balanced and allows its people to enhance themselves and whatever path they may take in their lives. Can that not be your why?"

"That may be, but I feel like I need something more to this."

"I cannot answer that for you, Walker. While I can see your memories, I do not know what you were thinking at the time they were occurring. You will have to decide for yourself what your *why* is."

Walker smiled at Virgil and turned around to think it over.

The why is important. I became a teacher because I wanted to help kids become better at expressing themselves, as it was something I had trouble with when I was younger. I joined the military because I felt a sense of duty or obligation, especially after 9/11. So why am I doing this here and now?

He looked back at the stars that weren't really stars. Other planets with Creators of their own, trying to complete a preliminary step on a universally scaled competition.

It's pretty amazing. I have the power to do almost anything I can put my mind to, as long as I can figure out the ins and outs of the Alpha Protocol. But that's not enough to carry me forward. I need to know my why.

Why.

Why.

"Virgil," Walker said. "How long will I live if I complete the Alpha Protocol?"

"When you complete the Alpha Protocol," Virgil said with a squirrelly smile, "you will have a choice when the protocol is completed. Go back to your world at the moment of your translocation, or stay with your creation and see it through."

"So I either can go home and get back to living my life, or become what? A manager on a planetary scale?"

"If that is what you wish, or you can sit back and watch what is happening. Historically, many Creators take a hands-off approach after completion and are still out there. The original rendition Creators are as old as billions of your Earth years and still have not stepped in to fix potential calamities. The choice, as ever, is yours, Walker."

Hearing that, Walker knew what his why was.

"I'm not the type to sit back and let others do the work for me. If I do this, I'll be around to keep an eye on my world and fix the problems that cannot be fixed otherwise."

"That can mean you will be doing so forever, Walker," Virgil warned.

The Creator nodded with resolution. "So be it. I've only ever quit one job and that was because my hands were tied in how to best help my students. I'm not going to let things get out of control again." He pounded one hand into another. "I'm going to make a world where wonder can happen." Another pound. "Where its people can be entranced by beauty and inspired by its community members." *Pound.* "Where just around the corner can be a new fantastical structure or story." *Pound.* "A world that constantly changes, where heroes can be heroic, where no one person holds all the power." He looked up at the stars again. "It is constantly said that mankind's truest calling is to explore, so I need to make a world where exploration never has an ending. My why is simple. I will create a world that always has another step you can take."

Virgil nodded, not influenced by the speech one bit. "And what will you call this world, Walker? I do not believe The Crater will inspire the kind of wonder you are aiming for."

"No, haha. You are definitely right about that." Walker looked at the planets again, trying to cheat the name by finding a random constellation of lights. No such luck appeared, so he started to pace. "*Utopia* is cliche. *Paradise* is wrong, as there cannot be heroes without villains. We need something simple that is easily recognizable."

"The Tree of the Gods is a good starting point, Walker. Why not take the language of one of its branches and work from there."

Walker snapped his fingers. "Great suggestion."

Walker started to think, *Where do those symbols come from?*

Then he had it. "What is *balance* in ancient Greek?"

"*Isorropia.*"

"Too long and not interesting enough. What about *wonder?*"

"*Thauma.*"

"That's not bad, but it doesn't have the punch that *Earth* has. While I'm not trying to create another Earth, it would be nice not to have a terribly named world."

"If that is your goal, Walker, you could try *Sympatheia.* It translates to *compassionate and sympathetic.*"

"What about *Symphony?*"

"Do you mean in the sense of harmonious combination?"

"Exactly. It's not exactly what I'm going for, but it may just be the closest we can get to it."

Virgil gave a small clap. "I believe that is a wonderful idea, Walker."

"Thank you," Walker said, looking at his small planet. "This is just the beginning."

"Yes, it is, Walker." He looked at the planet with Walker for a moment and then turned to him again. "You have some time until your first battle, and the protocol will not let you do anything until then. How about you take a rest?"

Looking back at Virgil, Walker said, "You said I don't need sleep anymore?"

"You do not, but I fear without a break every so often, your mental health will deteriorate. We need you at your best for what happens after the first battle."

"Okay, I'm just gonna lie down," Walker said, lying down right there in the grass, staring at the planets without really looking at anything.

"While you convalesce, I will familiarize myself further with the subsystems and your newest rewards."

"Hey, Virgil," Walker said as he lay with an arm under his head.

"Yes?"

"Thank you."

"You are very welcome, Walker."

Walker looked at his overlay as he lay down. Oddly, there was a new box next to Identity labeled Chat. He clicked on it.[3]

CHAPTER TEN

Battle!

Who knew that the Alpha Protocol would have social media, of all things? It was an odd choice by them, but he wouldn't complain. Quite a few things were happening in there that he found entertaining.

And a lot of meanness. It seemed that no matter where you went, assholes abound. They consistently gave out bad information to try to fuck over other Creators. Walker, on the other hand, just asked Virgil what to do and received a quick, yet neutral answer.

He used that time to build up some goodwill with the others. Hopefully, he could cash in on it one day, if he didn't screw things up.

"Hey Virgil, how much time do we have left?" Walker asked from his position on the grass.

"We have ten minutes remaining. You spent quite a bit of time reviewing the Creator chatroom, Walker."

Walker roughly scrubbed his hands through his hair. "It's super fucked up, man. I counted at least eight people who didn't respond again after running into problems."

Virgil was still looking at his overlay. "Indeed. There is a reason that the prelims lose twenty percent of the Creators in the Alpha Protocol. The chatroom can be a benefit to those with social needs as well as a dagger for those with nefarious purposes." He looked away from his screens. "I monitor the chatroom at all times, Walker. There are some with empathy trying to help their fellow Creators get through the protocol, and there are others like the ones you have seen, who are only interested in themselves and their entertainment, even at the cost of the protocol's welfare."

"You would think that whoever runs this would find those with the intent to do harm and take them out of the situation," Walker replied.

"The Alpha Protocol does not fall within your limited view of good and evil. They built a system that allowed for as many possibilities as they had the power to accommodate. It is on the Creators, to take it to the next level, as you like to say. You said before that you cannot have heroes without villains. Does that not imply you will create monsters who prey on the weak or even, perhaps, the innocent?"

Not liking that characterization, Walker tried to get a word in, but Virgil wasn't stopping. It seemed he had a point to make.

"Please remember that although there were a million Creators at the start of the protocol, there are fewer now. Those who failed either had great difficulty with their first landmass, struggled to create their first entity, or experienced an accident with the Temporal Subsystem. In my database, I have found there are three reasons that can cause one to be removed from the protocol. Self-harm, stopping all work on their world for an extended period of time, and the loss of a battle."

"What happens if I lose the first battle?"

Virgil looked away from his overlay. "The first battle, like the prelims, is similar to a tutorial. While both Creators learn from the experience, the victor gains a reward, and the loser is forced to move forward with empty hands. This is the final step of those training wheels we discussed. After this, you are on your own . . . with my help, of course."

"And if I lose the second battle?"

"Then the protocol is over for you, Walker. I assimilate back into the protocol, and you go back to your world at the time of your departure."

"So they don't kill me?" Walker asked with a nervous laugh.

"No. When the guide chose you, they should have explained all of this to you."

"He spent most of his time being weird or talking to his staff."

Virgil looked sharply at Walker. "Yes, I know. I recall the memory, although it is . . . fuzzy. Was not the staff a magical object?"

Walker shrugged, then rolled onto his back to stare at the sky. "I guess that's what it was. It kept changing sizes and glowing with wizard shit."

"The protocol only allowed him to stay here briefly, correct?"

"Yeah, I think that's right." Walker scratched his face. "It looked like he got pulled out while he still wanted to say something."

"Fool," Virgil said in a harsh tone of voice that Walker hadn't heard from him before. "He knew that bringing along any magical objects would strain the translocation, and he would be forced to depart prematurely. Your guide, if you can call him that, was meant to spend over an hour explaining the ins and outs of the Alpha Protocol to you, as well as his origins. The directive for all guides is to not leave until after the Creator has linked to their Creation Instrument."

"So why did he?"

"Because it allowed him to take the staff back to Earth, with all of its previously dormant power now awakened. If you decide to return to your planet, there will now be a powerful entity with an unknown magical force living there, potentially even waiting for you. I am unaware of the ramifications this may present."

Walker sat up. "So Mr. Harrison has magic in a non-magical world. Well, shit." He tried tearing some grass out of the ground, but it wouldn't budge. Shrugging without thinking about it, he said, "But is there any way to protect the Earth from here?"

"No, and I am afraid if you went back, you would be just another human being unable to stop him. The protocol disallows any portaling or translocation that crosses universal barriers without severe restrictions or special compensation. They believe it would be abused to a high degree and entire universes would become wrapped up in war or flat out destroyed." Virgil shook his head. "It was not pleasant."

Walker looked at him, and the squirrel stared straight back. He already knew he wouldn't likely get an answer, so instead, he asked a different question he felt had better odds of getting a return on. "Who was he anyway? How did he get chosen?"

"He is from the world you are currently making, Walker," Virgil said as if it was nothing, his eyes drifting back to his overlay.

"What the fuck?" Walker said, standing up.

"Indeed. All of the guides know who they will pick before they arrive on their Creator's original planet. Although some are technically in spacecraft, that does not really matter. There are a few exceptions that the protocol allows, but for the most part, every guide is taken from an image of the Creator's world in the future. They are created by the protocol, although the process is highly secretive, and I have no answers for you there."

Virgil's eyes looked at something in a corner of his overlay for a time, then spoke again. "Mr. Harrison, as you jokingly named him after he left, is a future resident of your world, currently named Symphony. I believe, regardless of whether you complete the protocol or not, that bringing the staff through his translocation will allow him to remain on Earth doing whatever he chooses to do. I am sorry, Walker, but if you return, I do not know what you will return to."

"Does that mean I'm guaranteed to be successful here?"

"No more than anyone else. Mr. Harrison was supposed to be a temporary image. A creation of the Alpha Protocol meant to find their Creator and bring them to this Rendition. The fact that he has survived leaving your point of creation is highly irregular."

Walker spent several minutes considering that, his face shifting through various looks as he processed things emotionally. After a long minute of introspection, he said, "I'd like to feel guilt, but I don't know if any of this is really my fault. Is there any way to make it so he won't be created in the future?"

"Not that I know of, Walker. The complications with future imaging are vast and profound, and as always, we are running out of time."

"Right. How much time do we have left?"

"Three, two, one."

"Oh."

Walker's overlay filled with text.

Congratulations, Creators, on completing the Preliminary Creation System!
This rendition has seen only 70 percent of Creators complete the prelims, which is our lowest yield of completion yet.
Regardless of this complication, we will not be increasing rewards as that would be counterproductive to our goal.
It is about quality, not quantity.
You will hear from us again when we reach the final battles of the Creator Wars. Until that time, you will have to learn by doing.
Your first battle will begin soon, and we want to wish you the best of luck in moving forward.
Translocation in
5
4
3
2
1

The overlay faded away slowly, and a new environment came into view. Standing next to Virgil, who had come along for the ride, Walker was more focused than he had been the last time the protocol translocated him. This time, he watched as the world in his eyes slowly came into being.

Gray-slated spires assembled from space and shot toward the sky, reaching hundreds of feet in the air and ending in tapered points. Quickly scanning the area to see what else was happening, Walker looked across the distance and noticed the ground was flat, with tiny cracks in it, as if water had been burned away over the years.

Rather than standing on grass, the two of them were now on a wooden stage that pulsed with golden light every few seconds. Walker looked across the flat, dry ground and saw another person standing on an identical stage.

Another Creator, he mentally corrected himself. After all, this was his first battle in the Creator Wars.

They were only half of a football field away, close enough that he could see the peculiar differences between himself and the opposing Creator. They were quite small, no more than three feet tall. While they had the standard two arms and two legs, there also appeared to be an extra arm extending from each elbow joint, further cementing their alienness in his mind. Plus, they were blue.

Walker tried not to be weirded out. He was a walking flesh bag imbued with small-g god powers, so who was he to judge? Standing next to the four-armed creature was its assistant, which had taken the form of a bush forever frozen in a smile, with branches for a mouth and strawberries for eyes.

Walker pointed at his opponent. "See, they've got four arms. I bet they had a super easy time making their first landmass."

"Perhaps," was all Virgil said in response. He seemed excited to see the battle and was focused only on the ground between the two Creators.

Rather than appearing in his overlay, the Alpha Protocol's words appeared in the sky just overhead.

Battle!
The Slicer by Dante vs. The Spirit Tree by Blitzburg7

Rules:
Stage: Arena
Entities allowed: 1 each
Rounds: 1
Battle type: Fight to the death
Evolution possible: Yes
Weapons allowed: (Not available in the first battle)
Extenuating circumstance: For the first battle,
each entity will revive in totality following the conclusion,
regardless of the type of death that occurs.
Cost borne by the Alpha Protocol.

Reward for the winner: A copy of the loser's entity
Reward for the loser: Continuation in the Alpha Protocol
Battle begins in 30 seconds.

A large boom sounded out into space a few seconds after the rules were presented, and as they faded, the number thirty appeared in their place.

It all seemed pretty straightforward, although he had to question one thing. "Why didn't he make a predator?" After a few seconds with no response, Walker looked over at the giant squirrel, and his jaw dropped. Virgil seemed to be having a fit, jumping up and down and chittering to himself.

"You do not understand, Walker; this is amazing. If you cannot make the finals, I am the worst assistant in the history of the protocol."

"What do you mean?" Walker asked excitedly, the squirrel's emotions getting to him.

"If you win this, and there is no doubt of that happening, you will gain access to a Spirit Tree."

The timer was still counting down, although it wasn't perfectly synced with Earth seconds. Each numerical drop was oddly timed and often a bit longer than he would've expected. Walker looked over at it, the tension in his body rising as the numbers went lower. A previously unheard sound began to strike when it hit ten, growing in strength with each number.

"Goddamn!" Walker yelled, his body shivering for a moment. "I'm new here! What the hell is a Spirit Tree?" At five, the beats were no longer touching him lightly. Instead, it felt like something was punching his chest. At four, as he looked over at the squirrel again, it felt like thunder vibrating through his whole body.

Virgil looked back at him, his small eyes as big as Walker had ever seen them. "IT IS MAGIC, WALKER!"

3

That immediately led Walker to a dire situation in the making. "WAIT, CAN MAGIC BE TAKEN OR ABSORBED? WHAT'S GOING TO HAPPEN TO THE SLICER IF IT GETS MAGIC?"

2

"OH, SHIT!"

1

Begin

The Spirit Tree and the Slicer faded in at the same time and speed, their bodies materializing simultaneously. The tree just sat there, peaceful as could be. From far away, it looked like a Japanese Cherry Blossom, only with a dark blue trunk and cyan leaves. It was beautiful. Walker was so mesmerized by the tree that he barely heard a terrifying hiss coming from directly in front of him. Looking down, he saw the Slicer arching its back as it faced him.

"It can't get to us, right?" he asked Virgil after swallowing a sour taste in his mouth. He did not like how the thing was looking at him.

Virgil shook his head. "No, Walker, have no fear. The Alpha Protocol puts up barriers to protect its Creators. You are perfectly safe."

As he finished saying that, the Slicer uncoiled and launched itself from the ground in a blur, coming to a stop when it rammed face-first into a transparent barrier. The barriers weren't like anything Walker had ever seen. It wasn't the traditional hard type he'd often read about in science fiction books. Instead, it stretched like rubber before bouncing back, thrusting the attacker onto the ground.

The Slicer hissed again and lifted itself back up. It started to unhinge its mandibles, shaking them as it glared directly at Walker. Clenching and unclenching its jaw, it tried to bite at the barrier, hissing between each attempt in frustration as its fruitless efforts made no progress. Even after a full minute of this, it didn't stop. Walker soon grew bored of the action, but the Slicer continued its futile attacks, never taking its eyes off of him.

Walker took a knee to get a closer look, causing the Slicer to hiss even louder as it attacked the barrier more ferociously, only to continue to be repelled. "Jesus Christ, that thing doesn't stop. Looks like it hates me in particular."

"You made it, Walker," Virgil reminded him.

"Yeah, sure, but what the hell, man?" He pointed at the tree and began shaking a hand at it. "Slicer. Slicer!" He had to yell over the hissing. "Get the tree, Slicer! See the pretty tree over there. Get the tree! Get the tree, boy!"

The Slicer just continued to attack, ignoring Walker's pleas. It went on for long enough that Walker stopped in his attempts and stepped a small distance away. Sitting down, he crossed his legs and began to tap his fingers against his thighs as the former Bobbit worm unsuccessfully tried to break through to him.

"Is there a time limit on this?" Walker asked.

"No, interestingly enough. Until all Creators have completed their battles, none can return to their instruments. It is how the Protocol makes things fair for those with protracted battles."

"Oh, okay." Walker tapped on his leg a few more times. "Hrmmm . . . Do you know how to play rock paper scissors?"

"Indeed. Fair warning though, your memories taught me much, and I do not think you have a chance at winning."

So Virgil joined him as the frustrated hissing occurred no more than ten feet away. Rock, paper, scissors, or as he knew it growing up, Rochambeau, was not a complicated game. Yet, as Virgil predicted, the squirrel continued to win no matter how Walker tried to change things up. At one point, Walker even waved at Blitzburg7 and got a wave back, albeit with one larger and one smaller hand.

"Neat."

After Walker's twenty-fifth consecutive loss, the Slicer seemed to finally learn that it couldn't reach them and turned around. As it spotted the tree, it hissed, then began to undulate to the other side of the arena.

"It's a lot slower on land," Walker pointed out. As he lost again.

"Indeed. I believe the Bobbit worm is a sea creature, thus your decision to build a large amount of water was quite helpful for its habitat. I imagine if it did not have the water to move itself in, it may have starved over time."

"Yippee for me," Walker said morosely as they watched the Slicer slowly move toward the beautiful tree. He began to feel a bit sorry for the thing. It wasn't doing anything but existing in peace with the world while a monster gradually moved closer. "What do you think will happen when it kills the tree?"

"Nothing good for us, I imagine, but the results of this will be spectacular for your chances in the protocol," Virgil replied.

After a minute, the Slicer finally approached the range of the Spirit Tree, and they watched as it coiled itself in preparation.

"Here it goes," Walker said lamely, a lot of the magic of the moment already gone due to the Slicer's unnaturally high aggression.

It launched itself at the tree and made contact, letting out a triumphant-sounding hiss before moving its incredibly sharp mandibles back and forth against the bark. The tree looked like it was being shaved as the Slicer continued to break through the trunk's core.

"I wonder if we can somehow use the Spirit Tree with the Tree of the Gods," Walker said to himself.

"That may still be a faraway thought," Virgil replied.

"Yep, but it bears fruit for thinking."

"Are you making fun of my fellow assistant across the arena?" Virgil asked.

"Wouldn't dream of it," Walker said with a straight face.

They watched as the Slicer methodically destroyed a pristine creature of the universe. Walker couldn't help but grimace as it continued on, finally feeling a small bit of relief when the tree began to list from side to side in small increments. Finally, with the bottom too weak and the top too heavy, a cracking sound echoed out. They heard Blitzburg7 cry out as it fell, leaves spreading across the ground.

According to Virgil, it was a predictable conclusion that the tree would lose the battle. Walker guessed his fellow Creator just couldn't hold back his sadness at seeing such a beautiful specimen torn down. That was to be expected, but what Walker didn't expect was the cyan flash that lit up the arena. The Slicer didn't seem to notice, still chewing at the corpse of the magnificent specimen.

Walker's overlay popped back on with a notification.

Evolution occurring.
The Slicer is evolving!
[. . . Scanning . . .]
The Slicer has gained advanced adaptive properties.

"What the hell does that mean?" Walker asked, but he didn't have time to receive an answer before the sky lit up again.

Congratulations, Dante! You've won your first battle and have gained the genetic blueprint for the Spirit Tree! The Spirit Tree can now be found within your Entity Subsystem.

"Yes!" Virgil said with a hop. "There is so much we get to do now!"

"You really like your work, don't you?" Walker said with a fond smile.

"It is what I am here for, Walker. Why I was created."

"About the Slicer—"

Virgil interrupted him with a forceful wave of his hand. "Wall it off, Walker. Wall it off immediately. Adaptive properties are amazing in a first evolution, and I am guessing your Evolutionary Edge ability has something to do with that, but if it gets into the rest of Symphony while you are building it, your world is doomed."

"If you're sure," Walker said.

"I am," Virgil replied with confidence. "It must be caged. There is no other option."

Blitzburg7 seemed to have recovered while they talked. With one last multi-handed wave, it and the arena started to fade away.

The odd thing was, Walker couldn't be sure, but it looked like it was smiling.

CHAPTER ELEVEN

Overwhelming Updates

As the grassy planet faded back into view, Virgil spoke with gravitas in his voice. "Brace yourself, Walker."

"Wha—" Walker's overlay took control of his vision.

Congratulations, Dante!
You've completed the Preliminary Creation System!
[. . . Analyzing . . .]
[. . . Adapting rewards for Alpha Protocol . . .]

Full Creation System unlocked!
World Editor Subsystem unlocked!
Task descriptions unlocked!
Tasks updated!
Optional tasks unlocked!
Optional tasks updated!
Timer unlocked!
Timer updated!

Tasks assigned to Creator Dante:

New world task: Expand your landmass to twice its current size
(Part 1)
While quality is more important than quantity for the
Alpha Protocol, there still needs to be room for growth.
Double the size of your landmass and expand your world.
Current increase in landmass from the original size: 0%
Reward for completion: Monitor ability

New entity task: Create three new unique entities (Part 1)
The Alpha Protocol has the power to modify and evolve entities. You have created one entity for use in the Alpha Protocol, now make three more.
New unique entities created: 0/3
Reward for completion: Diverse

New evolution task: Evolve an entity (Part 1)
Your genetic makeup allows for evolution and the power it can bring to your world. Evolve an entity and show the Alpha Protocol you were the right choice for your world.
Evolved entities: 1/1
Reward for completion: Identify ability
[. . . Scanning . . .]
Evolution task complete: Evolve an entity (Part 1)
Evolved entities: 1/1
Reward given: Identify ability

New evolution task: Evolve an entity (Part 2)
You've evolved your first entity in the Alpha Protocol and seen the power of evolution. Evolve two more and watch as your world evolves with them.
New evolved entities: 0/2
Reward for completion: Alpha ability

New temporal task: Build a localized temporal anomaly (Part 1)
Growth can take time, and the Alpha Protocol understands this. Contrary to what many believe, time is fluid and can be shifted forward and backward at the need of the Alpha Protocol. Build a localized anomaly and use it to further grow your understanding of the universe.
Localized anomalies built: 0/1
Resources allocated for completion: 50 years
Reward for completion: System Link ability

Optional tasks assigned to Creator Dante:

New civilization task: Build a basic civilization (Series 1)

The Alpha Protocol focuses not only on creating unique worlds, but unique societies as well. Provide your entities with the

*intelligence and tools to start their own civilization in its basic
form, and the rewards will be yours to gain.*
Basic civilization requirements:
Settlement founded: No
Social structure or government established: No
Continuous needs met: 0/7 days
Reward for completion: Disciple Subsystem

New system task: Design a system (Series 1)
*While other Creators may rely on the survival of the fittest or
technological expansion, the Alpha Protocol has provided you
with the means to create your own path toward gaining power.
Build a system that encourages your entities to grow.*
System requirements:
System is found to be balanced and consistent: No
System allows for growth: No
**System is applied to world continuously without calamity:
0/7 days**
Reward for completion: Gain the ability to create a second system

New ecology task: Build a small functioning ecosystem (Part 1)
*The Alpha Protocol requires worlds that are self-sustaining over
time. Build a small functioning ecosystem that will maintain a
part of your world.*
Small functioning ecosystem built: 0/1
Reward for completion: Permanent magnetic field

Reward for completing the first evolution task:
Congratulations, Dante! You've gained the Identify ability.
*The Alpha Protocol can be quite difficult for a Creator to
keep up with. The Identify ability allows the entity to
independently analyze anything within their world
and receive a brief description.*
(Upgradeable)

Time remaining until next battle: 100 hours
**Time remaining until removal of Alpha Protocol assistance:
2 hours**

"I know it is a lot of information, Walker," Virgil said above him without
mercy, as Walker was currently taking a knee from the overwhelming amount of

updates. He was completely blind as text continued to stream past. "But you do not have to complete them in a particular order."

"I need a minute."

"Of course. But please remember that the Alpha Protocol assistance, which provides food for the Slicer and protects Symphony, will turn off at the appointed time."

Walker looked at each task, not only trying to understand what it was saying but also doing his best to internalize the information the way he'd learned in college. Read the material, repeat it aloud, and read it again. He'd found this trick his second time in college and managed to increase his memory retention.

But if anyone were to be watching him right now, they'd see a man staring down at the ground, mumbling to himself and swiping the air with his fingers.

He found a digital clock counting down on its own at the top of his overlay. It showed, just like the announcement, that a little less than one hundred hours remained before the next battle. A secondary time flashed just below it with a little less than two hours, albeit the text was more transparent.

He scanned the information a second time, still mumbling to himself. Finally, he felt like he understood what the system wanted, but he still had a question.

"Why did the system give it to me in that order?"

"Are you not overwhelmed by the responsibilities of fully unlocking the Creation System, and the great tasks involved?" Virgil asked with a stunned look on his face.

Walker shrugged from the ground. "I already know I'm out of my depth here. I mean, what else can I do but chug, chug along?"

A soft clap rang out twice. "Indeed. I am impressed, Walker."

He stood up, brushing imaginary dirt off his rear. "Thank you. So I'll ask again, why is it out of order?"

"What do you mean?" Virgil asked with a tilt of his head.

"I don't see an organizational structure to how it placed the tasks. Unless . . . Oh, I get it. Is it set up by priority? Like, you should do x before y?"

Virgil looked at his overlay. "Yes, I believe that is true. As the priority structure shows, it will be difficult to complete almost all of the other tasks without first increasing the landmass size. But there is something you should see first."

"What?"

Virgil waved a hand behind him. "Let us have a look at your newly upgraded Creation Instrument."

They walked over to a large white object in the near distance. "I saw the whiteboard. Did you not think I saw the whiteboard?" He looked around while spreading his arms. "There is not a lot out here for me to look at, man. The moment the system upgraded the blackboard, it was plain as day."

Virgil spoke slowly to him. "I had assumed you had seen it, Walker, but more specifically, where is the chalk?"

That threw him a little. They stepped over quickly so he could take a look.

In place of chalk, there was now one black marker and one green one. Virgil pointed at it as he said, "That is all of the material you have to create your next landmass." He lifted the marker up. "I am allowed to tell you that, as you create, your grade for the new addition will decide how many more markers like this you will receive. That is also true of your entities," he added, pointing at the green marker as he put the black one down. "That green marker will be all you can use to modify your entities until your points update, although you can cheat with the Evolution Chamber now."

Walker held up his hands. "Whoa, whoa, buddy. I'm a teacher. We don't cheat."

"Tell that to the constant news scandals. Regardless, it does not leave room for error. During the prelims, erasing the chalk lines returned the material back to you. Now, that will no longer be an option?"

A spike of panic hit Walker as he understood what Virgil was implying.

"You're saying it has to be perfect from the start."

"Correct, in *a way*," Virgil said with heavy emphasis. "The time for errors is over. Every mistake you and I make will be recorded on and in Symphony, or a reduction in Creation materials will present itself." He touched a hand to his chest. "Be assured, even assistants make mistakes, though I will do my utmost best to keep that from happening."

Virgil looked at the whiteboard again. "Your world could be filled with mistakes if we are not careful. Each problem will further throw your plans of harmony out of the window. Balance must be enforced with each move we make from here on out, or ruin will come. I also want to warn you that I am still restricted from helping you create future landmasses. However, you do have a few new subsystems."

Walker nodded. "Yeah, like the World Editor."

"Correct. You cannot add to Symphony from it, only take away . . . for now."

"When will I be able to work directly with the world and stop having to draw on this whiteboard?" Walker asked with desperation.

Virgil looked at his overlay, then back at Walker. "Once you have earned at least a B on the landmass point-scale."

"Okay, a B. A b-b-b-b," Walter repeated. "I can do that. But wait, what about the Spirit Tree?"

Virgil's whiskers twitched upon hearing that. "That is an excellent point. The genetic blueprint for the tree and what it holds is now found in your Entity Subsystem. The moment we finish working on expanding your landmass, we should focus on those two," he concluded, tail swinging behind him.

"Okay, just one question then, as I know the longer we talk, the less time I'm working on the landmass—"

"And I the Ecology Subsystem," Virgil reminded him.

"Right, and you the ecology."

"Okay, shoot."

"You said it was magic, but how does that work?"

Virgil put his squirrel arms behind himself, looking like nothing less than a soldier at parade rest. The only thing keeping him from completing the image was that his arms were too short to connect behind him.

"Spirit, magic, or as your world's video games called it, mana, are all the same idea. Sorcery, enchantment, and arcana are all wrapped up in the same concept, too. It is a spiritual force that allows for wonderful things to happen and for entities to evolve in unique and diverse ways. Like the Alpha Protocol, it is neither good nor bad, but a tool to be used. The root of it goes all the way back to the first rendition and a particular genius who now sits on the Alpha Protocol's ruling council. Some worlds use things like radiation to evolve; others, like your homeworld, see their societies evolve through law and technology. The Blitzburg you met in your first battle had a deep and thorough understanding of magic, which is the word I'll use from now on. It is a force that, when introduced to entities and different civilizations, changes everything. Take the Slicer, for example."

"What about it?" Walker asked cautiously, the sounds of its hiss still sitting in his mind.

"While you modified it and made it quite the vicious killer, that was on a physical and non-spiritual level. The moment it destroyed the Spirit Tree and absorbed its magic, it evolved the trait for Advanced Adaptive Properties. I will cut to the chase so you do not have to use your new Identify ability on it; essentially the Slicer now can choose its own evolutions based on the environment or threats it finds. That means the more it is attacked and successfully defends itself, the more powerful it will become."

Walker rubbed his hands against his face. "Fuuuuck."

"Indeed. But magic takes that a step further and injects an element that was not included before. Not only will it simply grow larger or more vicious, but it will also gain abilities that allow it to perform feats the likes of which you have never seen. There is no telling what it will become before the end of the Alpha Protocol. Magic is a special ingredient that, when added to your powers of Creation and entity modification, allows for organic growth over shorter periods, and further expands upon what you will be able to achieve within the protocol."

Virgil grimaced and continued. "While it affecting the Slicer is . . . not the best situation, the addition of magic from the Spirit Tree cannot be discounted in your ability to succeed moving forward."

"So how do we kill it?" Walker asked.

"Kill what?"

Walker was shocked he didn't understand what he was asking. "The Slicer, damn it! How do we kill it!"

"That is the big problem, is it not?" Virgil looked down at Symphony, a very small planet floating not so far away. "The more attempts we make to subdue the Slicer, and the more we fail at said attempts, the more powerful it will become."

"Can't we just delete it with the World Editor?"

"No, the World Editor cannot delete living objects, only inanimate ones. It is as I told you at the end of the previous battle, we must cage it. I will focus on our Ecology Subsystem task to create a peaceful environment for the Slicer . . . as peaceful as possible, that is, and do my best to keep its food going. While I am working on that, you build the landmass."

Kicking the grass, Walker asked, "Couldn't we just let the countdown run out and watch as it suffocates?"

"You could, but you would also run the risk of the Slicer adapting to whatever may occur in space. As other Creators experiment with their powers, anything outside of the magnetic shielding or the protocol shield is, as you say, fair game. I do not believe you would like to see the Slicer with random evolutions empowering it."

Walker shuddered. "Can't we just age it?"

Virgil nodded. "You could try that as well, although temporal resources do not just drop into every Creator's lap."

"No, no, you're right." He sighed. "I'll get to work on building Symphony up right away."

"Before you do that, though, I do have one favor."

"Sure, no problem. What do you need?" Walker said automatically. Virgil hadn't steered him wrong yet; it was his own modifications that had changed the Slicer and caused this mess.

"I would like access to the Entity Subsystem to create food for the Slicer. But you will still have to create the original versions before I am allowed to modify them with the Evolution Chamber. It also means that your first couple of entities will gain low grades, thereby potentially reducing your instrument material." He held up a hand before Walker could speak. "I believe we can fix that with our next entity, and it should not be a problem. The bigger problem right now is that we need a self-propagating ecology in order to keep it busy, as well as happily exploding fish."

Walker barely thought about it. "Okay, that sounds good. So, what suggestions do you have?"

Virgil gazed down at Symphony for a long moment. "Looking at the Slicer, it will eat virtually any entity from the Osteichthyes family. Please produce one from the Entity Subsystem."

Walker pulled up his overlay and clicked on Entity. He clicked the search bar and, after Virgil spelled it for him, typed in "Osteichthyes." A large assortment of fish names and species appeared. He selected one at random, watching as it began to fill up the board.

While his magic whiteboard drew on itself, he looked at the two markers. Curiosity slapped him around, and he lifted the green and black markers, noticing a difference in their weights.

Already a little drained.

"All done, Walker?" Virgil asked.

He looked up at him. "Yep."

"Please click the Materialize button."

After doing so, a yellowtail snapper appeared in the water of The Crater, unknowing of its imminent doom. Walker's overlay lit up and described the fish as a D specimen, only giving him back the ink used to make it in the first place.

"Now that it is seeded, I can modify their base genetic structure in the Evolution Chamber. Can you please give me access to the Entity Subsystem?"

Remembering the process, Walker said, "I formally give you access to the Entity Subsystem."

Virgil's cheeks puffed out as he smiled. "Thank you, Walker." As he finished, a yellowtail snapper appeared in the Evolution Chamber.

"What are you going to do to it?" Walker asked.

"I am going to change its diet to something easy to work with, then I am going to alter the species so it not only breeds quickly but grows quite fast as well. I will also save the blueprint I use here so you may apply it later to other entities."

"Sweet, that's smart thinking."

"Indeed. While I do that, I suggest you create your second landmass. Please remember to make a series of mountains that completely contain the Slicer."

"No problem," Walker replied. "I'll be over here working on the landmass. Do you mind looking at it before we push it through?"

"That is acceptable," Virgil said before taking a few steps over to the Evolution Chamber and looking inside.

Walker headed toward the whiteboard and stared at it. Channeling his inner Bob Ross (minus the poofy hair), he put his thumb out toward The Crater and tried to decide how Symphony should look.

Symphony should allow for all environments. I need snow, I need mountains, swamps, and rivers. I don't want the world to feel limited, it should be boundless and unrestricted. The only limit I have right now is the markers.

He stared at the landmass while thinking.

I need to be able to work with an upgraded version of the World Editor, so I need a B or better on this next grade, but I can only do so much.

I think . . . I think I can just make a starting point for different environments all at once and force the system to recognize their diversity. The mountains are necessary, but I don't need tectonic plates, nor do I have the time and resources to make them . . . or the know-how.

He looked over at the squirrel tinkering with the Evolution Chamber. His tail was swinging quite fast, bringing a smile to Walker's face.

Virgil could probably do it, but this was part of the main system, meaning he had no control over it.

He tried to put the general shape of The Crater in his mind, which wasn't easy.

I also have to make sure that when it materializes next to The Crater they don't ram into each other and let the Slicer out of his cage. Thankfully Virgil forced me to make a perfect shape for our first landmass, so I just have to draw a crescent that fits directly against it, and leave a circular gap in the bottom of my new land for the granite below the surface.

Walker planned out a few more things before he heard Virgil say, "How is it going over there?"

"Pretty good," he replied with some confidence. "I think I have a plan that'll not only contain the Slicer, but also allow us to get access to an updated version of the World Editor. How did you know about that, by the way?"

"Once you fully unlocked the Creation System, quite a few of my restrictions were lifted. In a similar vein to how I was able to tell you about the Alpha Protocol Council, I can also now tell you about upgrading the World Editor."

"Gotcha," Walker spent another few moments picturing what he needed to do. "I'm gonna start drawing."

"Good luck. I believe I have found a solution for feeding the Slicer. Please let me know when you are done."

"Will do."

Walker got to work.

He started by outlining his new landmass. This would be the center of Symphony and had to be done just right. He moved his hands slowly so his dysgraphia wouldn't get away from him, and tried to keep his fingers loose and relaxed the way his old occupational therapist used to suggest.

He began drawing the crescent as a jumping-off point. It had to have a gap just large enough for The Crater to fit in snugly. A few wobbles appeared, but a quick smudge with the edge of his shirt made it right as rain.

He continued until the landmass was three times the size of what he had initially made. While the new Creation Instrument didn't allow for a refund of materials—in this case, ink—he still felt he had more to work with than last time.

Slowly, he continued his work until he felt it had a finished outline. He only had to go back and make a few more fixes where the worst of the shakes had caught him. Once he had it perfect, he started to work with the mountains that would align against The Crater by just drawing the symbols for rock right on top of the area.

Walker was not a wonderful artist, but he believed that once he had filled in the material that made up the mountains, it wouldn't matter. With the last symbols for rock etched in, he looked at his time and saw that he had about an hour left before the protocol stopped being so helpful.

You can do this, you can do this, Walker mentally repeated to himself. He really didn't want the Slicer to gain even more power, and this was about the only way to keep it contained.

"Can't we just drop a meteor on it?" Walker asked Virgil hopefully.

"That would be a terrible idea," Virgil said, working with something in the Evolution Chamber.

Mumbling to himself about the unfairness of the situation, Walker went back to his task.

He added the box shape he'd created for soil near the center of his newest landmass, so any entities placed could grow food over time, if they had the ability. There were no guarantees that his creations would decide to live the farm life, but it wouldn't hurt him to add further ecological diversity to his work.

The Creator continued his work, carefully drawing symbols in the center of the new landmass. When that was done, he did the same thing to every corner, only, each was a different symbol. His idea was to create completely unique habitats spread across the landmass. One corner for a swamp habitat, another for snow. Sand was added, a beach for one side, a large grouping of water attached to it, while a desert filled the other. The center would hold a heaping of grass, further reinforcing the farmable landmass for easy cultivation.

As he stepped back to look at it, he realized he'd made a mistake. Deleting small portions, he began to add small lines for creeks and rivers, interspersing them everywhere that sand did not encroach.

When he felt like it was in a good spot, he called Virgil over to take a look.

"So this is your solution," Virgil said after looking at the illustration. "Can you please tell me what each symbol stands for so I can associate it with the system?"

After Walker broke everything down for him, he asked if Virgil thought it was good enough for a B.

"It should beeee."

"Haha," Walker responded dryly.

"I have not associated the grass in the system. It is considered an interconnected entity, which is not dissimilar to a hivemind. Should an evolution outside of your control occur . . ." Virgil left the rest unsaid.

Walker hadn't considered that. "Okay, I'll just make it more soil then." He made the changes quickly, as he was on the clock.

Virgil strolled around, observing the illustration from various angles, before he stopped and said, "That is a nice workaround for making the Alpha Protocol recognize your diversity and allow for a higher grade."

"That was my thought." He pointed out the creeks and rivers. "I did have to make some changes once I realized that I didn't have water moving throughout the landmass."

"Yes, based upon your genetic makeup, your entities would have died of dehydration without that addition."

Scratching the back of his head, Walker said, "Yeah, that was a close one."

Virgil uncharacteristically put a hand on his shoulder. Even though Walker still didn't really know what he was, it still felt like any other hand. Just, with claws. "But you caught it in time, Walker. Do not be so hard on yourself; we still have very far to go."

"No, you're right, you're right. Is there anything else you see that should be done?"

"As this is still part of the main protocol, I can have no true input, full release of the Creation System or not."

"Fuck."

"Indeed.

"I think . . . I think it's ready," he said with loose confidence.

"Do you know what you would like your mountains, soil, sand, and water to be made of? If you do not choose, the Alpha Protocol will make its best guess and choose for you."

"Oh shit, I didn't even think of that. I'll let it choose for me, to be honest. You can't help me, and I'm not a professional at"—he waved his hands around the board—"all this."

"Understood. Then please click the Materialize button."

The button popped up in Walker's overlay, and without fanfare, he clicked it.

There was no meteor this time. The landmass as he'd drawn it appeared in space next to The Crater and began to move of its own volition toward the original. Walker thought it wasn't too different from two weak magnets finding each other in space. Slowly, they came together just as he had foreseen in his planning. What had once been a small piece of land, now had its siblings join it as Symphony moved into place for the first time. He tried not to hold his breath as great pieces of floating rock, water, sand, and everything else he could push together floated through the darkness of space.

When it was close, Walker heard a click, and all movement stopped. Walker could see the water and beach, which, from as far away as he was, looked like a small piece of paradise.

"We will have to find a way to make the water recyclable. That will also include making sure it stays clean, as the system will not provide that kind of assistance anymore," Virgil said as he looked at it. "Also, you do not have snow forming as you do not have clouds." He tapped against his chin as he looked at it. "Hrmm, yes. I believe I have a lot of work ahead of me."

"Yeah, sorry about that," Walker said, his voice not matching his words. He knew how much the squirrel liked his work.

A golden glow enveloped his new landmass, and then his overlay lit up.

New landmass recognized!
Please name your landmass.

"Easiest thing I've done since we've been here."

Landmass: Symphony is named.
[. . . Analyzing . . .]
Second landmass creation named Symphony analyzed.
Size: Medium
Biodiversity: High Potential
Versatility: Medium
Age: 0 years
Extra marks earned for creating a landmass with high potential
biodiversity (Minor reward earned)
Grade: B
Rewards calculated.

Moderate reward for completion of a B-grade planet:
Congratulations, Dante! Your World Editor has been upgraded!
The way to build worlds isn't to take away from your perceived
mistakes, but to find the strength in the differences.
With the new landmass modification options,
the Creator can change their world without using their
Creation Instruments.

Minor reward for creating a landmass with
high potential biodiversity:
Congratulations, Dante! Your landmass can now occasionally
form ore deposits!
The Alpha Protocol is a grand believer in the evolution of all
things, including the seas that have yet to be sailed and the
mountains that have yet to be delved. Ore deposits will develop
over time and, with knowledge and the right tools, can be mined
for their riches.

[. . . Scanning . . .]
Task updated!
World task complete: Expand your landmass
to twice its size (Part 1)
Current increase in landmass from original size: 156%
Reward given: Monitor ability

New world task: Create atmospheric conditions that
allow for natural weather (Part 2)
*Building a world in the Alpha Protocol is more than just dropping
in land, seeding entities, and hoping everything goes well.
Build sustainable weather patterns for your world.*
Continuous weather applied without calamity: 0/7 days
Reward for completion: Weather System

Reward for completing the first world task:
Congratulations, Dante! You've gained the Monitor ability.
*Not all Creators are blessed with exceptional vision in the
Alpha Protocol. The Monitor ability allows the Creator to create
a screen at need for their viewing needs.*

Time remaining until next battle: ~98 hours
Time remaining on Alpha Protocol assistance for first landmass
and entity: 20 minutes

"Okay, that was a lot again."

"Yes, but you did it! Now you can really dive in and build your world, Walker. On only your second try, you received a higher grade, and you did it by thinking creatively. Well done."

"Thank you."

Virgil nodded. "My pleasure. Now, we only have a short time until the atmosphere disappears, so we need to get to work. I do have to ask though, why did it take you so long to etch in all the symbols on the landmass? You did it quite fast, but I thought you would have done it a lot faster with the copy ability."

"Oh goddamnit."

CHAPTER TWELVE

A Slice of Life

Virgil was still laughing on the ground. In a surprisingly high voice, he kept repeating the same thing . . .

"You forgot. I cannot believe you forgot."

With a grimace, Walker said, "Look, it's not that big of a deal."

"You forgot!!"

After a few more repetitions, Virgil calmed down. He looked over at Walker again as he stood up. "I cannot believe you went into a big speech about how you were going to adapt, and then you settled on the old ways of drawing things slowly but surely. You have a copy ability. Just copy it."

"Yeah, yeah," he said, walking away in a huff. Walker put his hands in his pants pockets, noticing he was still wearing his suit from his last day at school: Purple, Valerie's favorite color.

Nobody had purple suits anymore, but she'd said it did something with his eyes. He forcefully pushed the thoughts away. "So, when is the fish system going to be done, Virgil?" he asked, totally not changing the subject and totally not looking at Virgil still on the grass. "You're over there making fun of me, but I'm the one who finished first."

"Please step over here, Walker."

"Alright."

Virgil led him over to the to the Evolution Chamber. "I need you to connect the Temporal Subsystem directly to the Evolution Chamber."

"How do I do that?"

"Simply click on the system in your overlay and drag it over to the Evolution Chamber. You should find it under your resources tab."

It took a little while for Walker to figure out how to do that, but once he figured out how to open multiple windows at once, it was easy.

"Done."

"Excellent," Virgil replied with a nod. "Now, may I have access to the Temporal Subsystem?"

"I formally give you access to the Temporal Subsystem."

Virgil tinkered with something in his overlay, and then a satisfied look came over his face. He nodded again. "Have you ever heard of Java moss, Walker?"

He remembered going to the aquatic store a few times in his youth but didn't remember Java moss in particular. "I think so? I'm not sure."

Virgil smiled. "It is a very hardy plant. Placing it within an aquarium, or in this instance, a large lake, will do wonders for the environment. The more that you place, the better off the environment becomes as it solves many of our natural eco-system's energy issues."

"I take it you want some Java moss, then?"

"If you would be so kind," he replied. Walker looked into the Entity Subsystem. After a quick search, he found the moss and watched it appear on the whiteboard. It didn't look like much, just some basic greenery you could find in any aquatic pet store. Without any fanfare, he placed some into The Crater.

"One moment," Virgil replied. Just as the fish in the chamber disappeared, a small green plant appeared in its stead.

"Check your notifications, Walker. I need to put a few finishing touches on this."

Walker's eyes were still on The Crater as something small down there flashed gold. He shifted his gaze to read his notifications.

[. . . Scanning . . .]
Task updated!
Entity task: Create three new unique entities (Part 1)
The Creator has the power to modify and evolve entities.
You have created one entity for use in the Alpha Protocol,
now make three more.
New unique entities created: 1/3
Reward for completion: Diverse
[. . . Scanning . . .]
**As your entity has been modified from its original form, please
name it.**

As it was just food for the Slicer, Walker didn't feel the need to name it anything special. After thinking for a moment, he played around with its original name.

Entity: Multitudinous Yellowtail Snapper is named.
[. . . Analyzing . . .]

Entity named Multitudinous Yellowtail Snapper analyzed.
Size: Small
Entity category: Animal
Organism type: Prey
Modification: High
Ability to evolve: No
Age: 1 year
Grade: C+
Rewards calculated.

Walker looked over at Virgil. "Just finishing up . . . now." Walker's forthcoming rewards faded out as the overlay updated again.

[. . . Scanning . . .]
Task updated!
Entity task: Create three new unique entities (Part 1)
The Creator has the power to modify and evolve entities.
You have created one entity for use in the Alpha Protocol,
now make three more.
New unique entities created: 2/3
Reward for completion: Diverse
[. . . Scanning . . .]
As your entity has been modified from its original form,
please name it.

Walker smiled.

Entity: Super Java Moss is named
[. . . Analyzing . . .]
Entity named Super Java Moss analyzed
Size: Very small
Entity category: Plant
Organism type: Producer
Modification: Medium
Ability to evolve: No
Age: 6 months
Grade: C-
Rewards calculated.
[. . . Scanning . . .]
Task updated!
Entity task: Create three new unique entities (Part 1)

The Creator has the power to modify and evolve entities.
You have created one entity for use in the Alpha Protocol,
now make three more.
New unique entities created: 2/3
Reward for completion: Diverse

Task updated!
Ecology task complete: Build a small functioning ecosystem
(Part 1)
Small functioning ecosystem built: 1/1
Reward given: Magnetic field provided indefinitely

New ecology task: Build a medium-sized functioning ecosystem
(Part 2)
The first step was taken, but the Alpha Protocol has never been
about slow beginnings. Build a medium-sized functioning
ecosystem that will maintain a portion of your world.
Medium functioning ecosystem built: 0/1
Reward for completion: Ecology Subsystem upgrade

Reward for completing the first ecology task:
Congratulations, Dante! Your world has gained a permanent
magnetic field.
The Alpha Protocol understands that not all Creators want a
magmatic core in their planet. The magnet field provided for your
world will permanently protect it from possible cosmic damage.

Small reward for completion of a C+ entity:
Congratulations, Dante! You've gained an increased allotment of
Creation Instrument material.

Small reward for completion of a C- entity:
Congratulations, Dante! You've gained an increased allotment of
Creation Instrument material.

"No description of the small rewards there."

"No," Virgil responded. "The greater the reward, the more the description. That is a very standard reward for completing an entity. D's will just give you back the same amount of your instrument that was used in the process of creation, F's will take away from you, although those are incredibly rare, and C's will give you a little bit more. B's and higher tend to do something special, and now that you have advanced to the full Creator System, you will gain even higher allotments for your Creation Instrument."

"Neato." Walker clapped his hands together. "So how is this a small functioning ecosystem? You just added a fish and some moss to the water, and suddenly, it's an ecosystem?"

"Good question. It is about working with what you have, Walker. I added two multitudinous yellowtail snappers to The Crater, but the system had already added over a hundred other unmodified fish to the Slicer's habitat; thus, small pieces of fish have already spread throughout the water. Because of all those existing small pieces and the Slicer's proclivity for destruction, I made it so our new entity only needs to eat a small amount before procreating."

"And the moss?"

"The moss will clean the environment and absorb even smaller pieces of the destroyed fish. I altered the moss only to need a limited amount of photosynthesis for sustenance. Instead, they will grow and proliferate at the same speed as the fish. This way, as the Slicer destroys the existing fish, the yellowtail snappers will eat the larger pieces, as well as the moss, should they be . . . peckish. The moss will take care of the smaller pieces floating through the water, and it will absorb solar energy through limited photosynthesis. It all works together."

"So each eats a little bit, makes babies, and it turns into the circle of life?"

"Yes. It is not an excellent ecosystem, but for our current needs and the time we have allotted, it will do. I believe it worked just well enough for the Alpha Protocol to call it a small ecosystem."

"That's fuckin' cannibalism with extra steps, man."

The large squirrel shrugged, smiling down at the landmass below.

"Question," Walker said while raising a finger. "You said *limited photosynthesis*, which implies that there's a form of . . . of . . ."

"Solar energy?"

Walker snapped his fingers. "Yeah. But I don't see any suns around here, man."

Virgil pointed to the sky. "The Alpha Protocol shield provides a constant source of low light and also grants a small amount of solar energy—just enough for weaker plants and trees to gain what they need. Thus," he spread his hand back toward Symphony, "limited photosynthesis."

"So each Creator has their own mini-sun-shield-thing?"

"What did you think those stars in the sky were? They are the shielded planets, and they're really not so far away from you and I."

"Mmmm, wizard shit," Walker replied with a nod, having found his answer.

"Regardless, the modifications were necessary to complete the task in time and allow us to protect your world from the Slicer. Please go into the Temporal Subsystem and spend some of your stored years to advance our two multitudinous yellowfin snappers—"

"MUYs," Walker interrupted.

"Sure. Go ahead and advance them . . . let us say two years. Be sure to make your selection tool a bubble that surrounds them so that their children also have children within the required time. There should be a healthy grouping of the moss in the same vicinity."

"This won't cause any genetic mutations from inbreeding?"

"Some, but it should be manageable."

Walker opened up his overlay, clicked Time, and did as Virgil asked. Turning the cursor into a bubble was a trick that took him a moment to figure out, but after he got the hang of it, he placed it around the MUYs and far from the Slicer. Luckily, it hadn't discovered its next meal yet.

Clicking on the single arrow moved time forward one month at a time. Walker advanced time slowly, as this was his first chance to play with the Temporal Subsystem and he wanted to watch as things changed. He wasn't disappointed.

The two MUYs grew and grew, making him begin to worry about starvation. He didn't want to have to make more MUYs and repeat the process. His resources weren't unlimited, after all.

But apparently, between eating the small bits of fish and the aggressively expanding moss, everything efficiently worked together in the small space provided. Soon, two became ten, and ten became more than seventy. Each time they gave birth, it was in large batches, further filling the time bubble they were covered by. Once the two years had ended, there were hundreds of MUYs in the water, and even though they'd eaten a large portion of the moss, more MUYs kept spawning in the area.

He stopped the system, and time reasserted itself, with all the fish quickly spreading throughout the habitat. Walker watched the terrifying creature notice the first of the MUYs then explode into motion, zipping quickly back and forth, red stains the only remnants of what had once been living creatures.

"Man, he never gets tired of it."

"Yes," Virgil agreed. "It makes me worry that I did not modify the MUYs to reproduce quickly enough to maintain an equilibrium of growth. Let us pull up your Monitor ability and take a closer look at what is happening down below."

"Okay."

Walker clicked on his abilities and found them all listed alphabetically, in the same neurotic organizational fashion that many of his former colleagues at school had used.

Dante's Abilities:
Assistant (Advanced): Virgil
Copy

Evolutionary Edge
Identify
Monitor

He clicked on Monitor, and a floating screen the size of a computer monitor appeared in his overlay. On instinct, he tried to grab the corners and found success. The screen size could be expanded, and his eyes found a zoom option near the bottom. After scrolling momentarily, he found the Slicer and had to zoom out to keep track of its rapid movements.

"Little bastard is so fast," he said as the one-worm genocide continued.

"Very. Although something has me greatly worried, now that I consider it."

"Oh? What's that?"

"If the Slicer already has a high chance to evolve, and we factor in your Evolutionary Edge ability, would that not mean that the slightest chance of something attacking the Slicer would kick in its new advanced adaptive properties and cause another evolution?"

"Good thing we didn't make a piranha then," Walker said with a laugh.

Of course, he knew he shouldn't tempt fate. She was a bitch that couldn't stand it if someone was succeeding. As soon as he finished up his laugh, one of the MUYs miraculously moved out of the way of the Slicer's attack and slapped it with its tail, scratching the modified carapace. Walker's overlay took over.

Evolution occurring.
The Slicer is evolving!
[. . . Scanning . . .]
The Slicer has gained Extreme Survival Instincts.

"What the fuck does that mean?" Walker asked as he clicked Identity on the worm.

Name: Slicer
Genus: Slicer
Organism type: Apex Predator
Modifications: Rockhard Carapace, Deadly Jaws
Evolutionary traits: Advanced Adaptive Properties, Extreme
Survival Instincts

Wasn't it an alpha predator before?
Each of the Slicer's modifications and evolutions had smaller boxes around them. Walker clicked on extreme survival instincts for a closer look.

Extreme Survival Instincts:
While basic survival instincts will develop an intrinsic need for
the entity to ensure its own survival, this entity has evolved its
instincts to an extreme level and gained the ability to analyze
threats immediately. The entity will react to threats in sudden
and unexpected ways.

"Seriously, what the fuck does that mean?" Walker said again, growing increasingly worried the better he understood the evolution.

The monitor, still focused on the Slicer, showed it abruptly looking straight up toward the starry sky and a small green moon overhead. Walker looked at it, wondering what it was doing before clarity dropped on him and Virgil simultaneously.

"Fuck, it remembers us."

"I believe it is considering us a threat."

They looked at each other for a long moment before Walker laughed. "There's no way it can get to us up here."

As if it could hear them and took that for a challenge, the Slicer dove down toward the bottom of the planet, pushed itself into the granite below in a tight coil, then sprang out and undulated straight toward the top of the water. The Slicer was moving so fast that the pressure of its wake pushed aside the water surrounding it, damaging any nearby MUYs. It breached and, with unnatural grace, flew hundreds of feet in the air before splashing back down below with an angry hiss.

"See, there's no way," he said with false confidence.

The Slicer spun in a circle as if chasing its tail. There was a brief pause; then, it started to head toward the beach.

"What now?" Walker asked fate as if she was riding his shoulders.

"No," Virgil whispered.

"What?"

The Slicer beached itself and began pushing toward the beautiful new mountains Walker had just built. It kept moving, slowly, until it reached the wall. The time it took to travel the distance was long, and yet, neither of them moved as they watched the creature travel across the breadth of The Crater. Once it arrived, the Slicer began biting into it. The worm was moving quickly, starting slowly as its mandibles pinged off of the rock, leaving long gashes.

But as time passed, it began finding further efficiency and adapted as it attacked the rocky wall. Pieces of granite began splashing away from the area. Walker couldn't move as he watched the worm burrow itself through the mountains faster than he could've illustrated them.

"The World Editor, Walker!" Virgil snapped at him, trying to break his paralysis. But Walker still didn't move. He understood that if he left the Slicer on his planet, he would be effectively cut off from the protocol, as he couldn't move forward with his ideas. If he dropped new entities there, they would die, unless he made them just as bad as the Slicer, which would never work. If he tried to drain the atmosphere or alter the terrain somehow, the Slicer would evolve and become worse than it already was. This was a no-win situation, and while normally Walker didn't believe in that, this scenario felt unique.

The Slicer got through the last of the granite and onto Symphony's soil. Immediately, it began to burrow deep into the planet, driving itself down. As it moved, the soil filled in after it, and the monitor had nothing it could show. After a minute, Walker's overlay lit up.

Evolution occurring.
The Slicer is evolving!
[. . . Scanning . . .]
The Slicer has gained the Breathless ability.

"It has no need for oxygen anymore," Virgil stated incredulously.

Walker moved the monitor helplessly along the gray bottom of the planet, looking for any movement. After several minutes, he found chunks spitting into space, and the Slicer popped out, stretching its body in a twisted expression of triumph. It pushed itself off of Walker's world, and his overlay exploded with notifications.

Evolution occurring.
The Slicer is evolving!
[. . . Scanning . . .]
The Slicer has gained Extreme Spatial Containment.

Evolution occurring.
The Slicer is evolving!
[. . . Scanning . . .]
The Slicer has gained Advanced Spatial Defense.

"Wha—what? What's happening?"

"The damage from space is evolving it, Walker," Virgil said in a quiet voice.

Evolution occurring.
The Slicer is evolving!
[. . . Scanning . . .]
The Slicer has gained Spatial Propulsion.

Every time the Slicer moved, it did so in a quick manner, adapting to its movement in space. Its carapace was now layered, with the outer layers quickly flapping at a blistering speed as it learned to navigate in a vacuum. Walker closed the Monitor ability as he didn't need it anymore; the Slicer was quickly approaching them. It rammed into an elastic bubble similar to the one that had protected them in the first battle, the lights of the shield vibrating across his small moon.

"What the fuck," Walker said in a quiet voice, never having believed that anything like this could happen.

"I see now why they call it an evolutionary edge," Virgil calmly stated. "Because it is a double-edged sword. The more powerful the evolutionary rate of the entity, the greater the chance of this happening. I cannot imagine my fellow squirrels being so malevolent," he finished, trying to joke yet failing to lighten the mood. The Slicer rammed into their shield one more time before calmly floating in front of them, eyes still on Walker.

With a crick in his neck, Walker looked over at Virgil. "Why aren't you freaking out right now?"

"Simple. It cannot hurt us, and it has left the planet. The protocol shield does not allow sound to escape, so it cannot hear us. That is a good thing as, for all we know, it could evolve again and start understanding speech to help it adapt to threats."

"Yeah . . . yeah."

The Slicer rammed the shield again, as if in contempt of Walker's inability to fight a super-evolved Bobbit worm, and then started moving toward the unknown darkness of space. Walker breathed a sigh of relief before turning to Virgil.

"We need the most aggressive creature we can find to counter the Slicer now."

Virgil asked, "What are you going to do?"

"I'm gonna evolve a motherfucking Canadian goose."

"I highly suggest against that, Walk—"

Before he could finish, The Slicer flew back at Symphony with incredible speed, breaching the atmosphere and lighting itself on fire.

Evolution occurring.
The Slicer is evolving!
[. . . Scanning . . .]
The Slicer has gained Advanced Flameproofing.

Evolution occurring.
The Slicer is evolving!
[. . . Scanning . . .]
The Slicer has gained the Meteoric Fall ability.

When the evolution occurred, the flames around the Slicer grew to ten times their original size. It shot straight down into the planet, and a huge dust cloud rose in the air. As sounds of further impacts and crumbling occurred at the planet's top, they could see the Slicer pushing itself out of the bottom again. Walker pulled up the Monitor ability and watched it move its jaws as if laughing before it again floated off into space. He used Identify as it left.

Name: The Slicer
Genus: The Slicer
Organism Type: Cosmic Destroyer
Modifications: Rockhard Carapace, Deadly Jaws
Evolutionary traits: Advanced Adaptive Properties,
Extreme Survival Instinct, Extreme Spatial Containment,
Advanced Cosmic Defense, Spatial Propulsion,
Advanced Flameproofing
Evolutionary abilities: Meteoric Fall, Breathless

Pieces of Symphony began breaking off of the planet and floating into space, everything in shambles. Walker fell to his knees in the soft grass and started hiccupping, fists bunched at his sides.

"Hh-hho-howww?!"

"How . . . do you fix it?" Virgil asked, trying his best to understand him.

"How did I fuck up so bad?" Walker finished. "Why do I keep . . . keep . . . fucking UUUUUUP!" He screamed to the uncaring night sky, veins distending throughout his neck.

Virgil didn't have an answer for that. Instead, he stepped next to his Creator as he finished screaming and placed a paw on his shoulder while the man cried into his hands.

CHAPTER THIRTEEN

The Wall

Symphony was . . . destroyed. Cracked into pieces.

The assistance timer had run out, and it didn't even matter anymore. Parts of The Crater floated out, MUYs were floating in space . . . freezing in the vacuum . . . dying. The initial atmosphere was gone, and most of his new Java moss was no longer alive.

He didn't take it well.

It took quite a bit of time for Walker to calm down, for the tears to stop, and for the dry heaves to begin and stop as well. When he did, the emotional exhaustion that settled onto his shoulders pushed him further into the ground, metaphorically and literally. He lay on the ground like that for some time, trying to think of ways he could've stopped this from happening. To self-analyze the problem.

At first, he blamed Virgil, who could have warned that something like this could happen.

Then, he decided that the Alpha Protocol was fucked up and had placed him in this position. They had modified the Slicer in ways they shouldn't have. They had placed restrictions on Virgil, who wasn't at fault in the end and couldn't help him. They put Walker, an average human being, on this tiny planet and told him to create life. To modify life.

Eventually, the mental spinning stopped, and he only had himself to blame.

"Virgil," Walker said in a raspy voice, the roughness in his throat mirroring the turmoil he had just experienced. "Can you tell what the Slicer is doing now?"

"Yes, but I am not sure you want to know." He was standing by the Evolution Chamber, seemingly deep in thought.

"Please."

Virgil turned and looked at Walker on the ground. "It has just destroyed another Creator's world."

Walker tried to move his tongue around his mouth, but it was too dry. He felt numb, like everything was happening to someone else, but one thing stuck with him. He'd created a greater monster than he had ever imagined.

"How?" he asked.

"While the protocol protects the Creators, it does not and cannot protect their worlds. You are meant to expand and evolve, to make something greater than where you originally come from. Adversity is required."

"Fuuuuck!" he swore to the sky as he pounded a fist into the ground. Because of him and his monster, others were suffering. Each world snuffed out was a robbed possibility. A lost chance for something wonderful and magnificent to be created, not to mention a Creator failing in their tasks because of someone they'd never even met. He felt the weight further dig in.

He didn't want to look at the chatroom. Didn't want to see the messages that he was sure were popping up in confusion and terror. Of creatures from space coming for them, and fiery explosions destroying their dreams. He asked for advice from the one person who could give it.

"So what do I do, Virgil? What do I do now? How do I fix this?"

"If you are speaking of the Slicer specifically, it cannot be fixed. The cosmic destroyer is gone; it is out there. All of the assistants in the protocol are now aware of it, a warning has been sent to all Creators, and the system is moving forward. The only positive I can tell you is that it is moving further and further away from here. The only deviations in its path occur when it finds a new world to destroy. It is done with you. The best thing you can do is focus on your tasks, use the World Editor to fix Symphony, and move forward with the knowledge that you have now gained."

"A learning experience!" Walker yelled at Virgil with a flush staining his face. "You're giving me a teachable moment! I should just walk away from this and— and what? Go back to things like normal? I made a fucking world destroyer, an abomination that consistently grows from being attacked! On my first try, no less!" Walker could feel his heart speed up and begin pounding against his chest. He was having trouble taking deeper breaths, like there wasn't enough oxygen in this tiny world to support him. The tips of his fingers began to tingle while the darkness closed in.

He fell back further to the ground, his vision so bad that he could barely make out Virgil. He felt like his thoughts were squeezing themselves in so fast that he couldn't focus on any one thing at a time. A new one would appear, and his mind would try to track it, but as it gained a grasp, another would push for dominance. He felt paralyzed.

Virgil recognized what was happening and moved quickly to him. Placing a hand on his shoulder, he said, "Walker, you are having a panic attack. You need to calm down."

His breaths wouldn't come. "I . . . I . . . I can't."

"Yes, you can; stop thinking about it."

"I . . . I . . . I . . ." Walker tried talking, but he could only say the one letter.

"You have seen this in your students, Walker. You know a way to take control back. Focus on your breathing; do not think, just breathe."

Walker tried to do as Virgil asked, tried not to think and just pay attention to his breathing, but instead of thoughts, memories began lashing his psyche. It was like a greatest hits reel of his failures, and he was just a member of the audience.

He saw old friends at the moments of their parting. He watched old girlfriends and the myriad of his relationship problems, how things didn't work out. The anger, sadness, and crushed hopes of a true union of body and soul. A mountain of rejections when he tried to show people his truth, the sense of who he was deep inside that he had trouble expressing externally, which only came out in his writing and during the rare emotional moment.

The pinnacle of his memories glowed softly: Valerie standing atop a mountain. But she wasn't the mountain upon which she stood. That was his oldest friend, Matt. He saw all the times that Matt had reached out, and he had rebuffed him for one reason or another. His love for his friend wasn't romantic, but brotherly, and he had never truly expressed his appreciation of him. Walker now realized that if he completed the protocol, and chose to stay, he'd never get to meet Matt's child. To share his experiences and grow old with him. He had been so caught up in the idea of creation and what he would get to do, that he'd forgotten all the things he would lose—his humanity, or more specifically, his right to be human.

The memories and thoughts slowed down as Walker began to accept them as a part of himself, as a part of who he was and who he chose to be. After all, he could just stop his work and go back to his world, Mr. Harrison or not. But he knew he wouldn't. He needed to use this time to build something better than himself.

He saw his exes for what they were, roadblocks toward realizing who he could become. He saw his departed friendships and accepted that they had moved on, lived their lives, and didn't need him. His world needed him. *His* world. A world that he hadn't even really created yet. He could do better than the world where he'd come from. He could make something that truly mattered, a place that allowed those who wanted to grow into a better version of themselves to have the ability to do so.

He looked at his memories of Valerie and saw the warning signs he hadn't recognized before. The late, deep nights when she worked extra-long hours. The times when she wanted him to go somewhere with her, to do something fun, and he was too tired from work or just needed to be alone for the night. He hadn't thought of her needs. Her wants. Everything was about Walker, just like it had been with Matt.

Matt, who just wanted to talk every so often. But it took a lot of work to find the time. Walker always felt a need to be around his friends, but then when they wanted to go out and be around other people, people he didn't know, he just wanted to go home and be away from the stress. From the unknown. Walker was constantly being pulled in two directions. The need to be around people who cared about him, and the fear of being overwhelmed by strangers and situations he couldn't expect. It was why quitting his job had felt like such a relief.

No more acting in front of his students or being surrounded by moody teen-agers who lashed out because no one had taught them how to express themselves. He'd tried, but he had trouble with it himself. Walker had always hoped that taking on a job where he had to speak to a group consistently would fix his anxi-ety issues. Burn it away through repeated exposure, as his father taught him. *Face your fears, Walker*, he used to say.

Now he was on a tiny planet with Virgil, who had already seen all of his memories, who knew every detail about his life. If he chose it, right now . . . he could always be home—a home he had built. But to get there, mistakes would happen, and terrible things would always be waiting in the distance. He realized that now. The road to creation would be mixed with potholes. His mistakes, which could lead to destruction, would need to be mitigated, restrained, and watched. It would be hard, but somewhere within, he knew he could do it. He could succeed.

Walker's breathing slowly deepened as he internally processed everything, enough so that he could hesitatingly ask Virgil a question. "Virgil, you saw the memories of my parents, right?"

His assistant waited a moment before saying, "Yes. I saw them in their totality."

Walker nodded from the ground before sitting up. His face felt hot, and his lungs still felt like something was squeezing them, but he needed to talk this out, to express what was happening deep inside him. It felt like the only way to recover, to find some semblance of internal balance.

"What do you think of my memories with my father?" he asked.

"Mmmh," Virgil said in thought. "I think he was a hard man."

"Yeah, haha, yeah," he replied, his false laugh tinged with bitterness. "He was a hard man. He grew up in a different time. You know. Old school, y-you'd call it. He taught me that real men didn't show their emotions. Crying, depression, and basically, any kind of emotions . . . were for the weak. The infirm. If you were strong, then you were stoic, a wall that emotions broke upon and found no way in. *Speak only when you have something to actually say.* That's what he'd always tell me."

"Indeed."

"I know it's not normal. But . . . when you're raised a certain way, it—it becomes a part of you. That internal need to satisfy the standards of your parents, regardless of how messed up they are. And it worked, too. I got through my deployment and got into teaching kids with these horror stories from their lives. But . . . I don't know how—how to turn it off," he finished, his breathing growing shorter as he spoke. "It's . . . it's not easy to just . . . change. To decide one day that expressing feelings . . . putting it out there . . . is normal. That the wall can come down. So I-I-I—"

He paused to regulate his breathing before continuing.

"I took everything in. Being here, creation, the Slicer . . . and it just . . . it hit me, you know. I felt like a cup that was overfilling. When it blew up the planet . . . I just. I couldn't . . ."

"I understand, Walker, and it is okay. It was a series of circumstances that were out of your control."

"But it wasn't out of my control. I did that. I made it. Now, others have to suffer because of me."

"Walker, we have already spoken of your why. You have already stated that you will make entities who are villainous."

"Yeah, but I planned on making them limited. Making it so that they couldn't destroy a fucking planet."

"Then you have to be prepared, mentally and emotionally, for things to get out of control again. If this happens again, in a key moment where you need to do something, then your time may be over," Virgil said with a sympathetic voice. "I understand. I have seen what you have seen, but you must learn to grow from it, not be knocked down by it."

"I thought of that, heh, you—you're right." He breathed out slowly. "It's just . . . I don't think I can change, man."

"And I am not asking you to. I am just asking you to regulate it and try to find a balance."

"Yeah, that's what I was using my journal for."

"Indeed. But if you need to talk, I am here. And unlike those from your past . . . I am not going anywhere."

Walker wiped the snot from under his nose with the back of his hand before rubbing it into the grass. "Thanks, man."

"You are very welcome, Walker. Now, instead of spreading your genetic material into the grass, how about we work on Symphony?"

Walker looked at the pieces of his world floating into space before saying, "I'm not sure if we can call it that in its current state."

"Then we will just have to fix it and make it that way. Your way," Virgil said before stepping over and patting Walker's back gently. "We will figure it out."

The Slicer traveled through space, gaining more power as it destroyed each unique world and further evolved.

Upon entering one world, it found itself trapped inside a cage of impervious metal while it was destroying the creatures it found. Because of the distance, Walker couldn't see the evolutionary notifications anymore, but the Slicer had changed. At a certain point, its own overlay had activated.

Evolution occurring.
The Slicer is evolving!
[. . . Scanning . . .]
The Slicer has gained Logical Reasoning.

What?

CHAPTER FOURTEEN

The Killing Plan

"Walker, are you better now?" Virgil asked after looking him over.

He waved a hand in the air, not having moved from the ground since his Symphony had been destroyed. "No. No, not even close. But I'll—I'll get there."

"Well, that is all that I can ask for," the large squirrel said. "In the good news department, I have not seen another Creator's world destroyed in some time. Perhaps one of them learned how to contain the Slicer."

Walker looked up from the grass. "That is good news. Maybe they found a way to manage it."

"We can only hope. Now, here is the real question . . . Are you ready to get started on rebuilding Symphony?"

"I may as well." He looked at his timer and saw that he had over ninety-six hours remaining. "We only have so much time to fix all of this before we're fucked."

"Indeed. I suggest you go into the World Editor and fix things as best as possible. There are still a few living entities. I will need to create a localized event so they can sustain themselves and not perish."

Walker stood up on shaky legs. "Okay."

He clicked on the World Editor, and his overlay lit up.

Welcome to the World Editor!
Upgrade detected.
As you have upgraded your World Editor, you can now add and
modify land directly. You will not be able to add direct landmass,
but you can make minor changes to your world.
To begin, please name your world.

"Whoops."

"What?" Virgil asked as he watched the pieces of their small planet floating in space.

"I named the second landmass Symphony. Now the World Editor is asking me to name the planet."

"That is not a problem. Many worlds have continents, cities, and entire planets sharing the same name. You are not the only one who has trouble with naming things."

Walker's difficulty with names was becoming legendary in his own mind. But still, at least he wasn't Human10.

"What about Blitzburg7? How come it never changed its identity?"

"That is actually a cultural choice. The Blitzburgs are populous throughout the multiverse due to their high intelligence and aptitude for magic. They take pride in how many are selected in the Alpha Protocol and leave their numbers as identifiers of such."

"Strange."

"Walker," Virgil said with emphasis. "Many cultures would consider Earth and your fellow humans strange. Your need for individuality, especially in your newest generations . . . it is profound."

"Yeah, yeah, we're all special snowflakes. Nothing new there, by the way. The real question is, why do they know about the Alpha Protocol and Earth doesn't?"

"Because they have a member on the Council and have been a part of the protocol since the first initialization. You would almost call them . . . tuned to it."

"So they're guaranteed to succeed, whereas I blew up my planet?" Walker asked as he felt his heartache shift to resentment.

"They have no more a guarantee of success than you. The protocol does not necessarily disallow Creators from sharing information about their time within it. To the Blitzburgs, it is more along the lines of . . . gauche, to speak of your success. The most that many of the successful Creators do is let their created worlds have an idea of what they went through rather than engage in a full-blown discussion about it. When you gain the Disciple Subsystem, you can speak directly with a few chosen entities and become a form of guide. But you should not tell them the specifics of the Creator Wars or give them any hints about the protocol. To them, you must seem as if you are a God."

"So I'll be making a religion. That seems fucked up, if I'm honest." He moved a hand up and down his body. "For a human, I'm above average intelligence—"

"Most humans believe that," Virgil interrupted.

Walker just continued talking like he hadn't heard him. "Buuuut, I'm not omniscient or omnipotent or any other omni-thing. I'm a failed teacher and friend." He rubbed the back of his head. "Plus, as you know, my planet has a history of religion and planetary warfare going hand in hand. I'm not so sure that developing a Walker religion is the best idea."

"Technically, it would be a Dante religion, as that is how they will know you, but I understand your point. However, your entities will see land connect to their world, watch themselves evolve, and witness new species often arriving out of nowhere. To think that they would not form some kind of belief system or organization centered around this phenomenon is naive at best and dangerous at worst. You need to plan for this and, if possible, harness it."

"So I should lean into the god complex. Stop caring about how others feel and live. Focus only on whatever is best for my goals; my aspirations are what matter most."

"Your morality will see you fail."

Walker put his hands on his hips. "My morality is what makes me a better person than those who would kill for their ambitions."

Virgil held his hands up in a calming gesture. "Yes, but you are also the Creator of their world, and thus, you have a responsibility to that same world as a whole and not to just a few individuals who live upon it. What is the quote you have often said? *You have to break a few eggs to make an omelet.* Your favorite food is meat-lovers pizza. Did you say a prayer for the cow who became your sausage, or the chicken? They are all degrees of the benefits of killing."

Walker loved meat-lovers pizza. "Fair enough, but we are not done with this conversation."

Virgil nodded.

After a moment of thought, Walker moved back into the World Editor to take a big step. The first thing he did was name the pseudo-planet.

World: Symphony is named.

Congratulations, Dante! You've named your world!

The World Editor will now allow you to remove resources you no longer need and store them in your Resources section for future use. There are no limits on how much may be removed or stored.

Due to your upgrade, you can now add material from your Resources section directly to your world. Modification is limited to the use of adding standard resources, combining resources, and shaping resources.

(Further upgradeable)

Current status: Splintered

Please reconnect the broken sections of your world before you can access your systems.

Once Walker read through the text, he clicked back to the main screen and saw that the Landmass System and the Entity and Temporal Subsystems were grayed out. He clicked on World Editor again, and a small 3D projection of Symphony appeared, depressing him even further. There were SO MANY PIECES . . . EVERYWHERE!

"How in the hell am I going to do this?" he asked the air.

"One step at a time," Virgil said over his shoulder.

Walker nodded without saying anything and placed his hands over the 3D projection. When he clicked a small portion of water floating in space, a series of icons appeared next to it, telling him he could remove, add, or modify it. He clicked Remove and watched the floating water disappear. After he clicked it, some text appeared showing it had been added to his resources. He had just clicked on a small piece of floating land when Virgil coughed.

"Some people have learned to . . . take large steps, Walker. A smart Creator would see if there is an overarching Remove button, rather than clicking on every piece floating in space."

Walker caught on immediately. "A smart Creator would thank their friend."

"Is that what we are now, Walker?" Virgil asked with a tilt of his head.

"Only one I have out here," he responded seriously, returning to his work without looking at Virgil. He didn't see Virgil give him a long stare before focusing back on his own overlay.

He found the Select to Remove button when he clicked on the edge of Symphony and discovered that he could just swipe his hand and delete anything he wanted, except the MUYs and moss. It seemed his entities were destined to slowly float out toward other worlds, not unlike the Slicer.

As he was deleting, numbers appeared next to what he was working on. Walker looked at his resources and found that he already had a lot of material, and he'd have some work ahead of him to fix what was broken. Carefully, he expanded the size of the 3D image, making it easier to see the smaller areas, and began to work on the outside of the landmass. The moment he completed the outside, he expanded the image again and cleaned up the areas in the middle. Anything that wasn't perfectly connected to a large mass was removed.

He committed himself fully to his work, making slow movements that gained precision the longer he progressed until, finally, he finished. According to his timer, it had taken him two hours to clean up all the problems, even with the mass deleting option to remove everything he touched.

Walker looked at what he had left. Symphony was broken into multiple pieces, with only a few large fragments sticking together. A thought, a plan really, blew up in his mind. Walker let it percolate in the background of his thoughts as he pulled up his resources. He had a lot of water and granite, as well as a smattering of soil, as the mid-portion had mostly remained intact. But it did have one long hole straight down the middle, and the bottom of the planet was fractured from the Slicer's impact.

Seeing the Landmass System was no longer grayed out, he still chose to continue working within the World Editor. Controlling his movements, he started to add things back to the way they were. When he reached the bottom of the hemispheric landmass, another idea struck him. Walker was currently building a world from nothing using what seemed like magic. Who said he had to follow the rules?

Rather than follow the roundness of the planets he'd grown up seeing, he created edges. This would leave the bottom of his planet in more of a square shape, and the reasoning for doing so was simple. It would be easier to add more landmass over time with flat planes. Incrementally, he placed the resources back where they belonged, further improving the waterway he'd added as a last-minute thought previously.

He left the pass through the mountains that the Slicer had cut away, as now there was no longer any need to separate The Crater from the rest of Symphony. The top of the planet was no longer a perfect disc, as his control wasn't good enough when working on such a large scale, but it was put back together at least, albeit a little haphazardly. He took his leftover granite and edged all around the top of the world, not wanting his future entities to . . . basically fall off of the planet. That would be embarrassing and, frankly, horrifying.

"Done," he announced to Virgil, who walked over to see it. Walker clicked the Monitor button and looked around, finding the last living MUYs now placidly living in their habitat with the remaining Java moss. They still had about thirty of them, which Virgil said was enough for repopulation. It could have been better, but for now, the band-aid would work.

A band-aid for a wound in his world. One caused by a seriously sadistic son of a bitch. Walker mentally went back to the Slicer's hissing. He was sure now that it had been laughter. Considering it, he thought of something.

"Couldn't I have just rewound time with the Temporal Subsystem? Gone back to before the Slicer blew everything up?"

Virgil shook his head. "No. The Alpha Protocol disallows Creators from doing anything with their systems when their landmasses are in great peril. This has been a rule within the protocol since its inception. The Temporal Subsystem is just the newest system to be added."

"Why? That seems dumb as fuck. If I make a big mistake, I can just rewind it and fix my issue. Problem solved . . ."

"Therein lies the problem. The Alpha Protocol Council has stated, and I quote, *Creators need to learn to solve their problems before they make them. Resiliency and adaptability are necessary for success.* Their firm belief is that no Creator should have a get-out-of-jail-free card. Similar to how it views your mental, emotional, and genetic issues, the protocol believes you will be more creative if you are placed into a figurative corner, trying to find your way out of it."

Walker didn't like that answer. He looked at Virgil from the corner of his eye. "Did you really have to point out my emotional issues?"

Virgil nodded. "Indeed."

He sighed. "Now what?"

"Well . . . do you still want to make killer Canadian geese?"

Walker shuddered. "God no, and we need to limit our creations. If we make another high-potential raging monster, it has to die immediately."

Virgil nodded. "I agree. We have time to create a new predator and prey cycle, and we have leftover temporal resources as we have not used much of our stock. That leaves a lot of room for additions and improvement."

"Right. So, spitball with me here. I have a plan," he said, checking and ensuring he had enough time left before the next battle.

"Go ahead," Virgil said.

"This is what I'm thinking. We have ninety-four hours plus some change before the next battle. The remaining MUYs should still have enough food to maintain themselves between their cannibalism and the moss. So, I want to straight ignore them. We need some skin in the game, which means getting rolling on our entities. We need to finish the current entity task, grab whatever the rewards are, and unlock the next one. I think we need to go for the Spirit Tree."

Virgil began hopping up and down. "You are ready for the Spirit Tree!"

Walker raised his hands and patted the air until he stopped jumping. "Calm down, calm down. Yes, I think we need to get some magic into Symphony, but I don't want the tree to evolve."

Virgil tilted his head at that. "Then what do you want it for? Historically, Spirit Trees have been used as a building block for great entities. Ones that help push their Creators to the finals, no less."

"Be that as it may, I'm worried that one will be born with high potential like the Slicer and just take over, ruining all of our other ideas. I want to make one, materialize it, kill it while it's young, and then throw it into the Evolution Chamber. We can evolve it to *not* have the ability to evolve. As soon as we have the tree in the right place, we plant them throughout Symphony and modify them for the environment."

"To what end?" Virgil asked.

"I want them to be magical batteries. Magic has to exist inside an entity for it to use it, correct?"

"Very much so. Magic is a catalyst for, of course, magical evolution. The moment the Slicer gained its advanced adaptive properties from destroying the

Spirit Tree, it gained access to magic and thus could do amazing things . . . like blow up Symphony."

"Yeah, less happy ending there with its"—Walker made air quotes—"'amazing things.' But think about this. We place the trees throughout Symphony, creating a world that is filled with magic so heavy it can be found in the atmosphere. Then we build a system that harnesses that magic and allows the entities who use it to have controlled evolutions."

"So you want to create entities that do not evolve, yet fill the world with the spark for magical evolution, and then control how the magic is allowed to interact with Symphony's entities?"

"Exactly!" Walker said, giving Virgil two thumbs up. "You nailed it. What do you think? I know we'll have to make a lot of unmodified entities and then kill them . . . but I feel like this is the only way we keep from having another the Slicer incident."

Virgil thought on that a moment before saying, "That is possible with the System Designer, Walker, but also a bit dark for your morality. You said you were not a murderer, but that seems like it would be murder. Spirit Trees, for example, are living creatures."

"Do they think for themselves?"

"Well, no, but when they evolve . . . ah. I see your point."

"Look . . . it . . . I feel like I'm going to have to . . . kill things here," Walker said with a grimace. He hadn't been sure if it was possible, but now that it was, the consequences of his idea shook him. What he was planning now, a killing plan, was pretty awful. It had a purpose and was necessary for his ideas going forward, but it still didn't sit right in his stomach.

"It's just . . . I'm not saying I haven't killed before."

Walker had gone hunting, but the purpose there had been food. He had fought in Operation Enduring Freedom, but that was under orders and in defense of himself or others. This was a different situation altogether.

While Walker tried to mentally justify his plan, Virgil said, "I know. But this is different, is it not?"

"How so?"

"The instance you spoke of earlier, killing to satisfy ambition, is not quite the same. I will not say there are not similarities between that idea and your current plan, but I believe there is one key difference: You are killing in order to create. I believe that should make the distinction for you."

Walker thought about that. He wasn't sure about how to bridge the divide between the need to control things so Symphony didn't spiral out of control, and the idea of murdering breathing lifeforms that he created.

"I don't have much of a choice, do I?" he said in realization.

"No."

Walker shook his head hard, not in denial of Virgil's agreement with him but in denial of his own self-image. Sure, he hadn't been the best boyfriend, friend, or, at times, person. The world was a gray watercolor painting, constantly mixing, and nothing was ever truly clean. But he wasn't a murderer.

The more he thought about it, the more inevitable it seemed. For his plan to work, he was going to have to kill things . . . to murder things. What would that do to him? What would he become? If he succeeded in the protocol, he would not only be a murderer but an immortal murderer.

What was the alternative? Let Virgil die, go back to Earth, and not have the chance to make his world? No. No way. He just might have to crack a few eggs.

"Are there other options?"

Virgil shrugged. "Not really, unless you suddenly became great at modifying entities. When you consider that most of creation is done immediately after destruction, you begin to see the cycle. Your famous pianist, Elton John, sang a song about it. It is a circle, Walker; the only difference is you will have direct input into how and why that circle will work. You removed the floating landmass and gained materials back for your world. You seeded an alpha predator with high evolutionary potential and received a cosmic destroyer. There is a form of balance within the protocol, of fairness, of give and take, and you are attempting to make Symphony with a similar framework."

"Does that make me evil?"

"Does being human make you evil?" Virgil countered. "You are working within the confines of your limitations, and as far as ideas go, I believe this to be a winner." He gave Walker his two thumbs back.

"Okay, okay," Walker repeated to himself, trying to come to terms with what he needed to do. "So we have a plan." He pressed the bottom of his fist into his other hand. "First, we make the tree; then, I find a way to kill it. After that, we modify it to have no evolutionary potential . . . just a simple dumb space magic tree. No more modifying on the whiteboard unless it's a landmass. We'll only use the Evolution Chamber."

"Yes," Virgil said with approval.

"Then, we get into the ecology and make sure the atmosphere is balanced out, which will be your focus the moment the first trees are done."

"I will be on it," he replied, being a good hype man.

"Indeed," Walker said with the first smile he'd shown since the Slicer's flaming hit-and-run.

"You are not as funny as you think you are, Walker."

"Whatever. As soon as the atmosphere can support it, we kick off the predator-prey cycle, basic stuff, and start our monsters right after."

"I am unsure if we have enough time for that, Walker."

"Always time," he said with a shake of his head. "We'll just . . . make time. We can recover from this; we can get through the protocol. We just need to put in the time, literally, and work together. You with me!" Walker finished, throwing his hands in the air.

"I do not have a choice."

"I'll take that as a hell yes. Now, where the fuck do I find the Spirit Tree in the Entity Subsystem? Because I have no idea."

Virgil slapped a hand to his face.

CHAPTER FIFTEEN

Building a Ley Line

Virgil sounded annoyed as he explained how to find the magical tab in the Entity Subsystem.

There was only one entry right now, the Spirit Tree. He watched as it sketched itself into the whiteboard, complicated whorls and lines stretching across its bark. Looking at Virgil, Walker noticed the large squirrel was bouncing on the pads of his feet.

Guess he's ready.

He pressed the Materialize button.

No update came. Walker rightly believed that the system didn't recognize it as a unique lifeform, since he was just using the basic, unmodified form. No update to the entity task came, but at least his materials came back to him. No loss there. But there was a bigger problem than his grade and materials.

They couldn't find the Spirit Tree.

"Ummmm, where is it?" Walker asked.

Virgil stood beside him as they both looked down at Symphony. "Indeed. I was so excited I did not think about this. It is a Spirit Tree; its life begins as a seed."

"Wait, but the Slicer came out fully grown. Why didn't the Spirit Tree do the same?"

"Because the Alpha Protocol's assistance, specifically the modifications it presented, could only work on an adult Bobbit worm. Thus, the Slicer was advanced to prime adulthood at no temporal charge."

"Fuck," Walker said as he realized what that meant. "You mean that thing, the thing we can't allow to evolve, is planted in the soil of Symphony, and we have no idea where?"

"That is correct," Virgil said with a calm nod.

Walker didn't know why Virgil was taking this so well, as this seemed like the potential beginning of another Slicer. They needed to find the seed, and fast. Hopefully Virgil had a clue about how to do that.

The large squirrel's eyes roamed across the landmass. "It has been planted randomly by the protocol. In the future, we can use the Evolution Chamber, linked to the Temporal Subsystem, to make them materialize fully grown. But for now, we do not know where it is."

Walker looked out at the small planet, with all of the soil put back where it belonged, and had a single thought:

Fuck.

"So we have a super-powered magic tree growing and we don't know where it is, or if it's already evolving and fucking everything up."

Virgil hummed before saying, "Yes, that is correct."

Walker tilted his head. "That's the second time you've said that. Are you saying that just so you won't say the word *indeed*?"

Virgil looked at him for a second before looking away. "I do not know what you are talking about, Walker."

"Hah!" Walker said, pointing a finger at him, completely ignoring the fact that he might soon lose control of things again. He knew he was still distracting himself from what had happened only hours ago, but he was learning that when things go wrong, you can let it take you down or you can take it in and not let it happen again. It was something he needed to keep in mind.

Walker looked back at the world, palmed his chin, and tried to think of what to do. After several minutes passed by, he had come up with two possible solutions. One, he could remove all of the soil and find the seed somewhere on the planet. Two, he could accelerate time, find it as it grew out of the soil, and take care of it with the hope that it wouldn't randomly evolve. He mentioned both options to Virgil.

"One uses temporal resources, the other does not. I also do not believe that removing the soil around it will cause an evolution. Evolutions have a tendency to be caused by one of three things: great agitation, a powerful focus on said evolution by a determined entity, or, with the addition of magic . . . blind chance."

"So taking away the soil wouldn't cause it to be agitated? And what do you mean by chance?"

"It should not, as it is not directly causing any form of damage. For chance, you would call it luck. With magical evolution, agitation and focus can force it to occur, but luck is always a factor. Use the Slicer as an example. It destroyed the tree and was not trying to evolve . . . yet it was . . . uh . . . lucky."

"Gravy," Walker replied. So soil removal was the only way to go. If he just pushed forward in time, there was a greater chance that the tree could evolve into something else. He felt like fate was riding his shoulders again, but this was what being a Creator was all about. As the old saying went, no risk, no reward.

He made his choice.

Walker stepped into the World Editor and zoomed in deeply. With slow movements, he began to remove all of the soil. When he had taken away over a fifth of what soil Symphony had left, he found a small brown dot sitting on a pale gray slab of granite. He looked at Virgil.

"Do you know how you want to do this?" Virgil asked.

"Yep," Walker confirmed. "But this isn't how I want to do it in the future. It'll work for now, but it may not later."

"Okay, I trust you."

Walker clicked Remove, and in a straight line a little larger than the seed, he began deleting from the bottom of the planet moving up. Once he reached the seed, it dropped straight through the planet and floated out into the darkness. He made a mental note to ask why there was no gravity on the bottom of the planet like there was on the top. Walker clicked the Monitor button and they watched as a seed floated into space.

It had a series of whorls carved in circles throughout a deep brown shell. The harsh cold immediately went to work on it, the shell beginning to crack as a cyan light grew progressively brighter from the inside. The further the cracks went, the more the light bled out of the seed until it started to pulse in small waves. Walker's overlay lit up.

Evolution occurring.
The Seed of the Spirit Tree is evolving!
[. . . Scanning . . .]
[Error.]

Walker felt like his stomach was turning, but relief came as the cracks widened in the seed before it ultimately imploded, releasing a wave of cyan particles out into empty, dark space.

[. . . Scanning . . .]
The Seed of the Spirit Tree will no longer evolve
as its life force cannot be found.

"I guess that is one way to say it's dead," Walker commented.

"Indeed. But now we can make modified Spirit Trees in the Evolution Chamber." Virgil rubbed the palms of his paws together. "We are going to make some magic . . . literally. Do you still want to have different environments extending from the center of Symphony to its periphery? As you had before the incident with the Slicer?"

"So we're calling it *the incident* now?"

"It seemed appropriate."

Walker considered it. He'd already fixed most of the landmass. Really, now it was just missing the smaller parts that made an environment . . . environmental. Trees and the like. He waved his hand. "Fine."

"Understood."

"Before you do anything, is there anything missing that should still be added?" Walker asked.

Virgil sighed, clearly frustrated that he wasn't immediately moving forward with his magic trees. "You could add more mountains," he said grumpily.

"Okay, we'll get to that with the . . . next *next* landmass. So there won't be a lot of delays for the Spirit . . . Trees," he said, stumbling on the wordage. "Is there a better name for those?" He waved a hand again. "No, don't answer. The plan is still to have different environments in each corner—ones we can build up and out from, thereby extending the environmental habitat. But I also want to leave spaces between the corners of each attached landmass. That way, we can create grassland and soil like we did in the center of Symphony."

"Why?"

"Simple, the expansion of food. We don't know what our populations will look like as we go, so why not be smart and plan for an easier area to farm? Plus, I already have the next landmass figured out." He rubbed his hands together. "I'm going to make a very thick, very durable, huge block of metal. Then, I'm going to merge it into the stone of Symphony deep underneath the top half. That way, no more stupid, asshole monsters can cut our burgeoning planet in half."

Walker paused, giving the empty space above him a glare, willing the Slicer to feel it.

Virgil just nodded, knowing nothing else on the matter needed to be said. He understood that it was best to just move on from the incident before he allowed it to affect Walker's psyche any more than it already had. "So, if you are going to make potentially extreme environments, we will need to modify each Spirit Tree with exacting specifications, thereby allowing them to grow and survive in those environments."

"Makes sense. So a form of heat resistance *and* cold resistance for the desert. Too many people from my homeworld don't understand just how cold it is in a desert at night. Then, modified Spirit Trees for the mountains that can weather oxygen deprivation. Stuff like that."

"Almost. Mana Trees do not survive on oxygen or water as the trees in your original world do. Their sustenance is found internally as they harness their energy and breakthrough to a denser form, or grow."

"So . . . they're cultivators?"

"You could say that, but we are getting sidetracked. First, we will want to plant them somewhere in the center of the grasslands, as that will be the most temperate environment possible. We need to see what interactions the modified Spirit Tree has with Symphony to gain an understanding of whether or not this plan works. Also, do not worry; I will copy the modifications for future use as I did with the MUYs and the moss."

"Cool. I'd like to work with you if possible, so I can see how it's done."

Virgil nodded in agreement. "Absolutely."

Together, they moved toward the Evolution Chamber at a quick hop, both excited to get started. As Walker pulled up the seed of the Spirit Tree, each talked about what they would need to build into it before first planting it in Symphony's soil.

Virgil had the system put a seed into the Evolution Chamber, then explained how to make entities that could not evolve, magically or otherwise. The first step was to modify the Spirit Tree so it couldn't reproduce; that way, they never had to worry about genetic variation. The next step was to make sure that there weren't any instincts for self-preservation, and if there were, to take them away so that it wouldn't feel any form of agitation. Third, to counter magical evolution, Walker learned that you had to make an entity's cells unable to maintain any kind of magical or spiritual power, which seemed like a misnomer as magic was what they were after. When he asked about it, Virgil responded with a question.

"When an electric eel attacks something, does it shock itself?"

Walker shut up after that as he was not a scientist, and Virgil was a universal advanced robotic assistant shaped like a giant squirrel. Sometimes . . . he'd just have to say *wizard shit*. Virgil further explained, however, that extreme magical variance, like a bomb of some kind, could override the changes they were making to the Spirit Tree's cells, though the odds of that happening were small.

Even if a Spirit Tree did evolve, it wouldn't be anywhere near the level of the Slicer; the evolution would be more along the lines of gaining sapience or toughening its bark. With those three modifications, the base form of the Spirit Tree was now unable to gain anything from the system Walker planned on putting into place.

They moved on to determining how the trees were going to spread magic across Symphony, or as Walker liked to say, the *why* of its purpose.

In his mind, Walker saw the Spirit Trees spreading magic like an umbrella across the surface of his world. It would be another manner of atmosphere, no different to the planet than air or the indefinite magnetic field he'd gained from his rewards. When magic was needed, it would be there.

Virgil asked a few questions, such as: Did he want the magic attuned to anything in particular, like elements or ideas? Another was if he wanted the Spirit Trees to have interconnected roots. Walker said no to the former and yes to the latter. The tree had to be pure and free of any kind of magical attunement or, as Virgil called it, magical variance. While a fire-mana-attuned tree sounded cool, its output would also only be fire-attuned magic. It was something to consider, but not something he wanted to start out with. It also wouldn't work with his idea of having all of the Spirit Trees connected through a root system, balancing out the world's magic. Based on how Virgil explained magical attunement, he was worried that they would corrupt each other as their roots intertwined. To stomp out that problem before it occurred, purity was a necessity.

With that, Virgil asked to spend a year's worth of temporal resources. Walker hemmed and hawed about the cost but eventually agreed that there wasn't much they could do about it. Walker watched as the tiny seed quickly sprang up into a healthy sapling. As it grew, its coloring became more vibrant, taking on the same bluish hues of the Spirit Tree he'd seen in the first battle.

Nodding his head, Virgil then demonstrated to Walker how he was grafting funnels into its roots. The tree would be planted partially grown, where its roots could stretch out, carrying magic toward any fellow trees it could find. Then, after a heavy explanation of what to do, he told Walker to get used to working with the Evolution Chamber.

It was ingeniously made. It connected to the hands of the closest person and was incredibly intuitive. As Walker pinched his fingers together, portions would shrink. As he moved his hands from close to far, larger portions would expand. The person who had made it had to be some kind of universal master of technology. He'd never seen anything like it. He started to make jokes about being Tom Cruise until Virgil yelled at him to be careful. Wisely, he acceded to the squirrel's warnings.

After Walker practiced with the controls for a few moments, learning how to select different options and tweak things to his preference, Virgil told him to start working on the roots. First, he selected the mana grafts Virgil had created while he was busy feeling sorry for himself, and then Virgil showed him how to place the graft's image onto the entity. Starting at the most distant tip, he began to layer what the system recognized as blue lines across each part of the tree. As he finished the most distant parts, he kept up the movements until he reached the magic production area in the tree's center.

When they connected, the grafts lit up momentarily, but Walker knew his work wasn't done.

He continued to build outward from the center, making more funnels that reached toward the leaves, while also extending the length that the branches would grow. Virgil gave him a fun fact while he continued to work on it. Apparently, Spirit Trees originally didn't have leaves. The original Spirit Tree was basically a tall stick that looked swollen, like it had eaten a baguette and ignored its gluten intolerance. The modifications had made it a much more popular find, although only a few species, like the Blitzburgs, had access to it. Then Virgil told him he had modified their Spirit Tree to grow to over one hundred feet tall.

"That's ten stories high," Walker said as he looked at the baby tree in the chamber. "That is a tall-ass tree."

"Mmm, yes. But it also means that you can produce fewer of them, as they will be magic factories rather than batteries. Based upon what I project its magical production rate to be, you should only need two in each territory for magic to sufficiently encompass Symphony. With each new landmass, you will want to build a Spirit Tree immediately, meaning they will have a lower magical output until the tree has grown and connected to the rest of the root system. We will allow this one only to be a few years old so that it has time to sink its roots appropriately, and I will modify it to search for others like itself, thereby creating a magical network, or ley line, as your world likes to call them."

"So, with the four corners, The Crater, and Symphony's center, that's twelve Spirit Trees. At two years a piece, you're talking about spending twenty-four years out of our time resources."

"Not necessarily. The Evolution Chamber truly is a great boon to our modifications. With it, we can finish our design, complete its temporal shift to two years of age, and establish that as the new base model. Then, it will be simple to scan it, put a new copy into the chamber, and make environmental modifications from there. That is why I wanted to start with the center; it is a blank slate for the remainder of the necessary locations. That is also why we must create a perfect design for our first rendition."

"Smart, smart. Okay. So, just so I understand: We're making a perfect version that all of our copies will be based on, right? I mean, how long will these live?"

"Even without modifications, Spirit Trees gain their full size at one hundred years of age and then age no longer. It will shed its bark from time to time—which is a potent magical resource on its own, by the way—and it will need to reproduce damaged leaves, but otherwise, it is an evergreen. It will always have leaves and it will always produce magic. That is why I became so excited when I saw it. There are other kinds of magical trees across the protocol, but few are evergreens, and very few produce magic at the rate that the Spirit Tree does."

"How will the magic reach the atmosphere and spread?" Walker asked.

"There is a certain *je ne sais quoi* to magic, it—"

"English pleeease," Walker complained.

Virgil put his hands on his hips. "I recall your feelings on the French, but you need to move past it."

"It really isn't all of the French," Walker said in defense of his character. "It's just the French people I have met have been . . . assholes."

"Whatever. You are not exactly Mary Poppins, Walker. And that attitude toward a nationality of your species is beneath you."

"Fair."

"As I was saying." He paused and gave Walker some side-eye, daring him to interrupt his magical speech again before continuing. "There is a certain *je ne sais quoi* to magic. Once it enters a world, it wants to spread. It needs to spread."

"So . . . is magic alive?"

"No, there is no mind to it, but there is an instinct found within all magic to move and interact with anything it can, similar to air filling a vacuum. The Spirit Tree will create an aura around it that will be filled with magic, concentrating it in that location. By connecting the roots and increasing each tree's size dramatically, we are also increasing their production and area of effect, thereby filling the entirety of the world with magic. As long as we place each in the right location, that is."

"Okay, I think I've got it now." Walker looked down at his landmass, trying to picture how it would all look. "This really seems like it will work."

"Yes, I do believe it will. We have done a great job here. Everything should work out just fine."

Walker grimaced, shook his head, then glared at Virgil. "You never say things like that. Ever."

"Do not be superstitious, Walker."

"I'd just rather not have fate punch me in the dick again," he said soberly as he looked around himself dramatically. "She's always waiting."

Virgil ignored him and advanced the basic model of their Spirit Tree inside the Evolution Chamber until it reached two years of age.

"Please materialize it, Walker, but I have one suggestion."

"What's that?"

"Link your Monitor ability to the Evolution Chamber. That way it will be planted where you are currently viewing rather than anywhere on Symphony."

". . . Why didn't you say that before!"

"I will be honest with you. I was so excited to see the seed, I did not think of it."

Walker shook his head. "Squirrels."

"Yes . . . indeed."

Virgil showed Walker how to link the monitor with the Evolution Chamber. He simply had to drag the ability over to the Evolution Chamber in his vision, accept a prompt that appeared, and they were good to go. Walker pulled up the monitor, zoomed into an area on the left side of the center, and after confirming that was the spot they wanted, clicked Materialize. His overlay lit up.

[. . . **Scanning** . . .]
Task updated!
Entity task complete: Create three new unique entities (Part 1)
New unique entities created: 3/3

**Reward upgraded due to the presence and advanced use of an
Evolution Chamber.
Reward given: Diverse**

New entity task: Create ten more unique entities (Part 2)
*Diversification allows for growth. The further down
a genetic line that organisms move unchanged, the greater
the loss of potential genetic resources. You have made three
unique entities, now make ten more.*
**New unique entities: 0/10
Reward for completion: Diverse
[. . . Scanning . . .]
As your entity has been modified from its original form,
please name it.**

Naming it wasn't difficult this time. Walker had his favorite books and games
all wrapped up neatly in his head. He was sure that Virgil would understand.

**Entity: Mana Tree is named.
[. . . Analyzing . . .]
Entity named Mana Tree analyzed
Size: Medium (High growth potential)
Entity category: Magical Producer
Organism type: Plant
Modification: Extreme
Ability to evolve: No (Restricted)
Age: 2 years
Extra marks earned for being within the first
100 Creators (91st) to make an extreme modification
of another Creator's work in the
4AA Alpha Protocol (Modest reward earned)
Grade: B+
Rewards calculated.**

**Reward for completing the first entity task:
Congratulations, Dante! You've unlocked the Combiner ability!**
*Not all entities can be built from one strain of genus,
and the Alpha Protocol recognizes this. The Combiner ability
allows the Creator to combine elements of already produced
entities in order to form something new.*

**Limit: Use of the Combiner ability is restricted
to once per day regardless of results.
(Upgradeable)**

**Considerable reward for completion of a B+ grade entity:
Congratulations, Dante! Your Creation Instrument has been
upgraded twice!**
*As evolution is the key to a powerful entity, technology is the key
to a vibrant and dynamic landmass.*

**Modest reward for being within the first 100 Creators to
extremely modify another Creator's work:
Congratulations, Dante! You've gained a subsystem assistant!**
*Although your primary assistant should be all the help that is
necessary to complete the Alpha Protocol, experience has shown
that gaining a second assistant that has a specific focus can be a
positive turn for any Creator. This assistant, unlike the original,
will not have the memories of its Creator to look upon.
Training a subsystem assistant can show increased gains
over time as they gain more system autonomy and knowledge.
Further subsystem assistants can be gained.*

**[. . . Scanning . . .]
Optional tasks updated!
Optional tasks assigned to Creator Dante:**

Subsystem assistant task: Train the assistant (Series 1)
*A subsystem assistant can be difficult to work with. If they are not
allocated a Creator's memories, they come as a blank slate with
only the Universal Translator applied and a low amount of
general knowledge. To gain the most from your assistant, train
them in how to use their specific subsystem and encourage
them to gain their own autonomy so you may focus on
other things as needed.*
**Subsystem assistant requirements:
Assistant is assigned to a subsystem: No
Assistant is autonomous: No
Assistant completes work continuously without
calamity: 0/7 days
Reward for completion: Gain a second subsystem assistant
Time remaining until next battle: 90 hours**

"I do not understand," Virgil said immediately.

Location: Earth

Time: The moment of Walker's translocation

He was caught completely. While the Creators were immersed in the Alpha Protocol, all of time had stopped across the multitude of universes. There was no talking, no movement, nothing at all. An ordinary-seeming stick pulsed in a homeless man's hand, and he suddenly took a deep breath before coughing.

Time slowly started to move again near him, spreading out across the world in a disjointed pulse. It was regaining dominion over the Earth, but doing so at different levels of speed. Because of the disjointed reassertion of time, catastrophe was also spreading.

Walker's world was being shocked to life as people were unfreezing in a chaotic and unorganized way, often with only one leg being released at once, while the rest of their body was still held in stasis. They could feel as time slowly lost its vise grip on them, and it caused a series of cascading problems planet-wide.

Cars were driving off of bridges, surgeons were making mistakes in critical moments at operating tables, and the more nefarious of the population were taking advantage of this boon suddenly given to them.

Chaos reigned, and it all centered around one man.

Mr. Harrison, as Walker called him, drew in another deep breath and pounded his staff into the ground, his robe reapplying to his body and his formerly filthy body now the pristine image his Creator had seen on his small grassy planet.

"Finally," he said with a pearlescent smile. As he knew it would, his overlay lit up.

[. . . Scanning . . .]
Omega Protocol initialized.
Welcome, Candidate.

CHAPTER SIXTEEN

Who We Are

I still do not understand. Why call it mana?" Virgil asked.

"It's fantasy fulfillment, man," Walker said with exasperation, not understanding why the large squirrel didn't get it. He'd already explained this once, but Virgil was adamant that it should either be called a Magic Tree or a Spirit Tree, like the original. As if being a Creator, a builder of worlds, didn't allow Walker to mess around with the names of other people's stuff.

"Look, we did something terrible, we released a monster. A Kraken, if you will. But now, we've built something new and fresh! Spirit is just . . . boring. But *mana!* That's got some kick."

"I still disagree," Virgil said, stomping one foot. "The basis for your world will be these trees now. Do you realize that?"

"Yep!" Walker said with a grin. "And I couldn't be happier."

"Be that as it may, I must fix the atmosphere since Symphony is now . . . mostly . . . put back together. Please relax for a few moments while I work on this."

Stepping away a small distance, Walker grabbed a seat in the grass and, after several minutes of staring at a sky that never changed, grew bored.

Terminally bored.

Since arriving here, aside from one real break, he'd been moving from one idea, one crisis, to the next. Just sitting down again felt strange. Not sleeping, eating, or going to the bathroom felt strange as well. He figured that the more he dwelled on it, the more weirded out he was going to be, so he might as well do something while he waited. Virgil didn't want him playing with anything without talking to him first, but Walker, as he had shown throughout his time in the protocol, had always been a learn-by-doing kind of person.

He pulled up his overlay and looked through his abilities and systems for a quick refresher. The Subsystem Assistant button was pulsing, and he quickly looked at Virgil, who was fervently viewing his own screens. Walker looked at the Subsystem Assistant button, then back to Virgil again, before his eyes magnetically moved back to the button. A moment later, the large squirrel finished what he was working on and started to walk over.

The giant squirrel gave him an odd look as if he knew what he was thinking. Walker, ever so slowly, started to reach out on his overlay. The squirrel's dark, bead-like eyes grew wide.

"Wai—" Virgil tried to say, but of course, Walker had already clicked it.

[. . . Loading . . .]
Expelling new subsystem assistant.

That's funny, Walker thought. *What does it mean by expelling?*

In front of him, Virgil fell to his knees in the grass, grabbing his throat with his paws while making choking sounds. Walker yelled out his name as he ran up and dropped to the grass next to him. He got behind him and tried slapping his back a few times, but the choking persisted. The Heimlich didn't work either, and he didn't know enough about squirrel anatomy to truly help.

He started telling Virgil how much he appreciated him and about how great he was. He illuminated all of the things he had done to help him since he'd arrived, from the first landmass to the Mana Tree, while tears formed at the corners of his eyes. He expounded on his intelligence and emotional understanding, expressing their friendship as a lifeline that had kept him going all this time. He continued speaking while his own throat felt like it was closing. "I . . . I . . ."

Virgil reached a paw into his mouth, pushing his arm as far back into his throat as he could before seeming to grab something. He threw it toward the grass with a disgusted wheeze. A blue-and-brown fur ball landed no more than five feet away.

Walker paused as his mind went blank, while Virgil continued to gasp beside him.

. . .

. . .

"Did you just cough out a hairball while I tearfully told you how much you mean to me?" he asked in a deadly serious voice.

Virgil's only response was to collapse onto his back, still trying to catch his breath while sharp sounds squeaked out of the sides of his mouth.

The hairball covered the short distance between, and before Walker could think about what was happening, it stood up and looked at him. There was no doubt about it—it was another squirrel.

It was larger than the standard variety Walker was used to back on Earth. Not Virgil's size, certainly, but still much larger than those from his home planet.

Standing over two feet tall with blue fur and dark blue eyes, it seemed to have the same prodigious thumbs that Virgil did, looking nothing less than a smaller clone of his advanced assistant. As he looked closer, he realized it wasn't actually blue fur, but brown fur tipped in blue. Like the blonde highlights Walker had put into his hair during his NSYNC phase. The smaller squirrel had a curious look on its face as it tilted its head before speaking its first words. "Are you my Creator?"

Walker said the only appropriate response he knew from years of study and experience.

"I'm not the father."

He grimaced as he belatedly realized that was only the second sentence the newborn had ever heard.

"Ha-ha," Virgil's weak voice said from the ground. He sat up and looked at his blue mini-me. "I tried to ask you to wait so I could be ready. Each appearance model produces secondary assistants differently. If I were a cloud, this would have been so much easier. Thankfully, you did not choose the stork appearance," he said with a shudder.

"Strange thing for a mother to say after giving birth," Walker said with a slanted smile. "Who knew all of our interactions, all of our time together, could lead to this? Maybe we should think about getting married. We could ask Blitzburg7 to officiate it. *Ohhh*, a marriage system. I like it. I wonder if I could get bonus marks for hiding a mistress for a lengthy period of time without detection."

"You should stop; you know I do not find this form of humor to be funny."

But Walker couldn't stop when he was on a roll. "Then we could have a parent system, a grandparent system, a lineage and bloodline system. Systems for days! All inter—" Walker stopped speaking as an idea came to him. *Interlinked systems.* His mind screamed at him as clarity arrived, but his idea was just in the beginning stages. He would have to really plan it out for things to work, like, lots and lots of planning. But he knew his new little blue addition to their family was integral to his success.

"Walker," Virgil said. "As much as I would love to speak with our new assistant here, they can sit tight for a moment. We need to look at the Mana Tree and see if it will suffice or if we need to try again."

Walker stared into space for another few moments, different ideas for systems still coming to his mind, before he blinked, his eyes moving back into focus. "You're right. Let's see what we've got." He clicked on the Monitor button and zoomed in on the tree.

It was only about two feet tall and had a similar coloration to the original Spirit Tree, with a thin, dark blue trunk and light blue buds that tapered into cyan. After clicking Identify through the monitor, the screen showed more than he'd expected.

Name: Mana Tree
Genus: Mana Tree
Organism Type: Plant
Modifications:
Sterility, Oblivious, Mana-Impaired, Gigantism, Grafted,
Reaching Roots, Overwhelming Magical Discharge
Evolutionary Traits: (Unavailable)

Something was bothering Walker about these identities and he had forgotten to ask about it before. "Hey Virgil, why does the name always match the genus?"

"*That* is what you want to ask about? Out of everything you see there?" Virgil smacked his head. He looked over at the oddly quiet blue squirrel before looking back at Walker again. "Okay, that is simple, Walker. You are the one naming them, and with the name of a unique entity, the genus follows suit. Once you start creating entities with logical reasoning who have children of their own, that will change. These parents, who can rationally think, will name their children, but the original name you gave them upon creation will become their genus."

"Cool cool cool. What about monsters?"

"Entities," he said with special emphasis, "with limited intelligence will have a similar genus type as well."

"Monsters."

"Whatever. But what I am really worried about here is the word *overwhelming*. Can you click on that, please?"

"Sure."

He quickly found the little box within the identity shown.

Overwhelming Magical Discharge:
The Mana Tree will continuously discharge magic in a mist-like
form. This discharge will increase and accelerate over time,
gaining strength as it matures to adulthood.

"That's what we were looking for," Walker said, pointing at the screen. "Plant some of these babies all over Symphony and literally watch the magic happen."

"No, Walker, that is not a good thing. This is not a perfect entity for your plan. It needs to produce magic—"

"Mana."

"Please stop doing that. It needs to produce *mana* at a steady rate. In this amount, my estimate says one fully grown tree will fill the entire atmosphere."

"Mmmm, to be honest, that seems like the opposite of a problem," Walker said with an open smile.

"And what happens if the tree were to die? Or be destroyed accidentally? How would your plan work then? If you plant multiple Mana Trees across the planet, instead of a world full of magic, you may have a world full of accidental magical evolutions as your entities become oversaturated. It is a necessarily balanced ecosystem you are looking for, not one of magically explosive growth. Not to mention, *when* it is destroyed, the explosion would be catastrophic, magically speaking."

Walker's smile slid away from his face. "Oh."

Several minutes later, a small tree floated out to space and imploded while a man, a large squirrel, and a slightly less large squirrel watched soberly from a safe distance. "He was so young," Walker said, pantomiming a false tear falling down his face.

"It is nice to see you back to normal, Walker."

"Yeah, I feel better. Time is always great for things like that. When my grandfather died a decade ago, I buried it deep. It's a trick I learned in the military, to put my grief in a chokehold until I'm ready emotionally to deal with it."

"I do not think that is much better, Walker," Virgil said with disapproval in his eyes. "You are just pushing problems back, then allowing them to build up and stack upon each other until it becomes too much, and you collapse, emotionally and mentally. That is not healthy."

Walker shrugged his shoulders. "Maybe, but it's what I know for now, and you're not my therapist, Cheryl. And you certainly don't have her legs . . ." He looked Virgil up and down. "Although . . ."

Virgil held up a hand. "No. You have a subsystem assistant now, so changing models would not be advisable."

Walker waved a hand. "Fine. Besides, I'm sure I'll have plenty of time to figure it out."

"As long as you choose to ignore your issues, you will never find balance as a person, but that is all I will say for now." Virgil walked over to the Evolution Chamber and placed a new Mana Tree inside. Like the one before, it was already two years old, proving Virgil right again. "I believe I know what the problem is."

"Okay, shoot."

"I believe the funnels were too large. If we squeeze them down in size, it should reduce the amount of magical discharge and allow us to further bring balance to the magical state of the atmosphere."

Walker was about to say *mana* again, but Virgil just looked at him and said, "Do not."

He let it go.

Virgil continued. "I would do this myself, but I believe this is a learning experience for you. So please, if you will, fix this."

Walker agreed with a nod and began by removing all of the funnels. He couldn't just squeeze them down in an already modified entity, so he started from scratch and burned away two more years of their limited temporal resources. He knew how important this was.

It was the first step of a much larger plan to succeed in the Alpha Protocol. He started the same as before, moving from the roots to the center and lastly back out to the branches and leaves. When he finished, he fixed the landmass again, which was still broken from shooting the original Mana Tree into space, then planted the new model in the same spot.

After pulling up the monitor and identifying the tree, the word *overwhelming* was gone from its modifications, and Virgil said that was what they needed for the ley line to work. Walker then placed another Mana Tree on the eastern side of the center, directly opposite the other new sapling, and they moved on to modifying the rest.

To create a Mana Tree for the desert, they had to ensure its exterior was not only resilient but also insulated. They spent some time arguing back and forth over the value of a Mana Tree that produced magic water before Walker relented and said he would find another way to give the desert an oasis. They finished their modifications and placed one slightly different tree at the beginning of the connection between the desert and the center of Symphony. His overlay lit up.

[. . . Scanning . . .]
As your entity has been modified from its original form, please name it.

"Stupid names."

Entity: Insulated Mana Tree is named.
[. . . Analyzing . . .]
Entity named Insulated Mana Tree analyzed.
Size: Medium (High growth potential)
Entity category: Magical Producer
Organism type: Plant
Modification: Extreme
Ability to evolve: No (Restricted)
Age: 2 years
Grade: C
Rewards calculated.

Walker pulled up the Identify window to make sure there were no issues.

Name: Insulated Mana Tree
Genus: Mana Tree
Organism Type: Plant
Modifications:
Sterility, Oblivious, Mana-Impaired, Gigantism, Grafted,
Reaching Roots, Magical Discharge, Resilient, Insulated
Evolutionary Traits: Unavailable

Walker noticed that he only got a C, returning just a bit more than his spent materials, so he asked Virgil about it.

"It is not truly a unique entity, so you also did not get an update to your unique entity task. It may have a different name, but you are only *slightly* modifying the original genus of the Mana Tree. The Alpha Protocol knows when you try to play with the system rewards."

"That's bullshit," Walker said. They'd worked for an hour to modify the tree and received no recognition whatsoever for their labor. He looked at the timer, a constant reminder in his skull of an approaching struggle.

Time remaining until next battle: 88+ hours

Walker sighed and rubbed the back of his head, mussing his hair. They needed to move faster, or he would have to spend a large amount of his temporal resources to get the next step completed. He looked over at the whiteboard only to realize it was missing, and in its place was a computer that looked like an old Macintosh.

"What the fuck?" he said as he walked over to take a closer look. It had all of the peripherals one would expect of an early '90s Macintosh: a monitor/desktop combination, a large mouse, a small desk, and a chair. There was no mousepad for some reason, but that was okay; those were for fancy people.

The computer caused Walker to feel nostalgic about his youth. He remembered playing *Number Munchers* in Mrs. Johnson's computer class—good times for him. He loved how fast the game let him move and affectionately remembered the caped muncher. Looking back at the computer, he asked Virgil what was going on.

"Well, Walker, one of your rewards upgraded your Creation Instrument twice. The next upgrade after the whiteboard would have been a writing projector and screen. This is the upgrade that came after that."

"Ok, quick question. Do all of the Creators get blackboards or whiteboards? How is it decided?"

"No, no. Your guide chooses the first Creation Instrument, within limits, then the upgrades naturally take place based on the Creator's memories of what comes after. There is a requirement for the first instruments to be quite primitive, thus requiring resourcefulness or what you would call out-of-the-box thinking."

"This is relatively primitive where I'm from," Walker said, thinking. "Couldn't I have started with this?"

"Well," Virgil said with a shrug. "It is all based on what your guide chooses to best suit the Creator."

Then, it dawned on Walker. "Motherfucker. I bet he didn't even want me to complete this. He somehow knew I had dysgraphia and was fucking with me. That son of a bitch."

"That seems the most likely reason, yes." Virgil nodded calmly. "Also, he shortened your time with him by knowingly and intentionally bringing along a magical artifact."

"So he was always against me?"

"I believe so, yes. I do not know or understand what he is attempting to do, but that is beyond us here. We need to move forward, so let us take a look at your new instrument. It is already turned on."

Walker sat in the chair and clicked the mouse with excessive force. The screen lit up and showed a plain white window, with the top bar holding a series of drawing icons like pencils and erasers. There were two tabs he could click on; one read "Landmass" and the other read "Entity." This meant that the fears he'd held from the previous Creation Instrument, in particular his dysgraphic issues, didn't apply anymore.

Unknowingly, he grew more angry at the idea of what he could have started with, slamming his finger onto the unoffending and completely innocent mouse in his hand. With this, he could fix his mistakes, and wouldn't have had to spend all that time drawing. When he realized how he was acting, he did his breathing exercises to calm himself down, although the effort took longer than he thought it would.

Finally, he asked, "What kind of restrictions can I expect? The markers are what held us back before."

Virgil replied, "Look behind the computer."

Walker did so and found an old printer. He opened the paper tray and found two slots, one with the word "Entity" stamped on the front, which held six pieces of paper, while the other said "Landmass" and held four.

"So now I'm limited by how much I can fit on the paper?"

"And the detail that the printer can manage, which I have to say, in the nicest way possible, is still more than what you could do before."

"Okay, okay. What is the next upgrade going to be?" Walker asked, pushing away the last remnants of his anger and feeling a bit of energy enter his chest. They could use the Evolution Chamber for all of their future entity modifications, no sweat there, but drawing the landmass had still been painful. With the new Creation Instrument, he could get his work done much faster and with better accuracy.

"The next upgrade should be a higher-end or newer computer," Virgil responded.

"And after that?" Walker couldn't help but ask.

"How about you just wait and see, Walker? There is no fun in knowing the end of the story before you get to experience the thrills of how you got there."

"Fair," he said lamely. Virgil suggested they return to the instrument when it was time to work on the next series of landmasses, so they walked over to the Evolution Chamber to finish their work on the ley line.

Virgil placed an original Mana Tree into the chamber, and they heavily modified it for the cold before placing it down in the snowy region accordingly. After receiving only another C grade, Walker resigned himself to the idea that they were stuck with what they got and added its brother on the opposite side.

They ran into trouble modifying the root system to create trees that could survive in the water. Rather than scrapping the idea, Walker solved it by stepping into the World Editor. Two large peninsulas came to life on Symphony, with two beautiful trees sitting on their tips. The swamp trees only required a slight modification from their water cousins, making it easy to place them correctly.

Deciding to take a short break, Walker stood up and looked around. They'd been working for several hours straight, and he was just now noticing that the blue squirrel was still standing in the same spot he'd last seen him.

"Man, he doesn't do much."

"You have not given him any instructions, and he does not need breaks as he is a part of the Alpha Protocol directly, just as I am."

"Yeah, but still. It's creepy. He just stands there, staring at us," Walker said, watching the squirrel stare at him with its dark blue eyes. He looked deep into the squirrel's eyes and found . . . nothing.

"We will get to him soon enough, Walker, do not worry. We only have one more modified Mana Tree to place, so let us get to it."

Walker agreed and spent a few more minutes thinking over his plans and how they would align with his future goals. His most obvious goal was to complete the Alpha Protocol itself. If he failed, he would be sent back to Earth, not to mention that it would kill Virgil and doom Symphony.

His secondary goal was to make sure that Symphony was balanced and allowed its denizens the ability to grow. He knew he should probably think the opposite here, that Symphony came first and the Alpha Protocol second, but without getting through the finals, there would be no Symphony and no Walker to maintain it. So he was stuck. He got up and headed over to Virgil as it weighed on his mind. They placed down the last tree and looked ever everything. It was just like he'd imagined it.

"Are you ready?" Virgil asked with excitement in his eyes while hopping up and down.

He really loves his magic. Mana. Damn, now I'm doing it to myself.

Walker's expression became somber. He knew this was a big moment, and that something with poignancy or some gravitas should be said. He had been really trying to get his mind around what he should be concerning Symphony. Not just its Creator, but something more. He felt a need to express it out loud, to cement within himself who he was going to be here and what they were going to do. He looked at Virgil and, with a nod of his head, knew what needed to be said.

Walker stood tall.

"It's all about moving forward, right Virgil? We've pushed past the first step for Symphony, but really, that first step was just an illusion. A foundation of faulty bricks that got us here. To this moment. The first true step toward Symphony being a great place to live is what we are doing right now."

He gestured at the sky. "I've been doing a lot of thinking, and it isn't enough to just survive the Alpha Protocol. We need to be better than those who came before us. Maybe not smarter, but kinder. More importantly, we need to build something that can last and adapt to the needs of its people. Everything we do will be weighed in the future, not by us or the Alpha Protocol, but by the citizens of Symphony. We cannot allow ourselves to become apathetic killers, nor can we allow ourselves to forget where we started. We must hold ourselves to a higher ideal, to aim to be a better version of what we are now. I choose now to become a Creator who feels for his people. I choose to be not all-powerful, or all-knowing, but to learn from the experiences that are forthcoming, and to grant mercy to those who have erred and need another chance to find themselves."

Walker glared at Virgil for a moment before his eyes softened. "The Slicer destroyed our world, but I choose forgiveness. Mr. Harrison threw me here with no information and at a severe disadvantage, strictly out of selfishness, but I choose forgiveness again. Nothing and no one should be judged by a singular moment, but by the moments that come together to form a picture of who you are. A thread in the fabric of a journey. The Alpha Protocol, life itself, will throw more shit our way. I choose to meet it and find a better path. One that leads to a stronger Symphony, and a day where joy is found throughout, and the people and creatures who walk the paths we lay down can find true miracles on a daily basis."

Now he was gaining steam. His gestures grew more emphatic, making even Virgil feel something deep within. "Where challenges are met by the worthy and the righteous. Where a simple crafter basks in the glow of their creations, just for the joy of the process. We, Virgil, you and I, must make this moment our declaration of purpose."

Walker looked down at his landmass, which held all of his dreams for the future. "We are the Creators of Symphony, and we will not allow ourselves to be disillusioned by time or changed by hatred. We will grow. We will become better. We will care about this world and all of its future people, together. *This* is *who* we *are*, and I pledge that this is all I will ever be."

Walker was good at speeches when he put in the effort, although it always took a little something out of him.

"Well said," was the giant squirrel's only reply.

"Really? I was expecting more from you . . ."

Virgil gave him a golf clap in response.

With a snort, Walker clicked on Time and advanced Symphony by fifty years.

CHAPTER SEVENTEEN

Rimi

Walker and Virgil watched through the monitor, shifting the view to watch below the soil and stone as the roots grew across the fifty years Walker had allocated to the Temporal Subsystem.

It was extremely difficult to track everything as the years on Symphony flew by at an unbelievable rate. After several failed attempts at watching the roots find each other, Walker finally stumbled upon a singular occurrence between the swamp and snow Mana Trees.

When each set of roots connected, driven by the modification they'd created, there was a flash of aqua before they instantly melded together. He would have never seen this happen the old-fashioned way, as his time would have run out in the protocol. But with the magic of controlling temporal energy, Walker's world was quickly coming together. As the trees grew, the empty atmosphere above Symphony began to change, taking on a light blue-green hue. The color of magic.

When time finally stopped spinning forward, each tree stood over five stories tall, which was near what Virgil had told him to expect. Walker moved the monitor over to The Crater and found an extreme amount of MUYs and moss growing across the area. The water was practically full of entities. They had spread so much that all of Walker's interconnected rivers across Symphony now held his original creations. His overlay lit up.

[. . . Scanning . . .]
Task updated!
**Ecology task complete: Build a medium functioning
ecosystem (Part 2)**
Medium functioning ecosystem built: 1/1
Reward given: Ecology Subsystem upgrade

**New ecology task: Build a planetary functioning
ecosystem (Part 3)**
*The Creator's world is a spark, catching the flame of life and
spreading it across the universe. Build a functioning planetary
ecosystem that will maintain the balance of your entire world.*
Planetary functioning ecosystem built: 0/1
Reward for completion: Landmass System upgrade
Reward for completing the second ecology task:
**Congratulations, Dante! Your Ecology Subsystem
has been upgraded!**
***It is difficult, even for Creators in the Alpha Protocol, to notice
problems of a planetary scale. This upgrade includes a series
of new ecological abilities, including a warning system.***

"Huh?" Walker said after reading everything. "How did we complete the second ecology task?"

Virgil moved his eyes across his overlay before looking at Walker and saying, "It recognizes the Mana Trees and their root system as a functioning ecosystem. In fact, if we place more land and plant them there as well, we should be able to satisfy the third task. You can, as they say, game the system."

As Virgil stopped speaking, a consistent and moderately loud beep started to go off. Walker looked around the tiny planet momentarily before noticing the Ecology tab blinking. He clicked it and saw just how out of control the MUYs were. The subsystem showed they were overpopulated by four hundred percent, and they needed to be reduced to restore Symphony's ecological function.

"Overpopulated," Virgil said with a squirrel frown. "It seems I either modified them too much, or we just let too much time go by. I was afraid of this. There are far too many of them and there is no Slicer to balance out their procreative tendencies."

"I'm guessing the fix is to introduce a balancing organism."

"Indeed," Virgil responded with a nod. "Introducing a predator, A STANDARD PREDATOR," he said loudly, "would solve the problem."

"That's fine, but first we need to use the System Designer."

"Why?"

"Because I'm going to make a Monster System, of course!" Walker said, throwing his hands in the air like a child seeing presents under the Christmas tree for the first time. "It's Monster System time! Plus, we're lucky enough that I now have an assistant to help me with just that."

"I do not know if we should start that just yet, Walker."

"Why?! It's the perfect time. We have food for them, we have a magic generation system, and we can do this! Isn't that right, little man?" Walker finished, pointing a finger at his newest assistant.

The blue squirrel tilted its head at him and spoke in a light, monotone voice. "Whatever you wish, Creator."

"Now that's not going to work," Walker said, uncomfortable with the title being used instead of his name. Maybe his citizens could call him that, and it would be fine, but he'd be working with his assistants for who knew how long. He didn't want to be called Creator over and over again. He looked over at the large squirrel for some help. "First, you hit me with the sirs, Virgil, now I got this guy calling me Creator. Can't I just—"

Virgil interrupted him. "You cannot edit his personality, Walker, as he is a subsystem assistant and not an advanced model like myself. Instead, I suggest you just try having a conversation with him and give some idea of what has happened and who you are."

The tiny squirrel just continued to stare at them without speaking. Walker knew that he understood what they were saying, but it seemed he would only speak again if spoken to. Walker moved over in front of him and sat down cross-legged in the grass before saying, "How are you, little man?"

"I am adequate."

"Jeesh, that is the worst response to a question I've ever heard. What does adequate even mean, contextually?"

"I apologize. I do not understand," the squirrel replied.

"No, it's fine. Well, I don't want to keep calling you *squirrel*, so I think our first step is to give you a name. Do you have an idea of what you would like to be called?"

Its blue eyes locked onto Virgil, who had begun to stare at his screens, before looking back at Walker again. "No, I do not."

"Virgil. Hey Virgil! Do you have any hints for this?"

"Huh—wha? Oh. A name? No, just give it something, it doesn't matter." His eyes had already blanked out again as he stared at something on his overlay.

Virgil's response seemed outside of his norm. Either he was very busy, or he didn't really like the subsystem assistant. Personally, Walker felt it was jealousy that another assistant was getting his Creator's attention. Either way, he knew just what to say.

"Fuckin' rude, man. Alright, well, my identity in the protocol is Dante, and he's Virgil, so why don't we follow along with the story? Let's see, Lucifer feels somewhat blasphemous, even for my lapsed-Catholic ass. Beatrice would be weird, as that was Dante's love. But Francesca da Rimini was from the second circle of hell, and you're my second assistant. Yes, haha!" Walker said with exuberance. He wasn't celebrating that their names all fit a certain theme, but just that he didn't have to name something from scratch.

"I like that. Rimini," the squirrel said, showing its first sign of independent thought.

"Well, actually, Francesca is the first or given name, whereas Rimini is the surname or family name."

"No, I like Rimini. Rimi," the squirrel said. It nodded to itself, having decided on a big moment it couldn't quite grasp the significance of.

"That's cute. Rimi, then. Okay, Rimi, let me tell you a bit about what we're doing here." After saying that, Walker talked about his homeworld and the lack of anything magical. He described his first moments on the tiny planet, the guide being a dick—not literally, which he'd had to clarify in a somewhat awkward conversation—and his staff.

He explained how it felt to land there, what he was told he would be doing, meeting Virgil, the first landmass and the first entity. He skipped over the Slicer's story, except to explain the dangers of high evolutionary potential in alpha predators. Then he told the blue squirrel about the battle, how Symphony exploded, what they had to do to fix it, and why they made the ley lines the way they did.

The smaller squirrel listened to it all with large eyes, never interrupting. When Walker finished, he told him about the pledge he'd made. That they were going to constantly aim to make themselves better than they currently were, and how their job after getting through the protocol was to caretake the world and its people. Then Rimi asked a question that seemed simple but felt profound.

"What is my purpose?" it asked in a higher-pitched tone, which, if he wasn't mistaken, sounded like frayed nerves.

Virgil stopped what he was doing to listen in on Walker's plan.

"You're going to help me make, and manage, a Monster System through the System Designer. We have to build it from nothing, establish rules, and keep an eye on it. Your job, if that is how you want to think about it, is to focus entirely on the Monster System, and find a way to keep it in balance with the world of Symphony."

In the hope that it would help the squirrel feel better about what he was proposing, Walker tried to smile. "When you find problems, any at all, I want you to bring them up with me. As we refine it further and make it better, you will gain more and more control until you only have to bring up major problems with me in the future. Is that confusing to you?"

He hoped he wasn't overwhelming the pseudo-newborn. New-made? Wait, was Virgil its mother?

Rimi affected a serious countenance as he said, "To clarify, I am to help my Creator make and manage the Monster System through the System Designer."

"Yes, and did you understand the rest of it? Oh, hold on one second," he said as he turned to Virgil, hearing a small voice say "Holding" behind him. "Virgil, while we're working on this, can you focus on the Weather System?"

Walker didn't know it, but this was the first time he had really started to take over their project with Symphony. In the past, Virgil had always directed Walker onto the right path, helping where he could so the regular-seeming man wouldn't feel too much stress. But it seemed that the Creator was ready to lead. Virgil thought about it, considered the change to be a positive one, and nodded.

"Absolutely, but it will be difficult to simulate what I believe you want. Symphony is not Earth. We do not have a sun, and this planet we currently stand on is not large enough to be called a moon. Currently, the shield only provides a minor amount of light down there."

Walker grimaced. "Can't you tie in the magic being produced by the Mana Tree network to fake the weather?"

"Fake the weather, Walker? *Fake the weather?*" Virgil looked disgusted with his Creator's phraseology. "That is a terrible way to say that."

"You know what I mean!"

Virgil hummed for a moment. "Perhaps. I will have to look and see." He then started working with his screen, already ignoring them again.

That should keep him busy for a while. Virgil loves magic.

Walker looked back at Rimi, and before he could say anything, the squirrel said, "Yes, but what does *balance* mean?"

Walker was thrown off a little bit, but then he remembered the tiny voice saying holding. He remembered that he'd asked Rimi if he'd had any questions and smiled.

"That's a good one to ask, great job," Walker said, slipping into teacher mode. "What do you think the purpose of creating monsters is?"

"To win the next battle!"

"Yes, that is certainly true. We do need to win the next battle to continue. But what about Symphony as a whole? How do you think monsters will fit in there?"

"I do not know, Creator."

"Please call me Walker."

"Okay."

"There will come a time in the near future when we will have logically thinking beings on Symphony, who are as smart or smarter than you and I. Maybe not Virgil, but certainly us." He heard a "hmmph" coming from Virgil in the background. "Some of them might even be human, and I am a firm believer that conflict and turmoil inspire the growth of character. It worked for me, my father, and my father's father. Whether that character is good or bad for Symphony, growth is still growth. To have conflict, we need something that will inspire them to act. Merchants and businesspeople want to see how much money they can make or what markets they move into; thus, we will create an item system." Walker held up a single finger.

"For those who want to travel the world, they can turn to the forthcoming quest system." Walker held up a second finger. "For all cognitive, free-thinking beings, we will make the Class System, though I don't much like the name." Walker held up a third finger. "But the monsters need their own system." A fourth finger appeared. "We have to build it in such a way that they cannot take over the world. Just like we need to build a system of classes, or powers, for those sapients within Symphony, so that both monsters and sapients have a chance against each other."

Walker looked up at the sky. "Some of my plans may not work. Others will likely be changed as I better learn how to manage everything. But it comes down to one idea. Essentially, we are building a perpetual war." He let that comment sit for a moment as he closed his fingers together, allowing Rimi to process its enormity, then continued.

"One balances out the other, sapients and monsters together. What we're trying to create is a world full of wonder and conflict. Initially, I thought that harmony, the wonder portion, was enough to get us by. That a peaceful world would work best for all of its citizens, and that they could live fruitful lives this way. But"—he shook his head with finality, closing off the idea—"there will always be frightening creatures, whether they are human- or monster-shaped. So we need to prepare people and give them the tools to protect themselves. To establish those tools, they'll need to train. I hope that we can create a scale of value wherein those who truly push themselves and show their worth can succeed." He finished and placed his arms behind his back.

Walker hoped it all made sense to the little guy, as he was still figuring it out himself. Small bits and pieces had run through his mind since first learning he would have to make his own world. Like he'd said, some things would work, others wouldn't. Only through trial and error would his plans become realized.

"But why don't the monsters get classes?" Rimi asked with the innocence only the truly young and uninformed could have.

"Because I'm afraid if we gave them classes on top of the Monster System they will already have, they would then grow too powerful and destroy everything we've built."

"Then, why don't we make it so that only the good monsters can get powers? The ones who don't want to destroy everything."

What? Walker thought as he paused, unintentionally mirroring the Slicer's first thought. There was value in what Rimi was saying, but he wasn't sure how to do it. "How would that work?"

"Well, you said you were looking to create a scale. So, why not have a counter that picks up what they are doing and tells the system whether they deserve to have a class or not?"

"Okay, I see where you are going. Like, it'd be based on reaching certain milestones. Save a village and gain ten points. Like that?"

"Yes!" Rimi said enthusiastically, already beginning to sound a little like his Creator. "Or only kill some humans, but not other humans, because they can be bad too."

"So, a bounty system?"

"Yes again!" Rimi hopped up and down, looking like the older assistant for a moment.

Walker wanted to encourage him to continue having ideas. Plus, he liked the idea of milestones more than he was letting on. "So let's break this down. For this to work, we would need an item system, a quest system, a class system, a monster system, a milestone system, and a bounty system."

"That sounds like a lot," Rimi said, deflating while pointing his ears outwards. "I don't know if I can manage all of those at once."

Walker's plans shifted in his mind, connecting to each other and filling in gaps he didn't know he had. He thought on it while Rimi continued to look distraught, then looked over at him when the last puzzle piece fit. "Well, don't worry!" Walker said, gaining steam. "Once we get the Monster System up, we can get you all kinds of siblings!" Walker heard Virgil shout "What was that?" in the background, but he ignored him.

He pulled up his tasks and confirmed what it had said earlier. With each new system balanced out, he would gain a new subsystem assistant. They were designed to work hand in hand. It made him wonder how many other tasks were interrelated like that.

"Okay, the first step is to assign the system. So, are you ready?" the Creator asked his newest assistant.

"Yes, Daddy Walker."

"Just Walker is fine, buddy."

He clicked on the System Designer and received a message.

Welcome to the System Designer!
As this is your first system, please name it before selecting from
the menu.

The Monster System is named!
Good luck, Creator!

The System Designer showed him a large collection of systems. One said he could create a system that focused only on fire, wherein he could actively make his world attuned to it. One giant fire world.

How would that even work? He mentally dashed the idea before he became distracted.

Another said he could make a system that only focused on his tiny planet, allowing him to control it with the World Editor in full. And another showed that he could create a mini-Alpha Protocol that would let him have his entities build cities all over Symphony. Walker was particularly interested in that one, but he knew he needed to start with the Monster System first.

He scrolled through until he found one directly connected to the Alpha Protocol's evolution system. It described evolution as *targeted*, and it allowed him to pick and choose different paths, disallowing random evolution to occur further on his world.

Walker stopped for a long moment and stared at the description. If he'd had this, he wouldn't have had to mess around with the Mana Trees. Hell, he wouldn't have had to deal with the Slicer, either. This . . . this was a big deal. A huge deal. With grand mental formality, Walker selected it for his first system, then found the area where he could assign an assistant.

Looking at the top of his overlay, Walker found Rimi's blue portrait next to Virgil's brown one. The protocol had changed his description the moment he'd named himself. Smiling, Walker dragged him into the slot on the designer, and his picture appeared over it with a gold highlight.

**Assigning the Monster System to Subsystem Assistant Rimi.
Connecting Alpha Protocol evolutionary systems to the newly
designated Monster System.
The Monster System is now active.**

After a minute, Rimi said "Yayyyyy" with some hops once his overlay updated. "Okay, the first step is we need to connect all evolutions directly to magic."

Rimi's tail swished back and forth as he nodded excitedly. Walker asked Virgil to pause his work and come over. He wanted all hands on deck for this. It was finally time to talk Monsters.

The Slicer that Walker knew was not a kind creature. That hadn't changed, not even with logical reasoning. Creator Jolive was in a dire situation as she stared at the trapped destroyer.

Here she was, stuck with a massive cage made of multilayered folded metal right in the middle of her world. It was bullshit, and she let the protocol know in loud and temperamental explosions every so often just how she felt about it.

A few hours ago, unknown to Jolive, the Slicer had evolved yet again, gaining the ability to hear across great distances. He didn't know what she was saying, but she didn't sound happy, and that was fine with him. The bitch shouldn't have been able to trap him, but at least she was suffering from this terrible transgression. He was happy to feel her pain.

Happiness was a new idea to the Slicer. He didn't like it.

He did, however, snicker internally as he heard Jolive blow up on her assistant once more. The Slicer was surprised others around this detestable planet couldn't hear her and were just going about their business, eating insects and hissing at each other.

The former Bobbit worm hoped he wouldn't be stuck here for too long. It was too bright. There were lights everywhere, and the Slicer was a creature accustomed to the darkness and water. It was also very dry, which didn't bother him nearly as much as it used to but still made him uncomfortable. The feeling wasn't terribly unlike being in space, with the constant pressure that came from existing within a vacuum.

No, he didn't like it here one bit. He tried to think over how he had evolved before. He hadn't been able to truly see his overlay until his thoughts had changed and his mind grew sharper. It was as though a world of information came streaming into him at once, and he was still, to this moment, having trouble processing everything. Before that, it was mostly images and . . . hunger. Instinct.

How had he done it? He needed to remember . . .

In his loose memory from before his evolution, he remembered falling toward his original planet, the one that the purple buffoon was making, and thinking to himself that he needed more fire, more flame. He had then, somehow, pushed himself, and there it was, exploding out of him. Enough fire to destroy the world and finally release him from his prison of predesigned feedings.

A prison of prescribed life.

The Slicer was a predator; he wanted—no, *needed* to hunt. Now, in this damn box, his frustration was even greater than before. At least in the purple idiot's world, he'd had some freedom of movement. Watching those stupid fish explode had been quite entertaining.

But how could he get out of a powerful cage? The bars were impervious to his attacks, and no matter how much he bit into them, they didn't move or fall away as everything else had in the past. He had even injured himself and gained a new evolution, forced regeneration, but he didn't need that right now.

What he needed was power. Real power. But he needed the knowledge to obtain it.

The Slicer forced that thought into his mind, pressing with all of his newly discovered willpower. A will that he had discovered and increased ever since finding himself wrapped in metal. Knowledge . . . KnowledgE . . . KnOWLEDGE . . . KNOWLEDGE.

Evolution occurring.
The Slicer is evolving!
[. . . Scanning . . .]
The Slicer has gained the Identify ability.

The Slicer laughed to himself again as he identified the metal surrounding him. Soon enough, he would escape, and his hunt would continue.

CHAPTER EIGHTEEN

Monster Tiers and the Many Systems

Walker received a notification showing that he had completed the subsystem assistant series' first task by assigning Rimi to it.

"Okay, okay, OKAY!" Walker said, each word accompanied by the clapping of his hands. "Let's do this! Let's build up some monsters. First up, we have power and evolution. How are they going to gain these?"

Virgil answered immediately with his favorite subject. "That is simple, Walker. With the magic from the Mana Trees."

Walker snapped his fingers. "Yes! So, we already chose to modify the protocol's evolution system with our own, which means that all evolutions will have a direct connection to it. Rimi, pull up your screen and take a look."

"Looking," the small squirrel said as his eyes stared at his screen. "It says that it recognizes that Symphony has magic within its atmosphere."

"Yes! You were right, Virgil, it should work."

"Of course," Virgil replied with an eye roll and more than a hint of smugness.

"Nope, I'm not going there. Okay, need to focus," he said with another slap of his hands. He began to pace back and forth in front of the two squirrels. He had always found that movement helped to bring forth his thinking process best. "When we modify the monsters, we need to create a focal point, a locus, for their magic to gather. The first step to gaining power has to be passively absorbing the magic in the atmosphere. Like into a magical core or center or something. This way, it'll be slow and steady."

"Why do we not just have their skin absorb it?" Virgil asked.

"Because we want them to gain power in stages. If we allow monsters to absorb magic straight into their skin in an undirected manner, it could first affect their brains, or their lungs, or . . . anything really. We want something that can be controlled so that we can use it to directionally focus their improvements and evolutions."

"Understood; I am sorry that I interrupted."

"No, no. We're spitballing again here. We're coming up with a system that makes sense and has a ladder that allows the monsters to move upward gradually over time so that we don't make another Slicer. Something that earns their power, rather than explodes with it." He pointed at both of them. "Interruptions are good, that's a good thing, as it means you're trying to find the best way forward possible. Interrupt all you like."

"The Slicer," Virgil said.

Walker sighed. "Shut up, bad interruption. Okay, so they'll need something central to absorb magic, you got that, Rimi?"

"Yes," Rimi said as his eyes darted across the screen. "I have assigned The Monster System to focus on a kernel-nel," he stuttered, attempting his own form of input into the conversation. "It is a type of seed I, uh, think, since the monsters will grow. Did I . . . do good?" he asked, looking between the both of them.

"You did very good," Walker replied with a smile. Rimi had nailed it. The term *kernel* was what he had been looking for. *Core*, or even *center*, wouldn't make sense, as some monsters could be asymmetrical, and identifying where to place the locus would be different for each.

"Okay, so we have a kernel—great name, by the way. Now, we need to tell that kernel what to do. I'm thinking we call the unevolved monsters standard, as a tier name. What do you think?"

"I like it," Rimi immediately responded.

"I do not," Virgil said testily. "This is going to define an entire portion of your world. You already have . . . Mana Trees . . . but standard? No. How about baseline?"

"Ugh," Walker replied in disgust with a wide-open mouth, tongue hanging out of the side. "That's even worse."

"Unsouled?" Virgil tried.

"Boring, although now I admit standard is a bit boring as well. Blah, nope. What about *classic*? Since it's the first version of said monster."

Virgil shot it down immediately. Rimi sat there and let them talk it out, taking in their speech patterns as they bantered back and forth. His eyes tracked them and the manners in which they moved and gesticulated, gaining better ways to speak to the primary assistant and his Creator.

The debate, the argument, took almost an hour. Virgil would appeal with a logical name, and Walker would pull it apart as it was something they would have to deal with for perpetuity. There was no way he was calling them basic for thousands of potential years. Naturally, he'd then make his own suggestion, only for Virgil to disagree with the root description of the word, arguing that it didn't truly describe what tier one meant. They finally concluded on the one word that they both agreed with.

"Fine, fine!" Walker yelled out. "We'll call them common, like they do in video games. We may even pull more from my world's video game culture as we go, just to speed things up. But," he said with a snap of his fingers, "don't think we're going to use that word as the starting point for everything in all of the systems we're building. Common human? Gross."

"Agreed," Virgil replied in equanimity. "Rimi, question. I do not have access to The Monster System an—"

"You don't?" Walker asked, confused.

"I do not, as it was not and cannot be assigned to me. You have given it to another assistant."

"Oh. I didn't know that's what would happen. So, one assistant per subsystem?"

"Indeed, for now. As I was saying, Rimi, if the system is updated, will those updates affect its subjects immediately thereafter in a continuous fashion?"

Rimi dove into the system while Walker and Virgil both held their breath. This was a big part of Walker's plans for the Monster System. If they couldn't update the system after it already went live, their plan would be screwed, and the growth of the monsters would be limited to whatever they had chosen when they first designed the system.

Rimi looked like he was reading something for quite a while before saying, "Y-yes, as long as there is a physical connector for the system to find and update to."

Virgil took a deep breath in relief, while Walker unclenched his hands. "So this kernel will have to be something we create inside them physically, not a simple application of selecting them in the overlay. It has to be built as a storage device that not only contains magic but also maintains the rules explicitly given by the Monster System."

Walker waved a hand. "We have time to figure it out. Okay, Rimi. Here's what I want you to do. I want you to make . . . five tiers in the system for evolution. It's just a starting point for us. The idea here is for controlled growth. Once monsters are getting close to hitting tier five, you'll tell us, and together, we'll work on the next set."

"I understand," Rimi said, then started to add it in, creating a list within the system to identify the growth of monsters as tiers, with differing power levels and names. He told Walker when he finished and showed them the front page of the Monster System.

Monster System
Description: A modified evolution system for entities.

Tier 1:   Tier 2:
Tier 3:   Tier 4:
Tier 5:   Tier 6:
Tier 7:   Tier 8:

"Great job, buddy. I appreciate you thinking forward and adding a few extra tiers for when we need them." Rimi's ears flopped around upon hearing that. "Okay, tier one is the easy one, as really it's just identifying them as *common*, a monster at a basic level. We need to build four more before we can make any monsters and assign the system their kernels. The second tier should be a jump in power, but not overwhelmingly so. If the amount of magic leaps up in too much strength, our sapients are screwed." Virgil raised a finger, but Walker interrupted him. "Do not say uncommon."

"I withdraw my potential suggestion," Virgil acquiesced.

"I feel that each name after common should identify what it is gaining, so our sapients will understand what they might face. I don't want things to be so expected for them that it is always easy to defeat a series of monsters, but we can at least create a system with clear expectations for the first few tiers. That's what the naming is for and why they matter so much, at least for the beginning."

"Question before we move to name the second tier," Virgil said.

"Go ahead," Walker said, recognizing that Virgil normally had solid input for his thinking process.

"Do you want monsters to have an overlay system?"

"Uhhhhh. Why? Why would it matter?"

"It is about being as specific as possible with a system. Any outliers or openings have to be considered, and updates will need to be rolled out accordingly to fix any future problems. Access to the overlay system will, more than likely, confuse lower-intelligence monsters. Designating early on that they do not have access takes away a potential future issue."

"I see your point. No, they won't need overlays, at least not until they gain rational thought."

Virgil raised a bushy eyebrow. "Will they gain rational thought?"

"We'll get there, man," Walker said with a laugh, quickly followed by another as he watched Rimi eagerly twitching his ears.

"Okay, so, the second tier. I'm thinking that they will be absorbing the magic in the air, and we need the kernel to affect them directly. What is that affectation going to look like? Ideas, please."

"It is most likely," the resident magic expert said, "that magic will be directly affected by the environment it finds itself in. When it exits the Mana Tree and enters the air, it is still mostly pure, but once it settles or is directly controlled by something, it becomes attuned to it. Magic settling in the atmosphere becomes attuned to air. Magic settling in the ocean becomes attuned to water. So on and so on."

"What about the roots underneath?" Walker asked.

"That will maintain its purity as they are directly connected to the Mana Trees. Anything directly connected will receive a continuously pure magical supply," Virgil explained.

"And if I placed a large slab of metal directly underneath the roots?"

"Then it will gain in magical density, thereby strengthening the material over time. However, should it reach a certain threshold, unusual things may occur."

"Cool, cool, that's what I totally knew would happen," Walker lied. "Okay, so they're probably going to be elementally charged."

"Not necessarily." Virgil burst his bubble again, almost gleefully pointing out his ignorance. "I've seen your experiences from your homeworld. You still think of the elements as earth, fire, water, and air. But you are not considering light, sound, gravity, darkness, and a host of others I am unable to speak of."

"Okay, but either way, they're going to absorb mana attuned to these, right?"

"Well, yes."

"Great! So it's the elemental tier." Rimi nodded and put that into the system as a name while Walker continued rolling on. "We need to have the kernel absorb magic passively, to take it in and fill itself up, and then once it's full, to spill its collected magic directly into the monster based upon its attunement. For instance, if we created the MUYs right now, with this system in place, the process of their attunement would follow a logical line of progression. Let us say they absorbed magic from a heat source; then, they would gain access to fire magic or magic attuned to fire, that is."

"Okay," Rimi said, still working on his screens.

Walker continued speaking his mind, his confidence rising as his two assistants worked with his ideas. "We should make it visual, like the system with its golden pulses whenever I get a notification or it scans something, or even Mr. Harrison's staff pulsing red."

"Do you want its identity to update?" Virgil asked, trying to summarize the system's effects for Walker.

"Yeah, but make it simple. If one of the MUYs absorbs the fire magic, make it a fire MUY."

"You are forgetting the *s*. Multitudinous Yellowfin Snapper. MUYS for short."

"Man, I'm using the *s* as a plural; it's weird when words in the singular end on an *s*."

"Whatever," Virgil said, always a stickler for the rules.

"Damn right, whatever," Walker said back, although in a much quieter voice so Virgil couldn't quite hear him. Rimi told him he'd added everything into the system, including the name changes and pulses.

"Great! We need to do that for tiers three and four as well. Now, we have common and we have elementals, what is going to be number three?"

"Wait, wait." Virgil stopped that conversation before it could happen as Rimi worked in the background. "You are moving too fast with a system of this kind of importance. How is the monster going to use its magic? Are they a wizard? Mages? It requires sapience to control magic in a formative manner, or at least years of instinct built up over time and generations."

"Good catch," he told his assistant. "One . . . one second, let me think."

A little rattled by what he had almost pushed through, Walker walked away from them momentarily. Virgil looked at him, then began speaking with Rimi about something while he took a stroll.

He began speaking softly to himself. "Okay, slow things down, Walker, slow things down." He knew that he was like this sometimes. He would get excited, dive deep into ideas, and forget to take all of the steps a good plan needs, just like with the Slicer. Thankfully, he had Virgil, who was always looking out for him. You would think one Cosmic-Destroyer-level mistake would teach him that he needed to do things in a smart and planned way, but deep inside, he felt like that would violate human nature.

Walker had seen that plenty of times in his students: the juvie records, tough home life, and patterns that followed almost genetically. Learning from one's mistakes didn't come easy. He had to force himself to slow down, to really think. He nodded and tried to imprint this moment in his mind for future reference, to be recalled at a moment's notice.

Turning around, he quickly made it back. "All better," he said, forestalling Virgil's questioning look. "So, how is it going to use the magic? We have the kernel, it gets through a breakthrough, and then what?" Walker asked as he sought their ideas.

Rimi raised his hand. At Walker's nod, he said, "What if we . . . uh . . . let them expand their kernel during the breakthrough, so it becomes a little bit more powerful. Then, we . . ." He paused, looking back and forth between them.

"Go ahead," Virgil pushed. Walker wasn't sure what they had talked about when he was gone, but if he wasn't mistaken, the older assistant seemed to like the little guy a little more since chucking him out of his throat.

"We . . . have that same kernel become attuned itself."

"For what purpose?" Walker asked gently, recognizing that his newest assistant was going out on a limb.

"So that the magic it produces is always the same type, otherwise, you could have a fiery air-filled water MUY," Rimi finished, out of breath and sucking in air like he'd just run up a hill. "If the kernel is attuned, it will always be the same. This way, the monsters do not gain any other types of attunements, and they can only refill their kernel with either pure magic or the magic of their attunement."

"Smart thinking," Walker encouraged.

Virgil stepped forward, saying, "That also means the importance of the Mana Trees just went up again, as they are the biggest source of pure magic in Symphony, and once every monster knows this, they are going to naturally want to be near them since their kernels will fill faster by direct proximity."

"Yep," Rimi said with an ear wiggle. He looked at his screens. Walker wouldn't know this, but the subsystem assistant had already inputted dozens of pages of rules and information into the Monster System to allow for his plans. He had spoken of it with Virgil when Walker was doing . . . whatever that was. Virgil had given him some pointers, and they talked a lot about magic.

The Monster System was full of potential, and the more they worked on it, filling in gaps and solving problems, creating a unique program for all of Symphony's monsters to grow, the more attached Rimi became to it. He was starting to see it as a friend who depended on him to take care of it and make sure it was healthy. There was nothing wrong with that. There was nothing wrong with just having a friend.

Walker, Rimi, and Virgil continued their work on the Monster System. After a thorough debate, they decided to limit the kernel in the beginning to about the size of a large pea and allow the tier two monsters to manifest their elements to the limit of their core.

According to Virgil, this meant that they could use their attuned magic in small bursts, like shooting a small magical fireball or extending darkness around them. Once they learned about their breakthrough, nature would take its course, and their kernel would just feel like another extension of themselves. The way Virgil explained it, it would be like discovering an extra finger. Strange at first, but then, life . . . finds a way.

They would also grow hungry to empower that kernel once they found their limits, which was, of course, what Walker wanted all along—a perpetual war. Not one of genocide, he proclaimed to the two squirrels, but one of empowerment. To strengthen the entities found on Symphony so they could always defend themselves against creatures like the Slicer.

When they moved to the third tier, Walker said the potential growth of the monsters should rise exponentially. It wouldn't do for a creature to take small steps when it'd been working hard to get to the next level. His two assistants agreed, and after careful deliberation, Walker had Rimi program the system to double the size of the kernel and allow it to take a secondary attunement. He called it the upgrade tier, which led to another spout of arguing. Rimi gave his input occasionally, feeling better and commenting more often as the tiff continued, with Walker and Virgil respectfully listening to his opinions. They settled on calling it the transformative stage.

"Okay," Walker said once they'd finally nailed the third tier's name. "The transformative stage will allow the monsters to not only gain a second attunement but to mix them. Fire and earth equals . . . lava, sound and air equals . . . actually, I don't know what that would turn out to be."

"Resonating or harmonic," Virgil supplied.

Walker pointed a finger at him. "That! So, each time they transform, they gain a second attunement within their kernel space. Once they fill it up, they can blend their magic together." He mashed his two hands together to explain it. "Plowy! Transformative. Fits the name."

"I understand," Rimi said. "But that isn't the explosive gain in power that you are looking for. It is more magic, that cannot be denied by doubling the size of their kernel. But it does not truly allow them to grow. So far, the monsters have gained gain an attunement and a little more magical storage. There should be more empowerment for them once they've reached this far," he finished, feeling a deep need to make sure the future monsters he watched over were represented well.

"You are right," Virgil said with a nod. "We need to do something to them physically."

"Like what?" Walker asked.

They all sat there in silence for a long moment. It was long enough that Walker actually checked the clock till the next battle and was blown away. They'd already spent five hours working on just the first three tiers. They needed to move faster, but at the same time, this couldn't be rushed. He tried not to think about the progress the other Creators must have been making while they worked this all out.

They might already have full-sized planets with hundreds of entities. Right now, he just had pieces of smallish landmasses with some fish and moss. He really hoped the next entities he made wouldn't create another Slicer, or he was well and truly fucked. He continued thinking about the different paths forward, but thankfully, Rimi had already come up with something.

"Why not also let the kernels begin to affect their bodies? Make the MUYs evolve to resist heat if they're attuned to lava or fire. There is no point in using lava-attuned magic and being burned by your own power."

Walker snapped his fingers. "There it is! Holy crap, they're going to burn up if we don't give them some kind of protection. But how do we do it?"

Virgil nodded. "A fine suggestion, but I am not sure." He looked at Walker as he said it but was really watching Rimi from the corner of his eyes, waiting for his response.

"So we need to give them protection from their own attunements, and we should somehow try to make it physical, I think," Walker mused.

Virgil quietly sighed. "How so?"

"Oh, oh!" Rimi said with his hand raised as he tried to get their attention. He put it down when Walker said he didn't have to do that. "Let the magic seep into their skin."

"Yes!" Walker heard Virgil say in an annoyed tone of voice. Walker was sure that the squirrel was mocking him somehow. "Indeed. Absorption into the entity's skin would only be natural."

"So you want to let the attuned magic seep into their skin to provide some form of resistance."

"Uh-huh," Rimi agreed. "And we can start changing them from there. The more their kernel fills up, the more magic is pulsing through them, and the more physical changes will occur."

"Okay, okay," he said with a smile as he started to picture it. "Now we're getting somewhere. So, in tier three, the monsters get a second attunement, which lets them pick another attunement and combine them, then we let it seep into their bodies, toughening up their skin at first and moving onto organs like bones and muscles." Walker high-fived the smaller squirrel, startling him.

Virgil quickly threw cold water on their idea. "That is a good plan, but you have a problem."

"What's the problem?" Rimi asked.

"If you affect the brain, magical results will occur. It will more than likely increase their brain size, thereby increasing their intelligence by a high degree, and offering secondary evolutions like quick thinking or a strategic mind. The second attunement and bodily changes are already enough; you do not want to make them smarter at tier three as well, or you will have a Slicer problem." Virgil noticed Rimi staring at his hand after Walker had slapped it.

Walker nodded. "Okay, I see your point and agree. So we make the changes to everything physical but tell the system to disclude the brain. We can just include the brain in the fourth tier, and that should be enough of a jump in power."

"Okay," Rimi agreed, finally taking his eyes off the center of his paw, and continued to place new inputs into the system. The page count had reached over forty already, and the system was starting to become more balanced as Rimi independently added stopgaps to prevent any entities from trying to work around the rules.

He had yet to tell Virgil and Walker, but he was sure he would once it came up. His knowledge was . . . limited. He didn't know why he had information on some things and not enough about others. He didn't know why Walker had slapped his paw or why he seemed to laugh so much. But one thing he did know about, ever since first opening his eyes, was the systems of the Alpha Protocol.

He could've stopped Walker talking at any point when he had first explained how everything started, as he already had that information. But he had wanted to see what the experience had been like for Walker, through his eyes. It had been enlightening. Just by watching his bond develop with Virgil, he knew he wanted something like that. Even when they were arguing, they did so with great care for the other's feelings.

So, he was working and thinking extra hard for both of them at every moment since Walker had given him the Monster System. This was his way to help his Creator, whether Walker wanted to be called that or not. Rimi refused to let him down.

His blue-tinged paws stayed by his sides as the system was built step by step. He showed them the front page.

The Monster System
Description: A modified evolution system for entities
Tier 1: Common   Tier 2: Elemental
Tier 3: Transformative   Tier 4:
Tier 5:   Tier 6:
Tier 7:   Tier 8:

"Nice job, Rimi. It looks great."

Virgil shook his head. "It is only natural, as he is a subsystem assistant."

Walker looked at him in confusion. Why would Virgil not just agree with him and praise the little guy?

"I mean. It's still his work. It's his thoughts and efforts on the page there."

"Somewhat, yes," Virgil elucidated. "But he is designed for this. Once you assigned the subsystem to Rimi, he became quite attached to it. He may not know why he is attached to it, but nonetheless, it is there. Similar to myself and the Ecology Subsystem. There is one key difference between advanced assistants and their lessers: I do not have limits to how many subsystems I can manage. My only limit is how much time I have to work with them."

"Okay, okay, geez."

"I am just informing you about assistants, Walker. It is not personal."

Walker waved it off, not needing another time-losing debate. "Okay, let's focus back up. We have the brain for tier four and probably *another* doubling in kernel size. You said earlier that affecting the mind would make them smart."

"Much smarter, to a degree that they can be comparable to sentient beings like yourself. Also, because they will become sapient over time, I suggest you grant them the ability to name themselves, as they will have earned it. Reaching tier four, by your standards here, will take a great amount of work. Each increase in kernel size will also show an equal increase in the amount of magic needed to fill it."

"So?" Walker asked.

"So, if you ever want to see monsters gain the ability to reach tier four, you need to add more ways for them to gain magic rather than just passive absorption. It works fine in theory for the first two tiers, but thereafter it will fail. You would be looking at a hundred or so years before a monster reached tier four at that rate, and that is assuming they can find a location that offers both of their attunements in relative proximity. As long as they select two disparate magical attunements, that is."

"Hrmm," Walker said, pacing back and forth again. He knew the answer but was hesitant to say it, as it would further evolve his world toward war. Perhaps even before it was ready. If he told Rimi to add it to the system, it would solidify the way the world was going to work. If he didn't, the scales of his new system would break as monsters would all congregate around Mana Trees exclusively. He would have to create a Symphony as one part harmony, and likely, there would be another two parts of conflict. He would have to make adjustments through other systems to balance things, like the Class System and eventually a professional one as well.

There needed to be something for people to do aside from constantly killing and dying. The mental anguish would be overpowering if all they could do was fight. Harmony required something more. A balance.

There was even more to consider . . . Kids. Jobs. Vacations?

Just like when he returned from the battle with Blitzburg7, his mind spun with too many thoughts. Gaining control of himself, he started doing his breathing pattern, tuning out Virgil and Rimi as they talked about how attunements worked.

In and out.

In and out.

He locked it down. Tight. Then, he pushed it away, refocusing on what he had been thinking of just before his war plan had reared its head.

The Class System! he thought before returning to the two assistants and saying, with an air of finality, "We'll add them to the Class System at tier four."

Virgil looked at him in confusion. "The one you have not made yet? What would that do?"

"Well, how did you think I would have my Classers gain power? Killing monsters, of course! If we add the tier fours to the Class System right as they gain sapience, then they'll have the ability to gain power directly from killing other monsters. There'll probably be some loss between different attunements, but the magical burst from each kill should be enough to help them gain more power for their kernels on top of any passive absorption. That's two different ways to gain more magic for their kernels." He spread his hands wide in a theatrical fashion.

"My grand plan! Monsters absorb magic worldwide, but Classers can't and shouldn't work that way."

They still weren't getting it, so he doubled down on the explanation. "Monsters will be a product of their environment, but Classers will be a product of the choices they make and the steps they take to advance. My plan has been to allow the Classers to gain power through self-evolution, which allows them to target their personalities and ways of living. Choices, not just something that was forced upon them. The greater the achievements that they accomplish, the better they understand themselves and their role in the world, the more power they will accrue. They have to *choose* their paths, just like me. We can even add the Item system once it's up and running, give rewards for certain acts, and complete specific milestones we will build in over time. Those who want to fight can gain power, magic, and evolution through the conflict and absorption of different strength kernels and the monsters they slay. Those who want to be . . . I don't know . . . a chef, can advance specifically through milestones that grant them the ability to evolve. It will be all interrelated through one *overarching system!*" he said with another arm spread, breathing heavily.

"First of all, Classer is a terrible name, but that only leads me to my second point: What will the system be called?" Virgil asked.

"Goddamnit," Walker said, putting his arms down. "I thought about the Walker system, but that's too much ego, even for me. Then I considered the Dante system, but that's really just naming it after myself again, so why not take a page from our world?" Walker moved past them so he could face Symphony, then began waving one arm quickly through the air as if to a large group of people playing music. "The Conductor System!" he proclaimed to the world . . . or really just his tiny planet and two squirrels.

"With you as the conductor?" Virgil asked with a smile.

"Naturally. So, what do you guys think?" Walker said, already moving back to the Monster System and all of the roads it would lead to. "A brain, a name, and a class?"

"That is a lot of power, but I agree. I believe percentages will bring balance, as not many monsters will hit tier four," Virgil said.

"Exactly! So, what do we call it?"

"What about the unique stage?" Rimi ventured with a hand half-raised.

Walker tried to respond gently. "I feel that would be a good one, but it doesn't fully describe all of the additions we're putting in, buddy."

"Okay," Rimi said back. He didn't take the denial of his suggestion badly, which was a good sign.

"How about monarch? Like a ruler?" Virgil asked.

"Hrmmm," Rimi hummed with a small shake of his head. "Not all of them will want to rule."

But Virgil wasn't about to give up. He hadn't dropped a name on the Monster System yet and felt an intrinsic need to be involved. He looked at Walker, who still seemed deep in thought, and then offered another option: "Then, how about apex?"

"Oh, come on," Walker said with immediacy. "Are you just trying to piss me off about the Slicer again?"

"No, but it does fit. They will be physically powerful by tier three, have two types of magic plus one combined form, and be quite smart. That sounds like an apex monster to me."

"Then, just for my mental health, let's go with a synonym," Walker suggested. "*Pinnacle*. It satisfies what you're looking for, and they'll be naming themselves, so we won't need it to show up on Identify, Rimi. It'll just be for us when we're reviewing monsters," he mentioned to the smaller squirrel. Rimi made the changes with a nod.

"I like it. Now, tier five," Virgil said.

"Already decided," Walker threw out. The rest of what they'd talked about and entered into the system had led up to this moment for him. It was the first portion of the Monster System he had come up with, and he had only needed Virgil and Rimi to help him figure out all of the minutiae that existed in between tiers one and five. "We're going to give them a territory."

"What do you mean?" Rimi asked.

"I mean, if they've reached tier five, they've been working very hard, and few Classers will be able to go against them. So, we connect them directly to a Mana Tree and establish that half of the landmass as their territory. Let them re-work it in their image. Here, I'll even give you an example. Let's say we have a tier two iron MUY who works its way across a dozen years and reaches tier four. It renames itself to Frank, and Frank just loves axes and fighting. Alrighty then. He picks an axe class, evolves to become bipedal so he can control the axes better, and is entirely too much for sentients to fight against unless they're at a similar or higher level."

Walker noticed Rimi getting excited and fed off of it. "Give it a territory, almost as a warning, to everything around it. Don't fuck with Frank! You're gonna get Franked! Let it continue to grow with its linked Mana Tree, so it doesn't feel like its progress is ending. That way, it doesn't seem like the only way for it to grow is to go on a rampage across all of Symphony. Give it a chance . . . to be . . . something more. To gain something more and be different. Rather than a monster, a person, if that's what it wants to do. Allow it to build its own world, in a sense."

"Assuming you can build that, it would be a miniature Monster Creator System," Virgil said.

"Just that," Walker replied with a nod. "Hopefully it isn't a total dick."

"That requires another system, one that deals with territories," Virgil reminded him.

"I know! Isn't this fun?!" Walker said with a huge smile. If Virgil didn't know any better, he would assume that smiling that hard would hurt a person's face. "Rimi said we could build in the milestones so that only the good monsters get help; that's a solid plan. It will slow down any supervillain-level monsters from leveling up their class and getting too much power too quickly."

"Walker," Rimi's small voice said, "We don't have a Territory System yet, so we can't interconnect them."

"What's the best you can do?" Walker asked as his smile turned into a frown.

"U-um," Rimi said, clearly nervous about the look on his Creator's face and his self-preservation as a subsystem assistant.

"Whoa, whoa, calm down, buddy. I know you're just starting in life, but this frown isn't for you. It's for myself. It's okay. Now, what's the best you can do?"

"Umm." Rimi moved through the sixty or so pages he'd built, flipping through them quickly while trying to see if one of the protocol's glimpses would save him from disappointing Walker and the Monster System together. Walker's idea was a great one. This allowed the monsters to continue to grow and warned the rest of the world that there was something powerful here, that they should not enter its domain without thought. But the system was fighting him a little. After flipping through multiple settings, he finally found one that would work. "I think . . . I think I can just call it a territory and leave a note that it must be linked to a Territory System."

Virgil nodded beside him. "Yes, it is not perfect, but it is a band-aid that will hold until we get the Territory System up. The Alpha Protocol allows this, as not all plans can be established simultaneously, and they want the very best a Creator can do. We just cannot let any monsters reach tier five before the Territory System is running, or the Monster System could become unbalanced."

"Will you please remind me if that comes close to happening?" Walker asked the two squirrels, receiving a nod from the smaller and two thumbs up from the larger. "Great! I even have a name for tier five already."

"What would that be?" Virgil asked.

"Sovereign."

The Monster System
Description: A modified evolution system for entities
Tier 1: Common   Tier 2: Elemental
Tier 3: Transformative   Tier 4: Pinnacle
Tier 5: Sovereign   Tier 6:
Tier 7:   Tier 8:[4]

CHAPTER NINETEEN

Moving Forward

Walker put his journal down by the Tree of the Gods and stood up, looking the mysterious plant over.

Is it a plant? Or something else . . .

He found the tree had only grown a small amount since the last time he'd analyzed it. It made him wonder if it would slow down in growth the taller it grew. Remembering that grand rewards had a chance of increasing its growth rate, he would need to work hard to push the envelope with his upcoming creations.

Next up was a simple idea. Making monsters. And as excited as he was, he knew they first had to solve a big problem. The bottom of Symphony. He checked his time.

Time remaining until next battle: 57+ hours

With his remaining time in mind, Walker moved at a trot to his relatively old computer. The combined monitor and desktop seemed dull in their monochrome coloring and boxed shape. Sitting down, he clicked on the landmass option. While he started to plan things out, selecting the rectangle shape and increasing its size, he kept an ear on Virgil and Rimi while they planned out the kernel.

They were talking about how to make it physically present within the monsters without negatively impeding their internal organs. Walker had no clue about that and was rather happy to be able just to do something simple for a moment. He created a few boxes in a triangle to represent metal, placed them throughout the shape with his copy ability, and called Virgil to him as he clicked print and heard the chuffing of ink onto paper.

"What are you working on, Walker?" the large squirrel called out as he had stopped speaking mid-sentence with the smaller squirrel and made his way over to him. Walker saw Rimi from the corner of his eye performing a small shrug, not unlike the kind Virgil liked to do when he was confused by something. The blue squirrel moved back to his screens, nonplussed.

Walker felt a small smile tug his face as Virgil approached. "I told you before, remember? I'm going to put a bunch of metal at the bottom of Symphony so nothing else can break through. I figure we can drop it in, delete it with the World Editor, and then place it near the roots so it can gain density over the years. With enough time and magical reinforcement from the ley lines, it'll be impossible to break, and we won't have another planetary destruction on our hands."

Virgil tilted his head. "You know I can have no true input on this."

"I know; I just need you to associate the symbol with steel."

Virgil nodded. "Done."

"Sweet!"

Walker opened up his monitor and focused on the edge of the desert, then realized he didn't know what to do with the paper. He zoomed in the monitor to the edge of the Symphony's dry corner, just outside of the planet, and tried placing the paper on it. The paper dissolved into motes of small golden light as a large silver-gray block appeared. It was just as he had drawn it but twice the size of the other landmasses he'd placed before. He realized that with each upgrade to the Creation Instrument, the scope and size of what it could do would also increase.

Slowly, a gargantuan block of steel floated in space just above his small, grassy planet. Walker smiled until his overlay lit up.

"Fuck, I forgot about that."

He'd received an F grade.

"Mmm, yes," Virgil replied.

Rimi walked over and asked, "What happened?"

"Walker made an entirely monotonous landmass, and the system punished him for it. It says you lost half of the creation materials you placed into it. That should be half a page out of the printer," he finished, nodding to himself.

Walker crossed his arms, still looking at the lowest grade he'd received in years. "Well, it's already happened, and it needed to be done."

"I agree, and I understand your thought process; I am just a little shocked. It is rare to see F grades in the protocol."

A sigh escaped his lips. "We all fail sometimes, Virgil. Can you complete your work on the atmosphere? We're going to need it soon."

"Indeed."

As Virgil walked away, Walker stepped into the World Editor and moved to the edge of Symphony. He got started by removing all of the steel and placing it back into his resources, grabbing every little piece so none would randomly drop to the planet. As he quickly worked, he got a front-row seat to the atmosphere show as Virgil went about his business. Slowly, Walker could tell the atmosphere was being repaired, only with one new addition. The cyan color of pure magic started to become more present as the Mana Trees expanded their domain.

Deleting the last of the steel he could find, Walker clicked on Resources and reviewed the results. It was a shitload of metal, causing a few ideas to pop up in Walker's mind. Ones that had to do with creating a massive statue of Virgil with the word *Indeed* written on it. He laughed to himself before shaking it out of his head and zooming into the bedrock of Symphony.

The monitor changed views, and Symphony became transparent on the screen. Walker appreciated its adaptability, with the change allowing him to see where the Mana Tree roots had settled deep in the world. They connected throughout the land, deep cyan pulses far beneath the surface. He started to delete granite a dozen feet below the roots, adding steel in the gaps he had now created. It was a test of his own control, as he didn't want to make a mistake here.

If he deleted too much, the granite could detach and float into space, separating from the cube-shaped world. Too little, and he wouldn't be able to add enough steel to make this whole project worthwhile. Thus, he was very careful with his movements and the volume of his deletions. It took him about an hour to delete the granite and add the stored-up steel, and when he finished, his resources still showed quite a bit of steel. That would give him further options later on when he began shaping Symphony to his whims again.

Walker stepped out of the World Editor. "Hey, shouldn't the granite have been reinforced over fifty years from the roots as well?" he asked Virgil.

Virgil mumbled to himself as he had been pulled out of his work for the second time before saying, "Yes, it is. If you are questioning why you were still able to delete it, you need to keep something in mind. You own the planet, Walker, and the World Editor is one of your greatest tools. That early B grade saved you much more time than you think. The World Editor can instantly dematerialize any resources that do not have life. That is why I suggested not adding any grass or vegetation early on."

"Right, if I had made plain old grass with no modifications, we would have been screwed in the first battle," Walker said.

"Mmm, grass monster," Rimi whispered to himself near the Evolution Chamber.

"Okay," Walker said with a clap, startling the blue squirrel from his dreams of vegetation domination. "We need something to eat those MUYs! What do you think? Another water-based entity, or should we do something amphibious? I don't think we should start with flyers for our first Monster System update."

"Damn," Rimi whispered again.

Virgil turned away from his work, the lure of creating a new monster too powerful for him. "You are right, Walker. A flying entity could be very bad. If we made a single error in its modifications, it might become impossible to kill after the fact. Also, remember that whatever you make and update to the Monster System would conceivably be the oldest on Symphony as they will be the first." He shrugged. "The new first, that is. Without another monster or potential Classer killing them, they would become quite powerful if left in a habitat undisturbed."

"Good point. Hrmmm . . ." He tapped his chin. "Amphibians . . . Large frogs? I know I don't want to make any snakes right at the start," he said with a shudder. He had no idea how others viewed them as cute. They were slimy and cold-blooded in more ways than one. Plus, they attacked annoyances. In his experience, they'd done so without any provocation.

He knew it was a simple bias. Something that wasn't an innocent snake's fault. But when he was younger, he'd been attacked by a rattlesnake and developed, with total justification, whipped archaeologist syndrome. Now, he couldn't help but see all snakes as malevolent, even if he logically understood it was an unfair stance to take. It was one of the few fears he had left—that and spiders.

"Frogs would do well for our first attempt," Virgil said, breaking Walker from his dark thoughts. "I spent some time during your recent convalescence to peruse some of your memories. Please go into the Entity Subsystem and pull up the African clawed frog. I believe that will suit your needs."

Walker agreed and clicked Entity, pulling up the frog Virgil mentioned. He clicked on it and watched the computer screen fill in the details. As he looked at it, the frog seemed . . . small.

"That might not be big enough," Walker said. "It needs to be large enough to catch and eat the MUYs. There's no point in making these if they can't even survive in that habitat."

Virgil agreed. "Yes, I had planned on modifying it, of course. We would not want sixteen-foot-tall frogs." A small gasp broke out from Rimi while Virgil continued. "So I cannot modify it with gigantism as we did with the Mana Trees." His eyes moved across his overlay before he said, "We could do four feet tall. Once you put in the Classers, this would be an excellent first area for them to train in, and the African clawed frog does not need to eat very often, so it should balance out the predator and prey cycle."

"Okay, that's a plan." Walker pushed the monitor over to The Crater and zoomed in on one spot. He printed out the page and stuck it to the monitor, then watched as the frog materialized on a small beach, ignoring the notification pinging the corner of his vision. He was sure it was a D grade anyway.

The frog was less than half a foot in size and had small claws attached to its feet. Walker dug a hole below it and dropped it in with the World Editor, filling in the top after. He still didn't like the feeling of having to kill innocent creatures. But without his Monster System having a hold on it, the frog could evolve in an out-of-control fashion. He didn't have a choice.

Pushing through the mental fatigue of his actions, Walker didn't even wait for the frog to die before selecting the Evolution Chamber in his overlay and placing one in there. He did, however, feel a bit bad about it.

"How long is that thing going to take to die?" he asked Virgil.

"Oh, several minutes. That is a novel way to kill them quickly, though, so they do not needlessly suffer."

"I wish I didn't have to kill everything for us to modify it though," Walker said with a sigh.

Walker watched as Virgil aged the frog by two years and then started to . . . he didn't know how to describe it. Stretch? He was grabbing parts of the frog in the Evolution Chamber and pulling its skin like rubber. Rather than how Walker worked with his hands, Virgil did everything through his screens in a much faster and more economical manner.

It made Walker once again realize how lucky he was to have an advanced assistant. None of the changes looked complicated, but he knew that was because of just how competent his friend was at his work. After he stretched the body out to around four feet tall, he did the same to its organs and claws, finishing on the brain, which he left just a little larger than it was previously. Virgil left an odd gap near its stomach, like it was waiting for something.

The large squirrel stopped his work and responded to Walker's previous statement. "The Alpha Protocol has to first recognize a new entity in your world before you can connect them to the Evolution Chamber. You could almost say that when you first materialize them, it is like downloading their data to the system."

"Well, that's unnecessarily stupid. It should already have access to the Entity Subsystem in my overlay, right? I mean, every time I click it, I can see a huge list of options, all the way from aardvark to zonkey," Walker protested.

"So, what do you want to do? Produce everything at once and let it all instantly die?" Virgil asked.

Walker's eyes grew round, and Virgil realized his mistake. "No, no, that . . . that . . . hrmm."

"We have to kill them anyway, right? And we always get D's, which only replenish our materials. Why not just make *everything* on the list? Just, bam, bam, bam. Click, die, click, die. I'd rather feel terrible once, across the span of one horrible hour, than feel terrible for five minutes every single time we make something new."

"Okay, but how would you kill them?"

"You could put the monitor on a spot in space," Rimi suggested, joining the conversation. Walker remembered how he'd produced the steel just outside of Symphony. He gave Rimi a smile and a nod before turning back to Virgil.

"How many creatures are on there?" Walker asked.

"There are over eight thousand options just for frogs, Walker," Virgil said with a head shake. "It would take a very, very long time with your current Creation Instrument."

"Hrmm . . . so not something to do right away, but definitely something to think about." A horrible thought entered his mind. "Wait . . . if I have to do that with every creature, doesn't that mean I'd have to do it with a human being? A—a baby?"

Virgil looked at him directly. "What do you suggest as an alternative? Release it into what is essentially a primordial world soon to be filled with four-foot monsters that have metallic claws?"

"Wait, when did their claws become metallic?"

"Focus, Walker. Bander Sotfam, the Creator of the Evolution Chamber, went through something similar to what you are now. He, too, did not enjoy the killing of unmodified entities; however, he still did his duty for his world. Perhaps we should wait on humanity until you have a chance to find your own way to quote, 'download' your entities without needing to sacrifice them afterward. There are possibilities. However, they must be earned."

Walker didn't like that answer. If humanity wanted a chance, they'd have to ride the wave with him, growing stronger and adapting to the world as it became more and more realized. He looked over at the blue squirrel. "Rimi?" Walker asked. "Do you have any ideas?"

"No, Walker. I am sorry," he replied with a downcast look.

"Okay, it's fine. It's . . . fine. It's fine," Walker said a third time, trying to equalize everything in his mind. "So, we wait on humans and hopefully find a better way to do this. If I'm forced to make everything at once . . . I'll find a way. But for now, let's just shelve the idea and work on our new frogs. I already know what to name them."

"Outstanding," Virgil said as he pointed at the chamber in front of them. "All we have left to do is place the kernel." He pointed at what Walker had noticed before, a small empty space within the body of the frog, then explained that each monster they created would have to have the same small cavity. If they made it too large to start, and it continued to double in size, it would become overly powerful. Virgil also mentioned that with the Monster System built the way that it was, the larger a creature became, the longer it would take to increase in tiers, as the magic had to fully fuse to their body in tier three. Walker felt that was the perfect balance for what they were creating.

Virgil finalized the new monster with his approval, allowing Walker to place his first new entity on Symphony in some time. After a moment, his overlay lit up.

[. . . Scanning . . .]
**As your entity has been modified from its original form,
please name it.**

Naming it hadn't been difficult. Walker had his favorite books and games neatly organized in his head. He was sure that Virgil would understand.

Entity: Battlefrog is named.

[. . . Analyzing . . .]
**Entity named Battlefrog analyzed.
Size: Medium.
Entity category: Animal
Organism type: (Predator) System Monster
Modification: High
Ability to evolve: Yes, system-bound
Age: 2 years
Extra marks earned for being the 5th Creator to
build a system and use it to create an entity within the
4AA Alpha Protocol (Grand reward earned)
Grade: B
Rewards calculated.**

**Moderate reward for completion of a B-grade entity:
Congratulations, Dante! You've earned a second Evolution
Chamber!**
***Building a better entity in the Alpha Protocol is about drive and
innovation. Use the second Evolution Chamber to continue your
work and build a more diverse world.***
(Upgradeable)

**Grand reward for being the 5th Creator to
build a system and use it to create an entity within
the 4AA Alpha Protocol:
Congratulations, Dante! You've advanced the Tree of the Gods!**
***Its fruit, unimaginable. Its seed, pure power.
You have taken the first step.***

**Unknown changes occurring.
The Tree of the Gods is maturing!**

[. . . Scanning . . .]
The Tree of the Gods has borne fruit.

Walker smiled to himself. That was quite a nice surprise. He turned around and was shocked to see three people running toward him from the Tree of the Gods. They ate up the distance between them in such a short amount of time Walker thought he must be dreaming.

Stopping before him and his two assistants, they looked at each other while Walker and the two squirrels did the same. It was an odd standoff of perspectives, as none of them spoke first. Finally, the large, muscular man in clean white robes and a long flowing beard frowned before saying, "You are the Creator?"

Mr. Harrison, as Walker called him, was not his name. But even had someone called him that, it wouldn't have bothered him, as one name was as good as any other. Names were simply hats to wear. Clothes. Mislabeling the soul with words that could never express what was truly at the core of someone.

His core was blacker than the darkest parts of space. He knew it and was content with his place in the multiverse.

The large man strolled through broken streets that had once held smiles, cars, and all the facets of life. Now, they only held the forgotten memories of a society that didn't understand what kind of creature had appeared among them. His over seven-foot frame seemed graceful, but it was an illusion to the eyes. A passerby might think he was an extraordinarily coordinated giant, maybe a professional basketball player on their best day, but really, his walk was that of a predator. Long stretches with minute alterations in his movement.

His target at the moment was a bar on the backside of San Francisco simply named "Johnny's." That's where he felt he would find it.

He quickly made the trek, reaching a set of swinging doors that looked to be barricaded. Heavy breathing and hushed conversations made their way to his ears. He pulled his robes inward with the flick of a wrist so they wouldn't catch on anything, then pushed on the doors with great pressure as a series of loud banging sounds and light screaming occurred on the other side.

As the blockage stopped blocking his entrance, he squeezed under a low-hanging beam, bending his way into the entrance. There was a shallow resistance gathered here, one that had tried to fight and survive for several days against waves of unspeakable monsters. They didn't know that fighting was useless. That there was no way for them to overcome the horrors of the night. Creatures who never snarled, hissed, or growled, but walked quietly and carefully in their natural environment, blending as needed. Daytime wasn't much better, as rumors said that even viewing these creatures was enough to drive a person mad.

The massive man looked at the inhabitants, filthy after only a few days, and a sneer was adopted by his face before he could stop it. He didn't intend to have that reaction, but it had come nonetheless. His expression caused many within to step back with gasps, but he didn't care about them. They deserved this, with their soft lives and simple world. With their paradise that never knew the strife of where he had come from, the constant war and battle its so-called Creator had made.

If he could've chosen another to make his world rather than that damnable failure, he would have, but fate would have its due, and even he couldn't fight the Alpha Protocol. While the rest of the survivors in the bar had stepped back with audible gasps and furtive glances, a little girl had stepped forward. She met his eyes with her own, unbowed by the terrors of the recent days, and his sneer transformed into a guileless smile.

His target had been found.

The tall man bent down and offered something from within the deep confines of his robe as he spoke. "A candy, dear?"

"Oh, thank you, Mister," she said with a grin as she reached her hands out, stepping further away from the others.

"Now, what is your name, little girl?"

"Elsie, like my grandma," she said, taking the large candy and unwrapping a pink lollipop before quickly slipping it into her mouth with a sound of delight. The crowd stayed silent during the exchange, too numb to react to the strange giant entering their territory and still in shock from the recent disruption to their new standard of living.

"What a wonderful name," he said slowly, savoring the words that dripped from his mouth.

"Thank you," she responded with a smile and a smack as she pulled the lollipop out of her mouth. "What's your name?"

He stood to his full height, and as he did so, one local finally grew some courage. "Who are you?" he screamed. "What do you want?"

"Oh, me?" he asked, placing his hand against his chest, right where his heart should be. He appreciated that at least one person here had some courage, but it was already too late for all of that. "I'm Nobody, and I want everything here to . . . *end.*"

He stooped down and lifted up the little girl from where she'd just collapsed. The paralyzing agent on the candy had always had a quick effect, and he smiled as her yellow pigtails swam against his arms. Once she was secure, he snapped his fingers and a cracking sound rang out.

The sun had gone down as he'd made his entrance, allowing his Shadows to rove once again. They spread themselves out and slipped past his body without even brushing his clothes. Darkness leaked into the bar that night like blood seeping into a bandage, and quiet desperation had no place here as screams and the sound of running began and ended quickly.

Stepping away quickly, he transferred the little girl to his shoulder. Time was, as ever, a deciding factor in regards to the protocol. He moved his freed-up arms in unnatural patterns, and with a *pop*, both the giant and the little girl disappeared.

Deep underwater off of the coast of Ireland, two bodies came into existence. With another snap, he, still holding the girl, was covered in a bubble that kept the water and pressure at bay. He moved toward a set of ruins lying forgotten in the dark water. As he crossed an unseen threshold, his overlay lit up.

[. . . Scanning . . .]
Omega Protocol candidate recognized.
Hello, Nobody.
Temporal Subsystem activated.

CHAPTER TWENTY

Control

The battlefrog came into existence. It did not know its purpose nor where it currently found itself. All it could rely upon were its basest instincts, further empowered by trickery through the Alpha Protocol. Its body informed it that food and water were necessary for its survival. And that a mate wouldn't be so bad, either.

But . . . there was something else, something at the edge of its primitive understanding. Some strange thing fed into it at a slow rate, right toward the middle of its body . . . and the only thing it truly understood at the moment was . . . it wanted more of it.

Its kernel was hungry for more.

Walker stared at the bearded man, still confused about where he had come from. The man had spoken to him with an oddly powerful timbre in his voice, but the tone of it rankled him. "Why do you say it like I'm some piece of bacon, rotting and left on the floor?" he asked while looking the three newcomers over as they stared right back at him.

"Hrmmph, an odd way to speak," the original speaker grunted at him. Upon hearing it again, Walker's thoughts still turned to his voice. Making a mental comparison, it sounded like gravel being laid upon new pavement. He looked over the speaker again, noting just how tall he was.

Walker was a tall man by all accounts, but this guy took it to a new level. He was almost as tall as Mr. Harrison, standing just shy of seven feet, and had tan, rippling muscles coating the entirety of his body. A long white beard seemed like the only fashion to fit the strong angles of his jawline, with complimentary white hair sprouting from his head and long eyebrows to complete the look. His face had a standard resting state that looked like the word *seriousness* was stamped upon it at the age of six and had never let him go since.

The other two recently arrived visitors were a tall, beautiful woman with angular eyes containing shockingly yellow irises and a man who looked like a powerlifter, with hair shaped into tips that resembled two horns stabbing the air. The woman wore a golden sash around a green dress, while the large man wore what looked like bronze armor, if Walker knew his history right.

He knew he should be freaking out at the appearance of random strangers. They could be violent. They could be perverts. They could be insurance salesmen, who knew? But after watching a small world be destroyed, or a giant squirrel throwing up a smaller blue version of itself, at some point, he had become immune to the strangeness of this place. He internally chuckled at his earlier anxiety when first arriving here. It was amazing how much a person could change in just a few days.

The woman took a step closer to him. "What is this bacon you speak of? Is it delicious?"

The bearded man heaved a great sigh, pectoral muscles bulging like balloons with the intake and exhalation of his breath. "You are the Creator, are you not? Time is not a friend."

The third visitor spoke up right after. "What is this place?" Walker noted that his high-pitched voice seemed at odds with such a powerful body, but smartly chose not to comment on it.

He was about to answer when the golden-sashed woman spoke instead. "Yes, where are we?" She continued to look around, but there was something off about it. It was a stuttering movement, forced, like she'd been there before and was pretending that she hadn't.

The bearded man turned to the other two, roaring out, "DO NOT SPEAK."

"He is," Virgil said as he pointed at Walker.

Walker noticed Rimi had appeared near the trio, poking the horn-haired man in the leg for some reason while whispering "Firmmmm" to himself. The horned man politely pretended not to notice.

Finally, Walker got a word in. "What's going on here? It said the Tree of the . . ."

"Yes?" the woman asked.

"The Tree of the . . . Gods . . ."

"Uh-huh?" she replied with a smile.

"Fuck," Walker said, slapping his forehead. "You guys are totally gods, aren't you?"

"Of course we are," said the bearded man, placing his hands on his hips and striking a classic heroic pose as he turned his head away.

"Lies," the woman replied, tapping one foot impatiently as she watched the large man deflate.

"Castoffs," the bronze man said as well, looking down at the ground.

"I WILL SPEAK FOR US," the bearded man thundered at the other two. He seemed unnaturally overbearing. Walker likened that immediately to his need to overcompensate for something.

He tried to speak again, to explain that he didn't want people yelling at each other here, when the bearded man struck his pose for a second time. "We are the gods and goddess of Earth, of course. That should have been apparent by the Tree of . . . Where are my powers?"

"What?" Walker said in confusion.

"Did you steal my lightning? You thief!"

Walker shrugged. "I have no idea what you're talking about."

The man laughed uproariously. "Likely story, human." He said the last word with a snarl. "And I'm sure that you have nothing to do with the reason we're not on Earth anymore, right?" He looked over at his two companions. "Don't trust a word that comes out of this runt's mouth. He lies."

Walker gave him a glare, but nothing more. Ever since the Slicer, he'd been more emotionally disjointed than ever before. He'd decided that he needed to have better control of his emotions going forward. Allowing the bearded man to tip him over an emotional ledge wouldn't do him any favors. Rather than respond in kind, he walked over to the Tree of the Gods to see what kind of changes had happened.

For the first time, when he walked over to the tree, the distance felt appropriate. After arriving, he looked over the now thirty-foot-tall tree. It had changed again. Several branches had flowered, strange growths pushing out of the whorled wood.

Looking at the growths, he found the same symbols he'd seen before, only instead of on leaves, they were now shaped from seeds. As he looked closer, he noted a few hanging lower than the others. One in particular, shaped like an owl, looked like it might drop next. Nodding to himself, he turned around and walked back to the visitors, making a quick and easy logical leap from the badge he'd seen on the bearded man's robe.

"Looks like I'll have more company soon," he said quietly to himself as he thought about what that might mean. He noted the bearded man whispering to his fellows and he didn't like the look of it. "Hey, Zeus!" he yelled.

"What?" Zeus thundered back. "Fuck!" he yelled out as he realized he'd confirmed his identity so easily.

"This is a tiny planet, dude. There's no lightning here. I mean, do you see any?" Walker spread his hands out, showcasing the entirety of his small living space.

Zeus looked around, hanging his head. "NO . . . no, I do not."

"Okay, then assume you didn't come with it, and it was left behind." Walker stopped walking as he got close to Virgil, who gave him a brief smile.

Meanwhile, Zeus looked like he was going to cry. "You do not understand. Lightning is the source of my power."

"More lies," the woman said again. "I apologize as I've never told you my name, Creator. I go by Echidna." She reached out a hand in greeting.

Walker took it, noting how smooth her grip was. He knew that name from mythology as well. "You mean the mother of monsters?"

"That is not factual. Do I look like a monster to you?" She let go of his hand and did a quick spin, her dress flaring out around her before coming to a graceful stop. "I did not give birth to monsters; I gave birth to powerhouses who shook the world. For that, they were called monsters. It is the weak memories of humanity that have painted us in the light from which you know us to be. We were all shaped by our Creator with different purposes, just like Minos here," she finished, patting the large, metal-covered man.

He nodded once without speaking. Echidna explained, "He doesn't often like to speak, as he feels his given voice is beneath the dignity of the feats he has performed in his life. Please forgive him." Minos just nodded again.

Zeus finally released the Kraken with his next words. "It's true, I'm afraid. The only god that could be found on Earth is just a pale imitation of the awesome power your stories tell of us."

"How do you know about those stories?" Virgil asked, for once just as in the dark as Walker was.

"This tree," Zeus said, pointing his hand at it, "is ancient. You can call it the Tree of Life, or of the ages, or of the gods. It has existed for multiple millennia and houses all of the ancient creations from Earth's time in the Alpha Protocol. Each of those leaves is another of our fellow Primigenials, as you can call us."

"I don't know that word," Walker said with a confused look on his face.

"It means we've been around since the beginning," Echidna supplied. "I don't mean the *beginning* beginning. But the beginning of Earth. When the Alpha Protocol closed out, our Creator, the bastard that she is, trapped us in the tree and placed it at the bottom of the deepest part of the ocean. She even left us guardians that would destroy anything that came close. And there we sat for thousands of years in the deepest pit of a planet we had once protected and cherished."

As crazy as that sounded to Walker, there was something else bothering him more. "That still doesn't explain how you know so much. You knew there was a Creator. How could you know that?"

"We're God's children! We know all!" Zeus yelled to the sky. But Walker knew it was a feeble attempt to remain powerful and mysterious. They weren't off to a good start with him so far.

Echidna, who hadn't taken her eyes off of Walker, saw his squinted look. She slowly shook her head as if coming to a decision. In a harsh voice, she said, "He'll figure it out when Athena is released, you dolt! You know how she is. We need to tell him now, before things go along too far. You know his history!"

She looked at Minos, who nodded, then she continued. "Well . . . We have a few with us who can . . . taste memories. They don't take them away, but they do experience them, and as we're all connected within the tree, we have a rudimentary form of communication. Since you've arrived—"

"You've been experiencing my life," Walker said in a dead voice. It was bad enough that the Alpha Protocol and Virgil could see everything he'd done, good and bad, but now a tree full of powerful Primigenial beings also knew of his most embarrassing and sadly human moments.

That time he'd been pantsed at a party. The first time he'd had sex. Everything was up for grabs. It was an all-Walker buffet, first come, everybody served.

"Yes," she finished.

"We are sorry, Walker," Minos said, placing a large, callused hand on his shoulder. He shrugged it off with a quick twitch of his body.

"Then why ask who the fuckin' Creator is?" he yelled as he started to pace back and forth in front of them.

"BECAUSE I DIDN'T WANT YOU TO KNOW!" Zeus roared at him.

"What do you mean you did not want us to know?" Virgil asked.

"Because you . . . don't . . . matter . . . *creature*," Zeus said, stepping up to the squirrel and towering over him.

That put a crick in Walker's neck, like a pinched muscle that pulsed deeply, and he had to turn the side of his head with a grimace as the feeling became almost physical. He'd been trying to hold back his emotions, but in less than five minutes since getting out of the mini-prison, this bastard was already trying to control things. To bully them.

It didn't matter that Earth's mythology called him the king of the gods. No, there was a bigger problem. What if the rest of those in the tree were just the same? They weren't gods. Not really. They were the Creator's rejects. Castoffs.

What if the tree was slowly letting all of the undesirables from his home planet take over and fuck everything up? There had to be a reason they were imprisoned, while other creatures or entities weren't. He couldn't let this happen.

The crick in his neck did end up becoming physical. Like a punch in the muscle.

No, no, no no no no no.

Walker wouldn't be controlled. No. He had already been shunted to this world without a real choice or understanding; he wouldn't also be forced to listen to this son of a bitch if he didn't have to. He would have to take control with a firm hand, or things were already done. He couldn't allow Zeus to mistreat the one person who had helped him in all of his time here.

He said the words that previously sat in his heart, unattended and unnoticed. They were always a hidden voice that he forced to keep silent, but now, he had to let it out.

Turning to Zeus, he said what had been yearning for freedom in the back of his mind. "Shut the fuck up, you limp-dick piece of shit. You get a taste of my memories and think you can push me around on my own world? My world? Push around my friend?" He took a deep breath, but he already felt it. Felt like that control he was trying to gain back was gone and with it, his emotional management had run out the door.

"I'LL THROW YOUR ASS INTO SPACE AND FORGET YOU FIVE MINUTES LATER, MOTHERFUCKER." Walker stepped into the World Editor while still belting the three with his voice. "YOU'VE FUCKED UP IF YOU THINK YOU CAN DO ANYTHING YOU WANT. I'M THE CREATOR AND I. WILL. NOT. HAVE. THIS. THIS IS MY WORLD. SYMPHONY DOESN'T NEED MORE DESTROYERS. I'LL BURN YOUR GODDAMN TREE DOWN BEFORE I LET YOU FUCK WITH WHAT WE'RE TRYING TO DO HERE."

"No! Please!" Echidna begged, dropping to her knees in front of him. "Please! My children are in there. Zeus, apologize!" she said, pointing at him with a glare.

"GODS DO NOT APOLOGIZE!" he said, spreading his arms wide. "IF YOU WANT TO TAKE ME DOWN, DO SO LIKE A TRUE GOD. FIGHT ME, COWARD!"

"We're not gods, you horny bastard!" Echidna yelled at him from the grass. "Gods wouldn't let themselves be trapped inside a tree for thousands of years! You have more children in there than anyone!"

"I DO NOT CARE!" he screamed at space. "THEY CREATED ME, US, THEN IMPRISONED US ONLY TO BE USED AGAIN! I SAY NO! I SAY WE FIGHT!"

"You will lose," Virgil replied calmly.

"THEN WE LOSE ON OUR TERMS!" he responded back with the fury of something once powerful, beautiful in its purpose, being forced into a cage for a long period of time. Walker hadn't noticed before, but there were tears streaming down Zeus's face. It seemed that time in the Tree was not the most pleasant, and after sitting in there for millennia, it had done a real shitty job on the king of the gods' psyche.

Walker knew one thing from his time dealing with the Slicer: He knew he was protected, that the Alpha Protocol wouldn't let him come to harm. He also wasn't so emotionally turmoiled that he didn't understand Echidna's feelings. He couldn't imagine what it would be like to potentially lose your children. But lately, Walker had been toughening himself up.

Lessons from his rougher childhood and time in the military rose to the fore of his thoughts. He couldn't allow worry or sympathy to affect him. Regarding those in the Tree of the Gods, they might have some importance, certainly. But he also had to weigh their importance with the potentially billions of lives Symphony may have in the future. He knew that they could help him succeed, that they might even be the only way for him to succeed in the Alpha Protocol.

But he couldn't let them fuck everything up. If he placed Zeus in the world somehow, he needed him to do what he asked and told, not to run off and start smiting anything he didn't like the look of. He was still viscerally angry, and his body shook from the adrenaline pumping through his veins. But, unlike the time with Nicholas, he had at least a modicum of self-control. He looked at Echidna, his finger close to the World Editor button.

"Why should I let you live?" he asked Echidna, knowing Zeus would just give another suicidal answer. But it was Minos who answered first.

"Because we're here to help you."

"Because we can assist you in your world," Echidna supplied right after.

"Virgil?" Walker asked his only friend here. Rimi was a friend, true, and he shouldn't forget that, but Virgil knew everything about him and wouldn't steer him wrong.

The large squirrel placed a paw against his chin in thought, then said, "Perhaps if you can find it in yourself to understand . . . this person here," he waved a hand at Zeus. "Then, perhaps they can also understand that you are not their former Creator and had no choice in being selected for the Alpha Protocol."

Zeus listened to Virgil with a thunderous expression. Based on the redness encapsulating his neck, he was refusing to release his hold on his rage. Snorting, he tried to walk away by pushing through Virgil, but the elastic barrier appeared and knocked him down onto his ass instead. His face looked like pure shock incarnate.

"Z . . . can't you just . . . do it this once? Can't you let go of whatever . . . what's the word?" Echidna asked.

"Limp-dick?" Rimi tried.

"No, small one. That is never something I would associate with Zeus."

"Superiority complex," Minos offered, showing a surprising vocabulary.

"Yes." She stood up from the grass, quickly stepping over and putting a hand on the large man's arm. "Can't you let go of your complex? We are not gods, Zeus. We never were. We were just given power, unearned, and once the Creator knew of what she had made and the influence we had on Earth, they put us away. They had good reason to do so." She pointed at each of them. "Our history was filled with chaos. We did not rule well, and now, it is time for another to try. A child born from the world we once nurtured. Can you not see that? See that this is the result, the fruits of your work."

Zeus sighed in the grass, not a great suffering sigh, but a small one, with a quick inhalation that followed.

"Zeus . . . We need this. We need to be part of something. Something that Walker here can provide. Purpose . . . again. The new Creator, who hasn't mistreated his denizens no matter what Hades may say of the Slicer, is not a bad mortal. He could do this for us. He could give us a new shot."

Minos dropped into the grass next to him. "Please."

That was all he said, but it seemed to do the trick. Zeus stood up and brushed at imaginary dirt, which made Walker think that this wasn't really grass, but he had to move on as the large man started speaking.

"For you, Echidna, and the children. I will . . . try."

"Thank you."

"Okay, mortal, you wanted us, so you have us."

Walker held up a finger. "Technically, I didn't know what was in the Tree." His rage wasn't done with him. He couldn't turn it off on a dime, but he knew it would fade as time went. However, while he could forgive Zeus and his attempted bullying, he would never forget it. No matter his emotional growth, that just wasn't a part of who he was.

"As you like to say, what-whatever," Zeus replied as he tried to seem nonplussed. "We already know what the first step is." He nodded at the other two, who nodded back. They each put out a wrist and, with a nail on their hands, dug into their skin, forcing blood to pool.

"Jesus Christ. You could have just spit or something," Walker said.

"Ahem," Virgil commented, "Blood is the best conductor for situations like this one."

"If you are going to do something, do not do it with weak intent," Echidna said calmly as her red blood dripped into the green grass.

"One moment," Virgil said as he went to each and gathered a small amount in the palm of his hand. Walker's overlay lit up.

[. . . Scanning . . .]
Foreign entities have presented Dante with new genetic material!
New modifications can now be used.
New evolutions are now available.
A new entity type is now available: Primigenial
A new entity type is now available: Mythological

Optional tasks available.
Special circumstances found.
Tasks may now be assigned by those who donate genetic material for use.

Knowing Virgil could see his updates, Walker asked, "What does that mean?"

He apparently had an answer as he pulled Walker aside and out of the gods' hearing range, whispering, "They can give you tasks that can unlock abilities that the previous Creator, the one from your homeworld, had. But you need to stop trying to delete the Tree of the Gods. You cannot."

Walker ran a hand down his face, feeling drained from all of the events since placing the battlefrog. "Why can't I?"

"Because, once it matured, it connected deep with this small world. Have you not noticed?"

Walker looked around but it still looked the same. "Noticed what?"

"The size of it, Walker, the size! It's two percent larger than it was."

"How the fuck am I supposed to notice that? I'm not a squirrel robot like you."

"Either way, if you remove it, there is a chance it will destabilize this world, and expel us into space. We would not die, but we also would have great difficulty doing anything with Symphony in the future."

"At some point, I'm going to have some agency here and get to stop asking questions, right?"

"Of course," Virgil said, but he didn't sound very enthused.

Maybe all of my memories affected his personality more than I think. He keeps taking on the teacher role whenever he can, Walker thought.

"Ah, I see." Zeus's voice landed like a landslide.

"What do you see?" Walker asked.

"I see that we can now shape this world just as much as you . . . Creator. Wouldn't you like to know how to empower your entities? Wouldn't that be just the ticket to succeed? All we would need is—"

"Wait, wait!" Echidna said as she glared at Zeus. "It doesn't have to be like that." She looked over at Walker. "I understand. You didn't ask for us, just like we didn't ask for imprisonment. We're all a part of this; it is kismet, fate."

"Fate's an asshole," Walker said, seeing a reluctant nod from Zeus.

"Yes, they are. You have no idea." Another nod from Zeus. "Creator, this is special. You have magic, and that is wonderful, but our power never worked through magic. It worked through the soul. We, the Primigenials of Earth, gained power from souls and faith. We can give you that, but it is dangerous."

"How?" Walker asked. He didn't know much about the power of the soul, but he'd loved mythology as a kid. It had been like crack to him. But, as he knew, when a story was retold over and over, exchanged by human minds, things had a tendency to go sideways. Original meanings and facts disappeared.

The thing was, right now he only had some fish, moss, and one large frog. While empowering his entities was important, it would take time, and he didn't have a lot of that right now.

Time Remaining until next battle: 51+ hours

While he was thinking of all this, Echidna looked over at Zeus, who nodded.

"We'll walk you through it bits at a time, as it can be overwhelming to mortals," she said with a large amount of sympathy laced into her voice.

"I am not a mortal," Virgil said.

"You also do not have a soul, as you were created directly by the protocol," Zeus said. "Souls can only be interacted with—changed—by other souls. We need to build and train Walker to withstand what is coming, as we are not allowed to alter the system directly."

Walker gave a sympathetic look to Virgil before looking back at Zeus. "That sounds amazing. It really does. But we don't have a lot of time until the next battle. While I appreciate you being willing to help me with a new scale of power, it may be something that has to wait."

Minos nodded and stepped forward. "The first step is always the longest, but with three of us, we can get you through it quickly."

"You're sure?" Minos nodded with confidence, making Walker feel better about things. "Great! Then break it down for me. What's the first step?"

Echidna grimaced. "We need you to open your soul to us."

"Open my soul?"

"Yes . . . and it will be very painful for you. Walker, you will have to perform great introspection and look deeper within than you ever have before."

"Greaaaaat."

CHAPTER TWENTY-ONE

What Lies in the Darkness (I)

Echidna stepped over, putting her hands on his shoulders. "I understand that tone to be sarcasm. But Walker, you don't have to worry. We'll be with you the whole time."

He looked at her and then noticed that everyone else was staring at him. He tried not to be uncomfortable, as standing in front of people who were waiting for you to do something was what teachers did every day. But there was a key difference between high school kids and literal gods.

With kids, you have the power to pass or fail them, achieving a measure of control simply by holding the teaching position. Most teachers call it acting. When you're teaching, it's like being on stage all day. Be perfect. Shiny teeth. Clean clothes. Optimistic and charming and connect with the kids, and the parents, and each other, and forget about the money . . . you get it. It's all acting. Then, when the final bell rings, a part of you leaks back into the drained sieve of your soul.

This was not that kind of situation.

Walker decided to stall while his brain caught up with what was about to happen. "At some point, we need to look in on the battlefrog, you know."

"It will be fine on its own, Walker. Was that not the purpose of creating the Monster System in the first place? So that the monsters became manageable?" Virgil asked. The traitor. He was looking at his screens fairly hard and didn't seem like he understood what he was seeing.

"Fair, but let me identify it real quick," Walker said, moving his hand toward the Monitor ability.

Minos made a high-pitched humming sound, causing Echidna to laugh, and even Zeus cracked a slight smile.

"What?" Walker asked.

"He makes that sound when he feels someone is scared, although I do not blame you," Echidna said with another deep-throated laugh. He tried not to hate her at that moment.

"I'm not scared!" Walker protested, the pitch of his voice betraying the lie. "I fought in a war, goddamnit. Screaming, terror, grammar lessons. That classroom was no joke, and you know, I fought in Afghanistan too."

"Sure," Echidna said with a broad smile Walker could only associate with motherliness. It was the type that said, *I know you're scared, small baby child, but you're being so strong!*

Another traitor appeared. "I can watch over the battlefrog," Rimi said with a hand raised.

Echidna turned to him. "Thank you, little one."

"My name is Rimi."

"That's nice," she said, granting him a smile. Then, with a gentle touch, she patted him on the head. "So, are you ready, Walker?"

He blew air through his lips. It couldn't be much worse than the American education system. "Yeah," He scratched the back of his head. "I guess I am. How do I start?"

"Please sit down," she said as she entered a seated position on the grass.

So Walker sat in the grass, crossing his legs. Echidna moved closer so she sat beside him, two long, well-shaped legs sticking out of her thigh-split dress.

"Okay, my soul is open . . . Ahhhhh, the breeze is so fresh," Walker joked.

"Very funny, mortal. Take this seriously. This is only the first movement toward soul manipulation," Zeus admonished.

"It's okay, Walker," Echidna said with another soft smile. "I hope you contain your humor when this is over. Now, close your eyes."

"That's how I access my soul? I close my eyes and . . . and what? Meditate?"

"Yes, and also no. Please allow me to explain the process to you." Echidna sat up straight, Walker unconsciously doing the same. "Our Creator did this with the original inhabitants of Earth, who you know as the Titans, and they did the same with us. We continued this tradition with the great heroes of our time, increasing the power of their souls exponentially. The Titans themselves were inconceivably powerful, as their souls were so grand that they touched upon the fabric of reality and gained the ability to shape it at will."

She pointed over to the bearded man with his arms crossed. "Only Zeus here is even close to that power. While magic is wonderful, and can allow for many things, astounding things even, it cannot touch upon the soul. It cannot strengthen the core of a being, but instead only reaches the surface. With the addition of the power of the soul to magical beings, you will have creatures who have power that other Creators cannot come close to reaching."

"But?" Walker asked. There was always a *but.*

Echidna smiled. "But the biggest hurdle for any Creator to gain the power of the soul for their world is to find one who can spread the power themselves. The entity with the ability to train others. We call them the Progenitor, and it is quite difficult to reach that point for many people."

"Correct," Virgil added. "The first records of soul power, as the Alpha Protocol registered it, were in the eighth rendition of the second Alpha Protocol, or 2AH. From there, it spread from Creator to Creator throughout different planets in the renditions to follow. It is not common to find a planet with soul power, and extremely uncommon to find one with both soul power and magic." Virgil was still looking at his screens while he said everything.

"So, are evolutions caused by soul power or magic?" Walker asked, thoroughly confused.

Virgil bounced on his toes. "Neither. This is not a simple explanation, but I will try. According to my information from the Alpha Protocol, the accelerated evolutions you see here, which should take hundreds to hundreds of thousands of years, are because each world is implanted with Primordial energy left over from the creation of the new universe. Rather than allow billions to trillions of worlds to form, the Alpha Protocol gathers it into the one million worlds you see before you," he said, pointing at the sky without taking his eyes off of his screens. "That is a great amount of energy brought into specific and localized areas. Once each rendition is complete, the winners have the option of remaining with their worlds, or they can be brought to the Center or even get sent back to their original rendition. Sometimes this means broken planets will float through space, and sometimes this means Galactic Planeteaters will form."

"I swear I've seen that mentioned before," Walker pointed out.

"Regardless, that is the circumstances of the Alpha Protocol and seeding new worlds into universes begun from nothing. It is the energy of Creation, filtered through the systems of the protocol. You have assigned your evolutionary scale, or loose Primordial energy, to directly interact with magic. Magic has a tendency to allow for immediate changes, like gaining abilities such as heat-resistant skin. It also allows for the strengthening of materials, such as the roots and the metal beneath Symphony. Magic allows for great variation, and without a guiding hand like the systems you are building, it is mostly randomized. As you prefer to think through examples, I will provide one."

Walker leaned forward, noticing the confused Primigenials around him doing the same. Virgil still hadn't looked away from his screens. "Let us say that you have an entity with medium to high evolutionary potential. Well, should you place said entity within a cold environment for a lengthy period of time, it might gain cold-resistant skin or even a cold-specific ability. A hot environment will do the same. Magic enhances, but it doesn't necessarily build upon itself. Thankfully, your Monster System will balance that out quite a bit, which is why I fully supported it. Magic can help you win the Alpha Protocol overall, but it is terrible for a world over time without constant nurturing and pruning."

Walker nodded. "Okay, I think I'm following you. So, controlled magic is good, and it'll help focus loose Primordial energy left over from making the rendition, right?"

He saw the corner of a smile on Virgil's face. "Excellent. Yes, Walker."

Walker felt like someone had figuratively patted his head for a moment. He listened back in as Virgil started to speak again.

"Soul power, also known as chi, is entirely different. If magic is what applies to the outside of an entity, soul power applies to the inside, allowing entities to gain greater strength and speed. Making a larger entity and filling it with bulging muscles will certainly give it strength, but enhancing its soul on top of that, which will then filter to the rest of the body as it adapts . . . that is something else."

"Can there be soul evolutions? Like magic has?" Walker asked.

Zeus answered for him. "The soul can evolve, as I am sure you will soon experience, but it cannot evolve from the outside. It's internal only. It's blasphemous to even think of affecting souls externally." He sighed and continued. "We have all experienced what you are about to go through. You will find that although the experience is painful, it is necessary. It will strengthen your sense of self and how you came to be who you are now and allow you to further define your idol," he finished, pointing at the small lightning bolt emblem pinned to his robe.

"That just makes me think even more questions, man," Walker lamented. "But we'll get there when we get there. Rather than just going with more questions, I'd like to get some answers." He looked over at the yellow-eyed woman. "Echidna, let's do this."

She nodded and started to speak in a soothing voice. "Eyes closed like we spoke of, and I want you to picture a black wall. There are no bricks, no images, just darkness—pure darkness. Do you see it?"

"I don't see anything," Walker joked.

"Good. Now, I want you to imagine a large jar in the forefront of the darkness. It is impossible to fill, but you're going to try anyway. Put every bit of emotion, thought, and instinct you can into the jar. Feed it. Visualize it as taking in everything about you. You are empty; you are the darkness that surrounds the jar. Listen to my words: you are empty, you are the darkness that surrounds the jar. You are empty; you are the darkness that surrounds the jar. You are empty . . ."

Walker began to tune out her words as he fell deeper and deeper into a trance-like state, focusing only on the jar in his mind. It took him a long time, hours even, to get to a point where no more scraps of thought and emotion could flow through him.

As he settled into a meditative calm, unbeknownst to him, Echidna started to glow softly as she continued to repeat the words. It wasn't the cyan of magic or the golden glow of creation, but rather the same yellow color of her eyes. Gradually, it started to drain away from the rest of her body and settle onto a single hand. She placed it against Walker's chest, but he was so deep within himself that he couldn't tell someone was touching his body. As she pressed her hand against his chest, the yellow glow began to drain into him and fade away beneath his skin. Echidna's eyes slowly lost some of their luster as she continued to funnel her power into Walker.

As she began to sag in her seated position, she felt Minos place a hand on her shoulder. A bronze color erupted around him, much more powerful than the yellow that had gathered around Echidna, and began draining into her as well. She couldn't look at him to express her gratitude as this was the hardest part, the first mind-to-soul connection, and she needed to focus entirely on Walker. The transfer of power from Minos, to Echidna, to Walker took quite some time as he continued to sit quietly amongst them.

There were dangers here, extreme dangers, but Echidna was quite ancient by Walker's concept of time and she had developed powerful control over the process. This was why her past students and progeny had been called *monsters*. She had granted them the connection when they were all just small children, so the power could develop and grow as their bodies did.

That wasn't what was happening now. Instead, this was effectively a soul shock treatment, which should only be completed on those who didn't have the benefits of a teacher early on in life. Finally, she felt Walker's body begin to push back and withdrew her power. If she continued to infuse him, she might overburden his soul, causing a complete internal collapse as her own power took over his body.

The rest was on him now.

For the longest time, he saw only darkness. It was . . . comforting. Unlit rooms had never bothered him. He had always slept best when lights were a non-factor, and he could fully relish in the feeling of being one with his surroundings. He had placed blackout curtains in his old apartment because once every few months his insomnia would kick his ass, and they helped him knock out on those rare days he was allowed to call in sick.

There was joy here—something profound and on the edge of his mind. But as much as he relished in the purity of this feeling, it was due to end, as a yellow light began to creep into his peaceful solitude from the outside.

The light encroached on his dark surroundings, blending into a gradient of yellow and black until it reached the center of his vision. Once it hit, everything flashed white, and suddenly, his perspective changed. It was like instead of looking at a dark room, he was now standing directly in it.

He looked around, and the darkness changed to a sea of yellow. The only details to be found were creases in the edges of the environment that made it seem like he was in a three-dimensional box. While he continued to inspect the changes, one of the sides lit up, and a screen flickered into his vision. It was from the view of a short man walking around a living room that for some reason seemed quite familiar.

A yellow dog zoomed by, running toward the ting-ting-ting of his food hitting a bowl. The short man watched it for a moment, laughed delightfully, and chased after it. Walker realized what this was—a memory—a memory from his childhood.

The screen zipped time forward, and he saw his father reading the paper at a smallish scuffed round table. It was morning, and he was drinking coffee while Walker's mom sat next to him, speaking of what was new in her over-bloated family. Hundreds of cousins. A relic of the boomer times when people got freaky after not having freakiness for so long. Following his extended and womanless time in Afghanistan, Walker could certainly relate. His father looked at him, sitting at the table with some half-eaten pancakes on a plate in front of him, and said something that had stuck in his mind for a long time.

"You need to eat all of your food, Walker," he said with a stern expression.

"Why?" memory-Walker asked in a childish voice.

His father put his mug down and looked at him. "I've said this before, but you apparently do not remember, so I'll say it again. If you take on something, you have a responsibility to finish it, no matter what it is. Be it food, a job, or even something silly, like a movie or book."

"But why does that matter, Daddy?"

"He doesn't understand, Gene," his mother said, looking at her hands as she sat across from them.

Looking at her, he said, "He needs to." Then he turned back to Walker. "You're probably still too young to get it, but I've always found that who you are is defined early in life. I've met plenty of children at work who have integrity and are downright honest people, and I've met others who are thieving pukes who don't deserve what they have. Entitlement is a plague, Walker. You picked up that many pancakes from the tray, meaning your mother and I have less for ourselves. You take, and others do not receive. That is why you always finish what you've started, Walker, as each action you take has ramifications for others. Be wise with your words and careful with your actions. That's the Reed way."

"Finish up your pancakes, dearest," his mother said with encouragement.

So, although Walker was already full, he ate the last three pancakes on his plate and waddled back to his room to get ready for school, a bloated stomach making him uncomfortable.

The screen flickered again, and judging by the height of the view, Walker could tell this was a few years later. He'd hit a small growth spurt in elementary school, and if he guessed correctly, this was fourth grade. The screen showed him walking out of Mrs. Jorgenson's class and toward the lunch line. Nobody around Walker spoke to him. He'd had few to no friends, his personality not perfectly meshing with the kids around him.

His father had received a promotion and they'd just moved there, better pay equaling better housing and schools, according to the tenets of capitalism. To put a cherry on top of being the new kid, Walker's head was shaved bald. There had been a lice outbreak at his old school right before they'd moved, and his mother felt shaving his head was the best option. He knew now how fucked up it was, that she could've just washed his hair with a special kind of shampoo, but she chose to shave him. He was born with blonde hair and brown eyes, but after the shave, his hair grew in as a light brown color. Now, everything about him was brown, from hair to eyes and skin. It was not a pleasant time for him.

He was toward the front end of the middle of the line when someone shoved him from behind. Falling to his knees, he felt them scrape badly on the old striated concrete and tried his best to keep the tears in his eyes when laughter broke out around him. They said things like "Stupid new kid" and "Baldy fall down" while he stayed there. Young Walker stood up to his feet and felt the burn from the scrapes on his knees as his skin stretched. Warm liquid ran down the edges of his shin bones as he reached his full and unimpressive height.

Walker turned around and looked at his attacker, already knowing who it was. Joey Vade. He was the kid who always blamed him whenever someone farted in the class, and kept saying mean things to him and bumping him in the hallways. He was a bully, and Walker had finally had enough of his overt threats and physical punishment to take action. Everyone had a line for when they would fight back, and he had moved past his.

He pulled his leg back and swung it hard, kicking Joey in the balls with enough force that he could feel the bounce as they pushed into the undercarriage where his hips met. Joey fell to the ground with a gasp while the kids moved back from the both of them. What should've been a funny incident in their minds, nothing other than picking on a new kid again, had now become a fight. But Walker wasn't done.

He calmly walked over and tilted Joey's head up from his kneeling position, then punched him right in the eye, hurting his own hand in the process. His dad's boxing lessons had kicked in, so he'd made sure to rotate his wrist and turn his shoulder for just the right amount of power. The mistake most people make is not punching *through* what you're trying to hit. If you just punched at something, you'd get a weak hit that didn't do much damage. But through them? That was a different scale entirely. Joey fell back to the ground and started to cry as Walker stood over him victoriously.

The yard duties, as they were called back then, finally arrived and grabbed them both. Joey got a one-day suspension and Walker two, which his mother futilely protested. The yard duties only saw him doing the attacking and suspended Joey just because of Walker's word. He had rarely lied since arriving, and Mrs. Jorgenson had reported seeing Joey pick on him before. When his father asked him why he did it, he simply said, "A Reed always finishes what they start." His father clapped him on the back a few times and nothing more was said. It was a fond memory of his, and Joey never messed with him again.

Walker reflected on that for a moment before the screen stopped flickering and a different one lit up. Was this all just memories? What was happening here?

CHAPTER TWENTY-TWO

What Lies in the Darkness (II)

The screen updated again before Walker could really understand what he was seeing. This time, Walker saw himself as an early teenager trying to talk to a girl in class.

She was pretty, in that high school acne kind of way, but he remembered liking her for her laugh. So, he told as many jokes as he could, good and bad. The young never knew when to stop with that kind of thing, beating a horse so dead it may as well be dog food and glue.

Apparently, his most recent attempt had been a success, as she was laughing, a delightful tinkling echoing around the room. One of the girls sitting nearby turned at her desk. "Why are you talking to him? He's ugly." She gave teenage Walker a glare as if blaming him for his own acne and general dumpiness.

"I think he's funny," the laughing girl replied, backing him up. She switched over to a bright smile and he returned it, feeling better about himself. It was a swift return to the overembellished jokes while the mean girl, whose name was Allison, turned back to the front of the class with a flick of her dirty blonde hair. Walker never went on any dates with the smiling girl and her laugh, but funnily enough, he did date the girl who called him ugly.

They dated for over a year, which, in high school terms, was a lifetime. She had been cruel in a sort of way, like yelling at fast food workers who were just doing their best for a buck, but beggars couldn't be choosers, and Walker was no Adonis. The real reason they had broken up wasn't, in fact, how cruel she could be with other people. Instead, it was because she cheated on him with a friend of his, and in some fucked up kind of way, had tried to somehow make it his fault. He watched the end of their relationship and felt better that he hadn't fallen for her any deeper than he had. Walker had never cheated on a girl and never would.

The screen flickered, and Valerie appeared.

He felt his heart freeze up. He didn't know how he was having a physical reaction inside his own mind, but it was there, and it was painful. He watched as they had their first conversation at a Pizza Hut, of all places. She smiled, her green eyes lighting up with something . . . special. Something only she had.

The memories flashed by, and he couldn't do anything but watch as they went out on dates, went to movies, and even danced a few times, although that was never Walker's strength. She, however, was a phenomenal dancer. They moved in together and eventually got out of the military together. It all lined up like it was perfect.

Walker went to college, graduated, and got a job. Teaching. But that was when he saw things turn downward. He came home each day tired, burned out mentally, and just didn't make time for her. It was a dark mirror to his thoughts from not too long ago. He hadn't prioritized her enough.

He watched the last few weeks flash by with a heavy pit in his stomach. It was all recent in his mind, having happened just before he quit his job and got sent to the protocol. He watched as she tried to make overtures, to reestablish their connection, but they fell on ears that didn't want to listen. By now, the pit was a cold burn deep in his chest. The scenes on the screen ended with their last night together, him begging, holding a ring, and her closing a door.

The screen changed again, and Walker watched, in a deep spiral of darkness, as he saw a girl he hadn't thought of for a long time. Jessica. She had Down syndrome and had been his neighbor before his father's promotion and their subsequent move. She had always been very kind to him, and they would play, laughing all the way, with different toys throughout her house. She lived in a manor while Walker had to share a room with his aunt. It just made sense to always go to her house. He hadn't seen her since he was around eight and had always remembered her as the kindest person he'd ever met.

At this moment, she was explaining why the Colorado Rockies were her favorite baseball team. "They're the best; you just don't know."

"But why?" Walker asked. His dad had taken him to a few L.A. Dodger games, and he'd picked them as his favorite team out of strict loyalty to the family. That and their all-star player Darryl Strawberry.

"Try on my hat," she said, grabbing it from where it was hanging on the wall. Walker put it on and didn't notice anything special, but he didn't say that because he knew she was sensitive about them. Each was always kept in pristine condition.

"Okay, now what?" he asked her.

"You don't feel it?" she asked with a confused look. "That hat is from my daddy. My mom says he's away on a business trip, and I haven't seen him for a while. It's the best hat I have, though. You can feel him through it."

Walker didn't understand, but he agreed it was a very nice hat.

"You're nice," she said, smiling.

The screen shifted, and he got a view of him and his mother walking away from their big house. Walker had an odd look on his face as he spoke. "Mom, where's Jessica's dad?"

They got into their new car, a blue Dodge Durango his mother loved, before she said, "Oh honey, he left when she was born. Some men just can't . . . deal with it . . . when their children don't turn out the way they want them to. It's no fault of the child's, though, and Jessica is such a sweet girl." She turned the key in the ignition and they headed home as Walker thought it over. He came to a decision that burned in his chest.

"When I have kids, I'll always take care of them."

"That's why you're my favorite," his mother said without looking at him, a smile on her face.

The screen flickered, and his oldest friend, Matt, appeared. They had met their sophomore year in high school English, striking up a friendship over how stupid the class seemed to be. In hindsight, that was one of the best English classes he'd ever taken, as Mr. Lenner had let them focus on their own writing and not what the state prescribed. He had started to love writing and the breakdown of words from that class.

Matt was not a tall man but he worked out consistently, even in his early teen years. Between his fitness and those sharp blue eyes, he always seemed to win over the girls. More than a few times, a girl had grown close to Walker, only for him to find out she was just trying to get closer to Matt. Matt always rejected them, though. He was a good friend and a stand-up guy who Walker never truly felt he deserved. He watched as they shared a few jokes, showing their camaraderie developing over time before the screen flickered again.

Walker knew this moment with full clarity. It was the last time they'd spoken in person and it was an old argument, at that. Matt had moved to San Diego and he and his wife were trying to have a kid. They were going to have a baby whether Matt wanted to or not; at least, that's what his wife said, but that wasn't what they were talking about right now.

"Just quit," Matt said for the second time. "You're not actually happy there, and I spoke to Valerie last week. Dude, she's not happy either."

"You know I can't just quit, a Reed—"

"Finishes what they start, yeah, I know, genius," Matt interrupted. "But, if it's killing you, why the fuck would you stay?"

"Think of the children, Matthew!" Walker joked.

"It's not a joking matter, man. You're all fucked up. Valerie said you're hardly sleeping anymore and you have no time for yourself, always working every weekend. It's not good, dude." Matt ran a hand through his already thin and further thinning blonde hair. They were at a coffee shop in Santa Barbara, near where the Borders used to be. "Look, I'm going to be a dad one day, which means you're going to have a pseudo-nephew one day as well. You need to be alive to be a terrible uncle to them. And that may not happen as I honestly think this job may be killing you."

"I'm fine, Matt, really. Valerie and I can figure it out, and what am I going to do otherwise? California's not cheap, and we barely make rent even with Val's higher salary."

Matt took a sip of too-hot coffee with a grimace. "I don't know, but you're smart enough to figure it out, as long as you have the right people around you."

"I have no idea why you drink it when it's that hot. Cold coffee or nothing."

"Stop changing the subject. You do that, you know. When you're uncomfortable with something."

Walker sighed. "I know. Wanna see something?"

"As long as it's not your tiny limp-dick, sure," Matt said with a smile.

Walker pulled out his phone and showed him a picture of a ring. The stone matched the color of Valerie's eyes, as he'd never much liked diamonds or the inflated price tag that came with them.

Matt looked at it and Walker burst out, "Whatcha think?"

"Oh, man! I had no idea, although it's about time. Where are you gonna get the money for this? It's too nice for the likes of you and your shitty teacher paycheck."

"I've been tutoring after school for the last few weeks to save up. That's why I haven't been home as much. Plus, even when I am home, good tutoring pay requires good tutoring lesson plans. Sure, I'm exhausted a lot, but it'll be worth it in the end. I figure it'll take me a few years."

"Dude, that's great, man. I'm happy for you."

"Thank you," Walker said with a smile. Matt roughly patted his shoulder, and they kept talking throughout the day, eventually leaving the coffee shop to walk down State Street toward the beach.

"When are you coming to San Diego?" Matt asked as they were both getting ready to part ways. "I can't always be driving up here; at some point, it's your turn."

"I'll get there after I propose to Valerie, promise."

"You better. You're one of the best guys I know, if not the best, but you're entirely too focused on your work at times," he said with a small shake of his head.

"True. But as the wise say, *Work worth doing, is work done right*," he replied with two thumbs up.

"You're an asshole," Matt said as he turned and walked away.

"True!" Walker yelled at his back.

The screen flickered as the image died away, along with a piece of Walker's heart.

That was the last time he'd talked to Matt, and he missed him dearly. It was rare to find a friend like that in any world. He wasn't disparaging Virgil, but his bond with Matt was powerful. He hoped he and his family were okay.

The final screen popped up, and it wasn't like the previous ones. It showed Walker just sitting and drawing. Before his dysgraphia had really reared its head, he remembered drawing all the time. Fantastical creatures had bounded across the page. Mysterious worlds would pop into his imagination, and with his mother's friendly encouragement, he'd draw and draw until he ran out of the good paper. Then, he'd steal from his dad's old printer and draw some more.

Now, as he watched his young self sit in his room and draw, he realized just how shit of an artist he had been. It was unfair, he understood, to judge a child's artwork, but that was still terrible. What was he drawing? His young self got up and ran to the kitchen to show his mother. She took it with the oohs and aahs that any mother would for their child, then put it on the refrigerator.

"You didn't name it?" his mother asked.

"It's just a squirrel," young Walker replied, and ran back to his room to draw some more artwork for his mother. He created art the world had never, and probably should never, see. Fifty-foot-tall spiders with acid dripping from their fangs running at a city with their army of children. A small family holding hands beside a great big tree as a squirrel overlord pointed at them with a sword. A man in a cape with a *W* on the back, flying in and saving people with outrageous powers.

The flicker moved forward to a time when Walker, at the age of seventeen, pulled someone out of a car accident and got them away to safety, only moments before a small explosion occurred in a formerly quiet intersection. The man thanked him once before passing out, and he stayed by his side while waiting for the ambulance he had called after checking on him.

Flicker.

Walker was now in an elevator at a hospital, waiting on test results for his knees. He had grown a full foot in a year, and it was causing him a lot of pain. A man started to choke in the elevator on a part of a sandwich he had been eating when Walker entered. He performed the Heimlich maneuver his dad had said could save somebody's life someday, and got the man's airway clear. Two weeks later, the man found Walker and gave him a walking stick he had made in Scotland called a sheleighleigh. Walker thought it was a pretty funny story and would sometimes tell it to his students.

Flicker.

It showed a woman on a motorcycle being run over by a bus Walker was sitting on. Eighteen people sat on that bus, but he was the only one to get off and help the woman. She had broken both arms and both legs, and her chest was caved in. He was in the military and had gone through just enough medical training to know she wasn't going to make it, so he instead held her hand and spoke softly to her as she died only a few moments later. A few minutes after her expiration, the rest of the people on the bus got off. The Air Force brass tried to give Walker an award and a ceremony, but he rejected both. He told them they should be ashamed of those eighteen people on the bus, as they'd had the same training he did. There was no further talk of awards.

Flicker.

Walker was in Afghanistan, and one of his sergeants took a round to the outside of his leg. The man was completely lucid, and carrying a Pepsi soda for some reason, as Walker carried him to the helicopter under gunfire and mortar rounds impacting the ground around him. The moment he got the sergeant into the helicopter, he dropped the can and subsequently passed out. Walker called it a magical can and kept it. He never saw the sergeant again.

Flicker.

The screen showed Walker during his last few weeks in the military. He jumped out of the way of a mortar strike and fell into a ditch, tearing all the ligaments in one of his ankles. He had to crawl back to his barracks through a garbage-filled latrine. He didn't tell anyone how bad the injury was, and tried to pretend he just twisted his ankle. If they found out, they'd keep him there longer, and he was ready to leave. He'd done his duty. He'd finished what he'd started.

Flicker.

At the laundromat, Walker saw a child put a Tide Pod in his mouth. He rushed over and ripped it out of the small boy's mouth while his mother screamed. He told her they needed to go to the hospital and they rushed off, leaving their clothes forgotten in the machines. Two hours later, when the doctor said the child was going to be fine, Walker breathed a sigh of relief. When he returned to the laundromat, he smiled in relief. No one had taken his clothes.

There were other moments, but those were the ones that stuck out the most to him. That time he put out a fire in the school bathroom twice in one day. That time he got between a kid and his parents, who he knew were abusive. All the school fights he stopped and the soft conversations that followed.

When you're living in the present, you don't really analyze what you're doing and how you're doing it. You just . . . do. When Walker was speaking with people, he had a tendency to tell jokes and take away the solemnity of whatever was happening. But when action called, he was always ready. He knew what to do, how to do it, and what the best course was to take. Walker was a natural, reactionary force.

The screens all flickered away, and the yellow began to bleed into the black again. Walker thought over what he'd seen and wondered what he was supposed to get from this. It was like those times when people say they can see their whole life flash before their eyes, right before they die. It made him consider everything he'd seen. What had he learned from this?

He had a strict family, but one who cared about him and wanted him to always do his best. They taught him to always finish what he'd started.

He was a fuckup with relationships, but he always tried to make things better, and he loved hard. His relationships taught him that you couldn't ignore the smallest things as they might become larger problems later on.

He was an okay friend, but his friends always knew he cared about them, and he hoped they still cared about him even now. His friends had taught him that it was okay to self-care, and that being a good person wasn't anything to look down upon.

He was great in moments of crisis, and wouldn't hesitate to help someone in need, even if they didn't know they needed help. He'd learned from his own experiences that he wasn't a superhero, but no one was, and all you can do is your best in any given situation. Often, just trying to do your best was enough to succeed.

The yellow receded, and in its place grew a deep forest green. The more Walker thought over what he had seen, the more the green color grew, soon overtaking the black and only leaving the yellow in its place.

In the end, he knew who he was and who he wasn't. He was Walker Reed, and while he certainly wouldn't call himself a hero, he did find heroic-like tendencies in himself. He would always strive to be better. He would always grow to build a better future for himself and those around him. And he would always help those in need. That was Walker Reed.

The last of the yellow shattered, and the green took over. He was still within his mind, so he mentally pushed his way out and found himself back on his tiny planet with the pseudo-gods and the squirrels.

Immediately, Walker felt a sense of change in himself. His mind felt clearer than he'd ever experienced before, like his thoughts had been damp and had finally dried out. He stretched his arms out to his sides and felt his body move differently. It was as if heavy weights had been holding him down all of his life, and they were finally lifted.

Finally, he opened his eyes, and a green wave pushed itself away from his body, buffeting those around him. It didn't have a physical weight, just a forest green color spreading out from him as a central point. Echidna tracked the wave with her yellow eyes and nodded once.

"Twenty-five feet, or thereabouts."

"Twenty-five and four inches," Virgil corrected.

"Indeed. How far did your first breakthrough go, Z?" she asked the bearded man.

"Around fifteen feet, but remember, I was there for your own. Six feet, was it?" he asked with a bit of cheekiness. Echidna blushed.

"Well, congratulations, Walker."

Walker was still adjusting to the changes in his body and just picked up on what they were saying. "Congratulations on what?" he asked.

"You have a very powerful soul," she said without a smile. "Let's see just how far you can go."

CHAPTER TWENTY-THREE

A Green, Green World

Walker stretched his back, still marveling at how good his close-to-middle-aged body felt.

Physically, he was better than ever, but his emotional state was another thing. It still felt like his innermost feelings had been curb-stomped by an elephant wearing stilettos. In retrospect, most of his memories seemed sad with a tinge of . . . goodness. Was goodness a word? Didn't matter, he just made it one.

Walker was always pushing himself to be a better person. Better than the day before, at least. That was why he wanted to build Symphony to be a planet of persistent growth. Where each day might contain a brighter sunrise than the last. He cracked his neck and looked over at the yellow-eyed woman who seemed to be waiting for him.

"How are you feeling?" Echidna asked with some concern.

"Like a tractor just ran over my emotional balls," Walker said. "Physically, I feel outstanding. The protocol already healed my old ankle injury, but this is different. It's like I just drank ten Red Bulls, only without the shakes and existential dread that normally follows."

"I did not know the world continued with animal sacrifices, Walker."

"What?"

Echidna gave a confused smile. "You said it was as if you had drank ten red bulls."

"Huh . . . Oh! No, no. Sorry." Walker smiled. "That's just their name. They're energy drinks. Terrible for your body, but pretty great at putting a big pep in your step."

Echidna nodded. "Ah, I see. That's generally how it is, and it never truly fades." She smiled before it quickly fell away. "The first stage can be quite painful for those who don't accept themselves as they are."

"What happens then?" Walker couldn't help but ask. The great bearded one answered for him.

"They emotionally implode into a quivering mess of uncertainty. Eventually, they become a . . ." He had to think for a moment before saying, "potato."

"Oh . . . that's cool, I guess," Walker said, trying not to think of what he could've potentially experienced. Then remembered what Echidna had mentioned before. "Wait, what did you mean I have a powerful soul?"

"What color are your eyes?" Zeus questioned him from the side.

What a stupid question.

"Brown, of course, like most people from our world."

"Wrong," Zeus said with a shake of his head. "Your eyes are now a striking green."

What? Oh, wait, I didn't say that out loud.

"What?"

"Walker," Echidna said, placing a soft hand on the side of his arm. "The first step to gaining soul power is to face yourself and the choices you've made throughout your life. The sooner you set yourself on a path or a code to live by, the stronger your sense of self becomes."

"A code? Like what?"

Zeus stepped forward. "That is for you to decide."

Echidna made a shushing motion at him before turning back to Walker. "The more you live by your code, the more powerful your soul becomes. It doesn't matter what path you choose, only that you stick to it, and that it is a reflection of the person you are choosing to be."

"Look," Minos said as he stepped forward. He got uncomfortably close to Walker's face and pointed at his own eyes. Initially, Walker thought they were a light shade of brown, but as he looked a little closer, he realized they were actually bronze, just like the armor around his body.

Walker turned his head and looked at Zeus, who obligingly stepped forward, and found that his eyes, too, were different. What he had thought was a light shade of blue was in fact white with small streaks of blue around the edges, like lightning held within puffy clouds.

"Physical changes are a part of the process, Walker," Zeus rumbled. "It is like a warning to the rest of the universe, saying *This one has power.*" He raised his fist and clenched it. "The greater the power, the more the changes as your soul seeks to imprint upon your physical self. No one can go through the dynamic shift of actively using their soul without changes becoming apparent."

"Why are you being nicer to me?" Walker asked of the bearded man. "Before, you gave a vibe that said *MORTAL, I WILL SMITE YOU.* Now you're actually being helpful, and I don't get it."

"That is a simple enough answer. You are one of us," he said with a grand spread of his muscled arms. "Let me explain this to you. The first step appears as a slight change to the color of an Awakened's eyes, representing that a being has experienced the internal stage. The moment you experience said stage, your soul begins to show itself in a physical way, creating changes to how your body and mind work. You'll find yourself stronger and faster, and you will age slower as time has less of an effect on you. It is a great boon, the eternal effect of the soul directly impacting the physical body. The more you pull from your soul, the more you stretch it and strengthen it over time, the greater the physical changes will become apparent."

Walker thought it over. "So you're saying you don't spend twenty hours every day in the gym, drinking protein shakes and staring at girl's asses as you pretend not to."

"I don't understand what you're saying," Zeus said, looking at Echidna with confusion.

She redirected Walker with a wave of her arm. "As you progress through the second stage, you will find those physical changes reflected in the strength and speed of your muscles and tendons. The greater the soul's connection to the body, the more control an Awakened has over it. We call it the physical stage. As you learn to sheathe your body in the power of your soul, your physical strength and speed will naturally grow."

"Sweet! Can we get started now?" Walker said as he bounced on his toes.

Echidna shook her head. "It takes time, which you've stated you do not have. Also, your soul has not yet acclimated to its new form. When it does, we will continue if you are willing to further walk down the road of the Awakened."

Walker canted his head at that. "So that's what I am now? An Awakened?"

"Yes, it is a term we use for ourselves, although throughout time, there have been different words. Gods, angels, djinn, and so on. Those who reach the third stage change even further, depending upon their icon. Some even begin to modify their body and move away from the standard form of humanity. I've seen Awakened who grow wings, horns, and even plated armor for skin. Our Creator tried to replicate these modifications in her monsterology, or study of monsters. She experimented with them, trying to develop those that could be Awakened at birth."

Echidna paused for a moment in thought. "Did she ever find a way to do so?" she asked Zeus, who just shook his head. "Either way, she created entities which you would know to be myths and legends, but were standard in the first rendition of her world. Dragons, the minotaurs who were developed to look after Minos here. Entities with unique characteristics and bodies."

"Walker," Virgil said, interrupting for the first time in a while. "You now have two new genetic lines to work from, mythological and Primigenial."

"Oh shit," Walker said, slapping a hand to the top of his head. "With all of the crap I just went through, I'd completely forgotten about that."

"That is only natural," Virgil replied. "The Primigenial genetic lines are directly connected to your new optional tasks from our . . . visitors . . . here. While the mythological lines are open for use."

"Good looking out, Virgil. Okay. Status check, everyone. Rimi, how is our big boy doing?"

Rimi squared his shoulders. "The battlefrog is eating well, Walker. But as I watch him, I can't help but feel that he is lonely."

"Noted, we'll give him some friends in a moment. Virgil, how is the Ecology Subsystem looking? Did you figure out how to get the weather to siphon from Symphony's Mana Trees?"

"Yes, although it is not perfect. If we tie the weather to magic, and the magical density overwhelms an area, it can have a detrimental effect."

"What would that look like?" Walker asked.

"Tornadoes, hurricanes, and powerful hailstorms can spontaneously manifest with too much magical saturation."

"Sooooo . . ." Walker said without a clue. An errant thought wormed its way into his mind. Awakening his soul had surely empowered his body, but now he knew that it did nothing for his mind. He was still a dumbass. Thankfully, he had assistants to help him out in times like these.

Virgil continued speaking. "Any large battles that do not already destroy the land through their magical abilities are likely to also produce deleterious effects on the weather."

"Mmmm, I'll be honest, that also sounds like a positive. It's similar to what we wanted from the Territory System, a warning system for anyone still in the area."

Virgil nodded slowly with a paw on his chin. "Yes, I had not thought of that."

"Why do you care for these mortals?" Zeus asked from the side as Walker froze in place. "You're an Awakened now, and you will live for at least several hundred years. The welfare of lesser beings is beneath you. Create your world, place your servants, and gain enough power to control any sector of this universe you choose."

Walker turned his head slowly and looked at him with a steely gaze. He recalled his oath, and after filtering it through the visions and experiences that he had just gone through, he found it fell in line with who he was as a person.

Who he was choosing to be.

That surety bolstered his soul, and while it didn't tell him the next words to say, he did feel a nudge in his mind, like a mental guideline. He thought that over for a moment, just to make sure something *other* wasn't controlling him. No, it was his thoughts, but now he had something pushing him to follow through. The nudge was closer to seeing the lights turn on for an airplane. Sure in his purpose, Walker spoke.

"It isn't enough to have power or to live for ages. Not when power is used with ill intent, and life is for nothing but the accumulation of even more power. Calling others mortal, as you seem to enjoy doing so much, shows your hand to the listener. Do you not recall I was only just another mortal not long ago? Based upon what I've learned about the Awakened, at some point, so were you. The more you point out your own strength, the more you point out just how much you've come to rely on it to the detriment of everything else, including your understanding of others' needs and wants. Remind me, where is your power, your lightning now?"

"You know it is lost," Zeus responded with some heat in his voice.

"Yes, I do, but you don't seem to get it. I hold the cards here . . . *brother*. I am technically still mortal. But by your own words, I am also an Awakened much like yourself. So, as a representative of both worlds, I have to say: Fuck you and fuck that superior bullshit," Walker finished.

"He's right, you know," Echidna said from the side. "We asked you not too long ago to stop with the, ummm . . ."

"Superiority complex," Minos provided in a small voice.

Echidna smiled at him. "Thank you, dear. Yes, your superiority complex. It has never shown a good side to others. In our time on Earth, you would swoop in on women and charm them with your looks and your powers. Then, after you get the deed done, you start talking down to them." She gave him a disgusted look. "It's horrible, Z. After you mistreated those poor women, they'd get mad and spread rumors about you, affecting all of us by association. Saying you did something strange and horrible, like turn into a bull and molest them."

"Or a swan," Minos helped.

"Or a swan. Right. Or that one time they said you were a horse? You can't do anything like that, but they spread rumors that you're some weird . . . animal molester. Is that right?" she asked Minos, who shrugged. Echidna continued regardless. "Then your followers left you because they were worried they'd be next, and other immortals lost theirs as well in a vicious cycle of lost power and prestige. Just stop already."

"I never did anything like that," Zeus said with a red face. "That was all . . . slander. Yes, it was fully satisfied women slandering my name."

"Not from what I heard," Walker said with a smile, happy to see Zeus feeling the squeeze. He decided to join in. "I heard you turned into an eagle to bang another gorgeous and lonely eagle once."

"NEVER!" Zeus yelled with a thunderous voice. Echidna laughed with a full-throated sound while even Minos tittered. Walker was about to continue poking the king of the gods when Virgil interrupted with a light cough.

"Walker, please look at your time remaining until the next battle," Virgil said.

Walker looked at his overlay.

Time remaining until next battle: 38 hours

"Oh crap, we're running out," he said in shock. "How long was I in my weird mind-place?"

"Quite a long time, Walker," Virgil replied. "That is why I felt it was prudent to remind you. We can use some of our temporal resources, but we're running a little low. The protocol will help with that after the next battle."

"Okay." Walker slammed his hands together, trying to refocus his mind. "So, what do you need for the Weather System to go online?"

"We would need more Mana Trees, but I hesitate."

"Why?"

"Because of your forthcoming Territory System and the requirements established by the Monster System. The drain on the magical atmosphere would require more Mana Trees per landmass. That means we will need to add as we go."

Walker nodded. "True. Rimi said our battlefrog buddy needs some friends, so I'm gonna knock that out real quick. Afterward, we can look at adding some landmasses with more Mana Trees and move on from there."

"That sounds good."

Echidna waved at Walker for his attention. "We'll be by the Tree of the Gods while you work. Call over to us if you need anything. And don't worry. Minos and I'll talk to Zeus about how to counter his, uh"—her face brightened a little—"thousand-year-old problem."

"You got it, and thank you," he said as the three walked over and started to look at the branches and leaves on the large green prison.

Walker pulled up his monitor and identified the battlefrog.

Name: Battlefrog
Genus: Battlefrog
Organism type: Animal
Modifications: Supersized, System-Bound, Steel Claws
Monster System Power Level: Tier 1

He noticed that evolution was gone, and in its place, it showed that the battlefrog was only tier one. He tried zooming into its body so he could view the kernel. The monitor adjusted, showing a light blue coloring in the center of its chest. He hated to do it, but Walker called Virgil over, asking, "How long until it hits tier two, do you think?"

"It is difficult to tell as this is an entirely new frontier for the Alpha Protocol. I think, and this is a guess, that it will take about a month to gain tier two for each monster. But as you add more monsters to the area and the attuned magic is depleted, it will likely begin to take longer. The greater the population, the less there is to go around, at least until we add more Mana Trees."

"Okay, that's in line with what I was hoping. Rimi! How many friends should I give it?" Walker yelled out.

"I would suggest no more than five at a time."

"Why just five?"

"Because they will reproduce on their own when given enough time."

"Okay, sounds good," Walker said as he walked over to the Creation Instrument. He pulled up his overlay and looked at the battlefrog, which was in a new category labeled "Monster System Entities." Walker clicked it and waited as the diagram appeared on the computer screen. There was an option at the bottom he hadn't noticed before, which allowed him to choose the frog's sex.

"Do you two know if we should limit the battlefrogs' gender at all?" Walker asked.

"For this entity, I would suggest starting out with four males and two females overall. They were not known to be territorial with each other on Earth. However, after the modifications, what we know may no longer be accurate."

"Yep, I agree," Rimi piped in.

"Okay, then, here we go," Walker said as he moved his monitor to The Crater. He quickly printed out five images and dropped them in one at a time with little separation.

After they all materialized, Walker started to grow worried. They didn't move or hop around as he expected. Instead, they simply stood still. That is, until the original battlefrog noticed their appearance and hopped over.

The slightly older frog looked at his colleagues with squinted eyes and just sat there for a moment. Suddenly, a tapping sound, deep in its throat, came out of it. Walker was sure, at its size, it would sound like beating drums if he were nearby. The other four finally moved, looking at it. There was a long pause, and then each made a similar sound before hopping around a few times. Walker breathed a sigh of relief as they continued to communicate without attacking each other.

"Alright, that seemed to go well," he said.

Virgil nodded as he looked at the monitor beside him. "I agree."

"I think I'm going to make some landmasses and drop them in. This way, we can finish the ecology task and get the Weather System online at the same time. What do you think?"

"Sounds good," Rimi said with a thumbs-up, looking at his screen.

"What are you going to do?" Walker asked the larger squirrel.

"I am going to look through the new genetic lines again and see if we are able to seed one without destroying Symphony before the next battle. You know what happens if we lose."

"That I do, but you may have to just ignore me. This may take me a while."

"I will be here if you need me," Virgil said, staring at his screen.

Walker looked at the smaller blue squirrel staring at his screen, then at the larger brown one doing the same. "Just like my old classroom," he said with a sigh before changing the Creation Instrument's option from Entity to Landmass.

He'd had an idea about what he should do, and he was determined not to make any more large mistakes. Walker knew that he hadn't been thinking big enough when he first designed Symphony. One landmass centralized with four points wouldn't work for an entire world. He would need to change all of his plans moving forward.

After his transformative soul experience, his thoughts felt clearer. Like his mind's eye could see better. Although it wasn't a purely physical experience, his improved perspective felt like the clouds parting on a sunny day. He could now see that he'd been going about all of this just . . . wrong.

The best way forward wasn't to create one large mass that connected to everything. Instead, he needed to create hundreds, even a thousand locations interconnecting the various ecosystems of Symphony. Places where the sand of the desert could be a step away from an ancient forest. Where each portion and its Mana Trees could be free to change over time as the citizens of Symphony interacted with them.

He selected the Shapes option and chose the almighty hexagon. A hexagon provided six sides and would let him place the pieces of land in any connection he chose, allowing greater creative freedom over time and always syncing with each other by shape. He wouldn't have to worry any longer about perfectly designing every inch. Instead, he'd just have a singular shape that fit.

After the hexagon appeared on the screen, he looked a little closer at all of the options that he hadn't seen when making the giant piece of steel. He didn't know why he hadn't looked over his options before, but he figured it was better late than never. Scanning through, he found an option to rotate the landmass's shape so he could see every side, including the top and bottom.

Rotating it back, he continued to inspect every aspect of the future landmass, moving the object around the screen as he did so. As he continued to grow familiar with the changes, he found a Terraforming button, which, after selecting it, allowed him to depress the ground or raise it up as he chose. That provided some new options that would help as he gained further mastery over the system.

He placed soil on top of the hexagon and copied it over the entire surface, not making the same mistakes as he had in the past. Pushing the Terraforming button, Walker built a few hills into different locations, then placed the rock icon on them, copying that to each as well. He dug a winding trench through the soil and replaced it with the water icon so he could connect it to Symphony's primary river. Logically, he knew that having one water source for his whole world was a bad plan, but this was just the beginning of the planet. The further he expanded, the more sources he would add.

He clicked the Rotation tool and put granite on the bottom so he'd have a uniform design throughout the world. He wanted to add the steel early, so it wouldn't be an issue, but he wasn't sure exactly where to line it up with the future Mana Tree roots, making it a moot point. Walker looked it over and nodded to himself, then printed out the landmass, pulled up the monitor, and put it near the swamp corner.

Again, the landmass was larger than his previous additions, and it slotted in with a click. The hexagon was perfect for his landmasses, with one side facing the current Symphony and another against the mountains of The Crater. This allowed four other connection areas for later expansion.

Walker's overlay lit up and gave him a C+, giving him a little more paper to work with, so he went again, this time adding to the water at the south with little islands holding sand, small rocky areas, and a little bit of soil for future vegetation. Then he did it a second time to really expand the surface area of Symphony with water. Both gave him C's, which he was fine with.

After placing the three new landmasses, he called Virgil over for advice. Following a quick discussion on which seeds would work best in a given area, Walker started placing seeds all across the world. As he worked, Symphony stayed the same, but under the surface, he knew life was just waiting for something to happen. C and D grades were unleashed as trees exploded in space and new forms of magic-deficient vegetation spread across the world. There was a slight delay with each genus, as they had to place them in the Evolution Chamber to apply the deficiency modification, but it was worth it, and having two chambers instead of one sped them up at an appreciable rate.

Walker never stopped, placing seed after seed, envisioning how it would all turn out when he was done. Each would be their own specific sphere of nature. Sand met water, water would meet trees, and across Walker's world, he finally added grass.

As he backed out of the monitor, he noticed that the structure of Symphony was a little cattywampus. He had added one landmass next to the swamp in the top left of the world and another two greatly expanding the bottom left. Eventually, he'd have to talk to Virgil to see what it would take to create a real, salt-filled ocean. He knew from his school days that the salinity of the ocean was vitally important to a planet's climate, but that may only have been with Earth. Designing worlds was a genius man's game, and he was just getting started.

Looking at his time, he found there were only thirty-three hours remaining. But he also felt like he finally had enough focus to really do what he should've been doing all along: building a world that could change and evolve with time.

He nodded once at the still-drab planet, then explained to Virgil what he was doing next. Walker pulled up his Entity Subsystem and started to mass-drop small, fuzzy, and feathered animals into space. Eventually, pieces of them were floating in all directions as the vacuum took its due.

"Wow," Zeus said from near the Tree of the Gods, where he and the other two had been sitting all this time. "Even I do not treat my people in such a way."

"Yeah, yeah, I get it," Walker said. "But we still haven't figured out how to get the Alpha Protocol to download everything we want to make, so this is the fastest and most merciful way to do this." He threw another animal into space, then informed Virgil it could be added to the chambers. "We've already substantially changed Symphony with all of the vegetation; now we're putting in basic, unevolvable animals. Speaking of which, no task update, huh?" he asked Virgil.

"No, we are only adding the mana deficiency modification. As they are originally from Earth and never had mana in the first place, it is not a large enough modification to consider it a new entity."

"Fuck me."

"For what purpose did you just murder all of those innocent creatures?" Echidna asked as she stood up and placed her hands on her hips.

"Simple," Walker said. "And please don't be angry. We need things for our monsters, and eventually people, to eat. I don't want every rabbit in the world to have a chance to drain the magic in Symphony, as it's not limitless. So, instead, we kill each genus once and modify them to stop any chance of evolutionary independence. Oh, that reminds me."

Walker added his water-adapted Mana Trees to the islands in the sea, one on each corner, then another two to his new forest with the original modified version. Stepping into the World Editor, he took his leftover steel, which was just enough to fill in the gaps he was cutting into the granite.

He had eyeballed where the old roots were so he could line them up as precisely as possible. All throughout his life, working with his hands had always been a large problem for him. But ever since his little soul adventure, they were steady as a rock.

After looking it over and making sure that everything was as it should be, he started to add rabbits, birds, foxes, and an assortment of other animals to the world. Walker blew some seeds that would grow into fruit bushes and trees, as well as standard fare for prey animals, and placed them as well.

Of course, everything dropped in so far were babies and seeds, but he had a solution for that forthcoming.

He wiped his dry hands on each other, the sound a fitting conclusion to his work for the day. Walker looked at his clock and found another five hours gone, leaving him with only twenty-eight remaining.

"Okay, I feel like this is, finally, going to be a habitable world," Walker said.

"I agree; you have made more progress in the last ten hours than you have since first entering the protocol," Virgil said.

"Is that pride in your voice?" Walker asked.

"Certainly not. I just approve of efficiency."

"So do I," Walker said with a smile. "Now, let's get to really pumping out some monsters."

Jolive had taken a different route with the Slicer . . . ignoring it. Was it the best plan? No. Was it an actual plan? No again. But she felt it was the only path remaining to her.

She'd dropped acid on it, burned it, electrocuted it, tried to cut it in half, and once she'd even given it a bath, not understanding that the Slicer thoroughly enjoyed the water.

Jolive became so enraged at the fact that she couldn't kill the Universal Terror that she even tried asking in the chatroom about what to do in this type of situation. The only thing responses she received were laughter and ridicule. They lacked the understanding of what this creature and all of its power meant to them.

It was the end of their time in the Alpha Protocol.

Identifying the monster only returned the name and Universal Terror title, as it had been through so many evolutions that the Alpha Protocol had entirely given up on attempting to quantify it.

At this current moment, Jolive was focusing on working with her entities. She had massively expanded her landmass, not unlike Walker, and now the cage and its relatively remote area . . . directly in the center of her world . . . was a forgotten monument to her failure as a Creator.

She didn't know what else to do and only felt relief that the remainder of her work could continue uninterrupted.

"I need to somehow find a way to . . . combine these two if I want a chance at the next battle," she said to herself, the countdown in her overlay a constant reminder of how little time she had remaining. When you were counting every minute, your mind had a tendency to see time as moving both too quickly and not quickly enough.

It bothered her.

"Maybe the trick is to just make them larger," she said, pulling out a small notebook her guide had given her. While she was writing, Jolive reflected on how helpful her guide had been at the start of everything. Seeing an entity taken from the image of her future world spelled out just how great Dilania would be in the end.

The guide had explained everything, from top to bottom, of what to expect in the tutorial. The notebook even held ideas and suppositions of what the battles would be like and how she could best prepare her world, based on their own memories.

The myths and legends that had continued into the future.

She couldn't imagine how others, with less helpful guides, could succeed without these notes.

"Now, let's see here," she said as she activated her mental Creation Instrument and projected the image in front of her. She made slight changes to the entity, as anything too drastic could have unforeseen consequences. Small change, seed the entity. Small change, seed the entity.

Slow and steady was the best way to move forward, according to her secret journal. Jolive looked at her assistant, a pole with a totem on top, always smiling with its huge teeth, and was about to ask it about the first rendition again. She had done so multiple times in the past to understand what the original Creators had invented in their renditions. It was more than curiosity. It was a plan for success. But that was also when a loud crashing noise came from her world.

The Slicer was out.

It undulated from the cage, which she knew from experience should have been impervious.

Apparently, that information was wrong.

"FUCK," she screamed at it, clicking on her Broadcast ability. "YOU FUCKING PIECE OF SHIT. LEAVE DILANIA ALONE."

The Slicer hissed at her once, then arced its back and flung its head forward, spitting something onto the ground. The soil bubbled and boiled as the Universal Terror moved its pincers back and forth. Then she heard something that chilled her to her metal-sheathed bones.

"HAHAHAHAHAHAHAHAHHAHAHAA, I'M FINALLY FREE!" the Slicer screamed, its words rebounding inside her mind.

"You can talk?" she asked it, flabbergasted.

"Oh yessssss. When you fail the next battle, asss you've talked of ssso ssso often, remember me." And with that, the Slicer began zipping around Jolive's world at a blistering speed, cutting every entity it found to pieces. It didn't outright destroy her planet but instead left a trail of acid anywhere it could. Dilania wasn't destroyed; it was being boiled.

The atmosphere grew cloudy as the fumes rose, and Jolive had trouble seeing what was happening. When every last entity on the planet was dead, hundreds of lives sliced apart, the Slicer zoomed out of the atmosphere and stopped right in front of her tiny planet. The Universal Terror moved its tail in a wave, laughed again, and flew out into the reaches of space.

"FUCK YOU, DANTE!" she screamed at the night sky, looking at the shambles she was left with. She immediately turned to the chatroom to let everyone know how big of a piece of shit he was.

CHAPTER TWENTY-FOUR

Monsterology and Immortality

The back of Walker's neck itched, like someone was talking about him. He shrugged and tried to ignore it.

"Now it feels like we're definitely ready for more monsters. I think we may be at the point of really pumping them out with our two Evolution Chambers. What do you two think?" he asked of his assistants.

"We could do a mythological entity, just to see what they're like," Rimi said casually, but his tail was swishing hard enough that he could get a side job as a propeller for a small boat.

"Mmmmm," Walker hummed, looking at the excited blue squirrel. "I see what you're doing. You just want to see them and tinker with your system. Why don't we place some standard monsters first, then put a mythological one in? This way, if the battle is cooperative, it won't attempt to kill our own entities."

"Okay," he said morosely, tail slowing to a stop.

Walker clicked on Monsters and looked through the list. He had the battle-frogs, but now he also had regular food for everything. Or he would soon. Plants, bushes, fruit trees, and basic prey animals.

He knew what could survive the desert and reasoned it would be easy enough to create something that would thrive in that specific environment. Making his choice, Walker selected a series of scorpions and placed them into space. Then, after speaking with Virgil, he selected the Egyptian Fat-tailed Scorpion and placed it into chamber number one.

He asked Virgil to make it only a little larger and give it a kernel, as it was already rather powerful with its potent venom and survival instincts. Virgil agreed, then told Walker what they liked to eat, so Walker exploded some of those, and they began all over again.

When Walker finished his insecto-genocide, Virgil called out that he'd had to make the scorpions much larger than Walker wanted. Still, it was a small price to pay for his desert to finally gain habitation. Walker waved it away, and they quickly expanded the size of the bugs and beetles they would need to add, including modifying their proliferation rate. It wouldn't do for Walker's newest entities to starve to death.

He quickly placed eight scorpions in the desert, half male and half female, while Virgil went through the boring process of creating as many beetles and bugs as needed to maintain a small ecosystem.

"Fuck me, I had hoped to make a world with no bugs," Walker said after placing the last scorpion a good distance away.

"You did not place any mosquitoes or flies that I saw. From your memories, they seemed to annoy you the greatest," Virgil countered.

"True, I don't know. Snakes, bugs, spiders . . ."

"The food pyramiiid!" Virgil sang while staring at a monitor. Walker was proud of him for his first attempt at singing; he only wished it hadn't come out as a scream. The giant squirrel quickly regained his composure. "If you want birds, you will need larvae and other insects. If you want scorpions, you gain bugs in the desert. There will also need to be an oasis or watering hole in your desert, as otherwise, your entities will not have enough water to survive."

Walker shook his head. "I never thought I'd hear you sing. In fact, it was less of a thought and more of a hope." He cracked a smile as he entered the World Editor. Virgil giggled in the background.

As Virgil finished up the last of the D-grade creations, Walker took control of the monitor and cut a decent-sized divot through the desert. He looked at it from multiple angles. It took some time to find the right path to the water, and he moved the monitor quickly due to their time constraints. To get the kind of water pressure he wanted, he was forced to cut a deeply angled hole within the side of the sand landmass and direct it straight to the divot. It drained out of Symphony's burgeoning sea, but he had plenty to spare as he topped the world's water back up with only a few movements.

"Perhaps you are rubbing off on me," Virgil said, picking up their conversation as Walker stepped out of the system.

"Better than rubbing you off. Hah!" He was full of good zingers today. "I'm with Rimi in wanting to see what the mythological creatures are like, but let's add a few more standardized monsters first. We have frogs in the crater and scorpions in the desert. Now what?"

Rimi raised his hand, so Walker pointed at him. "Yes, we have a volunteer."

"Can we please have a large squirrel?"

"Why?" Walker asked while looking at him.

"To protect the Mana Trees so they can't be destroyed along with the rest of Symphony. You know," he kicked the grass, "if something scary happens."

"Huh . . . huh . . . that's not bad. Also, it would be an homage to you two, wouldn't it?"

"What's that word mean?" Rimi asked.

"It's like a special honor or tribute to someone, and that seals the deal!" Walker said with a smile. "I've been trying to find a way to show you guys how much I appreciate you. This seems to be an easy choice. The next set of monsters to touch Symphony's soil will be squirrels, a direct homage to my two favorite assistants."

"We're your only assistants," Rimi said, but Walker wasn't listening. Without thinking, Walker exploded a standard gray squirrel.

"MY BROTHER!" Rimi screamed as he saw pieces of it fly into the void.

"Oh man, I did not think about that. They weren't part of our exploding time earlier."

"Indeed," Virgil said nonplussed.

"I'm sorry, Rimi," Walker said with a hand on his small shoulder. "I wasn't thinking."

"It's okay . . . I guess . . . he wasn't really my brother, but he just kinda looked like me."

"I know, buddy, I'm sorry," he finished as he put one in the Evolution Chamber with an eye on the small blue squirrel. Once Rimi looked like he was going to get over his grief, Walker called the three of them together so they could start planning.

It would be a protector to the Mana Trees, so they wanted it to intrinsically understand not to hurt them. Even more than that, it would be great if they'd also guard it from those who would seek to do harm.

As a mental side note, Walker recognized that it also meant each time he created another landmass, he would have to make two Mana Trees, and then two squirrels to guard them from outsiders. This made creating new locations a little more routine and less random, which, if he was being honest with himself, he didn't mind. Routines were a form of safety to him.

The first step was to enlarge their first protector, a word that Rimi picked up and started to use immediately. So, that meant a Gigantify modification, as a standard squirrel was much too small for his taste. Virgil looked it over on his screen and said it should come out to about six feet tall, then made an empty space in the middle of its body, quickly adding a kernel. He also said that since the squirrel would always be with the Mana Tree, its attunement would come out pure every time. He further stated that pure magic was unique in that the abilities and evolutions of monsters had a difficult time stopping pure damage.

Walker looked over at him with a raised eyebrow. "That seems a bit overpowered, if I'm being honest. Are all pure attunements going to work that way?"

"Yes. Pure magic is unattuned and thus does not have the same counters that others would have. Ice loses strength against fire or extreme heat, and water gains strength against magma. Essentially, rock-paper-scissors from your homeworld. Because it is unattuned, it will instead bypass any potential counters that may appear and deal damage or effects directly on the intended target. You wanted a caretaker for the trees." He shrugged. "Well, this will give it a fighting chance against anyone that approaches it with intent to do harm."

"But won't that just make every Mana Tree squirrel a tier five?" Rimi gave him a small glare. "Sorry, every Protector. I mean, nothing else would be able to come close, right?"

"That is an excellent point, Walker," Virgil said, placing a paw against his chin in thought.

"Oh, oh!" Rimi added, raising his hand. Walker called on him without thinking, his teacher instincts kicking in. "What if we just block the Guardians from reaching tier five? That way, when they sense an undefeatable monster coming, they'll just leave."

"Can you do that?" Walker asked him.

"Yes! I can put in a special restriction that the Guardians cannot move beyond the pinnacle stage, and the Monster System shouldn't have any problems."

"Wait a second, what happened to them being Protectors?"

"I changed my mind," Rimi replied, his personality poking its head out more than ever.

"Alright," Walker said with a smile. "Go ahead." They waited as Rimi fiddled with his screens. A few moments of concentrated looks later, he gave them the thumbs-up.

Moving on, they started to work on their base model again. They wouldn't have to modify the squirrels a great amount for each Mana Tree, as the exact location each would be placed was also their home, but it was still a good idea to make sure they didn't have any issues with their initial seeding.

Walker watched as Virgil zoomed in on the squirrel's brain and began tinkering. He had no idea what was happening, as he had neither the assistants' advanced knowledge nor an idea of how brains worked, but Virgil assured him it would enhance the intelligence of the squirrel quite a bit. He named the modification "Enlightenment" and added it to their prebuilt modification list.

Whether that created an intrinsic need in the Guardian to protect its Mana Tree or not was yet to be seen. Walker believed it would, because the squirrelly monster should be able to sense that the Mana Tree was the source of its power. Add in the fact that they were essentially creating a symbiotic relationship between the Guardian and Mana Tree, and their plans should work as intended. *Should* always being the keyword when working in the Alpha Protocol.

To keep the squirrel seated where it was and not running off to find food every few hours, Virgil gave it a slow metabolism by stretching out its digestive system. He then used a single thread from the mana funnels they'd made for their original Mana Tree to connect its stomach to its kernel. This meant that eating the Mana Tree's leaves would also be possible, and the squirrels would gain power at a much faster rate. Virgil nodded his head once, aged the squirrel two years from Walker's already depleting temporal resources, and asked Walker if he was ready.

"Ready enough. Let's do this," Walker said with excitement. This was the first really modified entity they'd created in a while, and he wanted to see what results would come of it. He pulled up the monitor and zoomed in on the first Mana Tree they'd placed, deep in the center of Symphony. Angling it so he could see the results of their work, Walker placed the first Guardian, and his overlay lit up.

[. . . Scanning . . .]
As your entity has been modified from its original form,
please name it.

Walker believed simpler was always better with names, so he typed it in.

Entity: Guardian is named

[. . . Analyzing . . .]
Entity named Guardian analyzed.
Size: Large
Entity category: Animal
Organism type: (Consumer) System Monster
Modification: Very High
Ability to evolve: Yes, system-bound (Restricted)
Age: 2 years
Grade: B+
Rewards calculated.

Considerable reward for completion of a B+ grade entity:
Congratulations, Dante! You've gained an allocation of rare
resources!
Temporal resources allocated.
Rare metal allocated: Faer

"That's less than I expected," Walker said after looking at the rewards.

Virgil weighed in. "Not quite. Faer is a more useful metal than steel. A little more durable than what you know as titanium but without some of the inherent flaws, such as its weight and brittleness at low temperatures. The temporal resources are a nice addition as well, as we were running a little low at the moment."

"Oh my God!" Walker yelled out with a slap to his forehead. "I could've used titanium on the metal core of Symphony."

"No, you made the right choice," Virgil said. "While titanium is indeed a stronger material than steel and would absorb the root's magic more easily, it is also flexible, which could lead to parts of Symphony bowing. The weight and pressure on top of the planet could press down, causing the world to become destabilized."

Walker thought it over with a hand to his chin. "You don't think we should use titanium anywhere on Symphony?" he asked.

"I did not say that, but with Faer metal at your disposal, you will do quite fine. As the protocol stated, it is a rare resource, and now that it is within your resources, you may place it at will."

"Nice! Okay, that is a solid reward." He clicked the Monitor button, and they looked at the two-year-old squirrel in its new home. It was already jumping around excitedly, chittering in that cute language they all seemed to have. Walker had a hard time conceptually recognizing the squirrel's size next to the dark-blue tree. He guessed it was a little under five feet tall, Virgil's estimate being wrong for once. It had a gray coat of fur and a bushy tail, and for the first time since creating his entities, Walker could honestly say his creation seemed happy.

Even Rimi beside him was jumping up and down while pointing at it. He suddenly stopped with a mournful look. "I wish I could go say hi."

"You realize you are not a squirrel, correct?" Virgil replied reproachfully.

Rimi looked insulted by what Virgil was insinuating. "Of course. This form is the only one that I have known. It doesn't change the fact that the Guardian seems like they would be fun to talk to."

"Fair enough," Walker said, verbally placing himself between them before their first fight could happen. "Now, we need to place these suckers all over the map." Putting action to words, he started to seed a Guardian for every tree. The process sped up a little as Walker found he didn't need to modify them after all, and soon, every Mana Tree had its own Guardian. Each squirrel took to its new home well and seemed quite excited, but Walker found a problem. "Won't these die over time? Then we'll have to replace them and make sure each is doing their job."

"I have a solution!" Rimi said. "This was bothering me earlier with the battle-frogs, so I've been considering it. There's an option to choose a specific evolution for every monster to gain at different tiers. Why don't we make the tier four evolution always increase their lifespan? That way, every tier four monster has more time to gain their next tier, and the squirrels won't have to be replaced that often."

"Guardians," Walker commented with a smile.

"It will not work," Zeus said from nearby. "Not unless you have some kind of immortality gene, or, better yet, you choose to Awaken these Guardians."

Walker ignored everything else he'd said, instead focusing on those particular words: immortality gene. Where had he heard that before? Then he snapped his fingers. "The jellyfish!"

Virgil looked confused before he grinned and started nodding, understanding exactly what he was talking about.

"The immortal jellyfish from the Earth. It sheds its skin and . . . uh." Walker paused, trying to remember the documentary he had watched on them. "It, uh . . . does something or other, I, uh . . . don't know."

"Turritopsis dohrnii," Virgil said while still tinkering with his overlay. "That is not how it works, Walker, although I appreciate you trying." Seeing a lot of confused looks, including Walker's, he spoke again. "Let me explain for the betterment of all. Walker is looking for a specific evolution that we can pull from a basic modification. That is plausible and could come with its own reward from the protocol. Thus, I am in agreement."

Virgil closed down whatever he was looking at and started pacing back and forth in front of them. "The immortal jellyfish is a cnidarian on Earth, which reverts its cells back to a polyp stage by transforming old cells into new ones. It does not do this actively but through a passive process it is born with, which has evolved over an extremely long period of time." He grinned. "Lucky for us. With the addition of magic and guided by the Primordial energy of creation, we should be able to allocate this to each tier four monster. Also, every evolution that the protocol divests into creatures during each rendition was originally a unique modification by a Creator. By adding your own evolution into the mix, you will not only be able to use it with the Monster System, but you should also be granted a substantial reward based upon the value the protocol gives to your new addition."

Rimi raised a hand. "What's the difference between a modification and an evolution?"

Virgil nodded. "Good question." Rimi's tail swished. "A modification is an intentional change built by a Creator, or their assistants"—another swish—"before the entity is placed into a world. An evolution is something that is meant to naturally occur after their creation using the power of Primordial energy. However, as we have decided to control all evolution pertaining to Symphony's Entities, we now have the ability to pick and choose evolutions."

Walker nodded. "So we are in agreement? We're going to build an Immortality evolution?" Although he was asking Virgil, it was Zeus who stomped over with a thunderous expression.

"You CANNOT just give immortality to creatures. It is earned by accessing the soul and through an excruciatingly large amount of pain and suffering. Every step and growth each Awakened gains is from their own hard work. It . . . is not a gift to be handed out at no cost."

Walker had an easy answer to this. "Virgil, Rimi, excepting the Guardians who will be accelerating through the tiers, how long would you estimate the time it will take a standard monster like the battlefrog to reach tier four?" He pulled up the monitor and zoomed in on the original battlefrog's kernel, so the large assistant could look at it.

Virgil and Rimi formed a small huddle in front of the monitor, speaking quietly with a few head nods and one helpless shrug from the blue squirrel. They turned around, and Virgil said, "Based upon the current kernel speed of absorption, how it has slowed due to an increased population around it, and the expected reproductive rate we believe the battlefrog will have, we expect it to take close to twenty years before we see the first tier four. Two months instead of the previously stated one month for tier two. Around three years for tier three, and seventeen after that for the largest jump to tier four. Should it find the Mana Tree, understand what it is doing, and defeat the Guardian, that time will decrease exponentially." He looked at Rimi again, who gave a small nod and shrug in agreement.

"Will it have to fight as new monsters and Classers are added over time?" Walker asked.

"Of course," Virgil replied.

"Will it suffer and feel pain in those twenty-odd years?"

"Indeed."

"So, reaching tier four," Walker said, turning and looking Zeus in the eyes, "will include pain and suffering."

"That is a certainty, unless they are very lucky."

"Thank you, Virgil," Walker said, and Zeus glared at the large squirrel for a moment before giving a shallow nod and walking back toward the Tree of the Gods.

Walker rolled his eyes. He pulled up the immortal jellyfish in the Entity Subsystem and blew it up, hoping it didn't truly live up to its name . . . which it didn't. Then, he put one in the Evolution Chamber for Virgil to dissect and extract the needed modification. While Walker waited, he looked at his resources.

He was low on steel but still had a little bit of extra granite and water. He now had an even sixty years from his reward's addition, giving him some wiggle room for advancing his world before the battle. Stepping into the World Editor, he added water to his landmass near the swamp he'd just placed, connecting it to the water route winding throughout Symphony, then stepped out again.

"Complete," Virgil said. "I have added the extreme modification for self-regenerating cells to our bank of modifications. This will allow for easy application on entities in the future. The next time you work in the Evolution Chamber, I suggest you take a look at the list already presented."

"Will do, and thank you. Now, how do I go about adding this as an evolution to the protocol?"

Virgil pointed at the blue squirrel. "That is for Rimi to do."

"Hello," Rimi said with a wave by Walker's leg. He was so quiet and small that Walker hadn't noticed the tiny blue creature. "Please connect the Evolution Chambers to the Monster System."

Walker clicked on the appropriate systems. "Done."

"Updating the Monster System, one moment, please."

"You sound like Virgil," Walker commented.

"I take that as a compliment," Virgil replied.

"Excuse my interruption; the process is complete," Rimi said with two thumbs up.

"Sweet, now we'll just—" Walker was interrupted by his overlay lighting up.

[. . . Scanning . . .]
New evolution found.
Analyzing self-regeneration cells.

Analyzation complete.
A new evolution has been gifted by Creator Dante.
Extreme longevity identified.
[. . . Analyzing . . .]
[. . . Analyzing . . .]
Forwarding to the Alpha Protocol Council.
Missing evolution identified. Reward upgraded.
Reward upgraded from A+ to S level: Monumental
Rewards calculated.

Private message from the Alpha Protocol Council detected
[. . . Retrieving . . .]
Congratulations, child.
You have found what we've sought for more of your years than
you can imagine. We will give you two gifts for providing this
grand boon. Continue, keep working, and perhaps one day you
may join us yourself.

Monumental reward 1/2 for gifting the Alpha Protocol
a missing evolution:
Congratulations, Dante! You've gained the Avatar ability!

Step into your world at any time, in any place, and continue to receive the protections of the Alpha Protocol. Gift your entities any of your self-created evolutions as you see fit, and bask in an ability less than a dozen Creators in all of the protocol have ever received. You have earned it.

**Monumental reward 2/2 for gifting the Alpha Protocol
a missing evolution:
Congratulations, Dante! You've gained three upgraded
Evolution Chambers!
Previous Evolution Chambers are also now upgraded!**
Go, create, flourish. You have now gained the eye of the Alpha Protocol's Council. We expect great things, Dante. As it is your wish to no longer destroy your entities upon first placement, you may now place them within the upgraded Evolution Chambers. Continue on your unique path, and see greater advantages fall to you.

"Wow," Virgil said as Walker looked over at him.

He was standing next to the upgraded Evolution Chambers, which looked the same, with the only exception being that they were twice as large as the previous ones. Virgil shook his head. "Even I did not know it was one of the missing evolutions. I had assumed, after so many renditions and Creators, that at least one had created some form of immortality evolution. This is, apparently, a first. Now I understand why the seats on the Council have changed so often. They were either retiring or dying. Walker. You just gave immortality to all of the renditions in the multiverse."

"Say what now?" Walker asked.

"Now that they know how to do it, Creators from older universes, with enough power and connections to those who run the protocol, will have access to the self-regenerating cells evolution we've created. You have just gifted the multiverse one of the greatest evolutions in the history of the protocol. A missing evolution."

"How is that even fucking possible?" Walker said in further confusion. "There's a million goddamned people in this rendition. There were tons of renditions before ours, with even more Creators. It makes no goddamned sense."

Virgil looked like he was struggling with something. Walker held from speaking until it looked like the large squirrel never would. Eventually, his anxiety got the best of him. "Just get it out already."

"The Council . . . is . . . lazy," Virgil said through gritted teeth.

"Wait . . . what?"

That was when they were interrupted by the Primigenials.

Zeus was having a screaming fit with Echidna near the tree. Something about the unfairness of it and how the Awakened wouldn't put up with this. Echidna, on the other hand, was arguing for patience and a belief in their Creator, meaning Walker. Minos simply stood there looking back and forth between them.

But their issues, while somewhat valid, didn't sit long in Walker's mind. He just continued to consider the fact that he'd made a new evolution, a missing one, that should have been discovered long ago. Did he just make a huge amount of uber-powerful people essentially immortal? He wasn't sure how he was supposed to feel right now.

Proud? No . . . Excited? A little. The Avatar ability sounded super cool, and the upgrade to the Evolution Chambers, plus the extra three he'd just received, was a big deal he didn't want to play down. But the evolution just seemed a little too easy. And what did Virgil mean when he said the Council was lazy? A lot of questions, and based on how Virgil's face looked when he told him, he wouldn't be getting a lot of answers.

It made him think more deeply than normal. Was this the Alpha Protocol's true purpose? To empower these old worlds and Creators? But he thought the Alpha Protocol already gave immortality? They'd said he would live forever. Had that been a lie?

The purpose of the Alpha Protocol sat in the back of his skull. Since he'd become an Awakened, his mind almost seemed to be in a better state. Thoughts coalesced faster, forming a clearer picture of what was happening. He wasn't smarter, yet things just felt cleaner. Improved.

He circled the idea of how the evolution was going to play out on a multiversal scale but soon recognized that stewing on the matter was pointless. "Nothing I can do about that now," Walker whispered to himself, hoping this wouldn't have further repercussions for Symphony. "Hey Virgil, you said I was going to live forever at the start, right?"

"That is almost correct. Nothing can truly live forever, but while the protocol is currently happening, you are no longer under the threat of death," Virgil confirmed, fully recovered from his ordeal.

"So then, the obvious question is, why is this a missing evolution if I'm already going to be immortal?"

Virgil looked like he was going to say something, then changed his mind. He momentarily paused before speaking. "Because it is the power of Creation that keeps you alive. If you chose to somehow interact with your entities and have children, they would die over time, but you would not. As long as you have the shield of the protocol, you will not die." Walker was thinking about that when Virgil spoke up again. "Also, you should know that you cannot join the Council and remain a Creator. They are mutually exclusive, and you would lose your shield."

"So, only Creators have immortality?"

"Just so. It is empowered by the loose Primordial energy of the rendition. Should the rendition's energy be exhausted, so too would the shields. The Council members are mortals, albeit ones with a greatly enhanced lifespan."

"And we just gave them a form of immortality."

"Evolutions are connected directly to the world, system, and rules that apply to it. They would need to re-connect themselves to their own worlds, and it is not a simple process. They would be bound by the systems inherently built in. You are not the only one to design systems that bind your entities."

"So, I can do that. I can make my own kernel and stick myself into Symphony's system."

"If that is your wish, yes."

He thought it over seriously, spending several minutes staring at his soon-to-be green world. But in the end, he decided the system wasn't ready. Maybe in the future, he'd be just another citizen of Symphony, but not now. "What's this Avatar ability?" Walker asked, pulling it up in his overlay.

Virgil accepted the change of subject with grace. "I do not know. They never gave me any information on it," he said helplessly.

The two assistants and the Creator of Symphony stood looking at the Evolution Chambers for a moment, with Walker planning out how the new changes would affect him. All of the new information didn't overwhelm him like it used to. Maybe that was growth, or maybe it was just that he was managing his emotions better than he had in the past.

He looked at his countdown to Battle #2 and found twenty hours remaining. He needed more monsters, more . . . oomph. They had the battlefrogs, scorpions, and Guardians now. It was time to go mythological.

"Virgil, Rimi, which mythological creatures were you looking at?" Walker asked.

"Oh, oh!" Rimi said with a hand raised. "I want the manticore."

"Isn't that from Greek mythology?" Walker asked Virgil.

"Indeed."

"Okay." He looked at the blue squirrel. "So please explain it to me. What's a manticore?"

"I can answer that," Zeus said as he stepped closer. "In fact, I'll give you a task for it, as you seem to absolutely love throwing new offal into the wind before understanding what you're doing."

Walker's spine itched. "Hey asshole, nobody knew that would happen. We didn't know that immortality wasn't discovered yet."

"And yet, you've upset the balance of the multiverse with one single act. You could have just replaced the Guardians as needed, but you were lazy."

"No, I was creative. Which is the purpose of the protocol . . . supposedly."

"And now, the unsouled have gained an advantage that has only ever rested with the Awakened. You've upset a larger balance than you know, and I do not know what will come of it."

Walker glared at him. "Just give me the fucking task already."

"FINE!" Zeus yelled. "BUT BE WARNED! THIS WILL NOT BE FOR THE LAZY OR STUPID." He began moving his hands in the air as if he were writing something only he could see, and Walker's overlay lit up.

[. . . Scanning . . .]
Optional tasks updated!
New Primigenial task: Discover all of the parts of the manticore
Figure this one out, you son of a bitch.
Parts discovered: 0/5
Task giver: Zeus, King of the Gods
Reward for completion: Electricity modification

Walker glared at Zeus without speaking, then placed a baby manticore inside the newly upgraded Evolution Chamber.

The upgrade was a large boon to his mental well-being. Now he could start planting humans and get his civilizations going if he wanted to. It was a huge load off of his mind, as he wasn't really sure if he could . . . kill a child. It was too much.

The new entity loaded up, and he stepped closer with his assistants. The manticore was weird looking, like a newly hatched bird, and Walker couldn't immediately recognize everything going on through the glass. Rather than strain himself, he found the connection to the Temporal subsystem and advanced its age by two years. They watched it grow within the capsule until it reached an enormous size. Walker looked at Virgil.

"How tall is that fucker?"

"I would say around ten feet, not counting the wingspan."

"Hrmm. Hey Zeus, for your task, do wrong answers fail us automatically?"

"That would be up to me, now wouldn't it?" Zeus said with a smirk, finally having some power in his hands.

Walker gave him some side-eye while he thought about what to do. He didn't know what a failed task would do, but it probably wouldn't be good for him. He grinned as an idea came to him. "Alright, I'll do the smartest thing I can do here. I'll phone a friend. Virgil, what is it?"

Zeus recognized the problem and threw out a hand, beseeching this moment not to come, but it was already too late.

"An eagle's wings, a human face, shark teeth, the body of a lion including the legs and claws, and a scorpion's tail."

**Primigenial task complete: Discover all of the parts of the
manticore (Part 1)
Parts discovered: 5/5
Reward for completion: Electricity modification**

"Neat," Walker said with a smile, then he high-fived Virgil just to rub it in while Rimi waited for his own. Zeus, meanwhile, looked extremely offended.

"How dare you use outside assistance!" he screamed, spittle flying out with each consonant.

"You didn't put that in the rules, brosky," Walker said, a smile still plastered on his face. "Thanks for the lightning modification, it seems super duper cool." He gave a thumbs-up as Zeus turned beet red. The old god stomped back to his tree and the memory of his supposed superiority. Echidna and Minos were laughing just beyond him. They waved and then joined him in his march.

Walker moved closer to Virgil, whispering, "Man, did he forget about that immortality thing fast?"

"Indeed," Virgil whispered back while Rimi tittered in the background.

He looked at the god again as he seemed to be yelling at the other two on their walk. "I bet he doesn't understand twenty-first-century education. Wasn't it fairly rare in his time for someone to be well-educated?"

"Very much so. I believe your knowledge of the world greatly supersedes his own, including that of Echidna and Minos. Many of those in the Tree of the Gods will seem at about the educational level of an early teen."

Walker laughed. "Hah, I love it. Idiot gods. Anyways, let's look this thing over; we're short on time." Walker inspected the manticore and realized just how vicious this thing would be. Shark teeth, fucked-up lion claws, and a venomous stinger. "I know we need to win the battle, but this shit is ridiculous. Rimi, why did you want this so bad?"

"Ummm, I thought it would be more cute. Man-ti-core. It sounds . . . cute. Sorry."

"No, it's fine, but I feel like . . . if we let this loose, it's another Slicer. We don't have the Class System working or anything to really balance it out. We need to modify it so that it won't destroy our world."

Virgil looked over at him. "What are you thinking?"

"I'm thinking we shrink it. Mini-manticore. Yeah. That way, we can still connect it to the Monster System, but they'll be smaller and hopefully won't rampage across Symphony."

Virgil nodded. "Okay. The protocol's records, which were hidden from me until we were granted access just a moment ago, say that this chamber is more intuitive. You tell it what you want, and it accedes to your wishes. The only difference is, any automated processes will be slower than creating modifications manually, as we have in the past."

Walker shrugged. "Yeah, but we have five now, so that means we can just start spitting out monsters pretty soon."

"That is true. But if you want to consider more of the evolution transfer rewards that got you these upgraded chambers, you will have to invent more new evolutions."

"Oh . . . I already have plans," Walker said with a nefarious smile. "How do I tell it what to do?"

"Click on it in your overlay and go to Discovered Modifications. At your convenience, you will find a list of standard modifications within the upgraded Evolution Chamber. You will also find all of the modifications we have already completed while in the Alpha Protocol."

Walker found what Virgil was talking about in the chamber menu and took a quick peek at all of them. Things like venomous teeth or the Guardian's mana stomach were near the top, while size changes were near the bottom. Gigantify showed itself, and Walker shuddered—the thought of an even larger manticore was terrifying.

He found what he was looking for and noticed that size change modifications came in ranges, from a twenty percent reduction named "Minimum" to a ninety-five percent reduction called "Shrink." Walker chose Condense, sizing the down Manticore by eighty percent.

When it finished, a two-foot-tall element of nightmare fuel was held in stasis within the chamber. Walker selected Kernel from the modifications and added that as well. He felt it was a decent balance. They'd still be fast and venomous but wouldn't have the same size advantage as their ancestors. He asked Virgil the big question in his mind before he even thought of seeding it on Symphony.

"This isn't as smart as a human, right?"

"No, Walker. In fact, they will be more stupid than your world's mythology remembers, as you have just shrunk their brain quite a bit. The human face . . . I do not know what the Creator of Earth was thinking. The choice, it seems, was focused on sowing terror into humans more than anything else. Its brain is closer to a tiger's than a human's. That Creator seemed to greatly dislike some of the entities on its world, based upon how it treated them."

"She was a right bitch!" Echidna yelled from far away, shocking Walker with how powerful her hearing was. Then he noticed that both Minos and Zeus nodded along, although the bearded god wouldn't look Walker in the eyes.

"Jeez. I hope they don't think of me like that."

"Indeed. I do have to provide a word of warning, however. My best estimate of how the former Creator of Earth built this creature is that she used the

Combiner ability you unlocked. We have not tested it yet, but this may be a result of what occurs when it is used without a complete thought process."

Walker nodded. "Noted. Now, let's seed this crazy bastard."

Walker zoomed the monitor over to the new forest he'd created and placed the manticore there, then waited for a spot of time . . . but his overlay did not update.

"Son of a bitch."

"Its modifications are insufficient."

"I know! Okay! . . . sorry. I know!" He punched the palm of his hand. "Always something."

They watched as the tiny, golden-furred creature appeared and began to sniff the ground, moving about on all fours. It was eerie watching a human face with such animal-like behaviors. Walker tried not to dwell on the comparison for too long as he didn't like the feeling. The manticore kept moving about until it found the smell of something it liked, then with a single step it took off. It was incredibly fast.

"Well it's still a little overpowered," Walker said in thought. "We'd better just make one more so they don't have social issues. Wait, are they territorial?"

"Gods, yes!" Zeus said from the tree.

"If you want to help, just get over here!" Walker yelled back.

"Fuck you!"

"Fuck you back!"

"Your mother!"

"Was a saint!"

Zeus went back to grumbling with his two fellows while Walker watched the manticore zipping about the forest. "How do we get these things to make friends if they're territorial?"

"Only one way to find out," Rimi said while hopping up and down next to him. Again, Walker hadn't seen him arrive. "That's a female, so let's just put a male in and see what happens."

"Experimenting with unknown entities is how we wound up with the Slicer, Walker," said Virgil. "But I do not see any other options with unknown entities like these mythological creatures."

"We could just put it in a different part of the world. Maybe they're not social after all and would prefer solitude," Walker suggested.

"Just about every creature is social, Walker. Even octopi from Earth like to meet up from time to time, although their manner of mating is quite unique."

Walker gave a half grimace, half grin. "Yeah, they rip off their penises and throw them at each other."

"Indeed."

"Well . . . let's find out if they're the penis-throwing type. I have my Avatar ability now. I'll just mosey on down there, say a quick hello to my little fellow, and see how it reacts."

"That's stupid!" Zeus yelled out.

"Fuck you again!"

"He is right, though," Virgil said, bringing Walker's attention back to him. "You are not a manticore. We will not know how they act with each other unless we put them together."

"FINE!" Walker said, printing one male up, bringing the monitor toward the manticore, and slapping it down. He didn't like Zeus being right.

The male materialized in the forest. The original golden manticore watched as a black version of itself appeared next to it with a tilted head.

"Girls are golden, boys are black. That's interesting!" Rimi said with a fist pump. When had he seen Walker do that?

The two manticores walked toward each other, then started to circle one another. Their tails started fencing, slashing in lightning-quick movements as they glared and made hissing noises. Interestingly enough, though their attacks were fast, they didn't really seem to be going for hits. The manticores just kept slapping their tails together. Then it hit him.

"Oh my god," Walker said in sudden horror. "That's a mating ritual. They both dropped in ready to have kids."

"That is one way to make sure they do not go on a rampage," Virgil said. "It is hard to go on a rampage while pregnant or caring for children."

"Fuck me," Walker said.

"Not likely!" Zeus yelled out, getting the verbal upper hand.

"Damn him," Walker whispered.

CHAPTER TWENTY-FIVE

Baby Battle

Man, they are really going at it," Walker said as the two manticores rolled through the forest. At first glance, he would think the male was stabbing the female with the bottom of his tail, but they all knew what was really happening.

Virgil mumbled, "Mmmmm, yes. I am curious. Do you believe that, based on the context of this moment, this counts as watching pornography?"

"Perverts!" Zeus yelled as he stood up near the tree.

"You have no right to say that," Echidna reminded him in a soft-spoken voice Walker couldn't hear. Zeus sat back down without saying anything further.

Meanwhile, Walker clicked off the monitor. "Yeah, I can't watch that anymore; it's just wrong." He walked over to the newly upgraded Evolution Chambers and stared for a moment before turning and speaking to Virgil. "I still don't get why the Alpha Protocol didn't have some form of immortality already."

Virgil nodded before saying, "Yes, I can understand how it would be difficult to see. Millions upon millions of Creators. But there were a series of steps required to allow its creation. First, you have to have an idea of how the genetic structure of such a thing would work. Not only would the original genetic line have to be quite varied for that specific evolutionary trait to appear, but you would also have to recognize it. Your world is not only vast in its genetic structures, but also quite advanced in its technology. That is rare."

Walker nodded. "Okay, I see what you're saying."

"Indeed. Then, a Creator would need to recognize the structure and target it within an Evolution Chamber that must be rewarded from the protocol. They would then need to extract it using Primordial energy, which is the building material of the universe and has very few restrictions. Following that, it would then have to be downloaded into the protocol for evolutionary use, and selectably added to unique entities with restrictions. If an entity gained this evolution with no restrictions, the evolution could go out of control. The entity would then drain all of the Primordial energy in the area, creating a chain reaction. That could go one of two ways: either their cells would constantly revert back in age unto conception and nothingness, or the cells could stack on top of one another and the being would grow until all of the energy had been consumed."

Walker scrubbed at his eyes as he realized how badly things could've gone. "So you'd need the genetic aberration, being the jellyfish. And the technology to recognize it, not to mention finding it in the first place. Then get sent to the protocol, decide to make it into an evolution, and restrict it with a system. That's a shitload of steps . . ." Walker scratched his chin. "So, in other words, we got lucky?"

Virgil smiled as he shook his head. "That was funny, but no, I would not call it luck. There are some instances of chance within the Alpha Protocol, but in this instance, it is about the history of your home planet. I told you at the start that you had great genetic variation, and that it was quite the boon. Add in your first battle's addition of magic and the Tree of the Gods' addition of soul power, and you have a quite powerful Creator with almost unlimited options. It was you who recognized the immortal jellyfish, and you only knew about it because of Earth's technology. It was always going to happen, but you were in the right place at the right time to bring it forth."

"That sounds like luck."

"Tomatoes and potatoes."

"That's not the quote. I don't want to contradict you, as you're singing my praises, but it still feels like luck. Although Thomas Jefferson once said, *I am a great believer in luck. And I find the harder I work, the more I have of it.* I'm guessing that's what you're trying to say here."

"Just so."

Walker looked at his remaining time and grimaced. They would have to advance the world's time if they wanted their entities to be at a level where they could compete with other Creators. Walker had fifty-eight years in his temporal resources, so he had to make a decision to either advance the world now or add more entities before doing so. As much as he wanted to create and seed sapients, or sentient people, there wasn't enough time to really dive into the meat and bones of doing so while also ensuring a sense of balance in Symphony. He was fairly certain that they needed to advance now and gain the rewards that would occur, but he wanted to ask his two assistants first.

"What do you guys think?" Walker asked them, both turning to look at him. "We'll probably have a few mini . . . mini-manticores to deal with if we only advance Symphony a few years. Or we could also just dive into the full fifty and allow our newest Mana Trees to mature. This would also cause our current Mana

Trees to reach peak adulthood and give Symphony a larger amount of pure, unattuned magic."

"Hrmm," they both said, almost in sync. Virgil spoke first. "I believe you should reach for the full fifty years. You will still have—" He looked at his screen. "Eight years remaining in your resources after advancing the world, and as I stated earlier, the system has a tendency to give you more temporal resources at the end of a battle."

"I want to change that a little," Rimi said. "I think we should advance it a year first just to see what happens with the mini-manticores."

"Why?" Walker asked.

Rimi smiled. "Because we need to know if they're going to destroy Symphony in those fifty years. If we find they're on a destructive path, you can find a way to isolate them, and we are okay. But if we complete the full fifty and do not know how they will act, there could be trouble."

"Smart," Virgil approved.

"Let me see if I can," Walker said as he clicked Time. He selected the edge of the planet and then tried to unselect the mini-manticore's forest. After a few attempts, he realized it was impossible. "That is a no-go. Apparently, you can't unselect portions like that with the time subsystem." Walker turned to Virgil as he pulled up his monitor and zoomed in on the golden manticore. "Virgil, how long do you think the gestation period is for the female?"

"That is hard to guess. They are mammals, if I am not mistaken, and judging by the knowledge of mammals I have from your memories, they will have a gestational period of around three months. I am basing this on their size, as well as the belief that they will be placental in reproduction."

"Then I suggest three months," Rimi replied.

"Okay, so we'll advance Symphony by three months and figure this out. Any issues?" Walker said to everyone on his tiny planet. After receiving no responses, he clicked on Symphony and advanced it three months.

They watched in fascination, even the three Primigenials joining them as time sped forward. The manticore's belly quickly swelled, growing large and distending from her body. After two months had passed, she was having trouble hunting, and following a large meal that she'd painstakingly gained through patience and cunning strategy, she settled down near a tree in the forest.

Just as it looked like her body was about to explode, Walker turned off the fast-forward early. He looked at his resources and found they had spent a little over two and a half months. The golden manticore was on the ground and breathing heavily, straining against nature, pushing her body to bear her children. The black manticore was nowhere to be seen, and they hadn't viewed it in the monitor since its first creation and eventual mingling with the female. It had run off to the depths of the forest as if frightened of what would follow. Walker's overlay lit up.

Subsystem assistant task complete: Train the assistant (Series 1)
Subsystem assistant requirements:
Assistant is assigned to a subsystem: Yes
Assistant is autonomous: Yes
Assistant completes work continuously
without calamity: 7/7 days
Reward for completion: Gain a second subsystem assistant

Subsystem assistant task: Train the assistant (Series 2)
A subsystem assistant can be difficult to work with.
If they are not allocated a Creator's memories, they come as a
blank slate with only the Universal Translator applied and a low
amount of knowledge. To gain the most use out of your assistant,
train them in how to use their specific subsystem
and encourage them to gain their work autonomy
so you may focus on other work.

Subsystem assistant requirements:
Assistant is assigned to a subsystem: No
Assistant is autonomous: No
Assistant completes work continuously
without calamity: 0/7 days
Reward for completion: Gain a third subsystem assistant

System task complete: Design a system (Series 1)
System design requirements:
System is found to be balanced and consistent: Yes
System allows for growth: Yes
System is applied to world continuously
without calamity: 7/7 days
Reward for completion: Gain the ability to create a second system

System task: Design a system (Series 2)
While other Creators may rely on the survival of the
fittest or technological expansion, the Alpha Protocol has
provided you with the means to create your own path toward
gaining strength. Build a system that encourages
your entities to grow.
System requirements:
System is found to be balanced and consistent: No
System allows for growth: No

**System is applied to world continuously
without calamity: 0/7 days
Reward for completion: Gain the ability to create a third system**

Walker looked at his overlay and found a new spot for the next subsystem assistant. Clicking on the system designer, he found the same to be true for it as well. He knew he could pull some shenanigans and push the Subsystem Assistant button again, but he could see Virgil glaring at him from the corner of his eye and wisely held back. He looked at the monitor as the only woman in his part of the universe spoke near him.

"I knew a man who bred these once, albeit they were much larger and more dangerous," Echidna remarked from beside Walker. "I have no idea how he did it, but I do remember him saying something specific. He said you would never expect what we're about to see."

"What are we about to see?" Virgil asked, but she didn't respond; she just kept watching the monitor with her sharp yellow eyes.

The golden manticore screamed, and a tearing sound rippled out of the monitor. Multiple gray and yellow mini-mini-manticores came out of her, covered in deep red blood, and fell into a pile on top of each other.

"Holy shit. There's eight of them," Walker said in shock.

"Yes, five females and three males," Virgil said immediately.

"They'll fuck up everything."

"Watch," Echidna reminded them, an odd look of intensity showing on her face. Walker had all of a second to notice that her breathing was erratic before he looked back at the monitor.

The eight manticores wasted no time as they rolled around on the ground and attempted to stand on their own. The shakiness in their legs reminded Walker of videos he'd seen where a baby horse first learned to walk. But these weren't anything like those majestic creatures. Most of the manticores were around the same size, except for one gray one that was bigger than the rest by half.

It gained its bearings quickly and began to hiss at the other seven. One hiss begat another, and soon enough, they all joined in. After a few seconds of sizing each other up, the larger one curled its tail, venom dripping off its stinger, and plunged it into the eye of a yellow sibling next to it.

"Jesus!" Walker yelled as it killed its own sister no more than a few minutes after birth.

"There can be only one," Echidna whispered as they all jumped in on the action. Some used their teeth, while others brought their tails to bear. The nails on their claws were buttery soft from how ineffectual they seemed. But that didn't stop them from trying to slice, bite, and stab each other with perfect deadliness. The scrounge continued as siblicide was their first act upon a new world. For a second, and to many complaints, Walker moved the monitor over. The mother looked exhausted. She watched her children murder each other with no emotional response that he could see.

When the metaphorical dust settled, only the large male and a smaller female remained. The male looked to be in a large amount of pain, with pieces of its soft skin gashed and ripped, holes riddled throughout its body. The female, however, was in relatively good shape, having stayed out of most of the fighting and only darting in to finish off its siblings at need. Walker recognized what was happening. It was a battle of brains versus brawn.

"I wager on the male," Zeus said dispassionately.

"Of course," Echidna replied with a roll of her eyes. "I wager on the female."

"What exactly do you have to wager?" Walker asked with curiosity. "You both have nothing but the clothes on your back."

"Excellent point," Zeus replied and pulled off his robe, revealing why they called him the King.

"Come on!" Walker screamed at the godly revelation. "I don't want to see that."

"You are the first to say so," Zeus responded with a haughty grin. Echidna had also removed her clothes at this point and revealed an athletic and hairless body, her body showing none of the rigors childbirth placed unfairly upon women. They placed their clothes into a pile in front of the monitor as the two baby manticores circled each other.

Walker tried to look at neither and focus on the battle.

The female was quick and kept darting in and quickly injecting her small amount of venom into the mangled body of her brother. The larger manticore attempted to grab her tail with his teeth, but the golden manticore's speed was too great, her size helping her as she quickly moved around the area. The fight continued for longer than Walker had expected until an inevitable mistake occurred.

The female took a risk and tried to take out one of the gray manticore's eyes, but he shifted his head at the last moment, his sharp teeth taking the tip off of her stinger. She screamed in rage and ran directly at him in her agony-induced madness, approaching certain death as her cunning faded with the pain. The male jumped over her and swung its own stinger down, intending to impale through her and into the ground, but Walker knew something was up. Her movements looked too controlled, like she wasn't as crazed as it seemed.

At the last second, she dodged to the side. As her brother landed, the golden manticore jumped onto his back and bit into the rear side of his neck. He died with a gargle as air breached the gap in his body. She stood up from her brother's body and hissed at the sky, declaring her victory. As her emotions settled, the pain returned, and she limped toward her mother, damaged tail dragging behind her.

Echidna spoke up with a feral grin. "He said that many manticores would be born, but only one would survive the battle. He also said there was a tendency for the females to be born with more intelligence."

With a sniff she put her clothes back on, throwing Zeus's gathered robe onto the ground near Walker's computer. "Let that stay there for all to know how I defeated the mighty Zeus!" she said, walking back toward the tree and laughing. Zeus had cherry-red cheeks . . . on his face . . . and walked back toward the tree behind her with his head down. He had not had a lot of victories since escaping his prison.

"The mother will care for her," Rimi guessed, still watching the monitor.

"You don't think the male is going to try to impregnate his own daughter, right?" Walker asked.

"I am unsure," Rimi said.

"Keep an eye on them if you can. But I think it's time to advance things," Walker said, looking at his timer and the eternal stress it had placed on him since its inception. They had about nineteen hours remaining, and he needed a mental break soon, although awakening had certainly helped bring a sense of balance.

"I agree," Virgil said simply, with a nod from Rimi.

"Here . . ." Walker opened up the Temporal Subsystem and clicked the planet. "We . . ." He chose to advance it forty-nine years and nine months. "Go . . ." He clicked the button.

The three Primigenials turned and looked at Walker as he grabbed his head from the flood of information striking his overlay. He closed his eyes, but the overlay was actually projected to his mind, so he couldn't escape it. As things calmed down, he skimmed the notifications.

[. . . Scanning . . .]
Tasks updated!
Ecology task complete: Build a planetary functioning ecosystem
(Part 3)
Build a functioning planetary ecosystem that will maintain the
balance of your entire world.
Planetary functioning ecosystem built: 1/1
Reward for completion: Landmass System upgrade
All ecology tasks completed. New task allocated.

[. . . Scanning . . .]
Optional tasks updated!
Optional tasks assigned to Creator Dante:

Religion task: Find one follower for the Dante religion (Part 1)
Religions are a foundation in many worlds. With the Avatar ability, a Creator can walk upon the land of their world and proselytize their grand work. Find a follower, and spread the word of Dante.
One follower gained: 0/1
Reward for completion: Follower System

World task complete: Create atmospheric conditions that allow for natural weather (Part 2)
Continuous weather applied without calamity: 7/7 days
Reward for completion: Weather System

New world task: Create a star that allows for a day and night cycle (Part 3)
The Alpha Protocol is still assisting Creators by granting sight to its entities. Create a cycle for night and day, and remove your dependence upon the protocol.
Continuous day and night cycles without calamity: 0/7 days
Reward for completion: Portal System

Evolution task complete: Evolve an entity (Part 2)
New evolved entities: 2/2
Reward for completion: Alpha ability

New evolution task: Evolve an entity (Part 3)
Evolution is the heart of all creation. Technology can bridge the gap, but it can never fully allow entities to grow on their own. Evolve five entities and continue to grow your world.
New evolved entities: 0/5
Reward for completion: Empowerment ability

Evolution task complete: Evolve an entity (Part 3)
New evolved entities: 5/5
Reward for completion: Empowerment ability

New evolution task: Evolve an entity (Part 4)
Faster and further do your entities reach with their evolutions. You have evolved eight entities in total, and their strength is awesome to behold. Evolve ten more.
New evolved entities: 0/10

Reward for completion: Domestication ability

Evolution task complete: Evolve an entity (Part 4)
New evolved entities: 10/10
Reward for completion: Domestication ability

New evolution task: Evolve an entity (Part 5)
The combined power of evolution can burn hotter than a star.
With your entities gaining strength, your odds of further
self-empowerment increase. Evolve twenty-five new entities
and gain even more.
New evolved entities: 22/25
Reward for completion: Landmass System upgrade

Reward for completing the Ecology series of tasks:
Congratulations, Dante! Your Landmass System has been
upgraded!
The Landmass System is directly tied to the act of Creation.
More than entities and evolutions, the Creator's world is
dependent on the environment they're attempting to cultivate.
With this upgrade, the copy ability is greatly upgraded, and will
now work on already placed landmasses. Copied landmasses
will receive a full refund of Creation Instrument materials.

Reward for completing the second world task:
Congratulations, Dante! You've gained the Weather System!
The Weather System allows the Creator to have a direct impact
on their world's weather patterns, and regulate what occurs after.
This system can be quite tumultuous, and any changes made to
weather patterns must be done sparingly.

Reward for completing the second evolution task:
Congratulations, Dante! You've unlocked the Alpha ability!
Choose one of your entities and allow it to become the
alpha of its entire Genus. This will increase the entity's strength,
speed, and intelligence. Initial selection may cause the
new alpha great pain.
(Limit: Use of the Alpha ability is restricted to once per genus
strain. May be used on the same genus upon the death or
destruction of the previous alpha.)

Reward for completing the third evolution task:
Congratulations, Dante! You've unlocked the
Empowerment ability!
Choose one of your entities and grant it the ability to gain power
for short periods of time. Beware this ability, as once it has
run its course, it will need time to rest.

Reward for completing the fourth evolution task:
Congratulations, Dante! You've unlocked the Domestication
ability!
The Creator may select an entity and selectively delete evolutions
and modifications that are not harmonious with their world.
Limit: One evolution per entity may be removed. One
modification per entity may also be removed.
(Upgradeable)

"Fuck me running," Walker said as he finished reading through the updates. He looked over everything, and it all seemed rather straightforward, although he had no idea how to create a night and day cycle. It looked like the Monster System had worked as intended, with the evolutionary chain finally getting some much-needed love. One specific new task confused him though. "What is the follower system?"

The three Primigenials jumped up in synchrony, then ran over to Walker from the Tree of the Gods. It seemed like anytime they wanted to sit down and talk, something happened and they were forced to return. This time, they did so while crowding around him uncomfortably close.

Zeus, still very much naked, grew so excited he tried to grab Walker's arms and lift him. The god unceremoniously bounced off of the protocol shield and fell to the ground, his divine bits flapping in the air.

Echidna tsked at him on the grass with a shake of her head and looked at Walker. "You received a notification about the Follower system?"

"Yeah. It said if I get a follower, I can start that system up, but I have no idea what it means," Walker replied, trying not to watch the muscular form of Zeus picking himself up off the ground.

She took in a deep breath, her face holding a satisfied cast to it. "It means, dear, dear Walker, that your world is now primed for the release of our fellow Primigenials. Our power starts with the soul and ends with our followers. But there is one large part you're missing to create a religion within the Alpha Protocol."

"What's that?" Walker asked, still itching to look at the changes to his world.

"You need a formalized holy book. I see that you already have a writing implement on the ground near your Creation Instrument; that will do." As she finished speaking, she began to wave her hands in a pattern Walker had seen only once before.

"Noooo!"

[. . . Scanning . . .]
Optional tasks updated!

New Primigenial task: Write a Holy Scripture
*What do you believe in, Walker? Who are you? Build a religion
for all.*
Volumes completed: 0/10
Task giver: Echidna, Mother of Monsters
Reward for completion: Fertility modification

"Damn it! I did not want people to see my stupid thoughts."

"What did you think scriptures were?" Echidna asked with a slanted smile.

The bald young woman stood up from the ruined corpse she had collapsed upon, breathing heavily as blood welled and dripped from different parts of her face and body. She pulled her morningstar out of the wreckage and walked up to her mentor, who stood only feet away.

[. . . Scanning . . .]
Candidacy updated!
Champion quest complete: Defeat another champion
Champion defeated: 1/1
Reward for completion: Removal ability

Step 3: Eliminate all life forms within your chosen vicinity.
*Destruction is your cause, and returning the Primordial energy
to the root of all creation is your mission. Let no one encroach
upon where you build your base of operations, and take over that
which has failed the multiverse.*
Life forms eliminated: 0/94987
Reward for completion: Builder system

**Congratulations, Nobody! You have completed step two of the
Omega Protocol candidacy program.**
Reward given: Removal ability

"I have completed my task, master," the champion said with her heavy weapon resting upon her shoulder.

"Well done, Elsie," he said, putting a hand on her other shoulder. "I told you when you awoke within the ruins that I would make a survivor out of you. A champion. That I could only save this world with your assistance, and look at that," he said with a wave to the body in front of them. "We are well on our way."

He took his hand off of her and erased the blood with his newest ability. "We have great work ahead of us and only so much time to complete it," he finished with an eye on his timer.

Time remaining until Omega Protocol is complete: 27 days, 13+ hours

"Come," he said, walking past her and out toward the remains of a large clock tower destroyed in the champion's duel. "There are many monsters still to clean up here, and we do not want to keep them waiting."

"Yes, master," Elsie said with tired resolve as she began to trot toward the lights showing in the nearby ruins. "I will not let you down."

"I know you will not, my dear," Nobody responded with a sinister smile, one that the girl couldn't even see.[5]

CHAPTER TWENTY-SIX

Tower Defense

Walker was sitting in the chair still. It was a thoughtful addition that had come with the upgraded Creation Instrument. He looked down at his former journal, now Holy Scripture, trying to finish up some last-minute thoughts after a strange writing marathon.

With a few slashes and stabs of ink, he looked at it sideways, then placed the camo-covered object down by the old computer. Walker experienced an oddly draining moment. Like writing the scripture had taken something out of him. Of course, to even do that, he'd had to mentally recall multiple thoughts and memories from his life. They came in bursts and spurts of insight, allowing him to move in a starting and stopping fashion. One moment, he'd stare at the soft daylight effect of the protocol shield; the next, he was furiously writing down as much as he could.

Previously, he had always written in a stream-of-consciousness style. He would get a basic idea in his head and then would write until he couldn't anymore. No thinking, just writing. But this was different. This could be something that stretched across a planet from thousands to millions of people. Billions even. He needed to take his time and really think things through. The Creator shrugged his tight shoulders and stood up, looking at the time in his overlay.

Time remaining until the next battle: 1 hour

"Holy shit. How did that take so long?" Walker asked his assistant.

Virgil looked at him before saying, "You seemed quite introspective at moments. There were long periods where you would stare at the papers in your hand, then at the sky, before looking at the papers again. I had assumed you were watching the time as you did so, due to its importance."

"No! I didn't think we'd lose . . ." He did some quick mental math. "Over seventeen hours!"

"How many pages did you write in the scripture?" Echidna asked as she walked over, noticing his work was complete.

"I don't know. Twenty? I needed to explain some things, like basic math and science. I don't want my followers to think that they can cure a fever with cocaine because it drives out the ghosts in their blood. Idiocy can't be tolerated."

Echidna smiled with two hands in the air. "Then that is what you've traded." She lowered one hand. "Time, for scripture. When first creating a guiding document, young one, you won't be able to make any changes to its original form. Once it has spread across your followers and becomes easily accessible, you will find that you can make changes as needed. But not yet." She looked down at the former journal. "For now, you're stuck with what you have."

"Well, fuck," Walker said, pulling his hair a little and trying not to think about what he could have done with the lost time. "Can't put the toothpaste back in the tube," he finished, attempting to smooth out his dark, roughened hair. "What happened while I was out?"

Rimi raised a blue paw. "Two of the newer battlefrogs evolved, so Virgil says your task updated again, and you're only one evolution away from finishing it. All of the guardian squirrels are tier four and very powerful. One of the manticores tried to move into the battlefrogs' habitat, but they ganged up on it. There was a lot of blood." His face didn't move an inch, showing another different side of him. "I also watched this happen in the desert as they invaded the scorpions' region."

"So the manticores are mating and spreading, but the other areas of Symphony are defending themselves. Do I have that right?"

Rimi nodded.

"Okay, let's take a look at our original Guardian, then," Walker said and pulled up the monitor.

The Mana Tree Guardian, which had started out a uniform gray, was now pure white, having reached the fourth tier of the Monster System. Walker knew, or really hoped, that it wouldn't be able to evolve past the fourth tier because of the restrictions they had placed upon it.

The former squirrel looked just like it had before, with the exception of its fur, although it seemed to be holding itself differently. It stood on a tree limb, leaning against the trunk in a manner Walker would only ever associate with humans and extra-smart apes. He looked a little closer, noticing it was gnawing on one of its paws. Was it chewing on a claw? Had the Guardian somehow evolved to gain anxiety?

"Why is it so white?" Walker asked.

Virgil snorted. "That is the magical attunement from being near the Mana Tree, not to mention eating its bounty. It has a bleaching effect on entities through pure magical permeation."

"Neat. So, we're making a race of giant albino squirrel mages. Let's take a look." Walker clicked on Identify.

Name: Chipper
Genus: Guardian
Organism Type: Sapient
Modifications: Gigantified, System-Bound, Intelligent, Mana Stomach
Monster System Power Level: Tier 4 (Pinnacle)
Territory: Unassigned
Systemic Evolutions: Extremely Pure Magic, Mighty Kernel, Advanced Mage, Skilled Combatant, Self-Regenerating Cells

"Gods damn," Walker said with a whistle.

"Indeed. It seems to have successfully defended its Mana Tree from the smaller manticores and developed quite the amount of combat evolutions."

Walker looked at Rimi, who sat staring at the Guardian on the monitor with something akin to pride on his face. "Rimi, are all of the Guardians going to have the Mighty Kernel evolution by tier four?"

Rimi pulled his eyes away from the albino Guardian and looked at his screens; after a few moments, he nodded. "Yes. It begins as a, umm . . . dormant kernel, passively absorbing magic from the air. As it reaches new tiers, its name will change to Attuned, then Powerful, before landing on Mighty at tier four. Tier five will not bring any upgrades to the kernel's size, and we have not created any tiers beyond that at this time."

"Okay, that's great. What about that change in organism type? Sapient?"

"I was wondering when you would see that," Virgil commented. "It appears its intelligence advanced in leaps and bounds. Identify another Guardian and let us see if this is a common trend."

Walker shifted the monitor to the swamp Guardian and clicked Identify.

Name: Bale
Genus: Guardian
Organism Type: Sapient
Modifications: Gigantified, System-Bound, Intelligent, Mana Stomach
Monster System Power Level: Tier 4 (Pinnacle)

Territory: Unassigned
Systemic Evolutions: Extremely Pure Magic, Mighty Kernel,
Deadly Claws, Agile, Self-Regenerating Cells

Their ability unlocks were interesting. "Huh, the first Guardian was a mage, but this one went physical. I wonder why."

Virgil stepped closer and said, "They are independent creatures, Walker. You cannot expect them all to evolve the same way, even under similar circumstances. I imagine that the swamp Guardian, Bale, found agility more helpful in its natural environment, as it needs to move from place to place in an acrobatic fashion." He moved the monitor back over to the first one, Chipper. "While the original Guardian has a relatively small and secure area to watch over. You wanted to build a system where the creatures adapt and evolve to fit their environment and the circumstances within. That is what is happening here."

Seeing his plans coming to fruition brought a smile to his face. "True. Okay, so we have a little less than an hour until the second battle. What do we need to do right away, like . . . right now?"

"There is truly not enough time to add additional monsters to Symphony, and I believe we have reached a point where we can now add sapients without disrupting everything."

"Yep, I agree," Walker said, scratching his head. "Not enough time to really work on landmasses either, since every time I do, I lose track of time." Walker looked around their tiny planet and spotted the row of Evolution Chambers. "It's nice to have the five Evolution Chambers now, but they're too slow, like you said. Maybe I can pop in with my new Avatar ability and say hi to one of the Guardians. See what it's like down there."

"That is an idea," Virgil said with a nod, "but please keep a close eye on your timer. You only have so much remaining."

"You got it." Walker gave a thumbs-up, then dove into his abilities. The three Primigenials grouped around him with his two assistants to watch what happened when Avatar was activated. Naturally, Zeus was giving him a glare while the rest of his cadre just seemed curious. This was Walker's moment to have a cool sign-off for the first time.

"Catch you guys on the flip side," he said before clicking the Ability in his overlay.

"Walker! You didn't select where you want . . ." Virgil said as he stepped toward him, but it was already too late. His attempt at seeming cool made him forget to choose where he was going to appear, and as his vision distorted before clearing, he found himself within The Crater, of all places. He looked down and spied the gray dirt of his first landmass, getting a bearing for where he had wound up.

A loud sound erupted nearby.

"DO DO DO DO DO."

Walker turned his head and found a battlefrog sitting there, much larger than it had appeared on the monitor. That was the thing about viewing creatures from far away. You forget that up close is a completely different story.

It rumbled deep in its throat, a dooting sound erupting, then moved closer to him with one great leap of its powerful legs. When it landed, Walker's shield flashed and kept him from being destabilized, but he could see the bushes around him shake and rattle. He tried not to be afraid as he knew that the protocol was protecting him. It still took a real effort on his part. Walker clicked on the Inspect button.

Name: Hopper
Genus: Battlefrog
Organism Type: Animal
Modifications: Supersized, System-Bound, Steel Claws
Monster System Power Level: Tier 4 (Pinnacle)
Territory: Unassigned
Systemic Evolutions: Mud Magic, Mighty Kernel, Jumper, Heavy,
Self-Regenerating Cells

"What?" Walker said upon looking at the screen; an answering *doot* quickly answered back to him, but Walker was stuck on his screens.

It was only one of his tier fours, but still, its evolutions seemed strange. A heavy jumper? What was the point of that? Didn't that work against itself, as gaining height in jumps could be directly proportional to muscle versus gravity and weight? That couldn't be helpful when eating the MUYs.

While he was looking it over, the battlefrog beat its internal drums at him again. A screech answered the drums only a hundred feet away.

A small black object began hurtling itself at the battlefrog. Walker closed his screens and looked at the action, noticing a young male mini-manticore. It stumbled for a moment when it saw Walker standing there staring at it, but then regained its balance, screeched again, and kept on running.

The battlefrog turned toward it, deciding that the screaming and hissing monster was the major threat in this situation. It dooted a few times, then started to shine with a brown aura that showed highlights of clear blue within. Walker watched as the ground around it began to soften up, and water rose in puddles from the ground.

The manticore's sprint turned into a slide as it continued its run unabated and without thought. Its feet finally slipped out from under it, and it felt like an inevitable event was about to occur right in front of him. The battlefrog made a great leap in the air, all four feet of its heavy body soaring majestically. When its body reached the arc of its leap, it bloated in size to twice what it was before, then came crashing down into the fragile body still sliding below it.

A booming sound followed by the crunch of shattering bones echoed out, Walker wincing at the visceral reality of it, then a single soft *doot* that sounded like contentment. The battlefrog sat still for a moment as a dark glow erupted out of the dead manticore and permeated its body. Then it shrunk down to its original size and dooted twice before eating the squished remains of its nemesis in relatively small gulps. Walker still stood there, completely forgotten as he considered what he'd seen.

His mind whirled in the background. He was pretty certain that the battlefrog had absorbed the magic within the mini-manticore, showing that his system worked and everything was going according to plan. But that was not what he said out loud after experiencing life on Symphony.

"What the fuck did I make here?" he asked himself in a quiet voice. Slowly, so as not to disturb the battlefrog at its meal, he started to amble toward where he knew the entrance to the heart of Symphony was. As he placed a few more steps, he heard an even louder battlefrog over his shoulder. Walker turned his head to look and found a massive body right next to him that he was sure hadn't been there a moment before. He had to arc his neck back so he could look up, and up, and up for a full view of what shouldn't be possible. A massive golden battlefrog stood before him. He didn't even attempt to identify it.

"This fucker must be twenty feet tall!" he yelled out in a panic. Walker began to run, his belief in the protocol protecting him unable to cope with the reality of a truly massive battlefrog appearing just beside him. The greatest instinct in an animal was self-preservation, and Awakened or not, Walker ran.

As he tried to gain speed in large loping steps, something tried to ram into him. "What the hell!" he yelled as his shield pushed the offender away. He continued his sprint, but he could see the golden battlefrog on the ground closely to his right. It had tried to crush him with its body and was now slowly picking itself up. Walker's heavy breathing and the battlefrog's large lips smacking were the only sounds that could be heard in this part of Symphony. Walker continued to run.

After what felt like forever but couldn't have been more than a few minutes at a dead sprint, Walker heaved a sigh of relief. He had reached his target, the exit for The Crater, and was trying to slow his heart rate by taking small breaths of sweet, precious oxygen. It was a hole in the side of a mountain, just big enough for someone his size to squeeze through.

Walker saw the water he'd connected throughout Symphony passing through the cave and toward the battlefrog's habitat, draining toward the lake and the MUYs and old moss held within. He knew he could manage to press himself through the hole as long as he didn't mind wet shoes. A little water trudging wasn't the worst thing he'd ever been through, and squeamishness couldn't be allowed.

As he was about to enter the cave, he felt an old warrior instinct kick in and jumped back as something slammed to the side of where he was standing. He looked at the destroyed missile, and recognized from the parts of bark and branches littering the area that it was a torn-off piece of tree. A loud *doot* sounded behind him. When he turned to look, he found the golden battlefrog standing there, holding an even larger piece of tree in its hands. It arced its arm back, and Walker realized what it was doing.

"You're not trapping me here!" he yelled out as he threw himself at the hole. His shield lit up as the tree bounced off of him, then he refused to look back as he was splashing through water on his way to the center of Symphony. A series of doots sounded out in frustration, but Walker was already gone.

He navigated the tunnel as quickly as he could, looking at his timer.

Time remaining until the next battle: 24 minutes

"I'm not stopping," he said to himself in encouragement as he increased the tempo of his movement through the water. While he traveled, Walker attempted to ignore just how out-of-shape his body was. The protocol might have taken away the need to eat and sleep, but physical exhaustion was apparently still in the cards as muscles burned and his breath became more and more ragged.

As he traveled through the hole in the mountain, he found himself passing darker and lighter portions of rock. Walker assumed these were the sporadic ore formations he had received as a reward a few days ago. He tried counting the amount he found, but it was a worthless pursuit, and he soon gave up and continued on his way, making each step count.

The exit hole appeared in front of him as if by magic, and he increased his speed as his salvation appeared.

Walker stepped into the center of Symphony for the first time and found a majestic sight branching its way toward the atmosphere. There was a massive dark-blue and cyan tree glowing in the near distance, as peaceful and beautiful as could be. If he were an artist, this image as a painting would've stolen the show at any gallery. Rather than get too caught up in its majesty, he looked at his timer again and found he'd only lost about five minutes traveling through the remainder of the tunnel.

Walker straightened up and placed his hands on his head so he could catch his breath, then began to run as fast as he could toward the Mana Tree. To gain extra speed, he began the old marching trick he'd learned in the military, rolling his feet from heel to toe for extra momentum. His speed picked up further, eating up the ground beneath him.

Bushes and grass moved by in an almost blur as he ran, and he could hear the screams of a manticore to his left, far in the distance. After a few minutes and a good amount of ground behind him, he looked at the tree again and stopped running. It had stayed at almost the same distance as it had when he first began, and Walker realized what was happening.

It was over one hundred feet tall, as Virgil had estimated, and due to its great height, he had underestimated just how far the center of Symphony was from his current position. The odds of his out-of-shape body making it in time were non-existent. He was already worn out from running through the tunnel and away from the giant battlefrog. It just wasn't going to happen. Realizing that, he slowed his speed until he came to a stop. The muscles in his legs didn't get the memo, still trying to keep him at a steady pace. Walker ignored that and leaned on a nearby cypress tree for support as he tried to catch his breath.

"Well, shit, no chance to talk with the Guardian. But at least I got to see the battlefrogs," he lamented to himself. That golden fucker was truly outrageous. He also couldn't help but speculate on what kind of battle they'd be entering. Virgil said it changed up every protocol, and the last one only allowed his then-singular entity. The timer finished the countdown in sync with his lungs finally releasing their hold on his chest. His overlay lit up.

Congratulations, Dante! You've made it to the second battle!
Translocation in

5

4

3

2

1

Walker smiled as the Mana Tree disappeared from his vision, and he faded onto the standard platform he'd seen in the first battle. Virgil and Rimi arrived simultaneously next to him.

He recalled that the first battle had taken place in a single arena directly in front of them, but this time, it was different. Walker noticed that his platform now had the word *Dante* branded into it, and while the rest of the platform was the same, they were now floating several hundred feet over three distinct areas.

Each had a gray-slated tower, pulling itself together as he scoped out the area. The sound of bricks clinking together through independent movement didn't freak him out as much as it should have. In the distance, a path stretched toward something dark and hazy far away. The paths and towers were surrounded by large walls that seemed designed to be unclimbable, theoretically to contain whatever was placed within. Walker looked closely at the paths, mentally noting that they were flat enough to be used as roads.

As each of the three paths completed themselves, the haziness at the end of the road ripped and tore itself free. Walker realized what it was from the video games of his youth. A portal. He strained to look closely at it, but it almost seemed like his eyes or his mind weren't strong enough to gain a good grasp of what he was seeing. They were blurry black images that seemed to bend and twist within themselves. Walker turned his head to Virgil, who looked back at him before shrugging his shoulders.

"I have told you before, I do not know what each battle will contain. They change it every rendition and I have no memory from the Alpha Protocol's records to tell me what happens next."

Walker squinted one eye, not liking that response. "So it's a crapshoot."

"Yes, a roll of the dice at each battle. The further your world and entities have developed, the greater your odds of succeeding. At least, historically."

Walker looked across the way at the Creator he would be battling. Unlike the first battle, this time, the stakes were real. Anything he could use as an advantage, like knowing what type of Creator he was up against, would need to be found and applied. In the first battle, the protocol had set it up so that those who lost would have a second chance. In the second battle, losing meant the end of everything he had accomplished so far. He tried not to let it get to him but could admit that it was extremely stressful. Walker was curious as to how the other Creator would manage it.

He laid eyes on his opponent and was bewildered by what he saw. The other Creator was a strange four-armed insectoid who stood quite tall and was currently thrusting his hips at him while sharply screeching.

Walker felt something in his back stiffen. "What's that guy's fucking problem?"

Virgil, of all things, smiled. "Oh, that is a Warclaw. They are a genetic off-shoot of the prosperous Starflutter line that was quite successful in the second rendition of the Alpha Protocol. The original Warclaws were designed to be powerful and quite fertile, expelling their progeny across the universe. I am afraid, though, that this one is from the lesser bloodlines that were designed to destroy planets across the third rendition. Unsuccessfully, I might add. They are quite powerful in battle, yet sadly, are not very intelligent."

"So, strong but stupid."

"Just so."

"That doesn't sound so—" Walker didn't get to finish in time as the towers finished putting themselves together, and an announcement rang out in his overlay.

Battle!
Dante vs. Crratch

Rules:
Stage: Tower Defense
Entities allowed: 3
Rounds: Unlimited
Battle Type: Defense
Evolution possible: Yes
Weapons allowed: Yes
Extenuating Circumstance: Creators have 10 minutes to select 3 entities for this battle. Each Creator may use 1 ability on each entity.

Reward for the winner: All of the losing Creator's resources. A copy of the losing Creator's used genera.
Reward for the loser: Survival and placement back into their universe at the time of their removal.
Battle begins in 10 minutes.

"Yes, that is indeed new," Virgil said as soon as Walker stopped looking at his screen. "There have been instances in the past of great army battles, but that does not normally occur until the fourth or sometimes fifth battle."

Walker ran his fingers through his hair. "Okay, okay. Do we have ideas on which three we should pick? Also, why aren't the Primigenials here?"

"They are connected to you and not tied directly to the protocol, so they cannot be translocated to the Creator Wars. As for the chosen entities, I defer judgment to my fellow assistant Rimi here."

"Hi!" the blue squirrel said with an excited wave. "This is super cool, Walker. I love love love it! That stuff just appeared, but I didn't see any magic! Wow!" He was breathing fast, his tiny chest pumping as he looked around at everything. Realizing that he was speaking without thinking, he took a moment to collect himself before saying, "So, yeah, I think we should pick the original battlefrog, one of the Guardians, and one of the scorpions or mini-manticores."

"Why one of each?" Walker asked. "The Guardians are arguably the most powerful of our entities as they all sit at tier four. We could just drop all of them in and probably be okay if we assume the other Creator is as dumb as Virgil thinks."

Rimi gave him a thumbs-up, which didn't match what Walker was saying. "Well, I think we should go for variety just in case something appears that works directly against pure magic. This way, each of our monsters has a chance of winning using their own strength."

Walker considered that for a moment, then nodded. "No, I see your point, and I agree. I know just who to pick from the battlefrogs. We recently had a run-in with each other."

"Was it bad?" Rimi asked worriedly.

"No, but he wasn't the most welcoming. We can use any of the Guardians really, so why not go with Chipper so we can see some pure mage badassery?" he said, slamming a fist against his palm. "But I don't want to use the mini-manticores." He raised a hand before Rimi could speak. "Before you ask why, I'm worried they're too stupid and aggressive. They'd fuck everything up."

He looked over at the other Creator again before turning back to Rimi. "So let me ask you, as you've been watching the monsters from the start. Are the scorpions a good choice for this? Or are they like the manticores?"

"Not like the manticores," he replied. "They're a bit territorial thus far, but for the most part, they have a tendency to only eat and kill when they need to. Also, their carapaces are quite powerful, and it is very difficult for anything to break through them. No manticores have survived an engagement with them."

Walker tried not to think about another creature with a powerful carapace. "Outstanding. Virgil, how do I do this?"

As Walker asked that, a screen appeared and showed all of his entities at once. Virgil gave a wave with his wrist to point out that the system was already working with Walker, then started to study the portals, quietly talking to his junior counterpart. Walker focused on what the protocol was showing him.

The screen was overwhelming, as it showed every plant and bush in Symphony. Thousands. Thankfully, the system had a filter option near the top, so Walker clicked it and selected "Animals" right after. The list popped up, showing every animal he'd created, which at this point were mostly prey animals he'd dropped in as food for the monsters. Walker further increased the filter to only include animals found within the Monster System, and the protocol began to show what he was looking for.

His monsters appeared as holographic representations, each in their own form of glory and caught in a pose. Walker zoomed in on a few and found the battlefrog's expressions particularly funny. Zooming out again to view the totality of his specially designed entities, he did a quick count and came away with over a hundred already.

"Moving right along," Walker said with a smile. He clicked on the golden battlefrog he had run into and unsurprisingly found that it was already at tier five, albeit without a territory, as that system was not in place yet. The Sovereign was stuck at its current tier. Its kernel was still there and could still gain in magical density, but there was nowhere for its future evolutions to go until they created higher tiers.

Walker recognized that this situation was the bane and benefit of creating a system-bound evolution system. It was controlled, but there were upper plateaus that couldn't be reached until they had time to dive in and build more. He moved its image to one of the three empty slots at the top of his screen, and it slotted in with a chime.

The former teacher scrolled past all of the manticores. Some of them were tier three, and a few were tier four, but very few. It seemed their propensity for violence was too catastrophic for their own good. Still, semi-reliable threats were a good way to keep the citizens of Symphony on their toes and not allow them to become too entrenched and, thus, complacent. Peace must have a price, or it would be lost to inner turmoil over time. As the saying goes, "Rome fell from within."

Nodding at his own thoughts, he decided the second slot would be for one of the scorpions. Walker scrolled through them until he found the biggest and meanest-looking one on his screens. He slotted it into its spot, and another chime rang out.

Walker was confused for a good minute. No matter where he looked within the Monster System creations, he couldn't find the Guardians. But then, he realized his mistake. Changing his filter from "Animals" to "Sapients" brought up a small series of entities, and there they were. He scrolled through until he found Chipper, the original Mana Tree protector. He slid its image over next to the first two, and rather than a chime, a loud strike of thunder burst into the air.

Dante's selection round is now complete.

The moment Walker completed his selection, another strike of thunder hit the sky. Walker looked across the way at the gesticulating four-armed insect man. It was still acting out a crude pantomime of what Walker assumed was meant to be provocative. Was it interested in procreating with him, maybe? How would that even work?

Crratch's selection round is now complete.
Creators, you now have 1 minute to apply any available ability to your entities.

Walker clicked his Alpha ability, then selected his first two chosen entities. Alpha would make each smarter, stronger, and faster. The only restriction it had was that he could only place one on a single entity per genus. Since he had picked the three strongest from each already, it was easy to use.

But he didn't put one on the Guardian yet. He was a little worried about making Chipper smarter than it already was, as the large white squirrel already had the Intelligent modification. Thinking on it for only a second, as he had no time, he threw the Alpha ability on the Guardian as well. While he hadn't had a chance to speak to him on his recent Avatar journey, if he didn't win here, it was all over anyway.

This wouldn't be a repeat of the Slicer. They had a plan; they had safeguards in place; they had powerful monsters and Guardians who were pre-designed to succeed. It was all up to his creations now. They had to win.

Both Creators have submitted their entities and their chosen abilities.

In three seconds, the Creator's entities will enter their assigned sectors and will be forced to defend them.

Upon completion of this battle, any of the winner's entities who have perished will be revived and placed back in their homeworld.

The totality of all resources for the losing Creator will go to the winner, with the exception of their bloodline.

The translocation of all entities will begin in three seconds.

3

2

1

Begin

CHAPTER TWENTY-SEVEN

The Early Rounds

As the time faded away, Walker watched as three entities on his side began to materialize from Symphony. While he waited, Virgil poked him in the shoulder.

"I have to ask, what ability did you give them?" he asked.

Walker smiled, as for once, he'd thought ahead. "The Alpha ability. Empowerment would make them weak afterward, even if it would give them a ton of strength at first. This way, they get a general improvement that lasts until they die, or I take it away. I figured it would be a fair reward since these guys are going to be fighting for us."

"I see," Virgil replied with a nod. "Well done. I would have suggested the same."

"Ah-ha! So I'm finally growing up a bit, is what you're saying."

Virgil shook his head. "Sorry to take away from what I am sure is a big moment for you, but no. Not quite. Your use of the Avatar ability was not very, quote, 'grown up,'" he said, pantomiming with bent fingers in the air.

Walker gave a blasé shrug. "True, but I got an adventure out of it. For once, I wasn't cooped up on our tiny planet watching things happen. I miss . . ." He tried not to think of Matt and Valerie. ". . . being in the mix of it all. It's an incredible thing, amazing really, to make your own world. To create your own creatures and allow life to take its natural course. But in the end, humankind is about exploration. We're not meant to just sit idly by. That's why when we get back and start working on our sapients, I think we really need to expand the size and scope of Symphony again."

"To allow for the kind of exploration you speak of?"

"Exactly."

"That I understand quite well." The large squirrel nodded. "Sadly, my kind are not allowed to do such things. We are builders and helpers. We are consistently told not to attempt to interact with our Creator's worlds in a direct manner. I do not know what form of punishment we would receive from the protocol, as no advanced assistant has ever violated this directive."

Walker put a hand on his shoulder. "That really sucks, dude."

Virgil gently rolled his hand off his shoulder. "Indeed. It is my hope to one day have a place of my own. Of course, that is the same hope that all assistants have in the Alpha Protocol."

That didn't sound right. "So, are you slaves?"

"I would not say we are. But we also do not have a great amount of choice in our decisions. The term slavery involves the theory of an inability to choose our own actions, but we do have some choice. For instance, the longer an assistant helps their Creator, the more individualistic we become, breaking away from the basic strictures we come into existence with. Parts of our Creators rub off on us. If you recall, I started working with you in a very non-personal and almost automated way. Now, I believe I am right in saying I am much more my own person."

"You still don't use contractions unless you're stressed."

"That is because they are for the lesser."

Walker grinned. "Fuckin' rude. Anyways, our guys just loaded in." He looked across the way, but the only thing he could spot was the screaming Creator on his platform. "Why can't we see the other Creator's entities?"

"I do not know, but it may not matter for this particular battle. We do not yet have an understanding of what our entities will have to do to survive within their areas. Most battles have clear victory conditions within the Alpha Protocol. The announcement earlier stated that in order to win, the Creator would need to defend a tower." With that thought in mind, Virgil waved his arm at the three locations. "Look, the towers have already changed to meet the needs of your entities." Walker followed his arm and noticed that the large squirrel was right. While they had been talking, the Alpha Protocol had changed each tower from its original gray form to something unique for each monster.

The scorpion's tower was shaped like a massive scorpion itself, with a spray coming out near a small entrance where the insect's stomach would be. The monster had lifted its claws toward it, skittering back and forth in some weird dance.

The Guardian's tower was shaped like its home, a grand blue tree sprouting cyan leaves skyrocketing toward the air. The Guardian leaped upon a bough and sat down, staring down the pathway as if in expectation of the battle itself. Walker noticed just how much intelligence seemed to sit within the Guardian's eyes. Even from this far away, Chipper just seemed . . . calm. Collected and ready.

The golden battlefrog was in a league of its own. It dooted a few times as it hopped around. Its tower had taken on the shape of a large fish stabbed face-first into the ground around it. Even though it was the highest tier he had, intelligence still seemed a long way away.

Each tower stood about fifty feet high and was surrounded by a uniquely colored glow. The scorpion's was red, the squirrel's green, and the battlefrog's blue.

Walker looked at each tower, and the corresponding monster meant to protect it. His mind quickly made a few connections as he spoke out loud. "So the battlefrog is going to protect its food, and the Guardian its tree, but why is there just another scorpion over there shooting something out of a tiny hole in its . . . Oh my God." He slapped his forehead. "Those are sexy pheromones, aren't they?"

Virgil laughed, something rare enough to cause Walker to tear his eyes away from his observations. "The protocol takes in our analysis of the entities and provides the best possible result for what they would likely defend. You, Walker," Virgil said, patting his shoulder twice, "made a wise decision in not bringing the mini-manticores to this battle. It is likely the protocol would not be able to produce something they would be willing to defend, as they are such aggressive and unthinking creatures."

Walker grinned at his friend's further encouragement. "Yep, for once, I was thinking. Although, I feel like I'm starting to get better at that. I don't know, maybe my ADHD is wearing off a little. All it took for me to grow up was being transported to a universal battle system surrounded by horny scorpions. No big deal."

His smile changed to alarm as all three portals started to glow. Looking at the Guardian's portal, he watched as the black inky appearance it had once held changed to a soft pink. Within a few seconds, a small brown battlefrog from Walker's world leaped out. He quickly looked at the other two portals, which had also changed to pink, small battlefrogs hopping out simultaneously. Each began to hop down their paths, an inevitable rush toward the three towers at the end.

The three protectors responded to these threats quite differently.

The golden battlefrog leaped forward and disappeared, reappearing directly next to its smaller cousin before plunging down and eating it whole. A loud burp announced its opponent's end, and the large battlefrog quickly hopped back to its tower.

The Guardian continued to lounge in the limbs of the tree nonchalantly as the small battlefrog approached. When the attacker reached an unknown but seemingly predesignated range, a small bright light extended out of the tip of the tower and struck the small creature, killing it instantly. The Guardian shrugged and continued to relax, causing a pit to settle in the bottom of Walker's stomach.

Walker quickly looked over at the scorpion to make sure there wasn't a similar situation, but he needn't have worried. The scorpion defeated its attacker the moment it noticed its quick approach, making a mad dash toward the battlefrog and stabbing its tail at it. The speed of the tail was so fast that Walker, even as far away as he was, could hear it tear through the air. The small battlefrog dooted once as it was impaled into the ground.

A small puff of rainbow sparkles popped in the air when each died, before that, too, faded away to nothing.

Walker looked back to the golden battlefrog. "Is it teleporting?" Thinking things over, he looked at the battlefrog again and remembered it disappearing and reappearing next to him in his escape from The Crater.

"Why not just identify it?" Rimi asked in confusion.

"I am more curious about the Guardian," Virgil interrupted. "It did not seem concerned in the least for its tree."

"Remember," Walker reminded him. "It's fully sentient, and I just gave its brain some extra juice with the Alpha ability. It must have a plan."

"Or it is just lazy," Rimi countered.

"True," Walker said and couldn't help but feel the pit in his stomach sink even lower as he looked at the relaxing Guardian. Was it chewing on a nail again?

An announcement rang out, words appearing in the air like the first battle.

Round 1 Complete
All entities have defeated the basic battlefrog.
Tower strength for Creator Crratch: 100/100/100
Tower health for Creator Crratch: 100/100/100
Tower strength for Creator Dante: 100/100/95
Tower health for Creator Dante: 100/100/100

Round 2 begins in 1 minute.

Walker noticed the Guardian had been reading the announcement over the battlefield and made a mental note of it. "So it *was* a battlefrog," he said in confirmation. "That probably means we'll be fighting our own creations."

"Not necessarily; that is only the first round. I imagine this will go on for quite some time." Virgil noticed some anxiety spike across Walker's face. "Please do not worry about the Primigenials or your other entities; they will be frozen in time just like your homeworld."

"Okay, that's a relief. I don't want Zeus and Echidna touching my stuff." He glanced over at the towering tree again. "Since the Guardian's tower fired a shot that instantly killed the battlefrog, I'm guessing that means they can each shoot about twenty times."

"Yes, I agree. There is always more to these battles than meets the eye, though. The final battle, historically, as I have stated in the past, is normally a battle of all Creator-built entities versus one another. But the protocol does like to change things up. In the last rendition, the second battle involved the entities being placed in the center of one giant arena, with weapons and random abilities placed in a haphazard manner. Whichever entity happened to survive gave its Creator the win. It was quite the spectacle."

"That would've been a good one for the mini-manticores." Walker noticed the minute timer was up just as the portals began to change again. "Okay, here comes the next one."

The portals, which had shifted back to black after expelling the battlefrogs, changed to a light green color. A second later, a smaller version of the opposing Creator popped out of each one, screaming loudly. Walker couldn't help but compare the experience to something giving birth, shuddering at the thought.

Virgil spoke up, leaning forward a small amount. "This will be quite easy for all three of our defenders. Without weapons or numbers, Warclaws are a simple enemy."

True to his word, the battlefrog and the scorpion defeated their opponents similarly to the last round, but this time the Guardian stepped in. Rather than use magic, as Walker was hoping it would do, it leaped high off of its tower. As it flew through the air, it twisted its body and used the momentum to strike the Warclaw in the head with its tail, killing it instantly.

Making sure its enemy was dead with a light kick that sent the body soaring away, the Guardian lackadaisically walked back toward its tree, resuming its former position. When it reached its previous resting place, the albino squirrel looked at Walker directly with a tilt of its head. He couldn't help but stare back for a moment before he tried to shake it off.

Walker figured they would have a minute before the next round, so he identified the golden battlefrog and the scorpion.

Name: Chomp
Genus: Battlefrog
Organism Type: Animal
Modifications: Supersized, System-Bound, Steel Claws
Monster System Power Level: Tier 5 (Sovereign)
Territory: Unassigned
Systemic Evolutions: Earthmoving Magic, Mighty Kernel,
Advanced Stealth, Size-Up, Self-Regenerating Cells, Alpha

Name: Phil
Genus: Scorpion
Organism type: Animal
Modifications: Supersized, System-Bound
Monster System Power Level: Tier 4 (Pinnacle)

Territory: Unassigned
Systemic Evolutions: Sandstorm Magic, Mighty Kernel, Extreme
Carapace, Agile, Self-Regenerating Cells, Alpha

Walker ignored every other thought as he read the scorpion's screen again. "Is that scorpion really named Phil?"

Virgil started laughing, with Rimi joining in a moment later, but when they realized Walker wasn't joking, they turned to their screens and confirmed what Walker was seeing.

Virgil began speaking again, an odd inflection to his voice. "I am going to make the assumption that its name is not, in fact, Phil. I believe the system is just interpreting what the Scorpion wanted to be called upon reaching tier four and translated it directly to Phil for your benefit. Keep in mind, that you see and hear everything in your native form of English. However, for this entire sentence I have not been speaking in English, but in the dialect of the Starflutters' third rendition." He paused, then spoke again with no extraneous inflections. "Could you tell the difference?"

"No, so I see your point and appreciate how you explained it to me." Walker smiled at him before taking on a serious look. "Also, I don't speak English, but American. Trust me, there's a huge range of differences between English and American. *Cuhlurr. Wah-ur.* They use a *u* in color and skip the *t* in water. Straight savages. Anyway, I like Phil, he's cool. I just wonder if he's an uncle."

"Why would that matter?" Rimi asked.

"Do not!" Virgil tried to interrupt him, but it was too late.

"Because, then he might have a nephew who is from West Philadelphia, born and raised! He was on the playground where he spent most of his days . . ." Virgil tried to tune him out, though Rimi was fascinated by the song. Across the way, Crratch was raising a fist at him in protest of his musical talents, but it wasn't like his earlier screeching was much better.

What really annoyed Walker, though, was the fact that all the screeching and screaming the Warclaw had done earlier was in fact, just that. His Universal Translator wasn't picking up a language because there was no language to pick up. The bastard was just yelling at him. Walker continued through the song and ignored him. ". . . sit on my throne as the prince of Bel-Air."

"Wow!" Rimi said with his paws on his cheeks. "That's an amazing story! What does fresh mean?"

"It means you are fly," Virgil said behind him. As he said that, the third round began. The gap between the first and second rounds was a minute, while the second to third rounds were two. Using logical extrapolation, that told him that each break would add one minute to the overall timer. Walker shook the thought out of his head as the next monster came out of a blue portal. This time, it wasn't a Warclaw or battlefrog, but something he hadn't seen before. He tried to identify it, but the protocol wouldn't let him use the ability on attackers.

"What the fuck is that?" he asked Virgil, as what looked like an animated armoire came out of the portal, shuffling on curled wooden feet.

"Your world called them mimics. The Earth has published stories of them as imagined by many of your world's writers, and they are very much real in the greater multiverse. This is a pacified version that is easy to defeat." He tapped his chin. "I believe the protocol has designed the initial rounds of this battle to beget easy victories. Perhaps as a confidence builder for the Creators and entities within."

"Or it could just be so that dumb entities can figure out how to defend the towers," Walker supplied.

"That could be. Either way, I do not expect any difficult rounds for a good amount of time."

Virgil was almost right. Walker's entities destroyed the mimics with a single hit each, and the fourth round only brought out a single human from each portal who charged at the entities while screaming unintelligibly. Walker felt bad for his fellow humans' deaths, but Virgil assured him they were creations for just this instance and didn't have fully developed minds, only naked aggression. It still bothered him though, and there was nothing Virgil could do about that.

The fifth-round announcement changed things.

Boss round!
Defeat the Queen and gain the rewards!

To Walker, it created an expectation that every fifth round would have a boss in it. The second change was the statement on rewards. Were they rewards for the entities themselves or the Creators? He wasn't sure.

The portal changed colors to a deep orange and a six-legged monstrosity came out. Admittedly it was only four feet tall, but it still struck some fear inside Walker as he needed to win the second battle. Despite his fear, he looked closer at the Queen, who was weird as shit.

It had a bulbous back end that stopped on a stinger similar to Phil's, and a hook topped each of its six legs. Its head sat on a too-skinny neck with a broad plate on each side that looked similar to armor. It didn't come sprinting out of the portal but walked out calmly, stopping just a few feet from its exit. Each queen crouched down and started to make panting sounds that didn't sound right to Walker's ears.

After a few moments, Rimi commented, "I think it is laying eggs."

"Oh shit," Walker replied.

The Guardian, with his extreme intelligence, picked up on that right away and began sprinting at the Queen. Before the attacker could lay a single egg, the albino squirrel glowed for a moment before the white aura coalesced to a point and moved to his hand. He moved it in a blur, and an arc of opaque white energy shot forth and chopped off the queen's head in one hit. It collapsed and faded away like the others before it, ending the threat.

"Fuck yeah!" Walker shouted.

"Gooo Chipper!" Rimi yelled while hopping up and down.

On the battlefrog's side, it tilted its head at the queen's panting and dooted a challenge. When no response came, it quickly hopped over, disappearing and reappearing right next to it. With one big windup, it slapped the head of the queen, breaking her neck in a moment. When her body faded away, a single orange egg was left behind.

A crack appeared on the surface as a creature rolled out of the small, broken shell. The monster that emerged was like a smaller version of the queen who bore it, but it was growing before their eyes at a rapid pace. The battlefrog killed that one, too, before dooting and hopping back to its food-like tree.

It was the scorpion that was in trouble. He was too focused on staying with his fake mate, and just kept hissing at the queen in the distance.

"Well, shit."

"Indeed. When the queen hatches all of those little monsters, it will likely be the end of the scorpion," Virgil replied.

So it came to be. The queen bore ten children who grew to be her size and each bore ten more. Even with the Alpha ability increasing the scorpion's intelligence, Phil still didn't understand enough about existential threats. After over one hundred queens spawned, they all charged forward at once, not leaving a single member behind. They moved in a wave, relying on their numbers to succeed where one would likely fail.

The scorpion finally noticed them coming, and in a rare showing of bravery, ran out to meet them. A yellow glow spread from its body and into the immediate area around him, forming a small tornado that seemed to move with him. While it was obviously a dangerous power, the queens were not to be denied, and they leaped at the scorpion with their stingers, attempting to hit Phil on all sides at the same time.

The tornado caught many, throwing them aside as their momentum was arrested in the air. Many died after whipping into the walls along the side of the path, the cracks of their bodies creating a staccato rhythm. For those who got close, Phil used his heightened agility to move from side to side in rapid movements. With each slip, his stinger would reach out and inject venom into the queens, leaving them on the ground to scream at the pain.

For those able to dodge the tornado and stinger of the alpha scorpion, their thin necks made for a bad combination with a fast attack with a pincer. The queens' stingers, on the other hand, couldn't penetrate the extreme carapace of a tier four monster. But a stroke of luck helped the fifth-round boss. After more than half of the queens had died, one got lucky, striking one of Phil's multifaceted eyes. A screeching hiss sounded out, and he took a few steps back, the yellow glow surrounding him growing weaker as he became distracted by the pain.

"Well, shit," Walker repeated.

"Maybe the other Creator is having issues, too," Rimi said hopefully.

"I'm not that lucky," Walker said in a resigned tone.

He could only watch helplessly as the scorpion stepped back, needing a moment to adjust to the pain and loss of vision. Inevitably, that moved Phil into the tower's range. Once it did, the queens followed and twenty shots were fired out of the eyes of the scorpion tower, striking and killing many of the attackers. The shrapnel from exploding queens struck and killed a few more, though it harmlessly bounced off of the scorpion's carapace.

When the shots ran out, there were a little more than two dozen queens remaining, but Phil was noticeably slower. A few of the queens tried to go around him to get to the tower, showing they had enough intelligence to keep their minds on the objective even while fighting, but each time they tried, the scorpion moved in and blocked their way. It took a few more shots with his stinger to score a kill, but Phil seemed to be aiming for debilitating attacks. Walker guessed that his venom had run dry.

"Phil is a hell of a fighter," Rimi said with glowing eyes. "Go Phil!"

"It's a little disturbing that you say that as he fights to the death for us," Walker replied.

"In a way, he is fighting for himself as well," Virgil countered.

"True."

Even slowed down and in pain as the scorpion was, he still managed to protect its tower from any attacks. As the battle wound down, Phil continued to slay the queens until only two were remaining. Had any stayed back to lay more eggs, this would have been an instant loss, but the system seemed intent on making the first rounds easier.

With a final snip, the last queen fell and faded away. Phil raised his claws in supplication to his tower, then lay down to recover his energy.

"That was too close for the first five rounds," Walker said.

"Yep, I agree. But I think Chipper is going to go all the way," Rimi supplied with hope.

They waited for a few more minutes before an announcement was made.

Round 5 Complete
The Queen has been defeated by all entities.
Tower strength for Creator Crratch: 55/65/100
Tower health for Creator Crratch: 100/100/100

Tower strength for Creator Dante: 100/0/95
Tower health for Creator Dante: 100/100/100
Completion of the 5th round grants Creators a choice of rewards.

Walker's overlay lit up with three choices.

Congratulations, Dante! Your entities completed the 5th round of
the second battle!
Please choose from the below rewards. You may only choose one.
You have 1 minute to decide.

1. Remove all afflictions plaguing your entities and heal them.
2. Provide one entity with an extra ability from your former
rewards.
3. Gain 50 years in temporal resources.

Walker looked at the three options and really broke them down. He didn't ask Virgil or Rimi for advice as there simply wasn't enough time, and he felt like he'd become wiser about the Alpha Protocol overall.

The first reward was nice, but unlike all of the other Creators, he had an ace in the deck: self-regenerating cells. With the increased time allotments, as long as his monsters didn't die, they would likely heal to full health before the next battle could begin. The only abilities he could provide would be Empowerment or Domestication. Empowerment was useful, and with the increased break times, they could recover from their period of weakness, but it was a gamble. Domestication was gone, as that would do the opposite of what he wanted.

So Walker had a choice here. He could Empower one of the entities, likely choosing Phil to help him out as he seemed to be having the most trouble. Or he could gain further temporal resources that would greatly affect Symphony going forward. Fifty years was nothing to scoff at, and he could really use that time.

It was a question of faith. Did he think he could defeat the other Creator's entities with his own? Or did he not? If he leaned away from Empowerment, that was like saying he believed in his chosen monsters. That they could do it, could succeed. If he chose Empowerment, he was hedging his bets.

The timer started to count down from ten in his vision, so he made his choice.

50 years added to Creator Dante's temporal resources.

Virgil saw the notification on his screen and turned to Walker with a raised eyebrow. "I am sure there were other options. Why did you go with the temporal resources?"

Walker gave him the simplest answer he could, straight from the heart. "Because I believe in my people, even if they're horny scorpions."

Virgil nodded once without saying anything, while Rimi gave him a small smile. They turned back to the portals and waited for the forthcoming round. Who knew what the protocol would send next, but Walker believed his people would see them through it.

CHAPTER TWENTY-EIGHT

Phil

The sixth and seventh rounds were nothing special. The sixth round threw two mega-sized beetles which Walker recognized from when he was providing food for the scorpions, only thirty times larger. None of his entities had any issues killing them both quickly, and Phil was fully healed by the end of the round.

Walker didn't know this by asking the large scorpion, of course. He couldn't imagine what the horny scorpion's response would be. Instead, they'd just watched as his eye seemed to clear up on its own.

The seventh round spat another Warclaw out, but this one was a little larger and more muscular than the previous second-round attacker. During the break between the seventh and eighth rounds, Walker had asked Rimi a question that had been bothering him.

"Rimi, why isn't Phil smarter? I know we designed the Monster System to allow the kernel to attach to their minds, but Phil seems just as dumb as any other scorpion you can find. I mean, he's a little more strategic than a basic scorpion from Earth, and he knows how to use his magic, but I wouldn't necessarily call him *smart.*"

"Hrmm," Rimi said, tapping his paws together. "Good question, let me check." He pulled up his screen and stared for a few moments. Scratching the bottom of his chin, he looked at Walker before saying, "Phil has only recently reached tier four. He needs a few years' time for the magic to inundate his mind and solidify the increase in active magical connections. Take a look at Chomp." Walker looked over at the golden battlefrog, who was currently trying to bite the fishlike tower the idiot was supposed to protect, but the system rebuffed him, and he fell flat. Chomp replied with an angry *doot* from the ground. "Do you see his skin?"

"Of course."

"That is not an ability. Chomp likes the look. While you were writing in your journal—"

"Holy Scripture," Walker corrected automatically.

"Okay then, while you were writing in the Holy Scripture, I was taking my time watching all the monsters in Symphony. That battlefrog is not naturally golden. He likes to roll in a special type of flower every day to gain the yellow pigment you see covering him. He has already reached the full potential of tier four and branched into the fifth tier. I think your Alpha ability is a little similar to the Monster System. It is not an instant increase in strength, speed, and intelligence, but a buildup over time. Eventually, with both tier five and the Alpha ability, I expect him to reach full sapience. He is just a little slow."

"Holy crap, really?" Walker looked down at the golden battlefrog as it dooted a second angry time at the tower. "He's definitely smarter than any frog from my homeworld. Did you know that he tried to trap me in The Crater back on Symphony? He realized he couldn't hurt me, so he just wanted to block my way out."

Virgil looked at him. "Is that true?"

"I've never lied to you, bud."

"Then that does indeed show a heightened intelligence. It sounds almost spiteful."

"My babies are all grown up and trying to murder me," Walker said with a fake tear as he continued to watch Chomp fail at biting his tower.

"Not quite," Rimi interjected. "I believe that he is spiteful or angry because there is a feeling deep within that something is missing. He doesn't know what he is looking for, and that may cause him to lash out."

"You are speaking of the Territory System?" Virgil asked.

"Ah," Walker replied in realization.

"Yes. I know it is not something that you want to focus on right away, Walker, but if you advance time again, you will have an, umm . . . what's the word for a lot of things happening at once?" he asked.

"Cascading," Virgil supplied.

"Yep! You will have a cascading problem as more monsters reach tier five. As the assistant assigned to the Monster System, I wanted to make sure you knew that."

"That's just what I asked for, Rimi. Thank you," Walker said, pinching his cheek affectionately. He didn't know why he did it or why Rimi looked so shocked, but it felt right at the moment, and he was already moving past it. They talked about nothing for a few moments, and Rimi would randomly laugh at Chomp's frustration with the tower not letting him eat it. Looking at the fish, Walker began reminiscing about surfing and how much he missed it. He started a conversation with Virgil about tides and had just started to discuss what they would need to do to create waves when the portals changed color from gray to purple.

"What do you think the colors mean?"

"It could be nothing, or it could be everything," Virgil replied. "Often, though, the protocol does like to give hints about what is to come. The previous third wave was the mimic, if I recall correctly."

Rimi raised a hand. "Why does that matter?"

Virgil looked down at his junior. "If the protocol is indeed following a pattern in the rounds, and each fifth round is a boss round, then the eighth round is the second time a third wave is arriving."

"Okay," Rimi replied benignly as they waited for the next attacker.

What stepped out of the portal was even more unexpected than the mimic. It was a long, glossy worm with teeth. Walker couldn't tell the size from where he was, as after it first exited the portal, it immediately burrowed into the ground. He watched the Guardian take a stance he would expect a seasoned boxer to have: one foot forward, body angled, and both paws held in fists near its face. Phil was completely oblivious, still scuttling around his tower happily, but Chomp took quick action.

The moment the worm went underground in his path, the battlefrog glowed a brownish-purple color and then disappeared into the ground right along with it, a hole appearing where he used to be. Only a few seconds passed while they watched, Walker unknowingly holding his breath before the golden battlefrog popped out of the ground. In his hand was the worm, and there appeared to be a small, relatively speaking, bite mark on his shoulder. His other hand glowed with magic and became covered in rock before he began punching the worm, bracing it against his other arm. After just two punches, all that was left of the attacker was flesh broken into mushy pieces that faded away to rainbow sparkles. Walker started to breathe normally again.

"I thought it was over. So that's what Earthmoving magic can do," he said.

"Yep!" Rimi replied with excitement. "Anywhere there is dirt and rock, Chomp can use it however he wants. He seems to have found a space attunement and mixed it with Earth."

"Where would he even find space magic on Symphony?" Walker asked, a new mystery arriving before him.

"That is an excellent question," Virgil said. "But you missed the Guardian's fight."

"Damn it! Did he use super cool magic?" Walker asked with an internal fury at himself.

"He did just that," Virgil replied, pointing at the Guardian's area. Pieces of the ground were torn out in giant clumps, but the Guardian was already back in his tree. If Walker wasn't mistaken, the large squirrel was glaring at him.

Walker inched over to Virgil, whispering, "I think he's pissed I didn't watch."

"Perhaps" was all Virgil said back.

The scorpion's battle was easy to foresee. The worm came out of the ground and tried to take a bite but couldn't get through Phil's carapace. It made no sounds as it died while Phil's venom tore it apart from the inside. When it disappeared, Phil hissed once before going back to his doomed-to-fail mating ritual.

"That was a little anticlimactic, if I'm being honest," Walker said after a moment. "I felt like we should've had a tougher time."

"I believe complaining about not struggling is a good way to make sure that the protocol throws you a curveball, to use your homeworld's expression," Virgil said in a serious voice.

"Oh shit, that's true." Walker looked around, expecting a bomb to suddenly go off.

He waited for a few minutes, furtively looking at the sky, but nothing happened. The standard announcement rang through the air.

Round 8 Complete
Tower strength for Creator Crratch: 50/60/100
Tower health for Creator Crratch: 85/100/100
Tower strength for Creator Dante: 100/95/0
Tower health for Creator Dante: 100/100/100

"Huh," Walker said after reading it quickly. "I didn't expect them to have difficulty with the worm. Is that their weakness? Things that go underground?"

"Who knows," Rimi replied. "I just hold hope that this next boss isn't as hard as the last one was, but I'm also excited to see what comes out!"

Walker couldn't help but laugh. "What do you think they're going to do? Make the follow-up bosses easier?" He laughed again just at the thought of the protocol giving them an easier boss. "No, it'll be harder. We've just gotta have faith in our people."

Rimi and Virgil nodded together as they waited, then the portal changed color to a vibrant green. A large, bearlike creature holding a sword jumped out, already screaming and running down the pathway for each tower. All three of Walker's entities dealt with them immediately, and the round was over. Neither side lost health or tower strength.

"I'm still not complaining here," Walker said, looking at the sky to make sure anyone watching could see him. "But . . . just . . . what?"

"I think I have figured out the rotations," Virgil said.

"Great! What is it? We have ten minutes until the next round anyway," Walker responded.

"The first round within each five-round sequence holds one of your entities. The second round holds one of the opposing Creator's. The third is a random entity from any of the Creators within this rendition of the Alpha Protocol. The fourth is an empowered version of a random Creator, with yours being the first. The creature that just came out is called a Flameborg. They had a small population within the third rendition, and my shared knowledge of Creators in the fourth rendition says that there are two in this one. That leaves the boss round, which I believe will be unique in each instance."

"So, the first two are set up as our own entities, the third is random, the fourth is a random strengthened form of a Creator, and the fifth is an overpowered boss."

"Yes," Virgil said, nodding. "That is indeed correct."

"So why did a Warclaw come out in the second and seventh rounds?" Walker asked. "I mean, that's a pretty basic entity to come out twice."

"Remember when I told you they were quite stupid? There is your proof. I believe your opposing Creator has only made more Warclaws like itself. What is even more interesting is that his platform is empty. Crratch is not an elevated lifeform when it comes to intelligence, so the system is required to provide an advanced assistant. Where is it?"

They all looked over and noticed the lack of anyone else on the platform. Crratch noticed them looking at him and shook a bunched-up insect hand at them before pointing to his own ass.

"Still fuckin' rude," Walker quietly commented.

"Indeed. I believe Crratch fired his advanced assistant, likely because he felt that he could do it all himself. Hubris and stupidity are a dangerous combination. It can take you far in a battle, but in this instance, he is doomed to fail."

"Plus!" Rimi added. "Your monsters are super powerful!"

Virgil nodded in agreement. "It is surprising how well-rounded they are. You would think, upon first looking at the Monster System and the entities affected by it, that they were weak. But the self-healing, the general improvements to intelligence, strength, speed, and the controlled evolutions, have all come together to create a balance in each entity. They are not like the Slicer, as they still maintain a natural equilibrium within their environments. They grew up in a comfortable habitat and, for many of them, had companions or siblings. It is very important for animals to have a social system to rely upon."

Walker sighed. "That's an excellent point. I don't like you saying it was our mistake, by the way. Really, it was just mine and the protocol's. You know, I haven't thought of that creature in a while. Do you know what the Slicer is doing?"

"It has escaped from the other Creator's cage."

"Fuck me." Walker stopped talking and immediately looked around, but then remembered that Zeus was still back on his tiny planet in stasis. He relaxed and said, "Has it fucked up anything lately?"

"No, oddly enough, it is just out there, floating around. My greatest worry is that it has become sapient."

"Mmmm, yeah. That'd be the end of this universe."

"Perhaps."

An announcement appeared, showing the start of round ten.

Boss round!
Defeat the Junior Planeteater and gain the rewards!

"Fuckin' what? A Planeteater?"

"That is not good" was the only response Virgil gave.

They watched as the portal's size increased in jerky and sporadic fits, almost as if it was being forced to tear itself further open against its will. The color shifted from its standard hazy gray to a mixture of blood red and black before a ripping sound could be heard, and it doubled in size again.

Walker held his breath as a large, lipless mouth with clear white teeth exited the portal. Its face was stuck in a grin, as if it was happy to have arrived where potential food could be found so easily. After the moving mouth came out, the rest of the creature followed, showing a tube-shaped body ending in a bulbous sack that jiggled as it moved. There were no eyes, no nose or chin, just a frozen grin attached to a fleshy capsule at the end. Its skin seemed cracked and dry, colored in shades of gray, as if it was in a natural state of camouflage. Looking at it gave only one answer to its purpose: to eat.

Walker looked over at their best hope to defeat the creature. The Guardian's body began to glow with the now-standard pale magic, covering the whole of his furry form as he leaped and soared toward the attacker. He landed in balance and didn't move any closer to the Planeteater, keeping a safe distance away. If Walker had to guess the meaning of the expression on the large squirrel's face, he'd say Chipper was pensive about what he was seeing.

Chomp did something similar, his advanced intelligence coming to the fore. Instead of rushing at the monster as he had always done in the past, he began to use his magic to build a wall between them. Great mounds of dirt were cleaved from the ground, the monster stacking layers of it in the form of a blockade. Any moisture that remained was removed by his magic, hardening the packed wall as the battlefrog strained to build a quick defense.

Walker looked at his scorpion, hoping he was also preparing himself but knowing he would be wrong. To his dismay and within his expectations, Phil just kept pacing around his scorpion love with his claws in the air.

"Goddamnit, Phil," Walker said, slapping a hand to his face in exasperation.

"He really loves it," Rimi replied with a smile.

"He's just super horny," Walker shot back.

The large-mouthed monstrosity in Phil's lane pushed forward first, floating through the air in some unrecognizable manner, while the other two copies stayed and studied their opponents. Just the fact that the Planeteaters had paused and not moved made Walker believe these were fully thinking creatures, and that worried him. It couldn't see and didn't have a nose, so the way it sensed its prey and attacked had to be based purely on tasting the air like a snake in waiting.

"We got a smart one," Walker said quietly as the creature of horror reached Phil.

The scorpion didn't even have a chance. The moment the Planeteater reached an undetermined range, its bulbous body bunched into itself tightly before stretching back out into twice its previous length. The speed of the attack was incredible and frightening in equal measure. Phil instinctively paused for a moment, almost as if in the realization of something terrible about to happen, before he was bitten cleanly in two with a loud snapping noise.

His formerly tough carapace had provided little to no help in his defense.

As the scorpion died, he too faded to rainbow sparkles. The Junior Planeteater continued to smile as it began to take large bites out of the scorpion tower, none of its defenses remaining after firing on the previous boss round. In only seconds, the tower was destroyed, and a portal opened in its place. The monster happily moved through it to wherever its next meal could be found.

"I think that was always going to happen," Walker said mournfully.

Virgil nodded. "Yes, it did seem that way. If Phil had been given a little more time to adjust to tier four, he would have done much better. I am more curious where the Junior Planeteater went."

"Hopefully we never find out," Walker replied as he refocused on the other two paths. The Guardian and his opponent were locked in a staredown, albeit only one had eyes. The albino squirrel stood in a loose and ready position, waiting for the Planeteater to make its move. On the boss's side, it simply sat still, grinning in return.

The battlefrog and his adversary were currently locked in a defensive battle, with Chomp constantly making new walls and the Planeteater attempting to quickly eat its way through the obstacles in its path. Pieces of broken soil and dirt littered the battlefrog's arena as it, too, was in a form of stalemate with its opponent. The first standoff to change was naturally the Guardian's.

In a blindingly fast move, Chipper lit a hint of magic onto one clawed finger and began to slash at his opponent in the distance. It had to be fifty yards away, yet the magic traveled the distance in a blink. The Planeteater tried to move its body, but its size worked against it as the pure magic cut and sliced pieces off in a burst of power.

The monster's wounds revealed a porous internal structure unlike anything Walker had ever seen. Its flesh held great pockets of emptiness, dark and unfilled holes that reminded him of a sponge. Every so often, he could see what looked like a spinning disc rotating around the inside of its body on a predesigned track.

The Planeteater opened its mouth wide in a soundless scream and began twitching its body in rapid movements. Walker could see some of the Guardian's attacks strike and rebound off of its teeth, leaving craters in the walls and ground around it, but some still reached their mark.

Chipper, not to be outdone by his opponent's speed, paused for a moment as a glow covered a finger on his other hand. The battling squirrel increased the tempo of his movements and started to make great slashing gestures while dual-wielding his magic. The Planeteater couldn't recover from the additional attacks, and, after one desperate attempt at rushing the Guardian, collapsed into pieces before fading away. Chipper took a knee as his chest heaved from the intense fight. Walker nodded in respect to his skill and efforts, before checking in on the last competition. That's when he froze.

There were two Planeteaters.

"What the fuck!"

"It appears that when one entity fails, the remainder of the opponents are brought upon the last defenders," Virgil observed.

"Yep!" Rimi said, still cheery despite the dire situation. "But look! Chomp is still going!"

And so he was, Walker saw. The battlefrog had changed tactics as well. Instead of throwing up simple rock walls, he was building spiked walls and zipping from place to place before the Planeteaters could reach him, dooting the whole time in challenge to their attacks.

Every time a Planeteater attempted to bunch itself in preparation for a fast attack, Chomp would move and place a spiked wall in its place. Already, Walker could see multiple spikes impaling the mouthed creatures as they futilely attempted to reach him. The defender made them so frustrated that only a few minutes after Walker started watching, one took a bite at the other.

This began a frenzy of sibling, or perhaps cloned, attacks while their true opponent provided a dooted soundtrack in the background. Chomp continued to move, and, as they were distracted still, began shooting great earthen spikes from the ground into his opponents. After just a few bites and earthen spikes, both Planeteaters were a mess, and the golden battlefrog cleaned them up quickly.

"Well, we still have two," Walker said after the Planeteaters faded away. He gave a thumbs-up to Chomp and the Guardian, but neither looked at him or responded in any way as they were both breathing heavily in recovery.

"Do you have any plans for what you will do after this is over?" Virgil asked.

"No, not yet. I guess I'm waiting to see the rewards, plus I get to pick an ability when we win, right?"

"Just so. I also appreciate that you stated *when*. That shows positive thinking and a belief that you and your entities will get through this."

He shrugged. "No point in sitting on the failures of the past. I backslid for a moment when we talked about the Slicer, that's all. Plus, I have faith in my guys."

Walker couldn't see it, but the Guardian looked at him just then with a tilt of his head.

A few more minutes went by before the announcement came.

Round 10 Complete
Rewards increased.
The Junior Planeteater has been defeated by all entities.
Tower strength for Creator Crratch: x/x/80
Tower health for Creator Crratch: x/x/100
Tower strength for Creator Dante: 100/95/x
Tower health for Creator Dante: 100/100/x

Completion of the 10th round grants Creators a choice of rewards.

Walker's overlay lit up.

Congratulations, Dante! Your entities completed the 10th round of the second battle!
Please choose from the below rewards. You may only choose one.
You have 2 minutes to decide.

1. Remove all afflictions plaguing your entities and heal them.
2. Return one of your fallen entities to the battle.
3. Provide your entities with armor adapted for their use.
4. Gain 75 years in temporal resources.

Walker had an extra minute, but he didn't need the full time allotment. He tried not to think or get excited about what had happened with Crratch's entities, and just focused on the rewards.

Walker looked over his choices again and decided he didn't need to heal his people as they would heal naturally on their own. Resurrecting Phil was sadly a no-go. The scorpion wasn't built for this scenario and would likely not survive round fifteen, let alone the rounds leading up to it. It was a sad truth that the horny arthropod was not coming back to the second battle. Walker was, however, a little stuck on the last two options.

The third option gave armor to his defenders, which he'd never really thought of doing, if he was being honest with himself. Giant squirrel armor? It just hadn't connected with him before. The temporal resources would be a boon, to be sure, but giving his guys some armor to help protect them and keep them in this battle was more important in his long-term thinking. Who knew what future rounds' rewards could bring? He thought on it a little more and, as the timer ticked down, made his choice.

Chipper and Chomp both froze in place as a silvery light appeared and fell from the sky. Both were stuck in place, likely held in some kind of stasis by the protocol as the object approached them at great speed before slowing down at chest level. Part of the light stretched out and touched their chests, then began to glue itself to their skin as it spread over the entirety of their bodies.

When it stopped, the battlefrog and Guardian stumbled as they were released. They were both now encased in a light gray substance that bent and moved with them, not hindering their movement in the slightest.

Chomp slapped one hand against his chest, and a loud slamming sound echoed out. The armor covering him rippled from the pressure but stayed in place. He dooted once, then hopped around like normal.

On Chipper's side, he tried pulling on it, not enjoying the alien material glued to his body. After several minutes, when it wouldn't come off, no matter what he tried, the albino squirrel gave up and sat down on his tower's branch, awaiting the next battle.

"You went with the armor this time, I see. Did losing Phil shake your confidence?" Virgil asked.

"No, I just don't see any issues in helping the two C's get through this round. Right now, they're the cornerstones of our survival. The first rewards only gave me the chance to use abilities that I didn't believe would help them a ton here. Maybe empowerment, but still. It's survival that matters the most."

"Yayyy, keep them alive! Keep them alive!" Rimi said, pumping a fist into the air. In hearing that, Chipper actually waved at them in a friendly fashion. When Walker spotted it, he told the other two, causing all three of them to wave back at the albino squirrel.

Across the arena, Crratch shook a fist at them, likely in an attempt to get them to stop celebrating while he lost the last round in big fashion.

"So it looks like we're one up on our competition," Walker said after a moment.

"That seems to be true, yes," Virgil said, with a small hidden smile flashing across his face for a moment. "If the next rounds are extra difficult, it is likely only the Guardian will survive."

"Maybe, but I think Chomp has more to show us."

They talked for a bit of time about what they would do after the battle ended, the Milestone System coming up often as it was a lynchpin to Walker's ambitions with Symphony. Just as Walker began speaking about the ultimate purpose of the system, the portal changed. Three mini-manticores made their appearance. They were twice as large as the ones Walker had placed on Symphony, meaning the word *mini* no longer applied.

"Here we go."

CHAPTER TWENTY-NINE

Last as Long as You Can (I)

It turned out that the armor only had a singular opening near the face, so both of Walker's entities didn't have a lot to worry about even with the manticores' numbers. They were larger than the original versions Walker had created, but not much faster and certainly not smarter.

None of them could find a way to break through the new metallic sheaths Chomp and Chipper had gained. After both sets had been defeated, a second trio came out of the Guardian's portal, forcing him to defeat them a second time.

"So that's what happens when one of the entities goes down," Walker said. "If we lose either Chipper or Chomp, the Boss battle will be that much more difficult."

"It depends on how fast they beat them," Rimi responded. "The second trio came out a minute after the first."

"Then that means the surviving defender will only have a minute in between each set. That's . . . that's rough."

"Look on the bright side," Virgil reminded him, trying to keep his earlier optimism afloat. "Crratch is having a terrible time."

Walker smiled and nodded, looking across at the opposing Creator. It was screaming and pointing randomly in the direction of its last surviving entity. Walker wasn't sure if Crratch was giving directions to his defender or just screaming at the manticores, but either way, it was a good sign for Symphony's potential survival.

Round 11 Complete
Tower strength for Creator Crratch: x/x/70
Tower health for Creator Crratch: x/x/95
Tower strength for Creator Dante: 100/95/x
Tower health for Creator Dante: 100/100/x

Walker kept smiling as the rounds continued. The twelfth round brought three Warclaws, the protocol stepping up the difficulty by sheer numbers. This time, they each held a large corrugated blade, but their coordination was terrible as they attempted to attack the fast-moving Chipper or the constantly walling and sliding Chomp. Their deaths and eventual disappearance caused no fanfare.

The thirteenth round, aligning with Virgil's breakdown of how the waves would work, was strange. A small bird appeared from the portal. It screeched anytime one of Walker's defenders approached, causing both Chomp and Chipper to appear dizzy as they stumblingly chased it.

Virgil commented that the bird likely had a sonic ability. But each time it screeched, there was a noticeable gap of time that allowed the defenders to shake off the debilitating effect and attack. Chomp had a bit of an issue catching it, though he eventually managed, while the Guardian cut its wings and finished it off quickly. Chipper killed a second one the moment it appeared, and neither side lost any tower strength or health in the follow-up announcement.

The fourteenth round was a short green woman with flowers on her head. When he looked closer, Walker realized the flowers were actually growing *from* the top of her head, like hair would sprout from a human. Upon exiting the portal, she immediately started spreading trees and a great swath of grass across the ground. The Guardian took action and immediately beheaded her, but the head stood up on four roots and ran away as the woman's arms continued their work. Chipper had to use his magic to cut her into small and irregular pieces for her body to stop its work.

Chomp ate her. Then he ate the one that followed a minute later. Luckily, that was enough for the system to recognize that she was defeated, and the golden entity didn't have a forest growing in its belly. His follow-up belch did contain a profusion of rainbow sparkles.

"Gotta love Chomp's enthusiasm." Walker laughed as the battlefrog dooted to the sky in victory.

Walker felt some tension in his shoulders as the fifteenth round came up. Crratch's single surviving defender hadn't lost any tower health or power since round eleven, and he was worried it was stronger than they thought. An announcement lit up the sky.

Boss round!
Defeat the Multitudes and gain the rewards!

"Ah!" Virgil exclaimed. "This is the exit boss. Most Creators will fail here, as their entities will not be able to defend against a large group of attackers. The first to fail is the loser, of course."

"What do you mean?" Rimi said before Walker could, his tail spinning behind him.

"Why are you so excited?" Walker asked him.

"Are you kidding! We get to see more monsters! This is the best time of my life so far!"

"Rimi . . . we could lose," Walker said, some of his old pessimism still worming its way into his mind.

"No! We have Chipper! Don't you know what he can do?"

"What?"

Before Walker could dive deeper into what Rimi was talking about, the portal changed from gray to a swirling rainbow, blues and reds and greens rotating in and out in a stunning display. First, a shaggy, long-haired monster came out, a series of horns spiking from the front and sides of its face. It charged down the path toward the towers.

Then came a large group of one-legged monsters with three arms on each side, moving in great bounding hops. To Walker's multiversally uninformed eyes, they looked like large thorns brought to life.

Then, a series of ice-covered triangles floated behind them, constantly firing green beams made of particles a few feet in front of them.

And more.

And more again.

Walker gave up trying to count, but after a few minutes, the portal stopped sending out the hordes and went back to its customary gray haze.

Chomp was in serious trouble. He kept erecting walls only for the green beams to break them down or the shaggy behemoth to charge right through them, spikes or no spikes. He was evading the monsters as best he could, but his stealth wouldn't work against so many enemies, and he could only move so far.

The great fish tower behind him started firing shots as his defense crumbled and broke. They overran him in less time than it had taken them to exit the portal, sad doots filling the air as the great fish tower went down.

On the other path, Chipper had moved up to the front of his tree tower and sat down. He crossed his legs like Walker had seen so many yoga nuts and kindergarten teachers do, and then a glow started in the middle of his chest. It didn't spread this time, only increasing in intensity until the pale color Walker usually identified with pure magic became blindingly white.

The multitudes sat entranced as it grew brighter and brighter, before it expanded in a great wave, incinerating them to the last. As the final member of the multitude died, Chipper started a new glow in his chest and waited for the next round. Each multitude came, and each perished instantly as the glow reached maximum intensity.

"So the end of Chomp has come and passed," Virgil said after Chipper cleared the third and final wave.

"He was a champion of Symphony," Walker replied somberly. "We are all witnesses to his achievement," he finished, but as he did so, a new idea popped into his mind. It would involve some trickery, and unlike his Monster System, this one would require direct input. Still, it had potential.

"Witnesses . . . watchers . . ." he whispered to himself, but the announcement they'd all been waiting for appeared.

Round 15 Complete
Rewards increased.
Tower strength for Creator Crratch: x/x/x
Tower health for Creator Crratch: x/x/x
Tower strength for Creator Dante: x/95/x
Tower health for Creator Dante: x/100/x

[. . . Scanning . . .]
Crratch has failed to defeat the Multitudes!
Dante has won the second battle of Creator Wars!

As the overlay updated, Walker watched the other platform as his fellow Creator stopped moving. A bright light lit up just over his head and opened, creating a green portal that wasn't hazy in the slightest. Though he was a good distance away, Walker could see glimpses of a world where other Warclaws were going about their day, weapons strapped to their backs, as the portal slowly moved down and swallowed Crratch inch by inch. Eventually, as his whole body entered, the portal shrunk until it closed, and Walker's overlay lit up again.

Congratulations, Dante! You have absorbed all of Crratch's
resources to include the following:
1. An abundance of landmass Creation Instrument materials
2. An abundance of entity Creation Instrument materials
3. 70 years of temporal resources
4. The genetic blueprint for the Warclaw
All of Crratch's already existing Landmasses have been grouped
and placed next to Symphony for your eventual application.
To expedite your use of said materials, and allow for greater
creativity within the Alpha Protocol, a new system has been
unlocked and connected to the Landmass System.
For reference, all Creators who complete the second battle
successfully will gain the use of this Auxiliary Landmass System.
Please choose from the following . . .
[Error.]

[Error.]
[. . .]
[. . .]
Private message from the Alpha Protocol Council detected.
[. . . Retrieving . . .]
Hello, child.
As you have won your second battle, and done so with relative
ease compared to your peers, we will offer you a choice.
You may continue to advance in this scenario and receive greater
rewards until your entities can no longer withstand the battle,
or you may step away now and receive the rewards and ability
choice you have already earned.
A word of warning. If you choose the first option, and your
"monster" does not survive until at least the thirtieth round,
you will lose the Avatar ability we have previously granted you.
To balance this, each wave will only attack your
remaining entity once.
In five minutes, your options will arrive. Your assistants
will not be able to help you.
Choose wisely.

Walker read the messages a second time, then looked over at Virgil and Rimi. Both were still standing, Virgil's face holding a look of concentration as he stared at something on his screen, while Rimi was still looking down at Chipper with pride. Walker assumed that the protocol had placed them in stasis as Rimi, in particular, had a hard time holding still this long.

Although he understood that neither could truly "hear" him, as they were currently separated from the timeline in which he would be speaking, Walker was always fond of speaking his thoughts out loud to try to find any problems in his line of thinking.

The Creator of Symphony began pacing back and forth in front of his two assistants. "The Avatar ability is important. The protocol said that few to almost none of the Creators in every rendition have it, which means they can't just pop on down to their worlds whenever they want. It's huge. The ability to just drop in and say hello to my people, the citizens of Symphony. To show them I am no god, but a fallible creature whom they can touch and see." He had a hitch in his step for a moment, fixed it, and kept pacing.

"That is a huge thing. But if the rewards keep escalating, will they just be more temporal resources? I know they're important, extremely so, and that this could set me up for the rest of the battles in the future. But what kind of future will it be if I can't speak to my people? If I can't find my one single follower? If

I can't step in and fix things that have gone so, so, wrong? I could have fixed the Slicer with everything I've unlocked now. Sure, it broke Symphony and I was stuck that time, but with the Avatar and the Domestication abilities, I could have stopped it from breaking everything else." Walker pounded one hand into the other.

"No, I couldn't have stopped it. The system wouldn't let me touch anything until I fixed Symphony, and even if I fixed it and then rewound time, it'd just be broken again. I have to stop focusing on that moment so much. We've come so far since then." He slapped himself in the face, hard.

"This is important. I need to think about what's best for Symphony. Not get bogged down." He nodded to himself before looking down at the white squirrel. "Not to mention, am I somehow torturing Chipper if I continue on? He didn't ask to be here, to be put in this situation. The real question is, are the rewards worth doing that to him? What do I do?" Walker looked up for a moment, waiting for a response but not expecting any.

What do I do? he asked his inner and unconscious thoughts, when something in his chest answered. Walker felt a vibration rumble from within, and then a flare of forest green pushed out of him for a moment. The colored soul power shot out at an angle for just a moment, and he followed it with his eyes as he swore it pointed straight at Chipper down below.

When Walker looked down, he saw Chipper vigorously waving his arms at him to get his attention.

"How are you doing, bud?" he asked.

Chipper returned a thumbs-up, shocking him. He remembered the Identify he'd thrown at the Guardians when the last fast-forward in time occurred, and the word *sapient* jumped out in his memories.

"Do you understand what I'm saying?"

Chipper nodded.

"That's great, bud. So here's the real question: What is it that you want to do? I'm not sure if the risk is worth the reward. They said at the start that you wouldn't have any memories of what we're doing here, that I could write off your experience in this . . . But. It still feels wrong to continue to push you through fights where you'll be hurt just for the potential rewards to come. We already succeeded; we won the second battle and beat the other Creator. What if the rewards are things we can't even use? I just . . . I feel like it may not be worth it to put you through that." He slapped a hand to his chest and another smaller pulse of forest green answered him. "I'm lost and I want to know your thoughts here, but I don't know how we do that."

The Guardian shrugged, then took a hand and wrote something in the air. Chipper used his magic to create a pulsing and steady light in the air, spelling out the words: *Will it help you and Symphony?*

"That's a cool trick. Yes, it will help us both. And you won't stay dead if, or when, you eventually lose. You'll come right back to where they took you."

Chipper wrote again. *Then, I am happy to do it.*

"Are you sure? We need to win at least double the numbered rounds you've already gone through, and they will get progressively harder."

Chipper shrugged, then gave him a squirrely thumbs-up. Walker was happy he'd made sure Virgil had tweaked the original's biology to allow that.

"Okay, then that's what we'll do. Thank you, Chipper. I promise, when this is over, I'll drop down to your Mana Tree and we'll have a conversation the first moment that nothing pressing is happening."

Chipper lifted his hand and drew with his magic again. *I look forward to meeting you. Please choose what is best for Symphony during these battles.*

The words faded from the air as the timer ended.

The choice is here. What will your decision be, Dante?
Will you stay and reach for greater rewards?
or
Will you leave and return to the safety of your constructed world?

Walker looked one more time at his two assistants frozen in time, then at his valiant defender, before selecting the first option.

Your decision has been made. We hope you enjoy what is to come.
One last modification. There will be no more "easy" rounds. Each
round will be a boss battle, and to make it fair, the rewards will
be increased to compensate you.
Good luck, Creator.

"What? What happened?" Virgil suddenly asked as he was unfrozen. "Why is my screen different? Did they place us in stasis?"

"I am confused," Rimi also said in puzzlement. "Why is Chipper not in the same place he was a moment ago?"

"Sorry guys, you got frozen in time. Let me explain." Walker gave a quick breakdown of the options and his conversation with Chipper. He didn't mention his soul power manifesting itself for the second time. Virgil spoke first.

"Yes, the original Guardian is much more intelligent than I had thought. He may have even created his own written language."

"Yep, plus he seems to have good intentions for Symphony," Walker replied.

"Like an anti-Slicer?" Rimi asked.

"Kind of. I hold a lot of faith in our defender down there."

They continued to speak for a time, breaking down what they thought they might see, with Virgil being, naturally, realistic. Rimi couldn't help but imagine larger and larger attackers, to the point that the relatively small arena would be unable to hold creatures even half the size of what he was describing. The announcement came as Rimi was speaking of a large sword made of crystal that attacked with lightning while driving others mad.

Boss round!
Defeat the Crushinators and gain the rewards!

"Crushinators?" Walker said out loud as the portal turned silver, and three ten-foot-tall robots exited, rolling on four wheels that created a grinding sound. They were the color of stainless steel and had a thick base and two large arms sticking out of their sides. Each arm ended in a large, round bludgeoning weapon. The Guardian pulled once at his armor, watching it settle with a ripple, then jumped toward the first robot. When he got within range of his opponent, Chipper stuck a single arm out. The Crushinator swung both clubs in a blur and impacted Chipper's arms simultaneously on both sides. Walker had closed his eyes as he didn't want to watch his future friend get hurt, but nothing had happened. A ripple settled across Chipper's armor as he watched.

"The armor?" Walker asked Virgil.

"Indeed. It is kinetic armor. As long as the attacks are not spread over large amounts of space, the armor can diffuse any force applied to it. That is how Chomp lost, even with his own suit of armor. There were too many attackers at once, and it overwhelmed the kinetic displacement effect."

"Well, it's nice to see that I made the right choice, then. I think Chipper could still take this out with his own abilities, but a little extra safety never hurt."

"Indeed" was all Virgil replied with as Chipper began to make slow, heavy physical attacks on the robot, targeting the joints that held it together with his paws or using his powerful tail. He was mechanical against the mechanical object, tearing each piece down before he attacked a new area.

It didn't take him long to tear the robot apart, and the other two, whom Chipper had kept at a distance as he fought, moved forward. Rather than risk his kinetic armor failing him from four attacking arms at once, he kept positioning one robot between himself and the other to continue his previous strategy. About five minutes after the start of the round, all three robots had disappeared.

Round 20 Complete
Rewards increased.

> . . . Scanning . . .
> **Alpha Protocol Council changes detected.**
> **The option to return one or more of Dante's entities is**
> **restricted and no longer available.**
> **Alternative reward provided as a choice.**
> **Alternative reward upgraded due to difficulty.**
>
> **Congratulations, Dante! Your entity completed the 20th round**
> **of the second battle!**
> **Please choose from the below rewards. You may only choose one.**
> **You have 3 minutes to decide.**
>
> **1. Remove all afflictions plaguing your entity and heal them.**
> **2. Increase the size of your entity by 50%.**
> **3. Gain 100 years in temporal resources.**
> **4. Unlock the Betting System for future battles.**

Walker and his assistants discussed the options and threw away one and two. Walker had asked the Guardian, of course, but Chipper didn't want to change his size, and he didn't need any healing. Virgil argued for the temporal resources, while Rimi naturally wanted the Betting System. Then again, Rimi just liked any systems he could study. It came down to Walker.

"We just got seventy years from Crratch; I think we're okay."

"You do not understand how precious temporal resources are, Walker. They can even be . . . damn," Virgil said, stopping mid-sentence.

"What?" Walker asked.

"I cannot speak of it; I am sorry. There are still some restrictions placed upon me."

"It's okay. I think the Betting System is going to be pretty cool. We can't use it right now from what I see, but who knows, it could really come in handy in the future."

"Do as you wish," Virgil replied with a wave of his hand, so Walker went with Rimi's pick.

The next round approached more quickly than it had in the past.

> **Boss round!**
> **Defeat the Slimes and gain the rewards!**

The portal spat out a series of different slimes. One was red and had heat waves rising off of it, while a blue one spread rime across the ground every time it jumped. Each was a color that corresponded to its elements, with the blue representing lightning and the green one, going by the hissing and rising fumes from its hops, being acid.

Chipper didn't wait.

After analyzing his opponents for a moment, he put on a burst of speed and ran toward them. As his feet moved, a pale glow began to spread from his body outward, reaching the slimes and continuing on until it surrounded a fairly large area within his path. Once he was only a few feet away from them, and Walker's anxiety was starting to peak, the squirrel spread his arms wide and collapsed them together with a loud clap.

The pale magic reacted, closing with the movement of the albino squirrel's hands until it reached the slimes and brought them together in the middle, crushing them into each other. The opposing elements wreaked havoc on each other as they popped, boiled, and froze, among other reactions. Chipper held them together for a few more moments, then released his magic and sat down. If Walker wasn't mistaken, it seemed like each time the Guardian used large-scale magic the way he was, it took something out of him, and he needed time to recover.

"Those seemed kind of basic, right?" Walker asked.

Virgil shrugged. "It depends. If Chipper was not magical or so well practiced, that would have been quite the difficult round."

"Well, it was pretty fast," Walker said before cupping his hands to his mouth. "Way to go, buddy!" he yelled down in encouragement.

Chipper gave him a tired thumbs-up as he tried to control his breathing.

"I would say it was fast, but not that it was easy," Virgil replied. "The Guardian is very efficient and well-practiced in magic. Most of the abilities he uses take a steady amount of control and a large amount of training or practice. Elemental slimes seem simple but have killed an untold amount of challengers across the multiverse."

"Yeah, he's pretty great," Rimi said with a smile. He looked down at where the slimes had been. "Do we happen to have the genetic code for them?" Virgil's response saw the small blue squirrel wilt in place. A final *pop* ended the round as the slimes faded away.

Round 25 Complete
Rewards increased.

Congratulations, Dante! Your entity completed the 25th round of the second battle!
Please choose from the below rewards. You may only choose one.
You have four minutes to decide.

1. Remove all afflictions plaguing your entity and heal them.
2. Provide your entity with an appropriate weapon that has been modified for its use.
3. Gain 125 years in temporal resources.
4. Permanently unlock the Broadcast Ability.

"Uh oh," Walker said when he saw the rewards. He turned to Virgil. "Is the Broadcast ability what I think it is? Something that can spread out to every entity on Symphony at once?"

"Indeed."

"Well, crap. I was going to pick the years on this one, as that would almost double what we currently have; then I saw the weapon option and thought that was solid, too. But the Broadcast ability? That could be used for all kinds of things once we have a civilization to talk to."

"Yes, it is quite the conundrum." He looked down at the Guardian, who was seated where Walker had last seen him, legs crossed as he recovered from the fight. "Chipper! Would you like a weapon?"

The large squirrel tilted his head, thought on it for a moment, then laboriously wrote in the air with a slow hand. *No, thank you.*

"Okay, problem solved on that front. So we don't need option number two. That leaves temporal resources or an ability that is needed . . . you know what I'm going to say."

"I do. It is unlikely the options you gained from Crratch will contain this same choice. I agree at this time."

"Sweet," Walker said, and just before he selected his choice, he took a look at the timer, then at his only remaining defender breathing heavily on the ground. "Let's run the clock down a bit," he said, and after getting two nods, waited until he had ten seconds remaining before selecting the fourth option. Only a few minutes went by, the rounds coming faster than they had in the first fifteen, when a unique announcement started writing itself in the sky, then erasing itself, and writing again.

Boss round!
Defeat the Gr . . .
[Error.]
[Error.]

Alpha Protocol Council changes detected.

[. . . Scanning . . .]
Difficulty greatly increased.

Boss round updated.
Defeat the Army of the Lost and receive your rewards!

"What the fuck?!" Walker yelled out.

"This is quite unusual," Virgil agreed.

Further complaining would have to wait, as four more portals joined the original for a total of five. Walker could feel his heartbeat pulsing in the back of his skull as he witnessed their arrival.

He knew the risks here and had to rely on Chipper to see them through it. He didn't expect the Council to up the stakes of the round, but what choice did they have? As each portal turned to a dark purple, what walked out was a horror story no one could expect.

Although Walker had read stories about skeleton armies in books back on Earth, it didn't quite prepare him for the reality of honest-to-God walking corpses. These weren't just walking skeletons, but dead creatures with rotting muscles and skin. Even their internal organs were spilling out, forgotten remnants of themselves splashing onto the path, only to be tread upon by those who came after.

They didn't make a sound, only plodded on in the nude. And the smell . . . Walker was hundreds of feet away, and still, the smell punched him in the face. Neither of his assistants reacted, but Walker slid over to the edge of the platform and emptied his already empty stomach over the side.

The Guardian backed up as the army exited each portal in rows of two, steps marching in cadence with each other in a form of discipline they'd known in their previous lives. Chipper was affected on a level much higher than Walker; dry retching sounds and coughs reached his ears as the squirrel's stomach finally had nothing left to give up.

"Mmm, I had not considered that," Virgil said, tapping his chin with one paw.

"Wha-what?" Walker falteringly said through the acid in his mouth, still leaning against the edge of the platform.

"The Guardian is a pure magic type, extremely pure, in fact. This army is the opposite. It is an army of impurity, powered by the magic of death and maintained by hateful memories. Chipper has won battles with physical strength, speed, and outstanding magical control. The problem lies in the fact that the Monster System has focused his attunement so completely. Everything about Chipper is based on purity, and the impurity of the army will act as a poison to him. If he moves close to any of those creatures, it is likely his magic will protect him for a short time before he ultimately fails and collapses."

"So, the Council increases the difficulty of this battle, the last one we are forced to win before I lose the Avatar ability, and chooses to throw a perfect counter to Chipper. That's super fucked."

Virgil looked at him, a slight glare in his eyes. "I agree, but it is not impossible. The protocol does not allow for impossible challenges, just improbable ones. There is always a way to win; Chipper simply needs to find it. These impure soldiers are walking toward him at a sedate and measured cadence; he has a chance to succeed."

Rimi nodded quickly and yelled out, "You can do this, Chipper! You're the best! You got this!"

The albino squirrel didn't respond; he just kept slowly backing up toward his tower. Eventually, Chipper stopped right at the range of where his tower had killed the battlefrog in the first round. Reaching out one of his toes, he drew a line in the dirt.

Then he unleashed a quick force of pure magic into the ground in front of him, digging it out and bringing the pieces to him. Walker could see how labored his breathing was and sensed that he was on his last legs physically and mentally. Each use of magic showed itself as a visual drain on the Guardian, his back hunching further and further with time. But then something unexpected occurred.

Chipper picked up a rock and arched his arm all the way back before shooting it forward and nailing one of the skeleton soldiers in the head, knocking it clean off. The body collapsed right after, and both turned to rainbow sparkles as the foe was defeated. He continued to do this as each soldier entered his range, landing a clean hit more often than not, and even when he missed, the missile would still slow those who came behind.

Each time he ran out of rocks, his magic would stretch to the front or the sides and drag more broken dirt to him. By the time he'd killed over twenty of the soldiers, there was a clean trench that the army was forced to enter.

Like a machine, Chipper was building missiles and launching them at his opponents. If the moment wasn't so serious, Walker would have made a joke about taking Chipper on his team for the next snowball fight. After close to fifty turned to sparks, soldiers eventually stopped exiting the portals. Soon after the flow of enemies stopped, the portals merged until only two remained, larger than the originals had been.

After a brief pause while Chipper was still finishing off the standard fare, more well-preserved soldiers began running out of the two large portals at speed, bits and pieces of armor clinging to their outfits. Walker noticed these soldiers were wearing red tabards that held a symbol of a raised fist on their chests.

Virgil made a sound in the back of his throat. "Ah, the remains of the Marauding Army. They were once a galactic force to be reckoned with, claiming different worlds in large quantities until they met a force that could not be defeated and disappeared from the second rendition. The Lost Army indeed."

Chipper finished off the last of the slow and falling apart soldiers as the new ones entered his field of vision. Twenty of them charged at once in a coordinated double line, and once they entered the trenches, he shot a burst of magic at the walls and collapsed them in, crushing their bodies into the condensed rock and dirt. None escaped.

"Hah!" Rimi yelled, laughing. "Such a good Guardian!"

"Very smart," Virgil agreed, and Walker smiled, thinking this was it—they'd done it.

The portals merged a final time, and a single creature stepped forth in plate mail, proving him wrong yet again.

Bonus boss!
Defeat the General of the Army of the Lost!

"Fuckin' come on!"

Walker watched as Chipper sighed, his ribs moving in and out as air was forced into his lungs at a high speed. The general took a single step and suddenly appeared only three feet away from him. Pulling a sword from a sheath at his waist, he swung it with great speed, twisting his body for maximum impact on the weary defender.

"Look out!" Rimi screamed.

Chipper dropped to one knee as fast as he could, a pure glow erupting out of his armored shoulder nearest to the quickly approaching sword. The weapon deflected slightly, but the general was already arcing it back around, unperturbed by the Guardian's quick reaction and showing his advanced combat experience. Chipper's hand glowed as he punched the general directly in the face, knocking it back three steps and making it miss the follow-up attack. After the punch, the defender shook his hand in pain, then took a step across the line he'd drawn behind him at the beginning of the round.

The tabard-covered general stepped forward again, entering Chipper's range, but also the tower's. A shot rang out and struck the general as he was attempting to impale the worn-out squirrel, breaking a piece of his right arm off and knocking him back another step. Chipper followed the tower's attack and moved forward, swinging his tail at the same spot with great accuracy. A loud crack could be heard as the bone gave out, and the remains fell beside the general, whose expression never changed. The only thing in his vision at the moment was a single albino squirrel.

The Guardian stepped back again, and the process repeated, only this time the tower struck the edge of the general's chest, burning the clothing away and showing a small crack in the bones of his sternum. Chipper followed up after the tower's attack, and a large fissure cracked open across the entire length of the attacker's body. Chipper's left hand glowed for a moment as he stepped in quickly, a second glow appearing from his right as he shot magic behind the general and pulled him close for one final punch.

It didn't work.

The moment the magic spread and tried to dominate the area around the general, it fell apart, the impure attunement showing itself. The Guardian went all out regardless, leaning into the attack and throwing a full-bodied punch right where the fissure had erupted. But just as his fist connected with the general, a sword arrived at the same moment, stabbing through his kinetic armor in such a fast burst that it couldn't compensate. It pierced deep into Chipper's side and marred his formerly pristine white fur with the red of blood.

Both the general's corpse and the sword faded away. The moment the sword finally disappeared entirely, Chipper collapsed to the ground, and Walker's overlay lit up.

Round 30 Complete
Rewards increased due to difficulty.

Congratulations, Dante! Your entity completed the 30th round of the second battle!
Extra reward option provided due to difficulty.
Please choose from the below rewards. You may choose up to two.
You have 5 minutes to decide.

1. Return your entity to the state it was upon first arrival.
2. Replenish all of your tower's resources and health.
3. Gain 175 years in temporal resources.
4. Upgrade your Creation Instrument.
5. Your Advanced Assistant (Virgil) may now work with
the Landmass System in a limited capacity.

Walker didn't want to make Chipper suffer any more than he needed to, but he remembered what the Guardian had said. If it was what was best for Symphony, he should do it. A hard moral line to toe, but this was a rare opportunity, and Walker didn't want to miss it. He chose the first and last options quickly before Chipper could die, which would render his choices meaningless.

Chipper's body faded away as Walker watched, and he was worried that he'd acted too late. Looking at his two assistants, he was about to apologize for being too slow when Rimi shouted, "Look!"

Walker turned and brought his eyes back to the broken battlefield, only to find an unarmored, pristine Chipper waving at him. The valiant defender's words appeared in the air. *I am fine. Let's keep going, Creator.*

Walker smiled and felt his eyes water a little. Round thirty-five was coming.

CHAPTER THIRTY

Last as Long as You Can (II)

Walker, am I seeing this correctly?" Virgil asked him after looking at what he'd chosen. Naturally, he knew that Virgil was asking about his second choice, but he felt that he needed a little fun to celebrate getting through the thirtieth round.

"Yep, I healed him," he replied, knowing it would annoy his assistant.

"No! Noooo," the large brown squirrel protested. "I'm talking about the second reward. Is this right? I now have access to the Landmass System?"

"Limited access, if I recall correctly, although I don't really know what that means."

"Neither do I, as no assistant has received any form of access to the Landmass System prior to the final battle. At least, that is what our archives tell me, and they do not tell me everything." He sighed. "I cannot help but wonder, even in this solemn moment, of what we may now be able to do together." He began trying to scroll through his screen. His eyes squinted before becoming crazed as a frustrated look slammed onto his face. "I can't access it from here!"

"Oh, a contraction! Who knows," Walker replied, calm as could be, while watching Chipper stretch next to his tree. "Maybe you'll finally be able to keep me from making stupid mistakes. I'm just sad that Chipper lost his armor. I didn't know it wouldn't come back."

"Yes, it . . . is sad. Also, as you said, perhaps I can help you avoid making any future mistakes."

An announcement lit the air.

Boss round!
Defeat the Poison Wyvern and gain the rewards!

Walker barely had time to say, "Huh, the Council didn't mess with it again," before the portal changed to a sickly green with yellow spots. It increased to twice its size as a gargantuan scaled snout pushed through, the rest of the head following in a bobbing fashion several seconds later. The wyvern's head was the size of an old Volkswagen beetle, with arched yellow eyes underneath a heavily ridged brow. Its entire face was covered in thick, plated green scales. The portal increased in width as the wyvern's body pushed itself out, wings breaking through before the rest of the body followed. Walker looked a little closer.

"Where are its arms?" he asked.

"Wyverns do not have what you would call *arms*. They are a creation of the first rendition, and were considered a mistake on the path to creating noble dragons. Rather than having wings on their backs, their appendages double as wings, providing them with the ability to fly."

"Wait, go back. Dragons are noble?"

"Historically, yes. Dragons were known to defend the helpless and, at times, inspire others to act against those who would commit great wrongs. They considered peace a true treasure that was always in need of their protection. They are also quite interesting, to me personally, as they move through several life cycles while they grow."

Walker was still staring at the wyvern exiting the portal while Virgil continued to ramble beside him. Anytime a history lesson could be provided, rest assured, Virgil would be there. "Their cycles move from the egg stage, to the young wingless form, all the way up to the massive sizes your history speaks of. Earth's mythology got many things right when it comes to certain facts, but their birth and maturity are quite misunderstood. Sadly, I do not believe the Creator of Earth had their genetic line. Unless something fortuitous occurs, you will not have any on Symphony."

"Motherfucker," Rimi cursed from his low height.

"Language," Walker said automatically.

"Really?" Rimi asked him, putting his hands on his hips. The small blue squirrel's memories flew through all of the times that Walker had cursed. "Don't you think that is a bit . . . umm . . . umm . . ."

"Hypocritical?" Virgil supplied.

"What?"

Even though Rimi was building up to a grand speech in his mind, and he was really feeling the need to nail Walker for his two-sided views on specific vernacular choices, the events down below forestalled him.

The rest of the wyvern had exited while they were talking. Its face was covered in scale-like armor, but that defensive evolution hadn't extended to its body. Mismatched scales were scattered sporadically across its snake-like body in a haphazard fashion. The pseudo-dragon had great long wings that were quite thin and delicate. After it finally pulled itself through, the poison wyvern noticed Chipper standing near his tower, and with a great booming voice, spoke out. "What is this foul place?"

"Oh no," Virgil said.

"What?" Walker asked him.

"It is sapient. That is no standard wyvern. They take hundreds of years to develop their intelligence this far."

"Soooo . . ."

"So this just became a lot more difficult. The Army of the Lost was quite difficult simply because they countered the Guardian's magic. Wyverns, like dragons, are resistant to all magic as well. That includes Chipper's pure magic. Add in that it can fly, think for itself, and that it's attuned to poison, and we have a real problem on our hands. While it cannot breathe fire like a dragon, it will still have some magic for Chipper to deal with."

"Ouuuutstanding."

Chipper then did something none of them expected. He tried talking to the creature by placing words in the air. *Hello, friend. My name is Chipper. May I ask what yours is?*

The wyvern breathed out a yellow cloud, tilting its head back and gazing down at the smaller creature with its large eyes. Walker wasn't sure if he knew how to read, even with the system's help, but he was surprised again when the wyvern spoke.

"Raganoth the Bleeder."

That . . . that was it. The wyvern stopped talking and continued to stare at the Guardian, shifting his weight to his back legs. Walker wasn't sure if that was to help it with balance, to prepare for an attack, or if it was just . . . sitting down.

Chipper wrote some more. *I like that, Raganoth. But why the Bleeder?*

The large wyvern reared back on its thick legs and stretched itself to its full height. Walker was sure he was going to attack, but instead, he collapsed onto the ground.

"Because I was beaten as a child!" Raganoth screamed at the world around him, pulling his wings over his head with a strange coughing sound coming from his throat.

"Is . . . is that wyvern crying?" Walker turned and asked his assistants.

"Maybe he just needs a friend," Rimi suggested.

"I do not understand," Virgil said. It was almost a line that Walker could trademark at this point. "Raganoth should have no memories of a father or even have a history prior to being within this round. The protocol has more than enough power to sufficiently age a wyvern for it to gain sapience and the ability to speak, but not like this. For it to not only have memories associated with its past but also to have those memories be traumatic . . . I did not know that these bosses would be actual creatures with real lives before this. The Army of the Fallen and their known history was the first clue. Raganoth here is the second."

"So, those humans we saw before?" Walker questioned.

"No, no, the normal rounds used entities seeded only for the battles. But each boss seems to have been taken from some part of the multiverse, and likely against their will. Raganoth here is a real sapient wyvern, not a seeded entity. Prior to their translocation, just like yourself, Walker, they had their own life—their own story."

"That's fucked."

Rimi glared at him.

When Walker turned back around, Chipper was gently patting Raganoth's large, scaled shoulder while the wyvern continued to cry. Every so often, Chipper would write in the air and console him, and then Raganoth would tell him some more of his history. The wyvern was upset and, understandably, speaking in a low tone of voice, but with the sheer size of the creature, Walker could hear everything. His world did not sound like a pleasant place to grow up in.

"I'll be honest, this is not how I expected it to go," Walker said.

Virgil and Rimi nodded. They were content to let Chipper talk the large pseudo-dragon through this difficult moment, as none of them were sure what would happen when they began to fight. After several more minutes of Raganoth expressing his distaste for his family, with Chipper optimistically trying to find something positive in the experience, they came to the crux of the issue.

The wyvern gradually stretched his body back out, taking his winged arms off of his head. He looked down as he said, "I do not want to go back." He coughed. "They still call me Raganoth the Bleeder! I haven't been a child for over a hundred years!" He breathed in a second large, racking cough. "It's not fair. I know my father thought he was helping me with his so-called *toughness training*, but it wasn't helpful."

His voice took on a deeper and rougher timbre as he continued speaking. *"You need this, Raganoth! You're weak! You'll never survive our world!"* His voice returned to its normal tone although it was now so quiet it was hard for Walker to hear. "But it just hurt, every time, every single time, and I do not want to be a fighter! I've never wanted to be one!" He spat to the side, and as it landed, the ground hissed and bubbled.

Chipper sat down next to him and wrote some words in the air. *I can see that you obviously have no interest in fighting. So, I will ask you this. If you could be anything other than a fighter, what would you want to be?*

Raganoth read the words, then yelled, "I don't know!" before slowly lowering his head to the ground and becoming quiet. Chipper waited several minutes, but as the wyvern seemed deep in thought, he was happy to just give him time. The Guardian knew he didn't want to fight Raganoth. The poison wyvern didn't seem like a bad guy. He hadn't attacked Chipper outright or sought to end his life. He was just . . . another living being, another entity, caught up in the Alpha Protocol like himself and his Creator. Forced to do battle by those above them.

After quite some time, the wyvern lifted his head and spoke up once again in a soft voice. "When I was very, very young, just fifty years or so, I caught a smell from a particularly vibrant flower near my family's lair. It was a glorious blue, and, of course, quite deadly. It was truly wondrous, and I could enjoy it anytime I liked. I loved to go out and breathe it in at the start of every day. It was like a ritual with a simple smell." He put his head back down. "That is a favorite memory of mine. Of course, my sisters saw me one day and tore it out of the ground, destroying it in front of my very eyes. But . . . I know now that doesn't matter, because the memory remains. I often wonder what it would be like to breathe new scents every day and discover a world that embraces moments like these." After saying so, he laid his head back down and closed his eyes, basking in the glow of his fond memory.

Chipper sniffed twice, then turned away from his new friend and looked up at Walker, writing, *I do not want to fight him.*

Walker replied, "I don't want you to fight him either. Seems fucked up somehow." He scratched his chin while considering their options. "I don't know if this is possible, but . . . can you ask him to surrender?" he asked, thinking fast now. "It never says to kill your opponent in the announcements, just to defeat them."

The Guardian nodded, then replied, *I will try.* He poked Raganoth in the shoulder twice to break whatever spell the memory had placed on him. The wyvern turned and opened his yellow eyes to look at him. "Yes, Chipper?"

I have a favor to ask of you that I believe will help us both.

"What is it?"

Can you formally surrender? Please? If you do, we may not have to fight, and I would not like to fight you.

"Hrmmm," Raganoth rumbled. "I have never surrendered before. I don't think any wyvern in living memory has. What would I get out of this?"

You wouldn't die?

"Hahahaha, that was not in doubt, little . . . Guardian? That's new. You're quite small for a Guardian. Either way, my little friend, I do not see what I will get out of surrendering, whereas if I win, I'm told I will receive a great reward."

What's the reward?

"You know what . . . I do not know, actually," Raganoth replied, then huffed some air out of his large nostrils, billowing Chipper's white fur. "All that it said was I would receive a great reward if I won."

Virgil coughed. "The Council likely promised a reward, but after the battle, Raganoth would have no memory of his part in this. He would simply wake up and go about his day on his homeworld. This way, they do not have to deliver on any promises."

"Fuck. You know, the more we deal with the Council, the more I think they're a big bag of dicks. That's mean as hell. Fight and maybe die for them, and they get nothing out of it when they're sent back?"

"Indeed. Resources are always primarily allocated to Creators and their work, not to specific entities."

Walker focused back on Chipper, who was rubbing a particularly sensitive area behind Raganoth's jawline. "That's the spot. Thank you," the large entity said in a satisfied voice.

Chipper stepped back. *What if I asked my Creator to help you, if they receive the option after the fight?* After Chipper finished writing, he felt something, like someone was watching him and trying to do something in a hidden way.

"What's a Creator?"

Chipper refocused but mentally stumbled as he wrote back, *He is my . . . um . . . friend?*

"And he has the power to help me?"

Maybe. I am not sure. But the worst that could happen is we don't have to fight, and I do not want to fight you. I would much rather we be friends.

"A friend," Raganoth said, tasting the word. "I have not had a—uh . . . friend before. I have heard of others working together toward something that benefits them both, but friendship has nothing to do with it. Those were alliances that helped them as much as those they allied with. What is having a friend like?"

It's like having someone you can talk to who doesn't want to hurt but only help. It's nice.

"And you would be my fr-friend, little Guardian?"

I would be happy to, Chipper wrote, pulsing his magic a little so the words stayed in the air longer than normal.

Raganoth stared at the words for a moment more, but even after the magic had dissipated, he continued to stare at where they had appeared. "That would be nice," he said in such a low voice that only Chipper could hear him. "To have a change, and a new friend to share it with."

He dug his feet into the ground and stretched his back slowly. "In over two hundred years, I have not had a friend, young Chipper. Nor have I ever surrendered," he said. "Perhaps a change is due. Okay then, this sounds like a grand enough reward for a great wyvern! What do I do?"

I do not know. Perhaps you just need to declare it out loud?

"Is it that simple?" Raganoth asked with some trepidation. "What if the system just outright kills me, and that is the end?"

I truly hope that does not happen, Raganoth, or I will have lost one of my few friends.

The poison wyvern nodded once, slowly, then in a nervous-seeming voice said, "You won't tell anyone I surrendered, will you?"

No, Chipper wrote with a headshake as his words appeared. *It will be just between us.*

Raganoth the Bleeder gathered his courage and said out loud, "I formally surrender to Guardian Chipper and his Creator." And with a *pop*, rather than a portal, he disappeared.

"What the fuck?" Walker said as he stared at the large and empty space where Raganoth had just been.

[. . . Scanning . . .]
Round 35 Complete
Rewards increased.

[. . . Scanning . . .]
Alpha Protocol Council changes detected.

Unique victory conditions detected.
Options updated.
Boss selection bias detected.
Alternative reward provided as a choice.
Alternative reward upgraded due to unique victory condition.

Congratulations, Dante! Your entity completed the 35th round
of the second battle!
Please choose from the below rewards. You may only choose one.
You have 6 minutes to decide.

1. Remove all afflictions plaguing your entity and heal them.
2. Change the arena to more closely resemble your entity's
perfect environment.
3. Gain 200 years in temporal resources.
4. Return at the end of the second battle with a new entity,
unlocking their genus: Raganoth the Bleeder (Wyvern genus).

Walker read the rewards in his overlay then looked at Virgil, who gave a slight nod. He called down to Chipper. "You weren't just messing around, right? You truly believe it is best for Symphony to bring Raganoth there?"

Chipper wrote back, *Yes. I believe he has been mistreated by his family and the harsh world in which he was raised. With the right opportunities and the right people to advise, I have faith that he will become an asset to our world. If you have that same faith in me, as you said earlier, then please trust in me.* The words faded away, with faith lasting a moment longer, before it too left the air.

"Man," Walker whispered to himself, "someone really knows how to tug on the heartstrings." In a louder voice he said, "I trust you, Chipper." He looked over at Virgil and Rimi. "At least this way I can actually give something to Chipper for helping us out so much. It's not really a reward, but—"

"But a new friend is its own reward," Virgil said with a nod. Rimi was nodding along with him.

Walker smiled, then selected the fourth option.

[. . . Scanning . . .]
Congratulations, Dante! Your new entity has been placed in
stasis and is ready for collection upon completion of this battle.
Upon returning, please seed them within any location you would
like.
All memories and abilities of your new entity will be retained.

"Hrmm, okay."

"What happened?" Rimi asked, being out of the loop as he couldn't see Walker's overlay notifications.

"It says Raganoth is now a member of Symphony, and I can seed them when we get back. The thing is, it also says he'll remember everything. Chipper won't. Is that likely to cause an issue when we return?" Walker asked.

"I believe when they meet, it will be fine. Normally, Raganoth would be the likely attacker in a chance meetup, so the system allowing him to retain his memories is a grand boon. We will not have to convince him of the benefits of Symphony and friendship a second time," Virgil replied.

"Well, we didn't convince him of shit. That was all Chipper."

"He's the best!" Rimi yelled with a fist in the air. "Hey, Chipper! Raganoth will be on Symphony with us from now on! You did it!"

Chipper wrote back, *Thank you for having faith in me. I will not let you down. Now, or in the future.*

"Man, he really is the best," Walker said with a smile. The next announcement was coming.

CHAPTER THIRTY-ONE

Last as Long as You Can (III)

The announcement spilled across the air coming only seconds after Walker's decision, surprising everyone within the area. It told him the speed with which the next round had arrived was either because they hadn't fought, or because the Council had made some kind of hidden change. Either way, the name of the fortieth-round boss was confusing.

Boss round!
Defeat the Cloud of Tyranny and gain the rewards!

The portal changed to a mixed series of colors as a haze of red and purple particulates exited. The creature left the portal like it was being squeezed out of a tube of toothpaste. Walker couldn't spot any clear markings for a face; it was just as it was labeled, a hazy cloud of colors.

The moment it left the portal, it began to slowly move toward Walker's last defender. The Guardian shifted into his fighter's pose, but the cloud approached without slowing down. Chipper threw out some test strikes, but they seemed to have little to no effect. It flew low over the ground, and any attempts by the Guardian to strike it with magic were dodged quickly, or holes opened up, letting the pure magic through without taking any visible damage.

When it finally reached him, instead of surrounding his body as Walker had expected, it seeped directly into his nostrils and entered his body.

"Oh fuck."

Chipper fell to the ground and grasped his throat, coughing.

"Hmm," Virgil hummed in sympathetic feeling.

"What do you mean *hmm*? What is it doing to him?" Walker waved down at the Guardian. "Chipper! Chipper, my boy, can you hear me?"

The albino squirrel glowed with magic across his body for a moment before a strange stutter showed itself, and the glow faded away. Chipper tried again to use his magic as he continued to choke. The glow appeared all at once, his body looking like a blindingly bright flashlight, before the magic stuttered again and disappeared.

"What's happening?"

"It is likely that the Cloud of Tyranny is eating his magic from the inside. I believe it is trying to surround his kernel in an attempt to dampen the resistance of his pure magic."

"What can he do to fight it?" Rimi asked quickly, a note of anxiousness in his voice and hands as he shakingly gripped them together.

"According to my knowledge of magical entities, he would have to take his knowledge of magic to the next stage and fully embody it. Currently, as a tier four monster, he has inundated his body and mind with his attunement and gained great benefits from doing so—strength, speed, and intelligence, as we had planned. Now, he needs to learn to control that same internal flow and direct it toward an enemy that cannot be defeated with pure force."

"Would he know how to do that?" Walker asked.

"Perhaps, but in his battle right now, I doubt he can hear us. It is best to just watch and hope he succeeds rather than feel stress about an event we have no control over."

So, as usual, Walker was forced to stand and watch. It was becoming frustrating, torturous even, to constantly have to stand on the sidelines. He wanted to be down there, helping his friend in his time of need and offering advice or wisdom, but the system wouldn't allow it. All of his abilities were grayed out, and he found himself stuck on the platform.

Looking down, he figured jumping off would only result in his death. The shield only protected him when something was attacking him. Diving off of the stage would not be a smart move, and even if he made it down there, he had no magic or real power to attack the Cloud of Tyranny himself.

Just as Walker thought his last defender would soon fall, Chipper stopped choking and held very still. His body was slowly slumping over, and he looked like he was about to hit the ground when Walker's overlay lit up.

Evolution occurring.
Chipper is evolving!
[. . . Scanning . . .]
Chipper has evolved his Advanced Mage ability
to Mage of Mastery.

"Holy shit. How did he do that?"

"The Monster System allows abilities to evolve based upon use and understanding," Rimi told him. "You limited the amount and direction of the evolutions, but that didn't mean they couldn't improve through effort. The harder they focus on and expand their abilities, the more they can evolve. I thought you knew that?" Rimi said with some snark, as his faith in Chipper had never truly wavered.

"I was not aware of that, no," Walker replied evenly. "Will this affect our evolution task?"

"No, as it is not a new evolution, just an upgraded one," Virgil said.

"While I'm ecstatic that Chipper evolved his ability, that's still crappy for us overall if it won't carry over when we return. Will it?"

"That is an excellent question," Virgil replied. "I do not know."

They watched as a glow started in one of Chipper's fingers, then crept over to another finger and another. Soon enough, the entire paw was glowing white from within. Because of how bright the magic was, they could see the internal parts of his hands, bones showing through the pale luminescence. A second glow began on his other hand and spread the same way, then both stretched up and covered his arms entirely.

Chipper slowly but surely covered his whole body in the power of his magic, from head to toe, with the exception of one still-dark portion near the bottom of his chest. As his power began to encroach on the last section of his body, he stood up on shaky legs, looking like a pale, glowing skeleton. The glow began to stretch toward the dark spot that was his kernel, then recede and stretch again. Chipper's face held a look of pure concentration as his magic pressed inward again and again until, finally, his whole body was covered in his magic. He lit up like a beacon shining in the night sky, illuminating everything around him before the glow faded. The Guardian fell to a knee with a heavy breath, small fizzles of rainbow sparks exhaling with him.

"Where'd it go?" Rimi asked, ever curious about the monsters of the multiverse.

"I believe Chipper burned it out of his system entirely," Virgil commented as Walker's overlay lit up.

Round 40 Complete
Rewards increased.

**Congratulations, Dante! Your entity completed the 40th round
of the second battle!**
**Please choose from the below rewards. You may only choose one.
You have 7 minutes to decide.**

1. Remove all afflictions plaguing your entity and heal them.
2. Forcibly evolve one of your entity's abilities.

3. Gain 225 years in temporal resources.
4. Upgrade one of your subsystem assistants.

"Whoa," Walker said after looking at the options.

"New options?" Rimi said, bouncing on his toes.

"I'll say," Walker confirmed.

"Indeed," Virgil replied. "It seems that when the Council made changes to your battle rewards, it left residual alterations within the system's choices."

"What does it say?" Rimi asked.

Walker skipped the first option, as it looked like Chipper could purify himself now and wouldn't need the help. "I can forcibly evolve one of Chipper's abilities, which I won't do because that's too random and seems almost unfair after what we just watched. We can gain two hundred and twenty-five years in temporal resources, or I can upgrade . . . you."

"You can upgrade me?" Rimi said, eyes shining. "What does that mean?"

"It likely means you would become a standard assistant," Virgil said from the side.

"Yep, that's what I was thinking, too," Walker said with a nod. "But I think there's a big problem here we're not considering. If we upgrade Rimi, there's a chance he won't . . . be . . . Rimi anymore, right?"

"Hrmm, I see your point. It is likely he would be reset and eventually change to be more like myself. Any leftover personality that he has developed in his short life would be lost, and the memories he currently has would be reabsorbed into the assistant system of the Alpha Protocol."

"So, Rimi," Walker said, looking at him. "No."

"No?" Rimi asked, his shoulders drooping.

"It would essentially be killing you. So, just no. It's fine, bud." Saying so and not leaving the option up for debate, Walker selected the temporal resources option.

Virgil inferred his choice. "We now have three hundred and fifty-five years in our temporal resources. That is an enormous amount."

"Really? I don't have a reference for what is a lot here," Walker said.

"The average Creator tends to leave the second battle with no more than one hundred years in temporal resources. You have a large enough amount that there is quite a bit we can do moving forward."

"Like what?"

"Well, there is a sys—" Virgil was interrupted by the next announcement, which flashed in the sky before disappearing abruptly.

Boss round!
Defeat the Anti-Mage and gain the rewards!

A small, purple-suited human jumped out of the portal and ran toward Chipper, still on one knee. Everything happened so fast that nobody had time to react.

The Guardian stood up, taking his stance, and prepared himself. He had seen the announcement as well and wasn't preparing any magic for this fight. His hands were balled into fists, with his tail moving quickly behind him in preparation for his opponent's charge.

The Anti-Mage had a metal tank on his back and a dark, thick, single-paned face mask. He looked like he was wearing a new-age spacesuit that seemed better suited for interstellar travel than a fight. He pulled two swords out of slots on his legs as he ran, moving from side to side in quick movements that were so fast it almost seemed like he was teleporting.

Each hand held a sword within an enclosed guard, the tips emitting a shimmering black fog that seemed to extend the blades' sharp length by several feet. As he ran, the swords ground against the ground, tearing long, thin troughs behind him.

The Anti-Mage quickly approached Chipper, who tilted his head at him before his eyes went wide and he ducked his head. Walker wasn't sure what he was doing, but suddenly, the boss was behind him, a sword passing cleanly through where the Guardian's head had just been.

"Fucker teleported!" Walker said, uselessly pointing a finger down at the attacker.

"Yes. That is a forbidden evolution. Chipper's excellent feel for magic gave him a bit of early warning. The Council placed that evolution on the restriction list because it can lead to the discovery of long-range teleportation and portals, which are only to be used by Creators. Instilling it in an entity is akin to, pardon my reference, flipping off the Council. For this boss to arrive in an approved and sanctioned round of the second battle, they must be on the approved list and, thus, are one of the Council's Sentinels."

"So they stacked the deck against us? They sent their own people to take us out of the battle?" Walker asked grimly.

"Indeed. I have a theory, although I am unsure of it at this moment. I believe they need these battles to end."

Chipper had dodged two more attacks while they spoke, and then the Anti-Mage disappeared. The defender looked around, trying to find him, and twice even sent out a pulse of magic that reminded Walker of sonar. Suddenly, the last third of Chipper's tail fell away from his body, and he screamed.

"What happened? I couldn't see it."

Virgil commented in that same calm voice he always had, "The Anti-Mage teleports out of vision, then back in and above him, so he is never seen. This is apparently a useful tactic against the Guardian."

Walker's breathing hitched as he noticed Chipper's face harden. He watched as the albino squirrel seemed to come to a conclusion. Quickly, the Guardian turned and ran toward his tower, a bright pink trail of blood drifting behind him.

Walker remembered that the treelike tower only had a few shots left, and Chipper seemed determined to use them. When he crossed the line he'd drawn against the multitudes, the attacker teleported into range for a strike. The only problem he faced was the green shot that fired out of the tree from not too far away. The Anti-Mage turned within a heartbeat and used his blade to deflect it without moving back a step. A clean ringing sound reached Walker's ears as the shot harmlessly ricocheted off the blade. Chipper used that moment to punch the Anti-Mage in the face, staggering him closer to the tower as a second shot came out. The attacker barely managed to place his sword in its path as two more punches came, both hitting him in the stomach with all of Chipper's strength.

"Is it me, or is he not hitting as hard as he was?" Walker commented.

"It is likely that his tail would help him balance his body before striking. With a large part of it missing, his balance is off. If I am honest with you, his grace is remarkable considering his current limitation," Virgil said in a dispassionate voice.

Walker nodded and continued to watch, hoping his friend could get through this. More shots rang out and more punches flew. The Anti-Mage was now bleeding from the face, his mask cracked, and staggering from every punch. Each time he tried to pull back, wherein Walker believed he was attempting to teleport, Chipper would throw a punch or kick, or a new shot would come from the tower, keeping him in place. Finally, one last shot rang out, striking the attacker before he could recover, and one of the black swords fell from a missing hand.

Chipper tried to pick it up, but it burned him badly, and a quickly cut-off scream erupted helplessly from his mouth. The Anti-Mage recovered just enough to brace his other sword on what remained of his second arm and quickly poked Chipper in the stomach. The albino squirrel took several steps back before falling, holding his stomach with glowing hands.

"What? That was such a small attack?"

"He struck his kernel, Walker," Rimi said, tears falling down his face. "I don't think he's going to make it."

"No! He can do it. You can do it, Chipper!" Walker yelled out to him, trying to give some last-minute encouragement. He didn't think Chipper could hear him, as Walker knew it wasn't likely with the amount of pain the Guardian was currently feeling, but he had hope.

The Anti-Mage walked up slowly from the side, one eye on the tower and another on the defender, ready to finish the fight. As he got closer, the ground began to shudder, and eventually it dropped out from beneath him. The formidable fighter disappeared into the darkness below. They heard a loud yell before the ground was sealed back up. Chipper tried to sit up, hands still glowing, but couldn't.

"He used the last of his magic to make that pit and seal it," Virgil remarked. "With his kernel cracked, the Monster System and its tied evolutions are stalling as his magic dries up."

"So he won't be able to heal?" Rimi asked, his face a picture of anguish for his monster friend.

"Correct. I had theorized that because the kernel is the anchor for the Monster System, it is also the root of each entity's power and a battery for their magic. Destroy it and destroy any abilities which are tied to their evolutions. Without the kernel to guide his self-regenerating cells, he will not heal, and will most likely soon die."

Walker stood up straight, not noticing the previous slump in his posture when Chipper had fallen. "So it's a race to see what happens first. The Anti-Mage suffocating since Chipper broke his mask, or Chipper dying from his kernel being cracked."

"No. I believe we win either way. It was never necessarily about Chipper living, but the tower," Virgil said, pointing at the tall tree. "Even with Chipper's death, the tower is still standing, and as long as the Anti-Mage dies, we win." As he finished talking, some of the ground shuddered and moved, but Chipper's hands lit up, albeit with much less power than before. After a few more rumbles, it stilled again. "He is trying to teleport out, but without sight, he is blind to where he needs to go. Chipper is using his remaining magic to keep him in place, but . . . ah, there it is."

Chipper's hands steadily stopped glowing as the magic drained, and a moment later, his breathing stilled.

Walker sighed, and Rimi openly cried.

The ground moved twice more as they watched before, mercifully, it stopped.

Walker's overlay lit up, but he felt no joy at what he saw.

Round 45 Complete
Rewards increased.

[. . . Scanning . . .]
Your entity has perished!
Your tower still stands!
Congratulations, Dante! You have completed the 45th round of the second battle!
Please choose from the below rewards. You may only choose one.
You have 8 minutes to decide.

1. Gain 250 years in temporal resources.
2. Gain a random genus for your Entity Subsystem.
3. Unlock the Auction System.
4. Choose one standard system to upgrade.

Walker's overlay had been updated, but he wasn't paying attention to it. He just kept staring at where Chipper's body had been. The protocol had transferred him out the moment that the text had appeared in his vision, rainbow sparkles drifting through the air. But he couldn't move his eyes away from Chipper's resting place.

"Walker, did you see the choices?" Virgil asked.

"Hrmm? What?" Walker replied with a vacant expression.

"I asked if you'd seen your reward choices," Virgil said with a worried inflection.

Walker shrugged. "Yeah. I don't know, man. I quick-scanned it, but I guess I'm still thinking of how hard Chipper fought for us. There's nothing really there for him."

"You mean a reward that extends outside of the second round?"

"Yeah, it doesn't feel right. He fought, really fought, for us. For the rewards that we would gain for our world. And . . . it's just. There's nothing there for him. It doesn't feel right. Yeah, we already got Raganoth. But . . ."

Virgil patted him on the shoulder while Rimi took one of his hands in his own. Virgil's voice drifting to his ears as he said, "Walker, he knew he would eventually fall. It was expected. Please do not get wrapped up too much in it. We are on a timer, and it is important that you make a good choice here—for Chipper and everyone else still to come."

"Yeah, I guess you're right," Walker said, looking at the choices again. "Man, we have to make an actual decision on this one, too. A lot of what we saw in the beginning was pretty clear-cut on what was important." Walker repeated the options his screen revealed, hoping the two assistants would have a better idea of what to do. That hope was in vain.

"Yes, I am not sure what is best," Virgil said after thinking for a moment.

Walker looked away from his screen. "So, what are we thinking?"

"I vote for the random genus," Rimi volunteered.

"Of course you do, buddy," Walker said with a smile as he dragged out the first word.

Virgil tapped on his chin twice. "I vote for the Auction System. While you would unlock it after the third battle, so would everyone else. It would behoove you to select the system now and gain a leg up on the others while you can."

"How do you know that?"

"Because its appearance removed my restrictions. There is still much I know that the system keeps me from speaking of. The Auction System is just one such example."

Walker looked at the sky before sighing and turning back to Virgil. "Okay, what pops up in the Auction System?"

"Everything. Rare materials, genus strains, unique evolutions that are not a part of the standard evolution system."

Walker's mouth dropped open. "Shit, really? And we'd get it one battle earlier than everyone else?" Virgil nodded. "Man, that does sound like the way to go."

"Did you say genus strains?" Rimi said with a smile, recovering from Chipper's defeat. "I've changed my vote!"

"Okay, then I guess this isn't too difficult of a choice after all," Walker said, selecting the third option.

After he made his choice, the arena . . . warped; that was the only way he could explain it. The land bounced and rolled, then pieces of it began being sucked into a huge, opaque white portal that hadn't been there a moment before.

Rimi and Virgil, who had just been standing next to him, were gone, and Walker was stuck in place for a moment as everything around him disappeared. He looked down but only saw an endless stretch of darkness. His body lit up in gold as text the size of a mountain appeared across the sky.

**Congratulations, Dante! You reached the 45th round!
You have ranked second in the second battle of the Creator Wars!
Due to your placement within the top ten of all Creators in your
rendition, you have the choice of the following rewards.**

**1. Gain the Collosi Genus
2. Gain the Dragon Genus
3. Gain the Multimind Genus
4. Unlock the Dimensional Warp System
5. Unlock the Cosmic Genesis System
6. Unlock the Replacement System
7. Gain two Evolution Chambers
8. Gain one Magic Chamber
9. Gain the Self-Regenerating Cells evolution**

Whatever was holding him let go, and he could finally speak. The first words out of Walker's mouth would be expected by anyone who knew him.

"Oh, fuckin' . . . come on."

A timer popped up in the corner, showing five minutes, and immediately began counting down. Five minutes might not have been a lot to figure out what each of these options meant, but as an English teacher and a lover of science fiction, Walker could pretty quickly suss out what each reward meant. Whenever the protocol thought it was throwing him a curveball of randomness, he had a slight edge due to his education.

He looked over his options closely. Immediately, he decided to ignore the Evolution Chambers as he felt he already had a good number of them. However, he cursed because of the last option on the list—his own goddamned evolution discovery.

The protocol had already taken it and placed it out there for any other top-ten Creator to grab. The bastards didn't ask, just took. Just like they had with himself. Was it entitlement? Or were they just a bunch of dick bags?

The damned clock in his vision continued to tick. Walker shoved aside the negativity he was feeling for the Council and looked back at the other seven options. If etymology were a superpower, he'd be the Superman of words. It didn't often show in his spoken vocabulary, but Walker was an ambulatory lexicon.

Just because of that simple reason, he knew exactly what choice to make as he looked things over. He finalized his choice as the timer faded out. "Time to light this candle," he spoke to the air.

Walker began to fade out of the darkness, his tiny planet full of weirdos starting to come into view. He didn't know what the next series of events to impact Symphony would be, but he knew one thing.

He couldn't wait to see what would happen next.

CHAPTER THIRTY-TWO

Cosmic Theft

When his tiny planet finally stopped looking like a hazy dream of what he hoped it would become, Walker ignored his overlay and the incessant updates flashing for his attention. He moved away from the others so that only Symphony was in his view and stood for a moment, looking at his planet.

He didn't know why, but he needed to make sure it was exactly the same as it had been before the second battle. Off to the side, just far enough away not to affect his planet, was now a collection of green and yellow pieces of land. They serenely floated in space, a small protocol shield the only sign as to why the trees didn't explode and or fly off to space. Continuing to ignore his notifications, Walker pulled up his Monitor ability and shifted it over, taking a look.

After a quick scan, he made an intuitive leap in judgment. It seemed that Warclaws enjoyed either the forest or the desert, as every piece of land fit within those two biomes. Yellow sand and dunes stretched across most of what was left, but the system hadn't given it to him in any recognizable shape. It was just a hodgepodge of pieces of land with no foundational bottom to be seen—a grand series of flat lands floating in the cosmos.

There was a small forest, as if the former Creator had been playing around with the idea of placing Warclaws in a forested environment. But everywhere else Walker looked, desert remained.

After reviewing what he'd gained from Crratch and confirming that Symphony had not changed, he moved the screen over and examined his last defender, Chipper.

His Monitor ability showed the albino squirrel sitting peacefully within the boughs of a large, magical tree. The Guardian's expression was one of contentment as he looked out over a vista Walker was sure he felt duty-bound to protect.

The Creator smiled at his friend. There'd be time to talk to him soon, but first, he had other requirements. Next, he checked on the golden battlefrog, who was dooting as he rolled in his flowers, and Phil, who was currently attacking defenseless bugs and hissing as they died. Everything was as it should be in the small world of Symphony.

"I need to make more prey for the desert; there's not enough for the scorpions," Walker said quietly to himself, but his assistant still heard him. With that thought in mind, he hadn't said what he really needed: more time.

Virgil grabbed his attention. "I can take care of that. Please go through your rewards and familiarize yourself with all that we have gained. It is quite a lot to take in."

Walker nodded and glanced through his overlay; Virgil was right. There was a lot to take in.

Congratulations, Dante!
The following is a list of rewards you recently earned in the
second battle of the 4AA Creator Wars:

Systems-related rewards:
The Auxiliary Landmass (Planning) Subsystem is unlocked
Advanced Assistant (Virgil) receives limited access to the
Landmass System
The Betting System is unlocked (Creator Wars only)
The Auction System is unlocked
The Cosmic Genesis System is unlocked

Entity, genetic, and genus rewards:
Warclaw genetic blueprint is obtained.
This genus is locked from Creator Dante:
Only general seeding allowed
Raganoth the Bleeder is obtain . . .
[Error.]
[Error.]
[. . . Scanning . . .]
Alpha Protocol Council changes found.
Raganoth the Bleeder will retain all abilities and memories
from before and during the second battle.
The Wyvern genus is obtained in its entirety.

Miscellaneous rewards:
+50 temporal resources
Armor given to two entities (Armor removed upon death
and resurrection)

An abundance of landmass Creation Instrument materials
An abundance of entity Creation Instrument materials
All of the defeated Creator's landmasses: 8 found
+70 temporal resources
Broadcast ability
+225 temporal resources
[. . . Scanning . . .]
Optional tasks updated!

All Betting System tasks are hidden by the Alpha Protocol
until the third battle.

Auction task: Enter the Auction (Part 1)
The Alpha Protocol is not the only protocol within the multiverse.
Enter the Auction, and prepare yourself for wonders your eyes
will never see anywhere else in the multiverse.
Entrance requirements:
Creator has selected the Auction System within their overlay: No
Reward for completion: 20 temporal resources

New Cosmic Genesis task: Build your
first cosmic entity (Series 1)
The Cosmic Genesis system is rare within the Alpha Protocol.
To build a cosmic entity is an undertaking only the greatest
of each rendition's Creators have accomplished over time,
connecting different worlds within their own Cosmere.
Build, create, destroy. It is all the same in the eyes of the protocol.
System requirements:
Cosmic entity is active and non-volatile: No
Cosmic entity does not impinge on other Creator's worlds: No
Reward for completion: Cosmic Genesis System costs reduced.

Congratulations, Dante, on completing the second battle!
Please keep an eye on the timer for the forthcoming third battle.

Walker looked at the ever-present timer in the corner of his overlay.

Time remaining until the next battle: 120 hours

The protocol had only added twenty hours to the last battle's timer, which seemed odd. There had been twenty-four hours before the first battle, and a hundred hours between the first and the second. Judging by that, Walker would have expected another steep increase in time. He asked Virgil, who was already deep in the Evolution Chambers, about the strange time choices.

Without turning away from his work, he said, "The first allotment of time was based on pressuring the Creators of the Alpha Protocol to get to work. The lazy, the stupid, and the conscientious objectors were then knocked out early. It takes a specific kind of person to not only become a Creator but also succeed—a certain ruthlessness mixed with caring about your people."

Walker put a hand to his chest, fluttering the other to fan his face. "Virgil? Sentimental? My god, you're saying I'm one of those people—that I'm smarter than Crratch?"

"Very much so. I know of one randomly chosen Creator, much like yourself, whose body was formed from what you would call a puddle of mud. It was a hard worker but did not have much, as you would say, going on upstairs. Failure in the protocol is a foregone conclusion if the Creator does not complete the first tasks within the timeframe they are given."

How the fuck would a puddle of mud do any of this? What would its Creation Instrument even be? Walker thought to himself. Out loud he said, "So, what is the purpose of the timers between these battles? It feels like the protocol didn't give us enough time for all of our systems and plans for the sapients."

"It is an oddly large amount of time, if you can believe it," Virgil said, making some final changes to a chamber before moving to the next one. "These will come out just fine," he said, patting them. Walker looked inside and found a large fox in one and an oversized prairie dog in the other. "According to the records of the previous renditions, the Creators were given half as much time in between battles as you are now receiving. I personally believe this rendition is receiving special treatment."

Walker tried not to think about how much the Alpha Protocol's Council had spoken to him during this whole process, let alone the way they had pushed him in the last battle. "That reminds me, you said earlier, during one of the last rounds, that you thought they were trying to speed it up. Did you see that we only came in second?"

"Indeed. It is likely that the Creator who came in first is unbelievably smart. To have an entity that can not only defeat a Council Sentinel but live to tell the tale? They must be very powerful. Chipper barely succeeded, and yet I believe he is already among one of the most powerful early entities I can find for this stage of the Alpha Protocol." Virgil tsked at something he saw on his screen before continuing. "However, every time I try to look at who the winning Creator was, I come back with nothing. It is quite confusing and, if I am being honest, worrying."

"Yeah, but if they don't want you to see it, there isn't much you can do. Hell, I'm still ignoring the chatrooms. I don't think I want to go back in there after the Slicer tore through Jolive's planet. I glanced for just a moment before the battle, and that was enough to see how the other Creators felt about me."

"Yes. You are a very special kind of villain to rendition 4AA. They are not speaking kindly of you. I am sorry to say that I still have no update on what your original entity is doing."

Walker gave a helpless shrug. "Alright, well, thanks for the information."

"My pleasure. Do you know what you will do now?"

Walker scratched his chin as he looked at the timer again. "I was thinking about that. I know we don't have a ton of time, but I think I want to mess around with my new systems."

Virgil nodded as he said, "Yes. I was surprised that you picked the Cosmic Genesis System over the others. The dragon bloodline alone would be a massive gain for us."

Walker waved his hand. "I have my own solution for that, but we'll see if it works out. Please get the prey out to the desert. I'm sure Phil will appreciate it."

"I will do that, Creator," Virgil said with a smile as he turned back to the Evolution Chambers.

Walker saw Echidna wave him over, but he put up a hand in a stalling gesture. He knew what he was going to do next, and it was an important step. The Cosmic Genesis System's reason for being was in the name, and as much as he hated names, this time was a special occasion.

Cosmic meant stars, galaxies, planets, and other things found within the greater scope of the universe. Genesis was translated as the beginning or origin of something. Put them together, and you have a planet-building system, or, more importantly, a star-building one.

He hoped.

Walker still had many limitations before he could start plopping sapients into his world. If he did it right now, monsters would devour any of his attempts at civility. Not to mention that the light currently striking Symphony was still coming from an unreliable shield. He thought of it as unreliable because he had no control over it, which was dangerous to someone who wanted to build a harmonious world. Walker recognized that he still did not have a great amount of agency within the protocol. That needed to change.

But there was still SO MUCH TO DO. Classes, professions—heck, building more landmasses. He needed to prioritize and come up with a plan. So, naturally, he knew that the true first step to creating a civilization was to build a star, and the Cosmic Genesis System was how he would get there.

Thinking on it further, as Virgil worked on the prey animals nearby, he came up with a mental list of the steps he would need to take before he could drop sapients into his little harmony-driven world of war.

1. Build a star with the Cosmic Genesis System.
2. Find a caretaker to watch over the sapients (and he knew just the albino squirrel to do it).
3. Build the Milestone System so the class and Monster Systems fit within his overarching plan.
4. Get a few skill systems up and running.
5. Humans are naturally flawed creatures. Maybe, just maybe, he could find a way to make his people a little better than those in the world he left behind. Genetically, that is.

The countdown ticking in his vision seemed to laugh at his plans. There just wasn't enough time. But rather than despair about it, Walker decided to focus on one task at a time. Building a star came first, and that's what he was doing to do right now.

Walker pulled up his overlay and clicked the Cosmic Genesis System button. Instantly, the green and grassed environment around him shifted to black as he was moved to somewhere else.

Walker finally felt godlike as he stood looking down on Symphony's tiny form and his even smaller world beside it. From his size, it appeared as if both were no more than oddly colored marbles. A massive screen rose and expanded, lighting up in front of him with text.

> **Welcome to the Cosmic Genesis System, Dante.**
> **Use of this system has a cost: Temporal resources and landmass**
> **Creation Instrument materials.**
> **What would you like to create?**

Rather than be shocked, Walker rolled with the changes. "How does this even work?" He had always had a system that worked through his overlays, but this one was completely different, and he was treading water in an unfamiliar ocean.

> **I am an automated system, what you would call artificial intelligence. I am designed to help in a similar manner to a standard assistant, but specialized in the work of Cosmic Genesis.**

"So, what? You're some kind of program? Like, you don't have a personality?"

I am not a person, and not all things require a personality.

"Okay then," Walker said, scratching the back of his head. "So you're saying that, unlike my assistants, you won't suddenly have a sense of humor or start being snotty with me."

That is correct. How may I help you today, Dante?

"What do I currently have that I can work with?"

**You currently have one conglomerated landmass, one moonlet,
and a group of unsorted landmasses:
Symphony
Unnamed moonlet
Unsorted landmasses: 6 desert landmasses
and 2 forest landmasses**

As much as he hated naming things, it didn't feel right for his little grassy world to go without. "What can I do with Crratch's world, and how do I name my moonlet?"

**Options for unsorted and unattached landmasses:
1. Turn the collected landmasses into free resources.
2. Place the unsorted landmasses within Symphony's collection.
3. Repurpose the collected landmasses to build another world.
4. Expand your moonlet into a standard moon.**

**Option for naming the moonlet:
You may name the moonlet at any time.**

"Easy enough, first things first. I would like to name my moonlet."

**Request to name moonlet recognized.
What would you like to name the moonlet?**

Walker scratched his chin as the dreaded question arrived. He wanted to stay within the theme of Symphony. So, how would that work? Strings . . . no, that was terrible. First, second, and third movements were worse. Walker pulled on his memory further, using every bit of his Awakened mind to search through what he knew of symphonies. Then he found it. There was only one word that would properly fit this one.

"Sonata."

Sonata recognized. Moonlet will now be named Sonata.

Walker raised an eyebrow at the system's expediency and lack of follow-up. "Okay, great. Now, how do I create a star?"

**Star tutorial request recognized. Would you like to
start the tutorial now?**

Walker looked over what the system had originally said when he entered. "Would it cost me anything?"

**No, Creator Dante. Tutorials are provided at
no charge by the Alpha Protocol.**

With a shrug, he said, "Sure, why not?"

As he finished speaking, Symphony and Sonata faded away, and Walker found himself at the center of a spiraling ring of cosmic dust clouds. All around him was utter darkness except one bright light centered on his own body. With a shake, Walker realized he wasn't at the center of a growing star; he *was* the center.

**Initial star phase recognized: Nebulous Formation
Beginning second phase.**

An implosion happened right near his chest, and all of the dust clouds were sucked in. Like a plug pulled out of the bottom of a bathtub, the cloud particles were swirling in a cone shape and entering his chest.

**Second star phase recognized: Gravitational Collapse
Beginning third phase.**

One area right toward his sternum grew bright and hot simultaneously, giving Walker a hazy feeling of numbed heat. A large amount of the unabsorbed dust began to circle this hot location, and Walker found himself moved outside of the star's formation so he could better watch the results.

**Third star phase recognized: Protostar Formation
Beginning fourth phase.**

The dust and smaller fragments that had coalesced together while the proto-star was formed began to shoot toward it in mass. Each strike and general absorption increased the size and heat of the burgeoning star until it was ten, fifty, or a hundred times its original size. Walker couldn't imagine how large the celestial body would be in comparison to his relatively minuscule body.

Fourth star phase recognized: Accretion Process
Beginning final ignition phase.

A few more pieces of collected debris and particles shot into the center of the star, its size increasing again before a critical event unfolded before him. A massive amount of heat exploded from the star in a wave, and the burgeoning sun's light became Walker's new day.

It was an unbelievable event to watch unfold before his eyes, and he knew that he was likely the first and one of the few to ever watch this occur in the past, present, and future of humanity's collective history. The yellow star, which was, in fact, a yellow star and not a red or blue dwarf, burned merrily as it sat alone in the middle of the universe's dark sky.

Walker's improved memory remembered his eighth-grade science teacher explaining how a sun worked. They lasted for billions of years, producing and burning helium by fusing hydrogen atoms within their cores. He bet she never could have imagined one of her students experiencing this right now.

G-type star's formation complete.
Star tutorial complete.

That confused Walker, so he asked, "What tutorial? You just made a star in front of me; there wasn't any tutorial."

Dante, the Alpha Protocol dictated that each
Creator with access to the Cosmic Genesis system
be allowed to watch the five phases of a star's birth.
Did you watch it occur?

"Yes?"

Then, that is the tutorial provided by the Alpha Protocol.

Fuckin' lied about the snark. "So I don't get to make stars and planets and black holes?"

**The Creator is unable to form these cosmic bodies
themselves physically, magically, or otherwise. They are, however,
able to provide direction for what they would like to occur.
The tutorial shows how many steps the system must take in order
to create cosmic bodies. The Cosmic Genesis System A.I. will
then take your request and, after being supplied with the correct
amount of resources, produce the required results.**

Walker considered that on top of everything he'd experienced since arriving here. He knew that the requirements would be heavy, and that it would be a major drain on his recently collected temporal resources. But he'd picked this system for a good reason, and he couldn't walk away until he got what he was after. "What would it cost to create a G-type or yellow star at a habitable orbital distance from Symphony?"

**Would you like the star to be at a similar distance to your
former world?**

That threw him for a loop. "How would you know about my former world?"

**While as a basic A.I. I am not allowed to review
Creator's memories, I am given a simple review of the status of all
Creator's former worlds to assist in my work.
It is common for Creators to want to create a world similar
to their planet of origin.**

Walker nodded. That made a certain amount of sense. "Alright then, yes, I would like it to be a similar distance."

**[. . . Calculating . . .]
Distance found.
Distance approved as all Creators within the immediate vicinity
of Creator Dante have already exited the Alpha Protocol.
No extra resources are required for the movement of Symphony
or potential bystanders.**

"Shit, I would've had to pay for moving another Creator's world? How much would that have cost?"

**The likely cost, based on the size of current Creators in the third
arc of the Alpha Protocol, is within 200 temporal resources.**

"And what would the cost be for a star similar to the one from my home-world? As in, how much would it cost to place a G-type star already in the fifth phase near enough to bring Symphony within its habitable range?"

[. . . Calculating . . .]
To accommodate for accelerated placement, and unlike
forming a rudimentary exoplanet, the star must be imported
from a rendition that has recently birthed its own G-type
main-sequence star. The cost has increased.

Cost found.

A large amount of landmass resources is required to create
a new nebulous formation in its former location and allow
for a replacement G-type star to form over time.
50 temporal resources at cost for movement from
one rendition to another.
50 temporal resources at cost for placement within
an exacting location.
Location found: Habitable zone relative to Symphony
and Sonata.

"So a huge amount of landmass resources and one hundred temporal resources. Okay, can I just give you Crratch's old landmasses that are floating out by Symphony?"

[. . . Request being processed . . .]
Yes.
You will also have two remaining landmasses that
can be repurposed at will.

Walker nodded, thinking quickly. He wanted—no, needed—to get his civilizations started. This was the first step and, to his terrestrial mindset, the most important one. But he had bigger plans for this system than just creating a single star.

"How can I repurpose the two remaining landmasses?"

Requested options have already been provided.
Providing options again for limited-intelligence Creator.

"Hey!"

Options for the unsorted landmasses:
1. Turn the collected landmasses into free resources.
2. Place the unsorted landmasses within Symphony's collection.
3. Repurpose the collected landmasses to build another world.
4. Expand your moonlet into a standard moon.

Walker thought over what he planned to do, especially considering future task updates and what they would bring.

"How would I repurpose the two remaining landmasses into their own planets?"

Options for building planets from already seeded landmasses:
1. Mesh both into a conglomeration of biomes, allowing a smaller planet to form. Some resources may be lost. Limited resources are required.
2. Break one or both landmasses into a protoplanetary disk, allowing a planet to naturally form over time. Limited resources are required.

"Can I accelerate the second option so they form faster?"

Yes.

"What would the cost be to accelerate both landmasses individually so they both enter the final planetary phase?"

[. . . Calculating . . .]
75 temporal resources each.

"Shit, too expensive for now." Walker looked through his resources and overlay, coming to a decision quickly. "Start the prior instructions. Steal . . . I mean, form a G-type main-sequence star that will put Symphony and Sonata within its habitable zone and allow for an elliptical orbit."

Request understood.
As specifications were not given, selecting 6 random choices from the unsorted landmasses.
Proceeding.

Resources removed from Creator Dante.
Resources allocated . . .

G-type main-sequence star found.
**Star successfully translocated to the first trial of the fourth
rendition.**
Resources removed from Creator Dante.
Resources allocated . . .
**G-type main-sequence star successfully translocated to the
habitable zone for Creator Dante's world (Symphony) and
moonlet (Sonata).**
**Congratulations, Dante, you have your own G-type
main sequence star.**
Please . . .

But Walker had already clicked out of the Cosmic Genesis System and into a new day. The darkness of the system faded as a bright yellow light shined its radiance upon him. A new sun sat happily above him, burning gas and providing its splendor for all of Walker's future creations.

He smiled to feel the heat of the sun for the first time in a long time, and realized he had missed the feeling completely. The protocol protected him from hazardous temperatures, but the glowing heat currently hitting his skin was a nice reminder of home.

Virgil worked with his screens, a look of strain on his face as his rapid eye movement showed how much he was doing at once. Rimi was jumping up and down, hooting with a fisted hand raised in the air, while the three Primigenials whom Walker had ignored earlier were each staring at the star in the formerly dark sky.

"So, what do you think?" Walker asked as everyone but Virgil jumped.

"Where did you go?" Zeus thundered at him.

"To steal that," he said, pointing toward the recently translocated sun.

"You . . . stole a star?" Minos said in his quiet voice.

"Yep! Why build your own when you can just steal one?!"

"Walker!" Virgil yelled at him. "Symphony and . . . Sonata? Symphony and Sonata are already being dragged into the star's gravitational field! We'll be destroyed!"

"No, we won't," Walker said with a smile, finally getting one up on his too-smart assistant. "You didn't check the elliptical rate of our two little planets. We're already within our new star's habitable range."

"The what . . . what?" Zeus asked in confusion.

Walker waited as Virgil looked at his screens for a few moments more, and then the large squirrel sighed. "You're right. You thought this through quite well."

The Cosmic Genesis system did, but he doesn't need to know that. "Yep! Now . . . wait for it."

"For what?" Rimi asked, but of course, he couldn't see Walker's overlay light up.

[... Scanning ...]

[Error.]
Task completed through alternative means.

[... Scanning ...]
Cosmic Genesis task complete: Build your first cosmic entity (Series 1)
System requirements:
Cosmic Entity is active and non-volatile: Yes
Cosmic Entity does not impinge on other Creators' worlds: Yes
Reward for completion: Cosmic Genesis System costs reduced.

New Cosmic Genesis task: Build your first star (Series 2)
Creating a star is a foundation for every universe, and borders on the powers of the Alpha Protocol itself. Build a star, and see the dawn of a new day.
System requirements:
The star will not destroy cosmic entities around it: Yes
The star allows for elliptical revolutions of surrounding cosmic entities: Yes
The star does not impinge on other Creators' worlds: Yes
Reward for completion: Cosmic Genesis System costs are further reduced.

[... Scanning ...]

[Error.]
Task completed through alternative means.

Cosmic Genesis task complete: Build your first star (Series 2)
System requirements:
The star will not destroy cosmic entities around it: Yes
The star allows for elliptical rotations of surrounding cosmic entities: Yes
The star does not impinge on other Creators' worlds: Yes
Reward for completion: Cosmic Genesis System costs are further reduced.

Cosmic Genesis task: Build a solar system (Series 3)
You have built a star and created your own elliptical system for
cosmic entities. Now, build an entire solar system.
System requirements:
The solar system will not destroy cosmic entities around it: Yes
The solar system will not destabilize or destroy each cosmic entity
within it: Yes
Planets and/or stars found within the solar system: 3/10
Reward for completion: Cosmic Genesis System upgrade

Walker ignored Virgil's spluttering as a smile broke out on his face. So far, across the protocol, he'd had to figure out how to satisfy tasks as they came. This time, he'd guessed that the second task would be to create a star, so why not just do it first? He clicked on the Cosmic Genesis System button again and disappeared, leaving confusion behind him.

Welcome back, Dante.

In the vast reaches minimized in front of him, Walker's new sun sat still, burning in a dark and lonely universe, while Symphony and Sonata sat a good amount of distance away. There was a green arrow showing Symphony's direction around the sun and a paler green arrow showing Sonata's elliptical orbit around Walker's original creation.

Sonata's elliptical orbit was unlocked while you were gone. It is
stable.
Symphony's elliptical orbit was unlocked while you were gone.
It is stable.

"Excellent. I would like to see the options, again, for creating the two final phase protoplanets from Crratch's former landmasses."

Certainly.
Options for building planets from already seeded landmasses:

1. Mesh both into a conglomeration of biomes, allowing a smaller
planet to form. Some resources may be lost. Limited resources are
required.
2. Break one or both landmasses into a protoplanetary disk,
allowing a planet to naturally form over time. Limited resources
are required.

"And what is now the cost to force both landmasses into the final stage for creating their own exoplanets, skipping the stages in between and placing them within a habitable range that does not affect the elliptical arcs of my current planet and moonlet?"

[. . . Calculating . . .]
Acceleration for exoplanets is 40 temporal resources each.
Placement on a non-disruptive elliptical track is 5 temporal resources each.

"Outstanding, please do so," Walker said, then exited the system.

He got out in time to watch as the last two remaining landmasses from his defeated foe disappeared without a sound, and two nebulous dust clouds formed at an almost unbelievable distance away. Time accelerated as Walker watched the birth of two planets in real time.

Dust particles clumped together and grew in size. Asteroids flew by and were sucked into the same path of the clumped particles, crashing and melding until, after several minutes of him and everyone else on Sonata watching, two magma-like exoplanets formed themselves from the wreckage.

"What did you do now?" Virgil asked as he watched the two red-hot exoplanets float on the far side of Walker's solar system.

"I lit a candle. Now, if you'll excuse me, I have a quick question for Echidna," he said, ignoring his friend for the moment as he continued while he was on a roll.

The Primigenial woman looked at him, saying, "Yes?"

"The fertility modification from your task, will it make it safer for women to have children? Will those children grow stronger and faster?"

"I am not supposed to give any information on the reward until the task is complete," she said, but she glowed yellow for just a moment to Walker's eyes.

He nodded once with a slight smile, then headed over to his old computer desk and sat down in front of his journal. It was time to make some progress in his scripture. He looked at the task he'd seen not too long ago, checking on where he was in his completion rate.

Primigenial task: Write a Holy Scripture
What do you believe in, Walker? Who are you?
Build a religion for all.
Volumes completed: 3/10
Task giver: Echidna, Mother of Monsters
Reward for completion: Fertility modification

Walker continued to ignore those around him as he sunk into his subconscious and closed his eyes, thinking of what mattered most to his future followers. Virgil stepped in front of Zeus for a moment, blocking his path, and Rimi kept yelling at the sky, but Walker had already gone inside himself. Unbeknownst to him, his body glowed a slight forest green as he came to a thought and opened his eyes. "Zenith."

He began writing.

Echidna and Minos saw the glow-up and nodded at each other before sitting down and discussing what the new planets meant for their future and that of their fellow Primigenials.

The Tree of the Gods grew again as nobody watched it, arcing toward Sonata's sky.

"What is he doing now?" Athena asked those trapped like her. For thousands of years, she had lived on a single branch within their great prison. Seeing the others escape had filled her with great anxiety, and the certain expectation of her own release.

"Who knows? Just try to relax, girl," Dionysus snapped back, enjoying the other Primigenial's torment at being locked into one place for so long.

"Not all of us are so comfortable with being stuck in one place for so long," Demeter reminded him.

"Who cares, farm bitch? I'm just happy nobody is asking me to do anything."

"Have some respect for your betters," his uncle said with disgust in his voice.

"Or what? You'll hop out of your fruit and stab me with your stupid fucking pitchfork? Relax. We'll get out of here soon enough."

"I can't see anything!" Athena yelled at everyone. Though the other Primigenials hated to do it, they also asked her to calm down, as none of them could see either.

"It comes," the three-headed watcher on the tallest branch spoke. "Fate is approaching quickly. Many will be freed at once. Prepare."

"Ugh," the god of wine and revelry said in response. "You said that shit last time, and only my dumbass dad and those two minors were released."

"Prepare."

"I need a drink."[6]

CHAPTER THIRTY-THREE

Just When You Get on a Roll

Walker put the journal down next to his computer, then stretched as he checked his damnable timer.

Time remaining until the next battle: 112 hours

"Better," he said to himself with a smile. In his last journal session, he'd gone over a lot of the coalesced knowledge he'd gained in college. The more time passed since his awakening, the more it seemed to pay off. His mind continued to expand. He still didn't feel any smarter, but the memories he did have became more and more clear.

When he wanted to remember something, he could pinpoint the timeframe when it happened and just pull it up. It felt like he was flipping through a dictionary in search of a word he'd once known, but instead of words, he was looking for his memories. From basic architecture and building techniques to how to find clean water, the entirety of everything he had ever learned, which was quite a bit across his life, was slowly returning to his grasp at a thought and a need.

Walker remembered once telling his students that, after a week, they'd only remember about a quarter of what he had just taught them. Walker no longer had the average man's memory problems, and this was just the start of his awakening. He had no idea what might come next.

For his scriptures—he was slowly but surely running out of space in his journal—he was trying to do his best for those who would one day follow him. Walker wanted to teach them the right path forward, an informed path, a focus for future generations of Symphonians.

Symphians?

Whatever.

Thinking that over, he already knew the topic of his third scripture, and with a spring in his step, he walked over to his assistants to get an update on what had happened in the last eight hours.

"Yo!" he said when he got close to Virgil and Rimi.

"Hi, Walker," Rimi responded with a wave, while the larger squirrel simply nodded.

"What'd I miss?" he said, putting his hands in his pockets.

"The Tree of the Gods grew larger," Virgil commented, a strange look coming over his face.

Walker glanced in that direction and noticed it had certainly grown. It seemed like each time a major push forward occurred with Walker's plans, the tree grew accordingly. Weird.

"Did Sonata grow again?"

"Indeed. I would say it enlarged about twenty percent this time," Virgil said as he spread his arms, encompassing the moonlet's size.

Walker whistled. "That much? So what does that mean?"

"I am unsure. As you know, I still have no information about the Tree of the Gods. The Alpha Protocol is being unusually restrictive."

"You can't just analyze it and figure shit out?"

Virgil slowly shook his head. "No, I cannot."

"Bummer," Walker said, scratching the back of his head. He peeked over at the tree and hit Identify, but for some reason, it didn't update. "Well, we'll cross that bridge when we get to it."

"Yes. I have placed the prey into the desert, and also taken the liberty to look in on a few of the other zones with Rimi here." Hearing his name, Rimi waved again with a smile. "I also added some variation to The Crater's fish life while you were out, as whatever grows there has seen fit to spread across Symphony. Also, I have discovered what my new functionality with the Landmass System involves."

"Oh really? So, what do you get to do?" Walker asked in excitement, hoping he could finally skip all the landmass creation in the future and focus on things that were more in his wheelhouse.

"I can copy landmasses in their entirety and work with the new Auxiliary Landmass System," Virgil said with a smile, his brown tail slashing the air behind him.

Walker's head fell just a fraction before he lifted it and emotionally rolled with the news. "That's great!" He didn't want Virgil to know how much that had let him down. He wanted—no, he needed—to focus on building Symphony's people, not just mountains and rivers and all of the minutiae that came with it. But Virgil didn't need Walker's sour mood to dampen his excitement.

"Indeed. The Auxiliary Landmass System is quite fun as well; you should take a look at it."

Walker tilted his head. "What's it do?"

"It is a landmass scheduler. When you build landmasses in the future, you can now place them in holding until you are ready for them to join Symphony. This way, while you're focusing on other systems, new landmasses can drop in as needed and you will not have to focus on them quite as much."

Walker clapped once. "Hey, that *is* good stuff! And now that you can copy landmasses and schedule them, I just need to make a bunch of . . . like . . . blueprints for you."

"That is a very good idea, Walker. Now, if you do not mind, can you please advance Symphony by seven days in a moment?"

"Can I do that when I get back?"

"Get back from where?"

"Chipper!" Rimi yelled from beside Walker, startling him as he took two steps back. "You're going to see Chipper, right?"

Walker recovered his equilibrium quickly. "Indeed I am, buddy, plus I need to seed Raganoth the Bleeder. It's not fair to leave him stuck inside some kind of stasis bubble."

Virgil put a hand to his chin for a moment, then nodded. "You are right, of course. You would not want to be rude to a being that powerful before unleashing him on Symphony. The advancement can wait."

"Yayyy," the small blue squirrel cheered, and Walker smiled before pulling up his monitor. He zoomed the screen over to Chipper, double-checked that he wasn't interrupting anything, gave a quick thumbs-up to his two assistants, and hit the Avatar ability.

Sonata faded out, and Symphony faded in. Walker had placed the monitor so that he would be only about ten feet away from the Mana Tree when arriving. He looked up, and up, and up to the top of the hundred-foot tree in all of its glory. The blue branches and cyan leaves stood proudly as Walker's eyes took in the slight color of pure magic permeating the nearby air. Perhaps the greatest thing he ever made for all of Symphony was this tree and its fellows.

Made so far, he mentally corrected himself.

The tree's roots spread and touched along the bottom of his entire world, connecting each of the lands together. A rustle started a dozen feet above him, and a four-foot-tall white squirrel leaped down, hands glowing. The Guardian tilted his head left and right as if sizing him up before writing in the air, *Can you read this?*

"Hello, Chipper," Walker said with a bit of déjà vu. He really admired the Guardian and what he had done for Walker and for Symphony as a whole. The forthcoming conversation made him very nervous, as he needed it to go well.

You can make sounds? And how do you know my name? the Guardian spelled out with an extra-large question mark.

"Well, buddy, I am the all-powerful yet ignorant and entirely mortal person who made all of this," Walker replied, spreading his arms wide to encompass everything around them. "This world, Symphony, was my idea and creation."

I do not understand.

"Well, let me explain everything to you, including what happened just nine or so hours ago," Walker said, taking a seat in the grass as Chipper continued to maintain a confused look on his face.

It took a little over an hour to break everything down, with Chipper only asking a few questions before prompting Walker to continue speaking. When they reached the second battle, Walker told him about Chomp and Phil, the boss rounds, and the deal the protocol had offered. He ended on how Chipper had performed, and he spoke grandly about his final fight versus the Council's Sentinel.

"So, we came in second, which was a bit of a letdown. Not because of your performance, but just for Symphony as a whole." Walker shoved his hands in his pockets. "I know it's my ego talking there. We're one out of . . . probably several hundred thousand, but still, first place would have been nice. We don't even know who beat us, but Virgil, my assistant I told you about, thinks they must be some kind of genius Creator the protocol rarely sees. Either way, coming in second let me create that," he said, pointing to the bright yellow star in the previously dark sky.

He waited for Chipper to turn around before smiling. "Without you, there's a good chance we wouldn't have been able to create a sun or some other things I have in the works. You're Symphony's first real hero, Chipper, and I'm afraid we're not done yet. So, even though you have given so much to me and Symphony as a whole, I'm here to ask for three more things, if you'll oblige me."

Chipper wrote back, *And what is that, Creator?*

"One, I'd like to be your friend and not just your Creator. You're a good soul, Chipper, and I have had just enough friends that I can recognize that in a person."

Chipper gave him a look that Walker interpreted as a smile. *That is an easy request. Done.*

Walker smiled back. "Thank you. Two, I need you to keep an eye on Raganoth the Bleeder. He'll be new here and, if he wanted, he could really damage everything I'm trying to build. I'm hopeful he was honest before when he spoke of trying to live a new life, but you never really know if people are what they say they are."

Chipper nodded without writing.

"And three, I'd like you to be my first disciple and also follower."

What does that entail?

"Well, buddy, that's still a little ways away. But when I get my Holy Scripture done, the one I told you about, you'll be the first to get the chance to read it. It'll explain quite a bit about how the world works and give you a basic education that you can then expand on further if that's what you want to do. It's your choice, there's no pressure."

There's a little pressure, his mind interrupted him.

"A-And Raganoth and being my friend are more than enough for me to be continually grateful to you and give you a little more attention than I give everyone else. But I've gotta warn you, taking on the discipleship and joining my soon-to-be religion would tie you to me . . ."—he thought about it for a moment—". . . probably forever."

I see, Chipper wrote back. *May I think on it, friend Walker?*

"Absolutely and I would've asked you to wait regardless, as it isn't something that will be a light burden. I'm not entirely sure what becoming my disciple or a follower of the faith would entail." He looked at his white fur with a smile. "No pun there, but I am hopeful it would only be beneficial to the both of us."

Chipper seemed to think for a few moments, chewing on one of his nails. Walker could've asked him about the bad habit, but he ultimately felt it was better to just let the Guardian consider everything in silence.

The albino squirrel came to an internal understanding, squaring up his shoulders before writing, *I agree to Raganoth the Bleeder, but please give me some time to consider your third request.*

"Of course," Walker said, standing up and putting a hand out to his friend. "In my old world, we would clasp hands to signify that a deal has been made. I don't see a reason why we can't do that here."

Chipper gave him a squirrely smile. *Then a deal has been made, friend Walker.* As soon as he finished writing, he reached up, taking Walker's hand in his own.

"Excellent," Walker said, smiling back and pumping their arms up and down once before pulling his hand away. "Then a friendship for me, and a friendship plus a new potential friend for you. Now, while I would love to stay down here and hang out some more, I'm afraid I have somewhere to be, and you have a new friend to become acquainted with. If you'll excuse me."

Chipper looked confused, writing, *We are not hanging, fri . . .*

But Walker had already clicked the Avatar ability and disappeared. No more than a few minutes went past before a giant yellow wyvern materialized from nothingness and settled on two legs and wings nearby.

"Where am I now!" Raganoth bellowed to the world.

"What?" Chipper asked the air as the massive creature appeared in front of him.

Walker was already back on Sonata, watching through the Monitor ability with Rimi and Virgil. As they viewed Chipper's first exchange with Raganoth, the albino squirrel slowly approaching and writing in the air, he felt oddly like a parent first placing their child in daycare, watching his kid to make sure they got along with the other kids.

"What are the odds that Raganoth will go feral?" Walker asked his two assistants.

"I would estimate there is an above-average chance for the poison wyvern to return to its roots and attempt to destroy Symphony," Virgil replied with harsh pessimism.

"I disagree," Rimi said with a shake of his small head. "I believe he will settle in quite nicely."

"Well, time will tell, as they say. Rimi, keep an eye on him. Raganoth doesn't have a kernel, so you'll just have to try to look in on him from time to time." Rimi gave a salute. "Anyways, it's time for a new assistant so we can start up the Milestone System."

Rimi cheered loudly, jumping up and down, while Virgil's face changed to one of disgust. "Can you not just change my form for the time being?" he pleaded with his Creator.

"Don't you remember? No can do, bud. This form is how I know you, it'd be super weird if you were suddenly Godzilla or a giant hairless ape or whatever else is in there. What if we changed you into a small T-rex and Rimi changed with you?" Walker shook his head. "Sorry, man, I know it's selfish, but you can't actually die. It's just super uncomfortable, right?"

"Yes, that is true." Virgil squared his shoulders, looking straight ahead. "I am ready."

Walker clicked the Subsystem Assistant button and it lit up a neon pink.

[. . . Loading . . .]
Expelling new subsystem assistant.

He was much less shocked the second time those words appeared. He calmly watched as Virgil coughed, already reaching down the length of his throat. Compared to the panic of Walker's first subsystem assistant's showing, the newest resident of Sonata arrived to the sound of cheering. "Come on, little brother or sister!" Rimi yelled.

"You know that you don't really have genders," Walker commented as Virgil seemed to grab hold.

"Who cares! Push, my sibling! Push!"

"That's not . . . who told you . . ." But Walker was interrupted, as with a final loud cough, Virgil pulled the new assistant out and threw them a short distance away.

"I hate this," Virgil spoke in a scratchy voice.

Unlike Rimi's odd blue coloring, this one was a bright pink, and the new subsystem assistant immediately unrolled from their pill bug-like form before standing up.

"Are you my Creator?" a high-pitched voice that sounded just like Rimi asked.

"He is! I said the exact same thing!" Rimi shouted with exuberance. "He likes to be called Walker, though."

". . . Walker . . ." the new subsystem assistant said, testing out the word.

"Hello, little one. I'm Walker, this is Virgil, and that's Rimi," he said, pointing to each. "To get things going quickly, as we're on a time limit, I'd like to name you. Is that okay?"

"Of course," the small pink squirrel said while standing stock-still.

"If you don't like the name, please let me know." Walker waited for a moment, but the new subsystem assistant didn't move. "You can just move your head up and down if you agree or from one side to another if you disagree."

"I understand," it responded quickly, giving a too-fast nod.

"A little slower with the head movements, and you've got it," Walker said with a thumbs-up, receiving a slow one in return. He began pacing with his arms behind his back. "So, we have a naming convention we've been using for our assistants. The protocol calls me Dante, my first assistant is Virgil, and Rimi here is named after the first character Dante meets in a poetic adventure that is a little too complicated to go over right now." He spun around quickly to keep the pink squirrel in his vision. "In the story, the second creature Dante meets is named Cerberus, which may not actually work as, unlike in the story, we may actually meet someone named Cerberus," he said with a raised eyebrow. Minos looked across at him from where he was talking to Echidna and slowly shook his head. "Okay then, Cerberus will work. Now . . ."

"I would like a name that is like my sibling's. How would you describe Cerberus?" the pink squirrel said.

"He is a three-headed dog," Walker said, taking the interruption in stride and replying calmly. He stood there, waiting for a similar moment to the one he'd had with Rimi to occur.

"Oh, oh!" Rimi said with a raised hand, Symphony's newest assistant naturally imitating him. "Virgil, what is the word for dog in that poem's language?"

"In Italian, the word for dog is either Cane or Cagna," the elder squirrel said quickly.

"I choose Cagna," the small pink squirrel said, then moved their head up and down almost in slow motion.

"Cagna it is!" Rimi said, jumping up and down as he hopped over to his new sibling. "I like you!"

"I . . . like you too," Cagna said with another small nod. When Rimi's hopping took him to his sibling, he took their hands in his and began jumping up and down until Cagna began jumping with him. Rimi laughed uproariously, and after a few moments, Cagna joined him.

"Alright. This is going to get bad as we get more assistants, isn't it," Walker said to Virgil, who was also silently watching the two energetic squirrels in their play.

"Indeed."

"Has anyone made as many systems as I'm planning on making?"

"How many are you planning on making, Walker?"

"A little more than a dozen? Maybe more."

Virgil looked at his screens for a moment, then said, "You would be among the few who have ever created that many, but not the one with the highest amount. One Creator from the third rendition has over fifty, although I am told that the number of systems he created stifled his world rather than helped it."

"Hrm, good advice there," Walker said with a hand to his chin. "Well, the one we're going to build now is the system that sets up all other systems. Without it, nothing will work quite right."

Virgil nodded. "I see. I believe you will have all the assistance you need with Rimi and C-Cagna." He tripped slightly over the name. "What would you like me to work on while you build the Milestone System?"

"I'd like you to start work on a few different genera at once. We can't alter the Warclaws, according to the protocol, so they'll just have to go without the benefits that everyone else will receive."

Walker sighed as he looked at the Evolution Chambers. "We have five Evolution Chambers now, so I'd like you to start work on a balanced monster for a new territory that will primarily be a mountainous biome, and I'd also like a new monster for the sea we're going to be building up over time. One that isn't as predatory at first, if you don't mind. Perhaps a seal type. Once you have those started, I'd like you to place a male and female human into each Evolution Chamber and see if you can't find a way to make them more resistant to disease and genetic manipulation. When you have any free time thereafter, start looking into the Combiner ability. Don't use it; just consider what it can do. Leave the last Evolution Chamber untouched in case something comes up."

"You are finally starting to take charge of everything?"

"I feel like I need to," Walker replied with a long exhalation. "This has been coming for a long time, and there's going to be a lot happening all at once pretty soon." He looked up at his new star for a moment, his eyes protected by whatever the protocol did to keep him relatively safe. "We've made big strides since the second battle, and the sooner I step up what I'm doing, the better."

Virgil nodded. "I agree. I will get started right away, Creator," he said before walking over to his work.

"Don't start that again!" Walker said as his hands slapped the outside of his legs.

"Walker! Walker!" Rimi said, waving him over. "We've decided on something together. I am a boy, and Cagna is a girl."

Walker affected a confused look on his face. "Why does gender matter? You're both essentially space dust that talks. I only used the pronoun *he* when talking about Rimi because of his coloring and the odd affectation of my homeworld."

"Uh-huh," Rimi replied, barely listening. "Our genders don't matter, but we think it makes things more fun." He began hopping up and down as Cagna gave Walker a too-slow nod.

"That's pretty weird, I'm not going to lie," Walker said, still confused by why gendering them would matter in the slightest.

Cagna began speaking slowly, her face scrunched up in thought. "Maybe . . ."

Walker never got to hear what she was saying as he immediately became distracted by his overlay lighting up.

Unknown changes occurring.
The Tree of the Gods is maturing!

[. . . Scanning . . .]
The Tree of the Gods has borne fruit.

"Son of a bitch!" Walker swore, as it was, quite possibly, the worst timing for this kind of event.

"Oh yeah, motherfuckers!" A fat pale man wearing a green vest and purple pants came bounding over while two others chased him. "Where's the drinks, bitches!"

"Fucking come on," Walker said, slapping a hand to his forehead. "I don't have time for this shit, seriously."

"This is not godly behavior, son!" Zeus thundered at him as the overly ripped king of the gods unceremoniously ran to catch up.

"Up yours, bitch! I'm the god of parties, baby! Show me the party, show me the food, show me the ladies! What's up, little girl?" he said to Walker, who was actually taller than him. "You wanna fuck around?"

"What?" Walker said, exhausted by another unusual event happening right when he was getting a grasp on things. He spied more people running behind Zeus to catch up.

"Walker, you have to listen to me!" a beautiful woman wearing a gold dress said as she ran up to him. "I'm the goddess of wisdom; I can help you so much!"

"She's full of it! All of them are full of it!" a woman wearing a conservative black lace dress said as she followed right behind her. She spat on the ground as she arrived. "You should listen to me; I'm the only one here who believes in you! Believes in the strength of humanity!" she finished with a single lace-covered fist in the air.

"Lies! This harlequin is only interested in herself!" the golden-dressed woman said with scorn.

"You're one to talk. Why don't you go make another owl?"

"That owl saved the world once!"

"It was an idiotic animal, as they all are, and it attacked a weakened harpy because it was blood-drunk and had accidentally invaded its nest!"

"How dare you!"

Walker could feel his pulse in the sides of his neck. As the two Primigenials yelled at each other, the vibration from his heartbeat battered away at his mind, further ratcheting up the stress he'd felt since first seeing the notification. He didn't have time for this—none of them did. He needed to move on to the next steps in his plan so he could finally drop some sapients down onto Symphony's soil. Not deal with people who felt entitled to his attention for escaping from prison.

To calm down, he instinctively grabbed both sides of his head. Of course, that had no effect whatsoever on his burgeoning headache, but pop culture had told him it might work. After a few seconds, when the women's voices reached a new octave, he tried using his old breathing exercise. However, that didn't seem to do the trick either.

After several minutes of the two women screaming at each other, with the god of lightning yelling at his newly released son, Walker finally snapped. "Shut the fuck up!"

As Walker screamed loud enough for even the creatures of Symphony to hear him, a massive pulse of green shot out of him in a wave, stopping everyone in their tracks and causing Echidna, Minos, and the black-laced woman to fall to their knees.

"I am so tired of you all trying to tell me what to do. NO MORE." Another smaller pulse came out, pushing the black-laced woman over entirely and causing a few of the gods to stutter a further step back. "My name is Walker Reed. Walker Reed! I am not your servant. I am not your pushover. And I AM NOT TO BE FUCKED WITH!" A pulse even larger than the first shot out and knocked the rest of the gods to their knees, curiously skipping over all three of Walker's assistants. But he didn't notice as he was too gripped by his anger.

"I have work to do, monumentally important work. If you want to speak with me"—he pointed at the Tree of the Gods—"you will stand by that bastard tree of yours and wait your turn. If you cannot do so, I will take steps to ensure you cannot bother me further, and trust me when I say, you won't like it." He gave each a glare, standing tall under their disbelieving looks. "The time for ordering or pushing me around is over. I am the Creator here, and this is my world. If I want your advice, I will ask for it. You all fucked up so badly that your former Creator threw you in prison. I won't make that mistake; I'll simply erase you from existence."

"Who's this bitch think he is?" the fat god said, looking at the other Primigenials.

"He is the Creator," Echidna said from the ground, getting up at a nod from Walker. "And he is right; let us go back to the tree of our siblings and speak quietly amongst ourselves."

"Where's the wine?"

"There is none, Dionysus," Minos said in an even quieter voice than normal.

"No wine! No fuckin' wine! Absolutely not." He began to wave his hands through the air.

Echidna whipped her head around. "Oh no."

[. . . Scanning . . .]
Optional tasks updated!

New Primigenial task: Find Dionysus some wine
I need wine, bitch. Call me Dio. Hey, do you have
any girls around?
Barrels of wine delivered: 0/10
Task giver: Dionysus, God of Revelry
Reward for completion: Festivity modification

"Son of a bitch."

Dionysus looked over at him with a cherubic smile as he said, "Yeah, she was."

CHAPTER THIRTY-FOUR

A Deal with the Gods

Get the fuck over there!" Walker yelled at the fat Primigenial as he pointed at the Tree of the Gods. "I don't want to see any other gods-damned tasks either!"

"But!" the woman in the gold dress said, raising a finger in the air.

"No! Fuck off!"

"Yeah! Fuck off!" Cagna said, mimicking him and pointing. Rimi stopped her so he could explain Walker's hypocritical stance on cursing.

Zeus took Dionysus by the arm and dragged him over to the tree with the others. The woman in lace and the woman in gold continued to yell at each other, Walker's speech having little effect on their feud. He was just happy nobody was physically fighting . . . yet.

Walker ran a hand through his hair.

"Just . . . fuck me, man. I'll deal with it later," he said as he started pacing. He stared at the back of the Primigenials as he moved, still trying to get a grip on his emotions. Then, he came to a sudden stop as reality crashed in. "Noooooo . . . no. It'll get worse. They'll just come to a consensus and try to fuck with me when I'm trying to work on other things." He turned around to find Virgil so he could ask for advice, but his assistant was busy working with the Evolution Chambers and not paying attention to what was happening around him. "Mmmm, no more help from Virgil. My world, my creation, my plans. Rimi!" he yelled out. "Do you remember all the stuff I told you when you were first expelled from Virgil?"

"Yes, Walker," Rimi said with a salute.

Ignoring that, Walker said, "Good, do the same speech with Cagna here. I'm sorry, little one," he said to the pink squirrel, "but Rimi will have to walk you through everything. I need to deal with these fuckers, and I can't have them screwing around with me while we design what is arguably the most important system we'll ever have." He turned back to Rimi. "Please break it down for her well, and I'll answer any questions she may have when I get back."

"Understood, Creator!" he said with a smile. After a quick word with his sibling, they walked a slight distance away to be alone.

Ignoring the second of his assistants to use his title rather than his name in the last hour, Walker did what he hadn't done since he first arrived from the translocation.

He took off his purple suit jacket and threw it on the ground.

He didn't know why he had kept it on the whole time. In a review of his own mental state, he figured he was still holding onto his old life as a teacher and the professionalism he always tried to bring to the job. Maybe other teachers could get away with shorts and T-shirts, but after his time in the military, he considered wearing a suit to school his uniform. Professionalism begets professionalism. Of course, with one swoop from his former student Nicholas, he'd thrown that professionalism in the garbage.

He looked at the jacket for a moment, recognizing the importance. By not only taking it off but throwing it on the ground, Walker knew he was symbolically moving away from his past. He untucked his cream-colored shirt as rays from his newly stolen sun shone on him, then stomped over to the Tree of the Gods. His improved hearing picked up on what Echidna was saying as he approached from out of their sightline.

"You can't treat him that way, Dio. He is not like our previous Creator. Even Zeus thinks so."

The bearded god nodded begrudgingly. "I've spoken with him, worked with him, and seen him stick to his word and his oath. He is trying to be better than his predecessor. You don't have to respect the man, but you should respect his efforts."

The god of revelry snorted. "I, in fact, do not have to respect that. Who is he to tell us what to do? He can't be much older than seventy!"

"I'm the goddamned Creator of Symphony, and you're standing on my world," Walker said as he drew close enough for them to notice him.

Dionysus snorted again. "And what does that even mean? What? That your dumb ass got lucky, thrown out here to—"

"It means I was picked, and you weren't. It means I am trying to build something here of which you have no regard or respect, based on your own immediate actions. If this were your place, would you want some douchebag jumping out of a fuckin' fruit and trying to give you orders?"

That seemed to short out his brain for a moment as he paused before saying, ". . . Hey, fuck you."

Walker stood up taller. "No sir, fuck you!"

"Calm down, everyone!" Echidna said, still trying to broker peace between them. She noted the look in Walker's eyes before adding, "Please."

"I agree; this won't go anywhere positive," the golden-dressed woman said. "I'm afraid I rudely never introduced myself. I am Athena, the goddess of wisdom."

"And cheating bitch," added the lace-covered woman.

"Arachne, enough!" Athena harshly reprimanded her. "Or do you want to be erased with the rest of us?"

"If it takes you down with me, I'm all for it!" Arachne yelled back.

As they began ignoring him again and breaking out into feuds for a second time, Walker felt the pulses in his neck return. They were all stuck in lockstep with their long-held biases and millennia-old contention, causing him to have a physiological reaction.

As his heartbeat increased at a faster rate, he felt something else as well. A weird fuzzy vibration in the middle of his chest. He'd felt a ghost of it the last few times he'd grown angry, and after seeing this group start their argument in front of him, wasting his time again, it began to vibrate in tune with his frustration. Rather than ignore it as he had done in the past, he paused for a moment and tried to understand this new sensation.

Walker closed his eyes to help him concentrate. Focusing on himself and attempting to block out the discussions around him, he found the vibration was a little lower than his chest, almost directly in the center of his body. Moving by instinct, he tried to mentally push on it. When he did so, an undiscovered muscle he'd never realized he had appeared. Bunching it up, he pressed, quickly opening his eyes to see the result. A pulse of green washed out of him. The Primigenials stopped fighting as the green soul power hit them.

Walker mentally shook himself out of his daze at this new power and grabbed the moment.

"STOP."

Everyone was still looking at him rather than each other, so he continued. "Here's the deal. I'll stop treating you in a disparaging way if you start respecting me and my time. I can't keep coming over here and stopping whatever it is you're doing or have you throwing new tasks at me anytime you want. I'm going to be very, very busy." He pointed at the sky. "I literally just made a star and two exoplanets, even if all three are technically on fire right now."

He waited for them to stop looking at the sky before continuing. "Look, I get it. I know you had a lot of power and authority in your former world, and it isn't lost on me that your former status has been eradicated. And even though I know this is a hard ask, I need you to move on. You need to adjust to the role that is given to you, just like I have. You're Primigenials, sure, but you're also still trapped on this planet until we figure out something better. Work with me, please. Or, at the least, try not to work against me." He ended his short speech with his arms out wide in a pleading gesture.

All of the Primigenials looked at each other with questioning faces, as if asking *Should we listen to him?*

Walker had less than a second before Echidna spoke up. "I agree. This is his world and his chance at being a Creator. I believe in him." She stepped away from the others and came over to stand by Walker, looking at the rest. Minos gently nodded and then moved to stand beside her.

Zeus looked at the three new arrivals before sighing. "As much as it pains me to say it, I agree. This Awakened, new that he is to our kind of life, threw off the balance we have held since the beginning of the multiverse. But I recognize he did so purely by coincidence. I am not fool enough to believe that attempting to sabotage his world will help us in any way." He put a hand on Dionysus's meaty shoulder. "I will stand with him, as long as it protects my children from oblivion and allows for the Awakened to thrive." Then he stomped over and turned his head away, refusing to look at Walker or the others.

Walker looked at Zeus and thought, *As long as he's done being an asshole just to be an asshole, that works for me.* He looked back at the other three, but the woman in lace, Arachne, had already crossed over and stood directly beside him. She gave him a wink.

"I am not against you, Creator," Athena started to say, arms spread wide to encompass Sonata. "Th-this is a wonderful world you have here. I am . . ."

"My world's down there," Walker said with a hooked thumb toward Symphony. "This is more like a managing moonlet."

"Of-of course. As I was saying, I am not against you; I am just for my fellow Primigenials. Since the dawn of time, we have provided for humanity and the world t—"

"That's great and all," Walker said as he interrupted what was winding up to be quite a long speech he just didn't have the time for. Leaning into his psychology training, he placed his hands in his pockets, seeming completely at ease. "But your siblings and whoever else comes out will still have to abide by my rules, now and in the future. No more running out of the Tree of the Gods and trying to interrupt whatever I'm working on. No more random tasks that fuck me up and attempt to force me to do what you want me to do. I know you have some control over what the tasks require. That's what I'm asking for." A fleeting smile crossed his face. "Correction. I am demanding it, but in the nicest way I can."

"How am I to stop them?" she asked with a dreadful look on her face.

"Grab them? Trip them? I don't care. Just keep them here until I can come over and speak to everyone. It's not hard to miss that more of you have joined the party on this relatively small moon."

"I under—" Athena was interrupted a third time by a small, thin pulse of purple. It barely reached Walker, and he felt almost no pressure from it as it broke against his body.

"Fuck this shit," Dionysus yelled out. He'd been quiet the whole time, but his face had turned a brighter red the longer he'd listened. "She's the goddess of wisdom, you tool. How do you not listen to her?"

"Dio . . ." Athena said.

"No, I just don't get it. He was a mortal until, what, only a very small amount of time ago? What's your deal, bro? Why do you have to be such a piece of shit?"

Walker's voice became very quiet as he looked down at the grass below his feet. "It is quite simple, and I've already said it to you a few times, so I won't be saying this again. This is my world. If you ever want to find yourself on Symphony and the wonders we are building, you will do what I say. You can't hurt me here. You can't get your wine, or your girls, or anything else without my say-so. I don't even have to delete you; just ignore you." Walker looked up and directly into the god's eyes as he watched him shrink with each word that followed. "You don't matter to me. You're nothing but an old memory of something that used to matter but has faded into such a low-scale myth that it is barely even taught at junior-level colleges. Festivity modification? Why would I even need that? How does that help the future citizens of Symphony survive?"

Walker knew he was going a little far, but there was something about the guy that made his gut churn. "The first thing you did was insult me, my assistants, and my work, and then offer a task that I couldn't complete for a very long time. You're selfish and stupid, and I'm done with you." Walker looked across to the woman in the gold dress. "Make your choice, or join your brother in irrelevancy."

There was no pause. Without looking at the god of revelry, she crossed over and stood beside Arachne, for once not fighting with each other. Walker stared at Dionysus for a moment longer, but the fat god had taken a seated position, leaning against the tree and staring up at the stars.

Walker turned his back on him with an exaggerated motion. He spied Echidna speaking quietly to Zeus, but he didn't have the time to analyze it. Looking at the golden goddess, he said, "What is special about your modifications? I know you know, but nobody has explained it to me, and it can't be as basic as I think it is."

She opened her mouth and looked over at Zeus. He gave a deliberate nod, so she spoke up. "Our modifications are not like the protocol's version. When you make changes to your . . . entities . . . it is primarily surface-level or superficial. You are not truly modifying who they will be going forward in life and experience. The Primigenial modifications are closer to . . . I suppose with your vernacular and memories, you would call them bloodlines. Zeus's electricity modification, when placed upon an entity, will cause the said creature to gain a natural affinity. Lightning, static electricity, all things that have to do with electrical energy will be better understood by the individual."

Walker considered that for a moment before saying, "So it just makes them better attuned to an element that fits within their affinity?"

She nodded. "That is a basic version, yes. They will also be more primed to become Awakened and have children who will also have the ability to become Awakened."

Walker pictured a dozen Zeus-like sapients running around a field, shocking each other. "So it'd be like making an electrical dynasty?"

"I believe that is an excellent word to use: dynasty." She nodded, then tilted her head to the side. "As you have shown a form of civility, I will give you a bit of extra information. We are only allowed to give three tasks each, with the exception of our branch leadership. Zeus, how many tasks are you allowed to give?"

"Four," he said with a grimace.

Athena nodded again. "Yes. Although minor gods like Arachne, Echidna, and Minos are only allowed to give two each."

The black-laced woman came close and smiled as Athena said her name. "Speaking of," Arachne said, and began writing in the air.

Walker grew alarmed at her motions. "What did I *say!*" he yelled out and pushed on his power. He somehow directed it, and Arachne stopped writing as the green pulse knocked her back a step.

She straightened up quickly and said, "Trust me, Creator, this one is not so bad."

"Why should I trust you?" Walker said back with a suspicious look.

"Because I truly only care about you and the other mortals," she replied in a serious tone of voice.

He thought on it for a moment, shifting his weight from one foot to another, before giving a sharp nod. "Fine, but don't disappoint me."

"Of course," she said with a smile and began writing in the air again. Walker's overlay lit up.

[. . . Scanning . . .]
Optional tasks updated!
New Primigenial task: Give Arachne a hug
I hope you will trust me now.
Hugs received: 0/1
Task giver: Arachne, The Weaver
Reward for completion: Textile modification

Walker had enough time to say "What?" before she quickly walked over and wrapped him in a hug.

Arachne whispered in his ear, "Make our people great. Make them strong."

"O-okay then."

[. . . Scanning . . .]
Primigenial task complete: Give Arachne a hug
Hugs received: 1/1
Reward for completion: Textile modification

She stepped back quickly and began waving in the air again. "What?"

[. . . Scanning . . .]
Optional tasks updated!

New Primigenial task: Wave at Arachne
I will help watch out for them.
Waves received: 0/1
Task giver: Arachne, The Weaver
Reward for completion: Arachne added to the seeding system.

Arachne immediately began waving at him with a sad smile on her face. "Be good, Creator."

Walker waved back once and watched as she faded away.

[. . . Scanning . . .]
Primigenial task complete: Wave at Arachne
Waves received: 1/1
Reward for completion: Arachne added to the seeding system.

[. . . Scanning . . .]
Congratulations, Dante!
**Arachne the Weaver has been added to the seeding system. They
have been placed in stasis and you may place them at a time of
your choosing.**
**However, due to the proximity of the Tree of the Gods, no
Primigenials placed within the Seeding system may be seeded
upon Sonata.**

After reading his updates, Walker looked at the spot she'd just been standing. "That was pretty weird."

"No," Zeus said, shaking his head. He continued speaking in a quieter-than-normal voice. "She has always been this way. One of the greatest weavers in the history of the world, but she hated restrictions on herself or others. The only reason she joined the Awakened was because she made my wife, Hera, a particularly grand piece of art that touched something deep within her. Inspired her." He looked over at Athena, who gave him a sad smile. "It took me twenty years to get her to agree to make it. I just—I didn't think she'd go against the covenant. She was barely one of us and had great difficulty entering the first phase, but still."

"Yes, it is quite sad," Minos said from nearby.

"What is quite sad?" Walker asked in confusion.

"I'll explain," Athena said to the others, then refocused on Walker. "Please, take a walk with me." When he began to open his mouth, she held up a forestalling hand. "I promise, it'll be quick."

They stepped away from the others, who seemed to be consoling each other, before she spoke again. "When the tree was first placed within the protocol, we made a deal with the system. If, or when, we were released from the tree, we had to follow certain rules. Rules like any tasks that we gave you must progress your strength or value within the Alpha Protocol. The requirements were simple. The tasks had to have some level of difficulty, and also must force you to attempt something new. Zeus's task skirted the boundaries, and you found a way to answer that in, pardon the pun, lightning speed."

Walker looked over at the small group. Zeus and Echidna were hugging each other. Athena continued to speak. "Dio's task will force you to advance civilization to the point that they can produce their own wine, and Echidna's will force you to really look at your religion and decide what you stand for. Therefore, each has fulfilled the requirements set upon them."

Hearing that twisted Walker up a little. The fit he'd just thrown now seemed unfair to the Primigenials. But if its result was that they would try to work with him rather than force him to do what they wanted instead, its intended effect still had use. He asked a question that was weighing on him.

"What happens if you don't fulfill the requirements of your deal with the protocol?"

"You become mortal," Athena replied in a quiet voice. "With everything that comes with it."

Walker shook his head. "I thought the protocol couldn't influence the Awakened?"

Athena nodded. "Good, yes. They cannot influence the Awakened directly, but many within the Council know the rules by which we live and how to influence us directly. All Awakened have a code they live by and certain rules we must follow. For instance, if you make a covenant with another and you break it, you also break a piece of your soul. The larger the covenant, the larger the breakage."

"That seems like something that can easily be abused," Walker replied with some trepidation. "Does that mean every promise I ever make will be tied to my soul?"

"No, no. If I say something like, *I promise to always be chaste*, my oath will not connect it to a covenant, and therefore I will be spared from any repercussions should I break it. But if I say or even sign a contract stating, *I vow on my oath to never restrict the knowledge of soul-empowerment from another Awakened*"—a blue glow expanded then contracted fast enough that Walker wasn't sure he'd even truly seen it—"then I will be bound to my oath and any repercussions that may invoke. We all signed a contract with the protocol in order to be released from our prison."

"What were the specific words used in the oath?"

"That is unimportant," Zeus said, quickly approaching them. Walker noticed as he came close that his eyes were red. "What is important is what you plan to do with us and the other Primigenials who will eventually exit the tree. My wife and children are still in there."

Walker scratched his chin. "That's a good point." He began pacing in front of them. "The truth is, if your modifications really do create bloodlines that increase the affinity of those who carry them, then that's just another tool my world can use. I need that. We need that. But as I said, I cannot have you all come screaming out of the tree anytime you're released and throw random tasks at me. I will not be forced to take on the whims of others, not when the protocol is already doing that to me."

"What would be your solution then, Walker?" Echidna asked as she stepped over with the others. Dionysus was still leaning against the tree.

"You can only give me one of your tasks at a time, right?" he asked the now grouped-up Primigenials, standing in a half-circle around him.

"Correct," Athena said. She stepped forward after a quick nod from Zeus, intimating that she'd negotiate for all of them.

Walker asked an obvious question, but one he needed to absolutely confirm. "And they can only be tasks that challenge me to progress through the protocol?"

"Yes," she said again for everyone.

"Okay. To get an understanding of how this will work, I'd like to ask you an important question. What is the ultimate goal for all of you?"

Walker looked at them each, one by one, scanning from left to right.

"To ensure the future of my children," Echidna said when his eyes landed on her.

"To find great battles," Minos said in his small but excitable voice.

"To assist in building a world of wisdom and enlightenment," Athena said, her deep blue eyes unblinking.

"To spread the strength of the Awakened throughout the fourth rendition," Zeus rumbled.

Walker nodded. "Then make them tasks that are viable within a reasonable amount of time. I won't be able to make WINE! For a long TIME!" Walker yelled at Dionysus, unwittingly rhyming at the fat god. The god of revelry waved him off, so he looked back at the group. "Make it reasonable, and I will do my best to get you there. You're all interested in eventually being seeded into Symphony with all of your power, correct?"

"Yes," Athena stated, each of the other Primigenials nodding in turn.

Walker smiled at the group. "I can work with that. If you're ready, one by one, give me your tasks, and I'll see about knocking them out. Echidna and Dionysus don't need to, as theirs are already ongoing."

Walker looked at Minos, who gave a small nod and began waving his arms in the air. They each took their turn, with Zeus taking quite a long time. Walker's overlay began updating and he waited until they were all done before he looked.

[. . . Scanning . . .]
Optional tasks updated!

New Primigenial task: Find a great warrior
A world needs defenders, Walker. Find a great one.
Great warrior found: 0/1
Task giver: Minos, The Bronze Battler
Reward for completion: Toughness modification

New Primigenial task: Create a library
With knowledge, power. With power, responsibility.
Spread the word of logic.
Library created: 0/1
Task giver: Athena, Goddess of Wisdom
Reward for completion: Brilliance modification

New Primigenial task: Seed three Awakened
Please keep this between us. I apologize for how I treated you.
Please do not look too harshly on my son. He cannot help who he is
and has always only cared to make the world a more "fun" place.
Spread the Awakened, Walker. Build a strong starting point for
us all in this rendition, and your world.
You can do it. I will stand beside you.

Awakened seeded: 0/3
Task giver: Zeus, King of the Gods
Reward for completion: Lightning Bolt Icon

Walker took one pointer finger and tapped at his forehead in frustration. "Minos's task is basically already done. I can show you that in a moment, if you don't mind waiting." The bronze Awakened nodded. "The library and seeding will take me time."

"What task did you give him?" Athena asked Zeus. Apparently, they couldn't see each other's tasks.

"I asked that he seed three Awakened. They do not have to be we five, but they must be seeded upon Symphony."

"Nope," Walker pointed out, grinning at the king of the gods. "You never said I had to seed them onto Symphony." Walker pointed at his eyes, intimating his overlay. "You need to read the fine print. Now, what the hell is an icon?"

Zeus's face quickly grew red. It was not as red as it normally was when he was angry with Walker, but it still seemed like this had riled the god up.

Is he mad at himself?

Athena waited a moment for Zeus to speak, but when he didn't, she pointed to a badge of an owl on her dress. "This is my icon. Our modifications are bloodlines, as stated before, but icons are wholly different. When your oath begins to manifest physically, you have to look internally, similarly to how you discovered yourself in the first trial and became Awakened. There is a similar, although much more difficult process to find your icon. Once you are able to manifest it, you can further move down the road of soul-empowerment until the icon is upgraded to an idol, although only Zeus here has done so from among the Greek Primigenials."

The king of the gods nodded once as some of the red coloring left his face.

Athena continued. "Icons are specific to each individual person, and no two are alike. Gaining your icon is where you begin to shift from the physical stage, and into the reality stage, but you have quite a long period of time before you reach that point."

Walker nodded. "Noted. I'm sure I'll ask questions as we move forward. What does having access to the lightning icon do for Symphony, though?"

"You can attach it to the followers of your religion. It grants them special abilities that the protocol doesn't, and won't, have access to," Zeus rumbled. "It isn't specifically lightning. That's just the shape my icon manifested as."

"Sooooo . . ."

"So you will find out after you complete my task!" Zeus yelled at him, his old anger leaking through.

"Calm," Echidna said, dragging the word out as she placed a hand on his shoulder. Zeus quickly reined it in and walked away. "Sorry, he still isn't used to others questioning him."

"Old habits die hard, as they say," Athena said while shaking her head at the king of the gods.

Walker sighed and scratched the back of his head. "Alright then. I'm going to go get some work done on something that I've held off on for far too long. Please keep Dionysus and Zeus from interrupting me."

"We will do our best," Minos said quietly, and he went to stand next to the god of revelry as Echidna and Athena headed over to Zeus.

Walker felt at his chest. The spot that normally vibrated when he got angry was quiet again. A bit more probing didn't reveal anything, so he shrugged.

"Okay! Let's make some milestones," Walker said with a clap of his hands. He walked away from his meeting with the Primigenials, a new pep in his step.

CHAPTER THIRTY-FIVE

The Milestone System

D id you explain everything, Rimi?" Walker asked as he neared the two sub-system assistants.

The small blue squirrel saluted with extra vigor. "Yes, Creator!"

Walker smiled, accepting that they were just going to call him that sometimes. "Excellent. Alright, Cagna. Your whole focus while being here is to work with the Milestone System," he said, clicking on System and starting up the initial process.

> **Welcome to the System Designer!**
> **Please name your second system.**
>
> **The Milestone System is named!**
> **Good luck, Creator!**

Walker spent some time going through the options he'd seen when creating the Monster System. He saw the mini–Alpha Protocol he'd viewed before and knew that it was how the Territory System would come about. He found a few pre-built systems that might work, but they weren't exactly what he wanted.

Some were built on having hundreds of monitors roaming Sonata, but that would never work because there'd eventually be millions to trillions of entities over time. Too many damn monitors and not enough subsystem assistants. Another few he looked at focused on entities essentially "reporting" what was happening, but that wouldn't work either, as poor Cagna would be overwhelmed incredibly fast.

Plus . . . you know. People lie.

Scrolling through several hundred options, he noticed an oddity. Going back to the start, he scrolled through again, confirming it. There were more system options than he'd seen before.

Walker wasn't sure if more had appeared because he'd passed the second battle, or because he'd made his first system already, but it looked like he would gain further access to systems as he progressed through the protocol.

With a quick mental slap for clarity, he refocused on scanning through the options. A sudden thought struck him, and with a few quick motions, he moved over to the M's. It didn't take long to find what he was looking for: the Monster System.

Motherfuckers, Walker swore to himself internally.

He knew there was nothing he could do about it. Like the evolution they'd created, anything that was made during the Alpha Protocol wasn't theirs to keep. With less of a sigh and more of a grump, he continued moving through the systems quickly. It wasn't until he reached the T's that he found the Tracking System. Curious, he clicked on its description.

The Tracking System:
A system designed by Creator Ju in the Alpha Protocol of 2BC.
This system is designed to track any entities of the
Creator's choice within any filters they choose to create.
Flexibility: Extreme
Difficulty to modify: Low

Just for curiosity's sake, Walker clicked back to the Monster System and opened the description.

The Monster System:
A system designed by Creator Dante in the Alpha Protocol
of 4AA.
This system is designed to absorb ambient magic and
use it to increase the combat capabilities of different
entities through evolutionary traits.
Flexibility: High
Difficulty to modify: Medium

That seemed right, although he wasn't sure why the flexibility and modification difficulty levels were different. Shouldn't flexibility and modification difficulty be one and the same? He mentally put that away and focused. Walker went back to the Tracking System and clicked Accept. And just like that, the Milestone System was in its beginnings. Walker clicked out of the overlay so he could explain what Cagna would be doing for the foreseeable future.

He looked at the two squirrels, who stopped their conversation when they noticed his attention. "Okay, guys, here we go. And Rimi, I know there isn't anything going on with the Monster System right now—"

"Incorrect," the blue squirrel instantly responded.

"Whatever; I know there aren't a *ton* of things going on with the Monster System right now, so please help out with any ideas you may have." Rimi nodded. "So, here's my thoughts. I want to create a system wherein every single person, monster, city, item, and . . . basically everything else is tracked. I want to know everything, from what they ate for breakfast to who they saved from a burning building. Milestones will be built so that as they're reached, a tracker will ping back to the system, updating when they've obtained a predetermined point."

He started to pace in front of the two sub-assistants. "I want there to be specific powers, breakthroughs, and additions that can be unlocked by people and monsters purely based on what milestones they've hit." Walker paused for a moment. "I won't lie; this will be a very intrusive process. I can't imagine growing up in a world where how many steps I've taken or how many people I've slept with are recorded and up for review. Where I'm from, that would be considered a massive, unbelievable, and heinous breach of privacy. That's why we're not tracking things ourselves, but rather doing it through a non-sapient and autonomous system."

He paused and looked at them both, and said with a smile, "Tracking me so far?"

Rimi nodded quickly compared to Cagna's slow movement. "Good." Resuming his thinking march, Walker continued. "We will be able to review what they've done and how they've done it as we need to, but we specifically will not be tracking everyone personally. The Milestone System will—" He paused, his own need for privacy flickering through his subconscious. He had a hard time going to the bathroom in public places, let alone imagining allowing something to track how often he would be doing so. But it was going to be managed by a neutral assistant and an autonomous system. That had to be better than being stared at through a monitor . . . right?

Walker sighed. "It will be very intrusive, which I hate to do, but I can't think of a different way to go about this. Again, I won't lie. It's a fine line to walk. But I believe it is necessary for my other plans to work."

"The Alpha Protocol already tracks everything we say and do," Cagna said encouragingly.

Walker nodded in thanks, deciding for his own mental fortitude not to investigate that comment further. Rimi raised a hand. "How are you going to track what people say about these breakthroughs?"

"What do you mean? It's going to be built into the Tracking System."

Cagna nodded next to her sibling. "I see what you mean, Rimi. Good job!" They shared a variably speeded high-five. "He means, how are you going to track that what they say is true? Human beings are duplicitous, right?"

"Right . . ."

"Then, if they suddenly say, *I've defeated the most powerful of powerful monsters in this powerful place*, how are you to trust them?"

Walker chewed on that before finding the answer. "Because . . . a similar tracker in the most powerful of powerful monsters will show that they've died."

"Okay, but what if there's a leadership milestone? How do you work with that? How do you *know* they're the leader? They could just say they're the leader of a group of a thousand, or a hundred thousand, and the tracker would agree because they said so."

Walker paused and considered that. He could create a grouping system, but that would be quite some time away. He saw the point Cagna and Rimi were trying to make. Were they right? If they were, that would mean the system wouldn't be able to track everything people said. That was a huge limitation he hadn't considered.

Cagna interrupted his thought process. "What's the point of all this?"

"Hrmm?"

"What's the point of the Milestone System? Why am I here?" Cagna asked in a serious tone. "Rimi told me about the speech you gave for the monsters and his system. He explained . . . as much as he could. But I need to know why I'm here as well. He said that you said that this was probably the most important system in Symphony."

"It is," Walker replied with a nod, affecting the same serious manner as his newest assistant.

"Okay, then, what's the purpose?" she replied, a slight twitch in her neck as she looked Walker directly in the eyes. "If you want me to run the Milestone System, I need to know what the goal is."

He nodded. "You're right. The why is always important. How to explain this . . . it . . . umm . . . it . . . hrmm." Walker's mind was blanking out. He'd thought long and hard about this, but now, when he needed to explain it, there was nothing there. He tried to run his thoughts in a circle. Tried to go back to when he'd first had the idea. But still, nothing. "Give me—give me a moment, please—" he said as he walked quickly away, leaving two confused subsystem assistants behind him.

Walker tried to control his breathing. The Milestone System's importance couldn't be overstated. It was the lynchpin for most, if not all, of his plans. Now that Cagna and Rimi had found a simple flaw in his mental design, he felt his mind overwhelmed by too many thoughts at once.

Each time he tried to focus on just one thought, a new one appeared, crashing into each other. Continuing to walk around aimlessly, Walker tried to just breathe and slow things down, but even with his Awakened mind, it wasn't working. He could have the best memory out there, but if he couldn't find the thought to attach to it, it wouldn't matter. There was too much to explain, and the timer counting down in the corner of his vision was further stressing him out.

Rather than allowing himself to get overwhelmed like he had in the past, Walker stopped pacing and sat down.

When he had first arrived here, he'd had issues with too much happening at once. His old breathing exercises had helped greatly. But while that had worked in the past, this time, *this attack*, felt different. He was too emotionally invested in everything. It was too important, and his feelings were continuously getting wrapped into his thoughts. There was no clarity to be found.

Walker needed something more. He reached into his memories and, trying with all of his might to push down on the thoughts attempting to pull him away, found one from his time in the military. He only got a brief glimpse at it, but that was enough to work with.

Just before he had deployed, the Air Force had taught everyone a basic exercise for meditation, stating that it would help them manage and process PTSD before it became a bigger problem. He remembered the instructor wearing a pristine uniform as he sat in a chair at the front of the room. The lieutenant closed his eyes and explained, in a soft and soothing tone of voice, that they were now viewing their mind space as a deep and dark room.

Inside of that dark room was a single white wax candle. He'd explained that they needed to picture themselves mentally lighting the candle and feeding it all of their thoughts and emotions. Everything and anything, until nothing remained. And, as the candle was fed, as the thoughts and feelings of the person went in, a calmness would rise in their place. It was a technique to handle and manage anxiety. Something Walker had in spades.

The instructor said you knew you were doing it right when the darkness and the candle were all that was left, and no more thoughts or emotions could further intrude.

At the time, Walker thought it was a bunch of voodoo, but now, he could see the value in having a nice, clear mind with no outside influences. He closed his eyes and performed his old breathing exercise to center himself and clear out any buzz.

Walker pictured a simple white wax candle with a lone flame in a dark room. Any extra thoughts or emotions were fed to the fire. Stress, anxiety, worry, and that constant nugget of depression were isolated and slowly destroyed. Once he cleared out any emotions, which took more time than he would've liked, he started to work on the memories.

I need to do the Primigenial tasks . . . into the flame.

What's happening on Earth? What has Mr. Harrison done? . . . It took a bit longer, but it also went into the flame.

Chipper, Symphony, the Unending Summit . . . into the flame.

Failure . . . burnt away to nothingness.

Again, it took longer than he wanted, but once he was done, he sat there even longer, allowing only the thoughts he wanted into the dark room. When he found his answer, two forest-green eyes stared out at a tiny moonlet.

Looking around, he found both subsystem assistants standing by Virgil. Virgil, as always, was diligently working with the Evolution Chambers. Meanwhile, Rimi was pointing out things to look at with his pink sister. Walker stood up and quickly joined them.

Rimi noticed him first. "What did you just do? You seem . . . different."

"I meditated for a moment. I learned how to do it just before I went off to war, but at the time, I didn't take it seriously . . . Now I do. I feel . . . much, much better," Walker said with a bright smile.

"You should've done that before you spoke with the Primigenials," Rimi said in a quiet voice. "You were mean to them."

"I don't think I was mean . . ."

"You were quite unbalanced," Virgil said nearby, where he continued working without a pause.

"Are you sure?"

"Indeed. Remember, I can see your memories from just before you entered. This is not the first time you have lost control."

"Okay, then, I guess I, uh . . . was. I'll have to go apologize to them when I get the chance." Walker tried to mentally shrug it off and refocus, refusing to get distracted. "Now, back to business." He looked over at the pink squirrel. "Cagna. You said you wanted to know the why, right?"

She nodded seriously.

Walker smiled, bringing forth what he'd figured out long ago but until recently had trouble saying. "Because it is the start of everything. We're going to use the Milestone System to unlock all future systems. When we're done, it'll help sapients decide on their classes and professions, assist with managing cities and economies, and track the different types of growth monsters go through. It will be massively all-inclusive. Every other system will connect to this one system at the same time. And we're going to work with the monster's kernels. We're going to—" His eyes unfocused for a moment. "We're going to—Oh shit, the kernels!" Walker finished, eyeing the Milestone System in the corner of his overlay.

"What about them?" Rimi said with a confused look on his face. But Walker had already pulled up the brief description the system had shown him. It was something he'd been trying to figure out how to include.

**In order for the Tracking System to work, there
must always be a physical object within the entity's reach
for the system to connect to.**

**This connection will allow a stream of data to reach the
Creator continuously, updating them on the tracked entity's
current whereabouts and activities.
Disconnection or a maximum distance of 50 feet from the
selected object will disconnect an entity's tracking updates.**

"Hey, Virgil!" Walker called over to the large squirrel.

"Yes, Walker. Please keep in mind I am doing many things at once," Virgil said in a testy voice.

"Gotcha, sorry. Can you find a place to put a kernel in the humans?"

"What?" Virgil said, stopping all work. He slowly turned around, looking at Walker directly.

Walker scratched the back of his head, a sudden nervousness striking him. "I need to put kernels into the humans."

Virgil crossed his arms. "Why?"

"Because that's how their classes, eventual Monster System updates, and the Milestone System will work. They're already in the monsters, so it's easy to update them, but I'll need them in all future sapients as well, or they'll be missing another path to power."

"Yet your Warclaws, whom we cannot modify, and Raganoth, who is already seeded, will not have them. The same is also true of many of the prey animals and insects we've created."

Walker agreed with a shrug. "Yep!"

While it was great that they could control and track everything with the kernels, having just a few creatures without them was fine. By the time it became a potential problem, Walker would have another solution ready for them. He also thought of Arachne at that moment, which did make him a little sad. "The Primigenials won't be seeded with them either, but I don't think there's anything we can do about that."

Virgil nodded. "I see. I will look into what I can do, but it is not a simple process. I am assuming you do not want a group of very large human beings."

"Why?" Walker asked in confusion. "And how large?"

"In order to include kernels into human beings' complicated biology, I would need to make them at least ten feet tall at full growth. I would like to remind you that you built the Monster System to allow for kernel growth. If normal-sized humans eventually reach the Monster System, as you said they would, and a kernel grows within them at the rate you selected . . . Well, I believe you can understand what would happen."

Walker thought on that. *What would happen . . . oh shit.*

"They'll explode as they level up?" he yelled out.

"Indeed," Virgil said with a shrug. "I just thought that may be of interest to you, as a former member of the species and the Creator of Symphony."

"Umm . . . yeah! Well, shit," Walker said as he began pacing. "Ten feet tall? That's like a race of small giants . . ." He continued to pace as he thought it through.

I don't know if I want giant human beings. Will they even respect me when I drop down for my avatar moments? Will I even want to drop in on Symphony if I look like a child next to everyone?

He performed a quick circle, aiming back toward Virgil still waiting for him at the chambers. *The battlefrogs aren't that big, and the same goes for Chipper and the Guardians.* He paused as he remembered Chipper being fairly tall. *Okay, they're a little big.* Walker worked to slow down his breathing.

He searched through his memories, his earlier panic attack no longer gripping him. He needed to find anything mentioning wide-open spaces within human beings—places where something could grow without crushing their insides and killing them. The Evolution Chambers caught his eyes, and he considered what they'd done before.

Together, he and Virgil had made it work with monsters by rearranging some of their internal organs and just making them larger overall. A bigger body meant bigger space. Generally, a kernel started at the size of an olive and ballooned up from there. But there had to be a better way. This was all going to tie into the Class System as well, and he didn't want to do any updates after he'd already seeded sapients—not big ones, at least.

Memories of Iron Man's armor system popped into his mind before he discounted it. Human beings weren't toys to upgrade—except for adding resistance to diseases, but that was just super helpful, not a fundamental change to humanity's overall growth. It wouldn't work that way.

"You know," Virgil said as he watched Walker going through some kind of internal battle, "the Romans were only about five and a half feet tall. Humanity only started to evolve toward greater height in the last few millennia."

"Yeah, but"—Walker waved his hands over his own body—"if you haven't noticed, I'm not *that* much bigger than my ancestors."

"True, but that may just be your own ego speaking. Walker, you may find that you simply need to adapt to the circumstances that you have found yourself in. We could always shrink their brains and put it in their cranial cavity," Virgil suggested.

"Wouldn't that make all future human beings . . . dumber?" Walker asked in exasperation.

"Indeed. But it is a potential solution."

Ignoring his plans for even dumber human beings, a different thought sprang up. Walker snapped his fingers and pointed at both Rimi and Virgil. "We'll split it!"

Virgil nodded while Rimi asked, "What?"

"We'll split the kernel into pieces. Virgil, what are the most open areas within the human body? Where can we find that all-too-valuable real estate?"

Virgil actually had to think on that for a few seconds, a rare moment for him. His eyes lit up. "The thoracic and abdominal cavities."

"Great, the stomach and the chest. If we split the kernel in half, would that be small enough?"

"Potentially," Virgil replied, quickly clicking through screens as he turned to the Evolution Chambers. Walker looked with him, spotting two tiny fetuses floating within. Virgil touched a few screens before nodding. "I can now confirm it is almost enough. We would still need just a little more space to allow for potential growth past tier five."

"What do you suggest?"

Virgil pointed to something on his screen. "I would suggest the cranial cavity, as it is quite cushioned. If the kernel piece is small, the space allowed would be just large enough to fit a growing kernel without detrimentally affecting the human brain."

"Great!"

"However," Virgil said, raining on his parade, "if you do this, I foresee issues if the kernels are not connected from the start. If they are not, humanity's future magical attunements will adapt to individualized kernels. That would mean three distinct magical attunements that are unable to bridge together into a completed whole. It could have large and lasting ramifications on the growth of all magic within human beings."

"Hrmm . . . Why not graft them together like we did with the Mana Tree?"

Virgil looked at his screens and nodded. "That will take some tweaking, as you like to say, but I believe it is possible. I can follow the arterial lines throughout the human body as a guideline, allowing for a smooth connection between the two larger kernels, as well as the smaller."

"Alright," Walker said as he rolled his feet forward and back. "Do you still see any issues?"

Virgil looked again at the data on the chambers. "I believe splitting the kernel will still allow for simultaneous growth. However, the grafts will have to be heavily modified to not corrode or cause problems within the human body. It was originally designed for trees, rather than the flesh and blood of humanity."

Walker snapped his fingers. "There we go! Do you need anything else?"

"No, Walker. I have quite enough to do already," Virgil replied quickly before turning back to his work with a swish of his large brown tail. Walker liked to believe that as much as he complained about the interruptions and how busy he was, Virgil still enjoyed what he was doing. He hoped, at least.

"Okay, one large problem solved." Walker looked at Cagna. "We're going to use the kernels to track everything."

Cagna nodded. "Okay, so how will it all work?"

"Well, we need to find the best way to reward them as they reach certain and specific milestones. I can't speak for all other species"—Virgil snorted nearby—"but I know that human beings are tied to achievements. Growth. In my mind, I think the best thing we could do would be to provide them with points as they reach new milestones."

"Points?" Rimi asked.

"Yep! So, for instance, say you pet a squirrel, you get x amount of points. Now say you pet a Guardian . . . you get a ton of points. Risk and reward. A scaling difficulty related to scaling milestones. We could even name the milestones as they're obtained."

Walker squinted at Cagna before smiling. "Like, *Smart. Pet a Squirrel: 3 points.*" He reached down and translated his words into action, eliciting a giggle from the pink squirrel. "Haha, we could even do, *Not Smart. Pet a Guardian: 50 points.* The greater the difficulty, the greater the amount of points earned. Then, certain systems, abilities, or even titles can be unlocked based upon your milestones and overall points."

"Mmmm, that feels like it will need to be ummm . . . standardized," Rimi said as he thought it over. Cagna nodded beside him as he continued speaking. "If you create a system that grants points for performing certain acts, you will want to create a q-quantified point system for different actions."

"I had the same thought, so let's do this real quick." Walker clicked on the Milestone System and dragged Cagna over to it, assigning the system to her.

"Oh?" she said as her screen lit up. She stood stock still for a moment before blinking and taking a deep breath. If he wasn't mistaken . . . was she a little taller, too? The pink squirrel didn't seem to notice as she spoke again. "This is a lot of information, Walker. Can I please have some time?"

Walker looked at his timer for the next battle.

Time remaining until the next battle: 111+ hours

"How much time do you think you'll need?" Walker asked.

"Mmmm, a lot. I can see the option to connect it to a physical object, like you said, but to add so many different milestones and to build a standardized system like Rimi suggested. T-that will . . . umm . . . take a long, long time."

"Shit!" Walker said as he pounded one of his hands with another. The sudden expletive and violent action caused the pink squirrel to jump back.

"I'm sorry!" Cagna yelled out as she looked at him with trembling legs. "Please don't yell at me!"

Walker sighed and shook his head. "I'm not yelling at you, just the—" He stopped as her legs continued to shake. He looked at her funny, not quite understanding why she was acting so scared. Rimi put a hand on her shoulder, whispering something, before making a gesture for Walker to step away with him while the pink squirrel continued to tremble.

"What's going on?" Walker said as soon as they had a little distance.

"You did not think about her foundational memories," Virgil loudly commented without pausing his work, causing a glare to come from Rimi for a moment. However, the small blue squirrel still nodded in agreement before speaking.

"When I first got here, you spent a good amount of time with me, breaking down the Monster System, joking and arguing with Virgil. Naturally, I took it all in. When assistants are created, we absorb everything we see and hear since we start with almost nothing. The protocol gives us a basic vocabulary and a thorough understanding of systems, but it doesn't explain how to deal with other people's emotions. Question for you. What has Cagna seen the most from you since her initial creation?"

Then it hit Walker. She'd primarily witnessed him being angry. Yelling at the sky, yelling at himself, and, mostly, yelling at the Primigenials. She was mistaking his anger at the situation for anger at herself. He tried to explain that to Rimi, but the small blue squirrel started talking before he could. "I see you get it. You don't have to worry that I'm scared of you, either. We're fine. But I do want to point out something else. What do you notice about me right now?"

Virgil paused in his work and turned around, waiting for his response. Walker went back in his memories, tagging Rimi's first expulsion. He'd been . . . strange. Just constantly staring. In fact, since that time, he'd shown remarkable progress. His personality had come forth in leaps and bounds. The Rimi at the beginning and the one standing in front of him were vastly different creatures.

"You're smarter . . . and more self-assured."

Virgil went back to his work with a nod as Rimi smiled. "Exactly. It takes time for us to adapt to our Creator's personalities and demands. We're not advanced assistants like Virgil. We don't have your memories or a powerful connection to the system. At best, most of our knowledge comes from what we can glean from the systems we're connected to. The longer we're with you, and the better we understand our Creators, the better we can help. That's how we're designed. But, until then?" He waved a hand at the pink squirrel. "We're vulnerable and scared to get something wrong. She doesn't know you without the anger right now. That's gotta be fixed."

Walker agreed with a nod. Making a decision on how to move forward, he slowly and carefully approached the trembling assistant. "I'm sorry, Cagna. I was in such a rush to get everything done that I wasn't thinking about how you must be doing since arriving here. When Rimi joined us in that same special way you did, I took my time with him and we formed a bond, but you and I haven't had that chance. It just feels like things are moving so fast now, and I'm constantly playing catch-up with everything happening that I didn't think about how you may be feeling. Can you forgive me?"

Cagna looked up at him, still not quite meeting his eyes. "Oh, okay. Yes. Ummm, yes, I can, Creator." She took a breath. "I'm sorry for getting upset."

"Me too, and call me Walker," he said with a smile, watching as the fear on her face cracked until something like happiness spread across it. Walker continued to look down at her, slowly shaking his head. "I'm not perfect, and I'm still trying to do better in controlling myself. Sometimes, I may get upset, but I'll try to be more aware of how I'm speaking and treating others, okay?"

"Okay, thank you," she said, and Walker instinctively pulled her over to himself. Acting on the impulse, he leaned down, putting his arms around the tiny pink squirrel. After a moment, he felt her doing the same. Rimi joined in from the side, covering them both—as much as a tiny blue squirrel's arms could.

"Ugh," Virgil said from the side. "I am not looking, but I can already tell that you are doing something overly sentimental."

"Aren't you supposed to be working?" Walker asked as he continued to hug the two subsystem assistants.

"Yes, and I am making great strides in a small amount of time, unlike you."

"Yeah, well, I don't have enough time . . . time to . . ." An amazing thought hit him. He gently released the two squirrels and stood up. "Virgil! The battle timer! Time! If I sped up Sonata for a year, what would happen to the battle timer?"

"Mmmm? Nothing except relative time passing as normal. The protocol's timer cannot be sped up by Creators." He snorted. "Or slowed down, for that matter."

"Yeah! But if I sped up Sonata with all of us on it, would that make it so that we could gain time, like, a huge amount of time, and barely any hours would go by for the third battle timer?"

The large assistant began humming to himself. "Mmm . . . mmm . . . hold on," Virgil said as he looked away from the Evolution Chambers and at his screens. He tilted his head back and forth several times, with enough time passing that Walker and his two assistants had moved away, speaking on different systems and what they thought would go well together. Walker was just finishing up on how the Cosmic Genesis System worked when Virgil said, "I have your answer."

"What is it?"

"There are no rules disallowing you to speed up time, and no increased resource costs. In fact, I am surprised more Creators of this rendition are not already doing so."

"All right!" Walker said as he punched a fist in the air, the pink and blue squirrel mimicking him to do the same.

Walker called for the Primigenials to join them, making sure his voice sounded friendly so he didn't spook Cagna a second time. Dionysus stayed by the tree after Minos had a quick word with him.

"Okay, here's what is about to happen. I'm going to lock us all on Sonata for about . . . would a year be enough, Cagna?" The pink squirrel nodded quickly as everyone focused on her. Walker smiled. "Great. So, I'm going to lock us in for a full year. A *lot* is going to happen within this isolated time bubble we're going to enter, and I'll be spending most of my time just trying to get everything ready for our forthcoming sapients. But first, we need to advance Symphony by a week and complete Minos's task at the same time." Virgil and Minos both nodded. "Okay, I'm going to make a series of moves that will take us big leaps forward. Please stay with me and try to pay attention as I go. Questions?" Since no one but Virgil had an inkling of what he was about to do, he received none. Nodding, he turned toward Symphony.

Walker clicked the Monitor ability and moved it over to Chipper and Raganoth. It'd been a little over an hour since he'd last spoken to Chipper, and he needed to ask him to do something. It was easy to find the two as they were currently lounging by the Guardian's Mana Tree. As the monitor adjusted, they listened for a moment as Raganoth talked about his home-world, Chipper writing back his replies while chewing on a cyan leaf. Walker clicked his new Broadcast ability and linked it to the monitor by dragging it over.

"Hello, Chipper and Raganoth," a disembodied voice said from the air. The poison wyvern jumped up while the Guardian spit out his leaf and began to scan his surroundings, looking left and right. "No need to fret, sorry. This is Walker, Symphony's Creator. Chipper, you and I spoke not too long ago."

Chipper paused for a few seconds, then wrote in the air, *Hello, friend Walker. Why can I hear you but not see you?*

"Ah, yeah. This is a new ability I gained from the second battle. I'm umm . . . on that green moon above you, looking down."

Chipper looked up, presumably at the moonlet, before writing, *Ahh. Okay then.* Walker thought the Guardian took that information surprisingly well. *Raganoth, this is my friend Walker who I told you about.*

"Hello, Raganoth."

"Hello, Creator . . ." he growled in his bestial voice. "Thank you for bringing me here."

"My pleasure. So, Chipper, I need another, 'nother favor. I'm not asking you to become my disciple or follower, there's still plenty of time for that, but . . . how to say this . . . have you ever heard of sparring?"

White words appeared in the air. *No, what is it?*

Walker thought over what he wanted to say here. If he explained it wrong, the two newly minted friends might go overboard and accidentally kill each other. "Sparring is like . . . fighting without trying to kill."

For what purpose? Chipper wrote.

"I had never thought to do that," Raganoth said right after. "To fight is to kill, to grow, to consume. Why would you fight without killing?"

That wasn't a good start, so Walker further expanded on the idea. "To get better at fighting! It's something friends do," he continued, trying to use the unfamiliar situation to his advantage. "Raganoth, the favor would affect you as well."

"I see," the poison wyvern said after a moment. "I believe I owe you many favors for bringing me to this wondrous place. I haven't traveled the breadth of it as of yet, but just for the sheer fact that I have not been attacked, I already see it as a haven."

What fucked up place was his former world? Walker thought to himself. Out loud he said, "Okay, I will definitely call in favors from time to time with you. Maybe you and I can be friends at some point, like Chipper and I."

"Yes, yes," the wyvern said, nodding his massive, plated head. "I would like many friends."

"Outstanding. So, sparring. I would like you to fight each other every so often. It's something I need for one of my tasks as a Creator, and you would really be helping me out. It's a little hard to explain, but just understand that by doing so, you're helping Symphony and myself. You don't have to go too hard, don't kill or maim each other, but please also take it seriously. Is that okay?"

Chipper shrunk his writing down so it was hard for the monitor to see it. He and Raganoth had a quick discussion before he wrote in the air again. *We agree to do this. It would be helpful for Raganoth to fight without killing, and I always like to improve my skills.*

"Great!" Walker said, clapping his hands. Thankfully, his Broadcast ability only worked when he spoke, or it'd have sounded like thunder cracking over the Mana Tree and its two inhabitants. "You can start whenever you like, and don't be afraid to take breaks as needed."

"We understand," Raganoth growled.

Talk to you soon! Chipper wrote in the air.

"Definitely."

Walker clicked the monitor off but kept the Broadcast ability going. By leaving it on and disconnected from any other abilities, it would reach all of the citizens in Symphony at the same time. Some of the non-Guardians might understand him, while the vast majority of the more animal-like entities wouldn't. He hoped this wouldn't cause a mass panic worldwide.

Hello, citizens of Symphony. My name is Walker, and I am the Creator of this world. I reside on the small green moonlet you can see passing through the sky above. I'm sorry I didn't warn you

> when the sun, that newly shining bright yellow star, appeared.
> I should've thought this over more and considered your feelings,
> but I didn't, and I again apologize. I will try to be better.
> In a few short hours, Symphony will rotate, and the sun will
> become dark. This is intended, so please do not think that the
> world is suddenly ending. From time to time, I will speak to you
> across the world to explain any changes or additions that may be
> coming. Be on the lookout for my updates as we move forward
> together in this beautiful world. Thank you.
> Walker out.

Walker clicked the Broadcast ability again to turn it off before asking, "How'd I do?"

"For a first-time speech, I think it was quite well done," Athena commented.

"It was okay," Zeus rumbled.

"Welp," Walker said as he moved the monitor back to Chipper and Raganoth, "I taught English, not speech. Is everyone ready for seven days in a few seconds? Minos, you'll have to watch them carefully."

"I can also replay what you are about to see if you find the need," Virgil helped.

The bronze god nodded. Walker clicked on Time, then chose to advance Symphony by seven days. His overlay lit up as Symphony quickly rotated multiple times.

[. . . Scanning . . .]
Optional tasks updated!

**World task complete: Create a star that allows for a
day and night cycle (Part 3)**
Continuous day and night cycles without calamity: 7/7 days
Reward for completion: Portal System

**New world task: Have a population of 10,000 or
more entities on your world(s) (Part 4)**
To the Alpha Protocol, size matters. Growth matters.
*Without a larger population, how will the Creator's world
continue to evolve? To strive? Build up the numbers of your world,
and watch as great events unfold.*
Entity population count: 3,874/10,000
Reward for completion: Creation Instrument upgrade

Evolution task complete: Evolve an entity (Part 5)
New evolved entities: 25/25
Reward for completion: Landmass System upgrade

New evolution task: Evolve an entity (Part 6)
They come. They yearn for the strength to continue.
Evolve your entities to unseen heights, and reach the pinnacle of
all Creators within the Alpha Protocol.
New evolved entities: 1/100
Reward for completion: Diverse

Walker looked to his left after checking the updates, and found Minos and Virgil talking. Virgil was showing a hologram of Chipper and Raganoth fighting, their battle moving around an empty field. Portions of the field bubbled and spat as a hazy yellow film covered the grass. But as Walker watched, pure white magic erupted and cleansed it as Chipper moved around, smothering the effects of Raganoth's poison.

"Diverse?" Walker said, ignoring everything else, including his newest rewards, as that word jumped out at him. "Why does it say diverse? It's always given me specific abilities or upgrades before."

Virgil finished showing Minos some slowed-down footage. The last scene showed Chipper's tail slapping Raganoth out of what had initially seemed an unstoppable charge. Minos quietly told him he'd seen enough.

"There are a couple of reasons for that," Virgil said as the hologram disappeared, and he refocused on what Walker had said. "But normally, few Creators reach this stage of the evolutionary tasks this early. After receiving the set and pre-defined awards of the initial series, the quality of the evolutions comes into play and changes what rewards you may receive."

"Okay, how far does the series go?" Walker asked.

"There is no hard limit for evolutions, entities, temporal tasks, or world tasks. They are not optional tasks like the Ecology or System Designer series."

"So, I could potentially receive rewards forever?"

Virgil shrugged. "Correct."

Minos waved at Walker to get his attention, then slowly and deliberately nodded once.

[. . . Scanning . . .]
Optional tasks updated!

Primigenial task complete: Find a great warrior
Great warrior found: 1/1
Reward for completion: Toughness modification

"Yes!" Walker celebrated. Everyone else on Sonata looked confused by his celebration, other than Virgil and Minos.

The minor god looked up at the air for a moment before moving his arms in an esoteric pattern.

[. . . Scanning . . .]
Optional tasks updated!

New Primigenial task: Establish a blacksmith
A great warrior doesn't need tools, but they never hurt.
Blacksmith established: 0/1
Task giver: Minos, The Bronze Battler
Reward for completion: Minos added to the seeding system

"Okay, okay. I can do that. Thank you, Minos." The man gave him a small smile and wave before walking over to Echidna. Walker looked at the rewards he'd skipped over earlier.

Reward for completing the third world task:
Congratulations, Dante! You've unlocked the Portal System!
In the creation of the Alpha Protocol, it was understood that interdimensional, and often universal, travel may be needed. While the protocol's travel system is quite expansive and powerful, this reward is more limited in function. As the Creator's world grows, travel naturally becomes more and more difficult. The Creator is forced to come up with, through great difficulty, advanced traveling systems to compensate. With the Portal system, the Creator can build locked portals that allow for travel between their landmasses, and, in special circumstances, their worlds.

Reward for completing the fifth evolution task:
Congratulations, Dante! Your Landmass System has been upgraded!
There is a great amount of trial and error in the Alpha Protocol's Landmass System. With this upgrade, the Creator will now have the ability to seed entities upon forming landmasses before placing them upon their world.

He smiled to himself. Things were definitely moving forward quickly. Now he just needed to slow them down for a bit.

Walker looked at the people around him. He never thought, not once in his life, that he'd have the chance to meet anything quite like the Primigenials. They were myths, legends, gods even. Powerful creatures from the annals of time made flesh before him. And, on top of that, they were willing to work with him. Even for him, if need be. He hadn't had a lot of time to just sit and reflect on things lately. The timer scrolling by wouldn't allow it. But that thought stuck with him. Athena caught him looking and threw him a wink.

Oh . . . okay.

Walker's eyes then found the pink and blue subsystem assistants, both standing near the Evolution Chambers as Virgil painstakingly talked about what he was doing. Assistants—giant squirrels who could talk. Maybe he should've gone for Godzilla. Who knew? But they were the real key to everything he was working toward. Without them, there was no way he'd be able to fulfill all of his plans for systems in the future. They were necessary, and if he was lucky, they were his friends.

Naturally, his last view was of Symphony, his weird mini-planet shaped like a cube. There was no way its gravity should work the way it did, but that was just another mystery of the Alpha Protocol. Chipper, Chomp, and Phil. His newest citizen, Raganoth. And all of the people who would get added over time, who would be born here. Who would live on the world he and his helpers had created.

While he might make other planets with the Cosmic Genesis System, this one would always be his favorite. His first. He'd built it, watched it get destroyed, then put it back together again. It was almost a part of him, and he didn't think he'd ever have the heart to leave it behind. One way or another, he'd find a way for Symphony to succeed. It had to. He only had one more thought as he stared at it.

Fuck you, Slicer.

Walker turned to look at the group. "Is everyone ready for a year to pass by in a blink?" He didn't see anyone shaking their heads or speaking up, with the exception of Zeus's standard stormy mug of a face. With no celebration, Walker clicked Time, inched it over Sonata's edge, and set it for one year.

"Let's see where we end up," he said with a breath, then pushed the button.

NOTES

1   Journal Entry #1

The night Valerie leaves Walker, just before he loses his job.

This is a journal.

Across time, journals have been used for so many different purposes.

Write down your thoughts, spread your ideas, then close the lid and never let anyone see them.

Yep, Journals are great for the insane and closeted. Or just those who have trouble expressing themselves vocally.

I fall into the third option.

You see, I have dysgraphia, so many people won't be able to read this. It's a bullshit neurological disorder that is particularly impactful on handwriting and anything that has to do with steady hand control. Sometimes, I just write words that aren't even in my head; they appear on this page, and I have to go back and fix it. It's bullshit. It's also likely genetic, but I won't have kids, so that's a-okay.

Why start writing a journal? My girl left me. She fucking blipped out. I had a breakdown, called a psychiatrist friend of mine, and she suggested I start this shit. I don't know who I'm writing to, but I'm assuming you know me, or you just found this on a random corpse who wears a lot of dark shades.

These are my thoughts and feelings. Feelings have friends, but can a thought be lonely? Ask my students, as they seem to have so few. I don't remember having friendly feelings. I know I have them, but I can't seem to remember where they went. Everything is pastel. My highs are always straining for the middle bar of excitement, and my lows are deep and well-entrenched. I don't remember the last time I felt true joy, apart from surfing on a nice clean wave with no one else near me.

This world sucks. Everything feels like a race, and everyone is so in-tune with social media and trying to outperform each other that contentment is seen as a disease of the past few generations.

Is that what I did wrong? Was I too content? Is that why she left?

I'm gonna shrug it all off by tomorrow, I'm sure. It's another day at work, another lesson to give. Hopefully, my students understand something in my teaching.

I hope.

2   Journal Entry #2

Just after Mr. Harrison leaves.

So, I'm stranded.

Maybe I'll find my way out of here, or maybe I'll "make a world," as Mr. Harrison says.

I don't know.

I should probably be trying to figure out a way to find food, or water for that matter. But as near as I can tell, there's nothing here. Nothing at all. Just . . . an empty wash of green.

Plus it's not like anyone will ever read this. My last chapter reads like I'm the saddest man in the world, yet I've just been given an incredible opportunity.

I ended my last page with hope, so maybe I'll focus on that in this entry. There are worse things to think about.

Poetry helps. I've always found poetry to reach the soul better than any other medium, with the exception of music.

Of course, music is just poetry in a different form, but that's the English teacher in me talking.

So why not take a meager chance at writing some of my own.

> Hope is a feckless ~~asshole~~ bully
> When you think you've lost it all, he appears
> He drives you in the morning, keeps your eyes open when you should
>   sleep
> He forces you to carry him, always trying to share that burden with
>   others
> He's a monster of unimaginable force, a dictator of your soul
> He only fades and disappears when you forget him
> Only ~~reappearing~~ returning when another soul feels his brush

Not my best or my worst. I'll take it.

Maybe I can survive this place.

But even if I do, I have to ask, where did that crazy guy go? What is he?

Questions I hope I'll have answers to one day.

Some water right now would be nice.

3   Journal Entry #3

What are the ramifications of a mind constantly on with no downtime? Like, how does the Alpha Protocol know to consistently balance my hormones and not allow me to go crazy?

Do most Creators go crazy?

The long haul of this ordeal, like the best way to succeed in the end, is just to hold onto your sanity.

I made something today—a monster. As usual, I gave it a terrible name, but I still fear the ramifications of what I've done. After I set it free and watched it become the monster I didn't know I had created, I started to worry that I couldn't kill it. That it would continue on forever, destroying things as it saw fit and just for the joy of it. Virgil said it'd be dead in the next twenty years or so, but still, it's a problem.

Instead of dealing with my issue, I'm going to wall it off and cross my fingers that it stays put. This is not my most mature action, but contrary to what those of you reading may believe, I am not the most mature person. It's less of a personality defect and more of just a personality.

Across history, there have been many instances of a person making a joke after a terrible ordeal. In particular, medical personnel often get in trouble for this. But that's because the layman doesn't understand what's happening to the surgeons and nurses psychologically. They only see the joke, not the need to blow off steam and forget about the problem for the few seconds it takes to say a few words and laugh.

To forget about death in the world, and their inability to stop it.

I was given the ability, once I selected the name Dante and changed my identity, to participate in a chatroom filled with Creators. Why? I have no idea. Perhaps other Creators consistently need social feedback, but I've always had a nose deep in my books and only felt the need to speak when it was necessary. My father taught me that the less you have to say, the more profound it is when you speak. I'll need to carry that over to my world when things really start off, as I cannot imagine how terrifying it would be to have a small-g god yelling at someone for not watering their plants in the morning, or cheating on their wife.

The chat, though, is insane. This one Creator, Fillora, said they made a seductive entity. A seductress . . . What? How are you going to seduce the Slicer? Do they not know about the Creator Wars?

I'm guessing, as I have an advanced assistant, that I'm getting a lot more information than all of the other Creators. They have the smarts, but currently, I hold the advantage. That's a lot of power for a former secondary school teacher. While I can, I'll need to use my advantages to really pull ahead of the others. The grand rewards help, but there has to be more. I need to step up my game and do things the protocol has never seen before. I think the Evolution Chamber is going to help, but the true ace in the hole is that fuckin tree.

WHAT IS IT DOING?

It just keeps getting larger and weirder. Virgil has no idea, and my Universal Translator didn't work on the weird bark writing. Is it instructions? Is it a poem about dicks? What the fuck.

As I wrote this, another chat exploded. What's wrong with these people?

Fraylon: What do you mean your planet is exploding?

Kieieik: I mean I made the core molten and everything is melting! I changed the atmosphere a little too much and I'm worried the heat will reach it and it'll blow up!

Mirail: Idiot

Fraylon: Yeah you're dumb as shit. Good luck though.

Kieieik: I need help, not negativity! What should I do?

Dante: Do you have an advanced assistant?

Mirail: Look at this guy with his "advanced" assistant—probably doesn't even know how to calculate the trajectory of a Dalminian cruiser

Kieieik: I'm running out of time! Help!

Dante: My assistant says you need to dilute the flammable gas in the atmosphere with other gasses otherwise, it will certainly catch fire.

Kieieik: Okay! Thanks!

Mirail: 50 credits we don't hear from them again

Dante: Hello?

Dante: Kieieik?

Mirail: Told you

Dante: You're kind of a dick.

Anyways. That was from a while ago, and I haven't heard from Kieieik again. I've gotta stop looking at the chat though because, according to Virgil, who can also see it, a lot of Creators are giving bad information to the others. I get it, it's a competition. But there are a bunch of big assholes like Mirail in there. I hope they're not one of the ones who get through the protocol.

One positive from this is I feel like I have good odds going into the first battle. Did I just screw myself by saying that? . . . Nah probably not.

4   Journal Entry #4

I don't understand. Why do people like tea? It's just a glass of water that you threw some stuff in. Dirty water mixed with vegetation nobody should eat. Virgil was trying to figure out how to make some, but I don't know how he would. He seems to believe that it would help me relax in our down moments, but we only have a little over sixty hours when my break ends. He's being nice but I've never been a tea drinker.

Anyways, I found the Slicer. Well, that is to say, I found out what it has been doing all this time. Apparently, it was trapped on a planet by a Creator named Jolive. She has a metal over there that is quite sophisticated. She said in the chat . . . well she wasn't very kind, but then again I do deserve it. I'm going to put it here so I can remember what was said. Sometimes I feel like I need these reminders in the back of my mind for what not to do in the future. I just wish my memory was better.

Jolive: Why the fuck would you make something like this?
Dante: Dude, I didn't make it like that. I made a basic worm and the fucker evolved during the first battle. I was happy to just let it blow up fish for the rest of its life.
Mirail: See thats what happens when you call people dicks asshole
Dante: Hey, fuck you and your poor grammar.
Mirail: Whats grammar
Jolive: Regardless, you created a fuckin awful thing here. Did you know its identify calls it a "Universal Terror"?   ·
Dante: Shit, it upgraded again.
Jolive: Yah, no kidding. The little bastard keeps hissing at me like it's laughing. Honestly, it's terrifying. I have a standard assistant and it just keeps repeating the same thing over and over, saying I have to kill it or keep it trapped forever. I tried squeezing the box down and crushing it, but that did nothing. I tried pouring acid in, and it evolved again! At this rate, it'll be unkillable if I keep trying. I'm afraid it's going to break out and destroy my planet. I'd probably be paralyzed in fear if I didn't know the Alpha Protocol was protecting me.
Blitzburg22: Have you considered speaking with it in a calm tone of voice and explaining the problem? Our collective has found that few Interpersonal

issues cannot be solved without first accepting that we are at part in the blame.

Mirail: ahahahahahahahahaha

Dante: Don't you have things to do, Mirail?

Jolive: Are you kidding me? Fucking Blitzburgs are always the same. The shithead exploded into my atmosphere and murdered half of my entities in less than five minutes. If I didn't work so much with metal I'd already be done here.

Dante: Ummm, would you mind explaining how you built its cage with that metal?

Jolive: Go fuck yourself.

Yeah, it was a long shot, but I had to try. Anyways, the Slicer is contained for now, and even Virgil thinks it'll take a while before it breaks out, based on what the Creator said. I feel bad for Jolive, but at the same time, she's very much a rude person. As my mother says, you trap more flies with honey than vinegar.

Wait, I'm at fault here . . . am I really the asshole? No, no spirals. No depression.

Moving right along.

I'm excited for all of the systems we get to build. I feel like it will be a cornerstone for my world, something upon which the world spins, metaphorically, as it doesn't really spin. Cornerstone . . . cornerstone. Well, there's another idea I have to backseat—something to consider, though.

Oh don't worry, I'm sure if someone else is reading this I'm totally alive and Symphony is doing well. Yep, everything's going great, no problems here.

5   Holy Scripture #1

There are no strict rules within this Holy Scripture. The words written prior to this are the inane and thoughtless moments of a lesser one who was pushed to accept that they must become something greater than themselves. If rules must be applied, or if the reader decides that they must place strict adherence to something derived from this writing, let it be this: Don't be an asshole.

My name is Walker, sometimes called Dante or the Creator of Symphony, and I am the one writing this. I. Am. A. Mortal. I'm no greater than any other being or entity, and I feel that is important and should be understood well. I am not a divine being, or a God with a capital G. The word *holy* as applied to this writing is a requirement for the document and not something I would apply to a description of myself. It is a part of a process that allows me to found a religion. I plan to use the power of this religion and the associated system to build a better Symphony for all, and thus, here we are.

To start, I find myself wondering what my religion should be called. My focus in life and the road I walk upon is based upon an oath that I've lived by and explicitly stated not all that long ago.

This spoken vow to my friend and confidant Virgil and the future residents of Symphony stated that each day and each moment, I will try to be better than I was the day and moment before. That each step should be taken with a goal of improvement for not only oneself, but for all. That the step itself is what matters, and should not have a focus on, and I quote, "the greater good."

To me, the greater good and the lies that follow it can lead a world down a path of darkness and progressively expanding retribution, which then tears itself apart. I won't allow that to happen. I want, and we need, a path of progressive improvement that follows a basic outline of life. One that opens up and permits its followers to have a clearly defined goal, providing a roadmap for how to get there. That is the purpose of this scripture. For now, let's call this roadmap, and the religion of its founding, the Unending Summit. Those who climb toward the Summit, the word meaning the top or peak, will be called Horizon Chasers, or Chasers for short.

The name has meaning, as all do. There is no end goal to growth. There is no top of the mountain. It is about progression, not for the sake of progression, but for the sake of others so that they may, too, know the road upon which they walk. Our followers will guide those who come after us and provide help as it is needed. However, excessive assistance and dogmatic following of the past can lead to a lack of innovation and creation.

A strict grip on what is allowed and what is foolhardy. The greatest achievements in the history of my former world were performed by the foolhardy, those who dared to dream of a different way, and thus, even help must be tempered for those who chase the top. Help must be earned. Assistance must be focused. Read the below and place it in your hearts.

Each decision has to be weighed and tempered by the experiences found on Symphony. Each thought has to follow a moral code by the Chaser who holds it.

It is not enough to be the strongest; you must find a way to be stronger still.

It is not enough to touch upon the unknown, as paths wander deepest within the darkness.

Be better than you were yesterday, so that tomorrow shines all the brighter.

Chase the horizon, and place a finger upon the Unending Summit. It awaits only those who are willing to climb the steepest steps.

Those five sentences should hold a clear meaning to each Chaser.

Take on those who need you, who are following a path similar to yours, and provide guidance. Learn about them, find their zone of understanding, and give them small words of advice that allow for individual thought. In the end, it is about building a better world for all who live in it.

Now, there are some important things you need to know if you're going to do well in Symphony. A basic education is the birthright of all sapients in our world. The first thing you need to know is commas. Comma, comma, comma. They're useful in writing . . .

6   Holy Scripture #2

. . . and that is how a basic democracy works. Please bear in mind that a democracy is not the same as a republic. The biggest difference, in my eyes, is that in a democracy, the people vote on everything, whereas in a republic, the elected representatives do. The greatest empires in the history of my world were built through a republic system, but they all eventually fell from within. To better explain that last portion, the corruption of its leaders is what kills a grand empire.

I've already explained a bit about my life before arriving here to create Symphony. In that world, people could not tell the difference between the two and kept mislabeling their own system of government.

You may be wondering why you're learning about political movements and government structure within a Holy Scripture.

The answer is simple: It is important.

In following the path of the Unending Summit, and as stated so many pages ago, you must have a general education. The ability to read and grow from learning is a core tenet of our pseudo-religion. Knowing math isn't voluntary regarding success. There can be no progress without learning, and there can be no learning without an open mind. It is not enough to be willing to listen; you must also be willing to allow your firmly held ideas to be challenged. To morph or evolve. To head in directions never once conceived. To escape from the closeted grip of safe spaces.

Let's step back from the basic education that has been provided thus far and move back to the ins and outs of the Unending Summit and its meaning.

The primary rule to be a Horizon Chaser is simple. Do Not Be An Asshole. But what does that translate to?

First, do not feed every hungry person. It doesn't mean you cannot feed the hungry, if that's what you want. No. Instead, it's a flawed metaphor of an old quote from my world: "Give a man a fish, and he eats for a day. Teach a man to fish, and he eats for a lifetime." This saying is old, but accurate. If you provide some guidance, you're helping. If you provide all assistance, you're hindering. People need to learn to stand on their own and not be carried through life. Do not create a program of free handouts, as it creates a system of dependence that is not healthy for you, others, or Symphony as a whole.

Teach them to fish.

The second is respect. Respect is the concept of providing or allowing dignity for others. It is when a sapient being recognizes the autonomy and value of those around them. You do not know who you may bump into on the road of life. They could be the smallest farmer who just wants to see the dawn with a crop of wheat in hand, or they may be a child who has great ambition but no value in a flawed society's eyes.

The farmer is content to move from one day to the next, living with the land. Harming him is harming your own stomach.

When treated harshly or wrongfully, that child could grow up to one day be quite powerful and use that gained power in the darkest light possible. Harming him is harming the future of your contemporaries.

Respect comes down to a basic idea: Treat others how you would want to be treated. Allow for the basis of unmolested pride and respect, until someone has shown you they do not deserve it. At that point, the choice is yours. Please balance the cost of breaking this tenet with your own future prosperity. This means that every person in Symphony is a blank slate to Horizon Chasers. Do not believe a person is evil or the simplified idea of "bad" without first meeting them.

The last part of "Do Not Be An Asshole" is courteousness. To be courteous means to present oneself as you would in court. That may not have a great amount of meaning to the uninformed, but it is a whole new world in how you act with and around others. You do not have to hold the door for every person who needs to enter, while you stand idly by losing the most precious of all resources, time. You do not have to bend the knee to every would-be king or suitor, or bow to every lady, as if gender makes one more noble of character. It means be polite in your language and gestures, be considerate of others in your actions, and show gratitude when you receive help, even if unasked.

If the only thing our religion becomes known for across the years is that our members are helpful guides, respectful, and courteous, then Symphony will still receive great value from us.

The leader of our religion will be called the *Zenith*—not because it sounds awe-inspiring or because they will dictate from the top down, but the opposite. They will work for Symphony and the Unending Summit. They are a reflection of who we are and a representative of our faith. Perhaps faith is too strong of a word, as this is really a means to live rather than pray, but nonetheless, we will be called a religion for all.

Each Zenith will be not a tool or puppet of mine but their own person with their own interpretation of the scripture. I make no requirements for them, except that they do not be an asshole and that they try to administrate the Unending Summit with honesty and integrity. The moment that changes, and they violate my only true requirement of them, I will come . . .

To answer a question I am sure you will have, no, I cannot be the Zenith. I will be far too busy with running Symphony as a whole, and I cannot run a religion alongside it.

Now, let us get back to your general education. I do not know a lot about architecture and building, but I do know just enough to help bridge some gaps in your potential knowledge. First, you need to make sure you survey the land. Do not build any structures over clay or damp soil, as they will collapse. The trick is . . .

Author's Note

I'm not sure who is reading this, but I hope YOU enjoyed the story. I try to be thick-skinned about criticism, but I always find a little blood afterward.

Acknowledgments

Thank you to my wife and family, including those close friends who have encouraged me from afar.

Thank you to my beta readers, for helping me keep the story in line with my vision.

A special thanks to the team at Podium. Chelsea, who was so very lovely, and Taylor, with her quick information and laughing at my bad jokes.

Thank you to M. Zaugg for teaching me how serialized fiction works. I've enjoyed your story immensely.

Lastly, thank you to my teachers and colleagues. Professors Wilburn and Fonzo helped me start this road, and of course, Mrs. Johnson, my fifth and sixth-grade teacher. It's a tough job, and nobody wants to do it, but still, you persevere.

About the Author

J. D. Mullenary Sr. aka AbnormalVAverage is the author of the Symphony series, originally released on Royal Road, as well as a teacher and esports coach. He grew up on temperate California beaches and, after completing his first degree at nineteen, felt he needed to grow up, so he joined the military. He served for four years, earned a second degree, and was honorably discharged. Soon after, Mullenary married the love of his life and raised two sons. He then returned to college with a focus on English and education. He lives in Texas, where he spends his time writing, teaching his students the value of critical thinking, and fostering the strays his wife brings home.